Francesca Clementis degree in Philosophy from Sussex U ten years in advertising before becoming a full-time writer. Her first novel, *Big Girls Don't Cry*, was published in 1999 by Piatkus. She lives in London with her husband and daughter.

Also by Francesca Clementis

Big Girls Don't Cry

MAD ABOUT THE GIRLS

FRANCESCA CLEMENTIS

PIATKUS

For more information on
other books published by
Piatkus, visit our website
at *www.piatkus.co.uk*

First published in Great Britain in 2000 by
Judy Piatkus (Publishers) Ltd of
5 Windmill Street, London W1T 2JA
email: *info@piatkus.co.uk*

The moral right of the author has been asserted

A catalogue record for this book is available from the British Library

ISBN 0 7499 3212 0

Set in Times by
Phoenix Photosetting, Chatham, Kent

Printed and bound in Great Britain by
Mackays of Chatham PLC, Chatham, Kent

For my mum and dad.
Does this make all those sleepless nights worthwhile . . .?

A challenge: I give you the story of my life in under a hundred words. You have to guess what comes next. Pay attention.

1) Born thirty-six years ago to a wonderful mother and devoted father – or so I was told. I was handed over to a different mother and father five days later.

2) Didn't get into grammar school of my choice. Went to local comprehensive where rolling tobacco was most popular product in tuck shop.

3) Didn't get good enough A levels for Cambridge. Went to Sussex University. (Watch for the clues, they're not subtle.)

4) Dreamed of becoming a magician. Became a teacher.

5) Wanted husband and four children.

6) Happily settled for ten years with husband and four children – now you supply the tag . . .

What did you guess? Something on the thwarted dream theme, of course. After all, I gave you enough pointers. So what did you come up with? Someone dying, husband betraying me, leaving me, kids turning out badly, disfiguring illness, miscarriage of justice landing me in prison? Good suggestions, all perfectly plausible, all wrong. I'm fine. Husband and kids are all fine. All healthy, all happy, all well adjusted.

It's just that they are actually somebody else's husband and somebody else's children.

And that somebody else wants them back.

Chapter One

It is eight sixteen a.m.

'Mum! Where's my lucky Biro?'

'Mum! Can I have a sleepover at Peter's house?'

'Mum! Why can't I have a bra?'

'Mum! I've given up meat. Do smoky bacon crisps count?'

'Biro is on the floor by the video, Phoebe, no sleepovers at boys' houses, Claire, you can have a bra as soon as you need one, Jude, and smoky bacon crisps don't count, Ali, but pepperoni pizza does, so put it back in the fridge.'

Four daughters. Four questions in twenty-eight seconds all answered without breaking my stride from the tumble dryer to the ironing board. Four lunchboxes on the table packed with the perfect balance of the healthy, the chocolatey and whatever is currently advertised on TV. Two dogs of indeterminate parentage hoovering the terracotta floor with licky tongues. The house is all cosy clutter, happy lives mapped out in photos and fridge magnets and Post-it notes. There is enough mess to reassure the kids that I am not neurotic about housework but the occasional whiff of disinfectant to reassure myself that I am not breeding E-coli on the breakfast bar. Radio One is playing and I know the words to Prodigy's latest hit. I am truly supermother.

Eight nineteen a.m. The girls are running late for school as usual. But not too late. They rush out of the door, kissing me quickly and barely making contact with my cheek. Except Phoebe, my eldest and strongest and neediest girl. She is currently weighed down by adolescent burdens and hugs me at every opportunity. Poor Phoebe, she's got the lot: spots, orthodontic braces, greasy hair, a constant sense of existential doom and the biggest bust in her class. She hasn't needed me this badly since she was four and I love this renewed dependence even while my heart shreds at her suffering. She smells of medicated shampoo and Clearasil.

She is my favourite but I've learned how not to show it. It's one of those parenting skills that are never taught or even mentioned in books. 'I love all my children equally.' 'I may *like* one more than another, but I *love* them the same.' Like children learning the Lord's Prayer, we recite our lines in monotones, hoping that the words alone will convince. But we don't mean it. I share my love equally between the four girls but I always find additional scraps and extras from some-where inside me for Phoebe. Maybe it's just that she asks for more. I stroke her hair as she pulls away from me and we exchange a look that makes me feel complete.

'Bye Mum!' they all shout. And then they are gone.

It was pretty much the same routine yesterday. They'd all left for school and I'd switched the radio off. For a few moments I allowed my ears to adjust to the silence. Then I metamorphosed into my other self – the one who dusts to *Kilroy*, who shouts out the answers to *Supermarket Sweep*, writes down the recipes on *Ready Steady Cook* and sews name tags on gym kit while watching Richard and Judy bicker about hysterectomies.

4

These are my domestic sins, to be confessed only after a few glasses of wine with other mothers. It is our shared secret, one that we conceal from our husbands and, indeed, from our other friends who not only have their radios tuned to Radio Four but actually listen to it.

Sometimes, when I remember that I once read Stephen Hawking's *A Brief History Of Time* (and understood at least seventy-five per cent of it), I worry about the effects of Vanessa Feltz and Australian soap operas on my soul. But I console myself that perhaps I am really watching daytime TV from a postmodern critical viewpoint. It's a lie but at least the word 'postmodern' is still part of my vocabulary after years spent in almost continuous communion with Postman Pat.

The truth is, I just like TV. Always have done. Indiscriminate television-watching is my nicotine, a slow drip-feed of reliable pleasure. I love it all, soaps, dramas, sitcoms, game shows, documentaries. Good or bad, I don't care. I love the synthetic parallel universes that punctuate my own linear existence; I love the vicarious lives the box allows me to experience; I love having a common point of reference to share with strangers. Being part of an audience is a form of belonging and I like that. I love being able to join in conversations with strangers at checkouts about Ken Barlow's bizarre commitment to wearing inappropriately tight denim jeans. TV straddles the class and education divide in a way that the Labour Government can only dream of doing. So here I am. I've come out. Hello, my name is Lorna and I watch *The Bill*.

Yesterday morning was sublimely normal. I had a huge pile of exam papers to mark and I was making myself a cup of tea and scrambling about in the biscuit tin for something like a digestive or a Rich Tea finger that wouldn't leave tell-tale fingerprints on my work. (I *am* a professional, you know.) Then I heard a key in the door and I was terrified.

Not terrified of some unknown intruder. I knew it was Rob. When you've lived with someone for ten years you know exactly the sound of their key in the front door. It's one of those familiar touchstones that still thrills me with its intimacy. No, the terror came because it *was* Rob. He never came home in the morning. Not even when he was ill.

Rob is a dog behaviourist. It's how we met. All those years ago, I had a psychopathic German Shepherd called Shipshape who had developed a fear of gravel. I had to carry her over my drive every day and my back was packing up. Even then, Rob was well known (in Clapham doggy circles, that is) so I took Shipshape to him. His wife had left him him two months earlier and he was in a desperate state.

I sometimes wonder if it was his situation that attracted me in the first place. I admired the way he coped with the children, I liked the way they all needed me, I enjoyed the drama. I moved in within a matter of weeks with cured dog, a vanload of possessions and a deaf ear to friends' warnings that this could not possibly work out. And then there were the girls. I'd always wanted children, not necessarily for the birthing business, that didn't really bother me one way or another, I just wanted lots of kids, a big loud all-encompassing family of my own. I loved this family on sight. They came as a complete package, Rob and the girls, and it was exactly the package I wanted.

It took a while but their lives eventually all got back on track. Now Rob has a national reputation and a suite of offices in a local vet's practice. He has back-to-back appointments every day which is why, for him to come home at ten o'clock on a Thursday morning, something terrible must have happened. I didn't want to know what that was. Not when our lives were so good, so secure.

I heard the dogs scrambling over him in excitement. 'Hello JR. Kili. Come on girls! Where are you, Lorna?' he called from the hall.

'I'm in here.' I quickly switched off the TV and composed myself. Whatever was going to happen, I intended to handle it bravely, with grace, with style, with humour. That's one of the advantages of a life founded on early, consistent disappointment – you end up with a well-tested armoury of punchlines to deflect most attacks.

In the short time it took Rob to walk the eleven steps from the hall to the kitchen, I'd imagined most of the possible scenarios, played them through to their inevitable conclusions, amazed him with my stoic acceptance of the grim situation, comforted him in some strong, wise, womanly way that I like to think I possess and come up with practical solutions to every problem. (Note to myself: I *definitely* watch too much daytime television.)

Then I saw his face and I knew, I just knew, that it was more serious than anything I'd contemplated. It wasn't pain on his face, or devastation or resignation, but confusion. He took a deep breath. 'There was a letter waiting for me at the office. From Karen.'

He waited for me to respond but this wasn't one of my scenarios. I had responses for redundancy, cancer, repossession of house and death of distant family member but not a letter from Karen. And a letter from Karen did rather imply that she was alive. Which was very bad news for me indeed. It was bad news for us all, but particularly for me.

Karen was – is – Rob's ex-wife, I mean wife. They've never been divorced so she's still his legal spouse. And she's the girls' mother, birth mother I mean, since she hasn't been a 'mother' to them in ten years; not in person, not by phone, not even by post. Walked out on four children under the age of five. Does that sound like a mother to you?

'What are you thinking, Lorna?'

I decided to filter out the bit about Karen not being dead and that being bad news. Even with spectacular comic delivery, I sensed that it would not raise a laugh. And I wasn't joking anyway. So there.

I tried to remember what agony aunts and TV shrinks do in situations when highly charged questions are fired at them. Perhaps answering with another question was safe. At the very least, it would buy me time to sort my feelings into a cohesive, non-threatening stance.

'Why did she write to you at work and not here?' It was a reasonable question. It was not as if she didn't have this address. This had been her home for six years before she abandoned it so it was safe to assume that she remembered where it was.

'She knew that it would be a shock for me to hear from her after all this time, so she thought it best that I get the letter at work where my reaction wouldn't upset the girls.'

'Wow. That must get her through to the next round of "Mother of the Year".'

'I'm not defending her, Lorna. I'm just answering your question.'

And so the first microscopic wedge of division was tapped into our relationship with that ever-so-slightly impatient tone in his ever-so-slightly defensive reply. All at once, Karen morphed from some translucent phantom of the past into a fleshy substantial threat.

For the first couple of years after I met Rob, I lived in permanent terror that his wife would come back, remorseful, laden with presents and well-documented excuses for her outrageous behaviour. But she didn't come back. She communicated via her parents that she was making a new life for herself in the USA and would not be returning. There was talk of a nervous breakdown and, by the time she recovered, she was aware of my existence and concluded that the children were better off with me.

To be honest, during those early months when I first took on the care of Rob's children, I understood her actions entirely. I know they weren't *my* children and, so the story goes, that makes a difference, but four children under five – I was demented with tiredness, frustration and awesome responsibility. Not only did I understand why she walked out, I was amazed that she'd stayed as long as she had. Without smothering them, that is. And if that shocks you, then you've never lived, month after month, on no more than two consecutive hours' sleep at any time. You've never been tyrannised by four small creatures twenty-four hours a day, demanding and rejecting your attention in alternate onslaughts. You've never known what is to be tortured by inconsolable crying and whining and screaming for days on end. You've never been a mother.

I only survived it because I was simultaneously demented with love for Rob. Our love was a distraction, a coat of emotional sustenance that provided a potent salve to the torment of child-rearing. Maybe that's why couples who have children to buoy up a struggling marriage inevitably find that the marriage dies under the pressure of a new baby. If you weren't laughing before the baby came along, you can be sure that you'll find precious little to amuse you when it does.

9

But all these generous assessments of Karen's desertion evolved in the certainty that she was gone, never to return. Now she's back and I don't feel so generous any more.

Rob sank into a chair, weighed down with decisions. 'It was only a short note really, not a letter as such.'

I went over and put my arms around him. He was a tall man, over six feet, and yet he looked small right now. He looked so vulnerable as he slumped over the kitchen table. It was hard to believe that he would turn forty in a few months' time. He was one of those ageless men who looked about thirty from the age of eighteen until sixty. His hair was the same style that he'd worn since puberty, thick, naturally curly and settled comfortably around his face. His eyes were blue, blue, blue and so, so, so kind. His skin was totally unlined and I realised, in a shocking revelation, that this was probably because he didn't laugh a great deal.

I mean, he's not miserable or gloomy or anything, it's just that he has a quiet, dry sense of humour that doesn't often express itself in belly laughs. He's the smiler and I'm the laugher. Rob always said that he most loved me for bringing laughter into his family. There hadn't been a lot of it in the year leading up to Karen's departure and there was none at all after she'd left. I squeezed him a little more tightly, hoping he'd interpret the hug as comforting rather than proprietorial.

He came from a family rather like my own where, when he was sad, his mother gave him paracetamol rather than hugs. This left us with a thirst for physical reassurance that we both tried to satisfy in each other. There were other similarities in our backgrounds, comforting coincidences that we chose to make the foundations of our relationship. We were both only children, both lost

10

our fathers when we were eighteen and took on the unwelcome responsibility of looking after mothers who had been utterly dependent on their husbands for the practicalities of life. We'd both escaped to redbrick universities a few years later than our peers and had consequently felt displaced by the gap in age and maturity between us and our fellow students. We both needed an excuse not to return home so Rob got married and I just carried on studying. You know the rest.

'So what does Karen want?'

'The note just said that she wanted to meet up with me to talk. That I wasn't to worry, she isn't planning on causing trouble etc. etc. She's staying at her parents' house.'

Two miles away. Oh God. 'How long for?'

Rob shrugged. 'She didn't say.'

There were too many meaningful silences in this conversation for my liking. I lightened my voice. 'Well, there's no point in getting worked up until you find out what she wants. You *do* have to see her, don't you?' I added a false laugh to this last, rather desperate question.

'Of course I have to see her.' He touched my hand as I flinched at this. 'Sorry. I didn't mean to snap. Anyway, look on the bright side. Perhaps she's met someone in the States and wants a quick divorce so that she can go back and marry him.'

Now I'm not famous for looking on the bright side. I'm quite good at finding the funny side in a bitter, ironical sort of way. But bright sides have always eluded me.

Divorce. No. I wouldn't even think about it. I wanted it too badly and we all know what happens when you want something too badly. Well, we know what happens when *I* want something too badly.

11

'You should have known this would happen sooner or later!' you scream from the dress circle. But don't be too quick to heap scorn on me for being the author of my own circumstances. The outcome of the choices I made ten years ago may appear to be more dramatic than your average tale of Suburban Sue, but am I the only person who's dared to hope that she might beat the odds, buck the trends, win the prize?

I know how easy it is to spot behaviour patterns in somebody else's life. God, I do it all the time, anything to take my mind off my own mistakes. When was your first time? You know what I'm talking about. That first stab of panic when you looked ahead towards your dream or your goal or your destiny and it wasn't there. It wasn't in front of you because it was behind you or over there or anywhere else except where it was supposed to be.

And dreams are the whole point, aren't they, the arrow-head on the shaft? They give you direction, purpose, meaning. If we didn't have something to aim for, we'd all be flitting in and out of parallel lives, toying randomly with hobbies, careers and partners. We all know what happened to my dreams, so let's look at yours. Please. Indulge me. Humour me. Don't let me carry the banner of female fallibility all by myself here. How did you lose sight of *your* goals, the original authentic ones, not the ones you've tweaked to fit your present situation?

It started early, didn't it? When you longed to be Mary in the nativity play but were cast as fifth sheep; when you asked Father Christmas for a Sindy doll and you got an encyclopaedia; when you asked for a piano and got a stylophone – a second-hand one without Rolf Harris's accompanying instruction booklet. And thus the pattern was forged.

You were going to marry in white in a pretty village church when you were twenty-one, weren't you? To a man who looked like David Cassidy (my own choice – insert pop icon appropriate to your personal era), was sensitive, faithful, wrote and read poetry, was also a promising executive with a car, a flat and a mother who lived at least three hundred miles away. You actually got married, when? Were you thirty-one or even forty-one? Did you wear green? It was probably in a registry office in a new town civic centre and you had to pretend that you didn't mind, really, and white weddings are just silly teenage fantasies. And no, of course you didn't want a lot of fuss. And your husband? A nice man, I've no doubt but . . . but . . .

So how could it have happened? Where did that dream disappear to? Somewhere along your squiggly lifeline you'd meandered off and settled for second-best. Or sixtieth-best. Whatever. And you didn't mean to. Nobody does. Pink bedrooms all over the world are full of little girls dreaming of being ballet dancers who will end up becoming aromatherapists. Or maybe there are children who dream of being aromatherapists. There's a scary thought for our new millennium.

I didn't plan things like this but I've done all I can to make the best of it. I've found a life I like, a man I love, the family I've always wanted and I'm not going to lose it now.

Rob was brightening up. 'If you think about it, why else would she get in touch after all this time? It must be about a divorce. Wouldn't that be great, Lorna? The girls would never even have to know she'd been in touch!' He kissed me cheerfully. 'Look, sorry I was in such a state. I just needed to see you and talk to you. I've calmed down now. I'll call Karen this afternoon,

13

get everything sorted out as quickly as possible. Don't worry. Everything will be all right.' Then he was gone.

He'd been in and out in fifteen minutes. I still had exam papers to mark, the washing to sort out, shopping to do. All I could think of was Karen taking away my daughters. Even taking away Robert. I couldn't breathe. I was becoming irrational. I needed a drink, a dessert and a friend. I picked up the phone and called Andrea. I left a message on her answering machine. 'Hi, Ange. Me. Listen, when you get back from the school run, give me a call. I need to meet up for lunch.'

I instantly felt better. Andrea would understand. She'd know how I felt and she'd know what to do.

She was a mother. Like me.

Chapter Two

The restaurant in Debenhams was packed with women. We were the only ones without shopping bags and the only ones drinking wine. We were almost through our first bottle and it wasn't even midday.

I loved Andrea. She mirrored the me I pretended to be. Her hair was naturally blonde and wavy where mine was highlighted and blow-dried to the point of desiccation. She was slim. I was skinny. She was confident. I was good at acting confident. She was beautiful. I had an interesting face. She had one daughter of her own. I had four of somebody else's.

She emptied her glass in one gulp and stared at me in mock-sincerity. 'Right. Let's sort this out then we can get drunk and start embarrassing the waiter. First things first. Have you set your video for *Neighbours* and *Home and Away*?'

I laughed despite my misery. 'I'm not that bad, Ange!'

She raised an eyebrow. I held up my hands in defeat. 'OK, OK, so I am that bad. But so are you.'

She considered this accusation. 'Not quite. I never set my video for soaps.'

I snorted. 'That's because you know that I always do, so, on those rare occasions when you miss them, you can phone me the next day and get the updates.'

'I rest my case,' she proclaimed in triumph. 'I can wait twenty-four hours for the latest gossip whereas you don't go to bed until you've caught up with it all so that makes me much less sad than you.'

She's right of course but I forgive her because I'm so grateful to have found a co-conspirator to share my passion for low television. 'Well anyway, on this occasion you're wrong. I was too stressed to set the video. Besides, I can watch the repeats this afternoon with the girls.'

'So how are the girls?'

I answered on autopilot. 'Phoebe is the victim of every cruel trick puberty has in its repertoire, Claire has discovered boys and, even worse, they have discovered her, Jude is looking for a way to rebel that doesn't involve self-mutilation or any kind of deprivation and Ali is working her way through an A-Z of alternative lifestyles.'

Andrea looked puzzled. 'That's it? You haven't found dope in a pencil case? Condoms in a backpack? No sign of anorexia or pregnancy?'

'It's not the girls.'

Andrea laughed. 'It's always the girls with you, Lorn.'

'Not this time. It's Karen. She's come back.'

It took a few seconds for the name to register with Andrea. When recognition surfaced, it pushed Andrea back in her chair like a body blow. I watched her dredging memories to the front of her mind, memories that I couldn't share. Because Andrea had known Karen, really known her.

They'd been friends, more than friends, I suppose. They'd been in the same maternity ward, in adjacent beds, when their first babies had been born. It seems to have provided the setting for the birth of most of the friendships between the mums in my circle. Andrea and Karen had been inseparable, meeting up every day in the park or playgroup or swimming pool. They'd shopped together, breastfed together, swapped nipple creams and weaning tips. And when Karen embarked upon her successive pregnancies with mind-boggling speed and regularity, it was Andrea she turned to for support.

I thought I'd got over my profound jealousy of this bond between Andrea and Karen that I could never replicate, but now it was all creeping back, washing over me like nausea.

When Andrea finally spoke, she seemed to be talking to herself. 'After all these years. Karen Danson.' She sighed and shook her head. I waited patiently for her to remember that I was here. When she did, she was mortified. 'God, Lorn, I'm so sorry. You must be feeling terrible! So what's she doing back? What does she want? I can't believe she's got the nerve to just turn up like this with no warning!'

I swallowed my jealousy and reminded myself that the length of my friendship with Andrea far exceeded the four years she had shared with Karen, however intense those years might have been. 'Rob only heard from her this morning. We don't know what she wants, just that she needs to speak to him. Rob thinks it might be good news. You know, she might want a divorce.'

Andrea snorted at this. 'Has Rob actually *said* that he thinks that's good news?'

I bristled at this. 'Don't start all this, Ange. I'm not in the mood. Not today.'

'Ten years, Lorna. He could have divorced her after five years without her consent. He could have contacted her through her parents. All he had to do was—'

'Thank you, Andrea. I'm painfully aware of British divorce laws. You know it's more complex than that.'

'No, it's not complex at all.'

'Ange, please!'

'OK, OK. So Karen's back. It's a bit of a shock but you can handle it. You and Rob and the kids, you're a family. She can't hurt you. Rob's probably right. She probably just wants a divorce.'

'You just accused Rob of *not* wanting a divorce.'

Andrea raised her hands up in resignation. 'Don't take any notice of me. I don't know what I'm saying. I'm premenstrual, maybe even premenopausal. I'll probably have to shoplift tins of pilchards from Asda after lunch.'

She smiled and so did I.

The drink was making me reckless. 'What do you think she'll be like?' I asked.

Andrea shrugged. 'Two years of therapy. Eight years in America. She'll be taking Prozac and have big hair. Shall we get another bottle?'

I was going to be all right.

18

Chapter Three

The hangover kicked in during the afternoon. I marked my exam papers in a Distalgesic haze, adding ten per cent to every student's marks to compensate for my total lack of commitment to the exercise. All the girls got back in time for *Home and Away*. I fell asleep. They tiptoed around me knowing that, if I didn't wake up to get dinner started until their dad got home, we'd all go to Pizza Express.

I didn't wake up. Rob came home. We went to Pizza Express where I drank a litre of mineral water and ate five packets of breadsticks. Somehow I made it to my evening class where I delivered an incomprehensible lecture on the philosophical implications of the Second Law of Thermodynamics. I didn't understand it myself and I was giving it, always a bad sign. But I'm confident that the lecture was good. I was performing on pre-programmed autopilot and my students applauded.

It's an impressive skill but this is not a rare feat, even or especially for a mum. It is commonly accepted among women (and among men – although they dare not mention it in female company) that a mother's brain cells die at a rate in direct proportion to the growth of her children from embryo onwards. It makes little difference whether you've actually given birth or not,

19

the erosion begins whenever you pick up the parenting process. Once you accept this fact, and we all do, believe me, there are only two possible outcomes: total cerebral atrophy or a carefully planned sacrifice of the less useful half of your personal cortex.

In my case, I needed to preserve my salary-earning teaching and analytic skills at the expense of my spatial awareness and physical coordination. Hence I can produce a competent discourse on Aristotle, even when drunk, but I will never get the hang of line-dancing. I have divided myself into two different, separate women – the mother one and the other one. And it's absolutely essential for my professional and emotional wellbeing that the barrier between the two remains defined and unbroken.

As I packed my notes and books away, I began my soft-shoe shuffle back from teacher to mother mode. It was a short, easy, much-travelled bridge.

'Are you OK, Lorna?' It was one of my students, looking concerned. I clearly hadn't applied enough make-up to my ravaged face.

'I'm fine, Simon, just a bit tired, you know how it is,' I replied cheerfully. What an imbecilic response. How could he possibly know how anything is? Simon Flynn is twenty-nine, single and his biggest responsibility seems to be keeping his rather magnificent head of curls in order. In one of my rare moments of enhanced self-esteem, I had considered the possibility that he might have a crush on me. Ridiculous word, crush, for one grown-up to use about another but the whole notion is a bit ridiculous in itself.

I'd never got very involved personally with my students. I was always too tired to join them for a drink after college and the course was sufficiently demanding that the two-hour sessions allowed no extra time for any chit-chat. But Simon had often walked out to my car with me and, over the nine months that I'd been teaching him, we'd covered quite a lot of each other's lives.

He was the classic example of the bright student who was never encouraged at school and left with all his potential untapped. After drifting from job to job, he found he had a skill for computing and design just at the time when Internet website-building was emerging as a growth industry. He was soon earning a lot of money and started to look at improving his education so that he could broaden the application of his skills.

He was finally spurred to enrol on my course when his girlfriend left him after a live-in relationship. He mentioned that it was something to do with his wanting kids and her preferring cats. This was as intimate as we'd ever got.

Simon didn't appear convinced by my assurances that I was fine and he was reluctant to go. 'Well, if you're sure.'

'I'm sure.' If I sounded curt, it's because I was suddenly exhausted and wanted to get home.

He took the hint. "Take care then. See you next week.'

I smiled in compensation for my abruptness. 'See you next week.' Then he left. I allowed a few minutes to avoid having to walk to the car with him and make conversation.

I tried to relax. I unclenched my stomach muscles, visualised Rob and the girls and made a mental note to myself to check Teletext when I got home to see what had happened on *Home and Away*. But this time the muscles clenched right back up again. I remembered Karen.

When I got home, I'd completely forgotten about checking Teletext. (Must be in shock.) Rob was on the computer, chatting over the Net with a dog trainer in Delhi. He raised his hand to acknowledge my presence and made some gesture that translated into something along the lines of: 'I won't be long, sweetheart, but we're just discussing techniques to correct territorial defecation among border collies during the rainy season.' Something like that.

My headache had settled into a polite throb and I felt calm. Rob wouldn't be on the computer if something dramatic had happened. He would be examining the sell-by dates on the tins in the kitchen cupboard. That was his thing. In times of difficulty, I got drunk with my friends and Rob sorted out the fridge.

I made us both some hot chocolate and switched on the television. Rob came through just as I sat down. 'How were your students?' he asked.

My mouth dropped. 'They spontaneously combusted. What difference does it make? What happened with Karen?'

He was casual, too, too casual. 'Fine. No problem. I'm seeing her tomorrow for lunch.'

I waited for him to elaborate. He didn't. 'And?' I prompted in exasperation.

'And what?' He didn't do coy innocence very well. Few men do.

'What did she have to say for herself? You must have spoken about things. Our daughters, for example. *Her* daughters? Or would you rather not tell me? Fine. Be secretive.'

Rob pretended not to hear this. He picked up the *Radio Times* and started turning over the pages, head down, with that metronomic regularity favoured by people who are trying to avoid attention. There are 130 pages in the *Radio Times* (excluding the Christmas/New Year double issue, obviously) so I didn't anticipate waiting much longer than two minutes and ten seconds (two seconds per double page flick) before he would either have to speak to me or feign interest in *Casualty*'s latest love triangle.

He didn't even make it to two minutes. He threw the magazine down in resignation. 'We didn't exactly have a pleasant chat, if that's what you're getting at. It was very awkward, if you must know.'

'Did she ask about the girls?'

'Of course she did!' he snapped back. 'It was the first thing she asked. But she knew all about them. Her mum's kept her posted, sent her photos and things.'

I'd guessed that but I didn't like hearing it. I didn't want her to know about our lives, not the details, anyway. They belonged to us, to our sealed family unit. She was not a part of that. She'd left, I'd joined and we'd locked the doors behind us.

Rob went on. 'She just wanted me to know that she's back and to discuss a few things.'

'What things?' I asked quickly.

Rob exhaled with forced patience. 'Lorna, I don't know. I've told you. I'm seeing her tomorrow. We'll thrash it all out and then we'll all know where we stand.'

He threw me what was supposed to be a reassuring glance. Insecurity must have been emblazoned on my face like a hideous warty growth. He walked over and hugged me tightly. 'Oh Lorna, I know how difficult this must be for you. But I love you. Do you hear me? I love you and the girls more than anyone or anything. This is *our* home now and Karen isn't going to break it up. I love *you*. Only you.'

23

I let myself believe him. I did believe him. I'd believed him before the letter from Karen arrived and nothing had effectively changed so I had little choice.

I wanted to talk through the hundred 'what ifs' that were flooding my worry centre. I didn't because I knew that would annoy him. And I didn't dare risk that, not until I knew what I was up against. Oh yes, I already saw Karen as a rival and I was preparing myself for the contest. I decided to wash my hair before I went to bed so that it would look fluffy and tousled when Rob left me in the morning. It was a look he'd always loved and I wanted him to take it with him into the meeting with Karen.

I briefly contemplated seducing him with wild abandon but I knew that he'd just fall about laughing. I couldn't make up my mind what this said about our sex life and now was not the time to analyse the issue.

I switched off the television and kissed Rob gently. 'Sorry to cross-examine you like this. I'm just a bit . . . you know.'

He knew. 'You look tired, Lorna. Good lunch with Andrea?'

'How did you know I had lunch with Andrea?'

Rob laughed out loud. 'I can always tell!' He started listing the clues on his fingers, with obvious satisfaction. 'You always fall asleep on the sofa afterwards; you always root around for Distalgesics and leave the bathroom cabinet door open; you always drink up all the mineral water and juice in the fridge; Teletext is always set at the soaps page, so you can catch up on *Neighbours* and/or *Home and Away* which you will have missed; there are fruit pastille wrappers sticking out from between the sofa cushions because you falsely think they will mask the smell of alcohol with a less obvious aroma than mints. Need I continue?'

I laughed until it hurt. Or maybe it was the Distalgesics wearing off and the original hangover returning. A thought occurred. 'Do you want me to cancel tomorrow night?'

Rob looked baffled. 'What's happening tomorrow night?'

I was exasperated and only my new insecurity stopped me from saying something accusatory. 'Don't you remember? We're having Andrea and Dan over for dinner. And the Jacksons.'

'Oh yes.' He tried to look enthusiastic but just looked vacant.

'So do you think we should cancel?'

'Of course not. I've already told you, there's nothing to worry about. Who knows? Maybe we'll even have something to celebrate tomorrow night.'

We both pretended that this was a real possibility and the tension of the moment dissipated. I was exhausted. We spent a few minutes discussing the girls, something we always loved to do at the end of each day, then I went up to bed. I usually went to bed before him and, suddenly, it was absolutely vital that everything was as ordinary as possible for this one last night.

I washed my hair gently, trying not to aggravate my headache into a migraine. Migraines are not attractive features in women outside Jane Austen novels. I applied a generous dollop of my most expensive hair conditioner and even waited the full recommended five minutes before washing it out. And let's face it, who does that?

I spent the five minutes rummaging through my nightie drawer. I had to choose carefully, not wanting to make it obvious to Rob that I was answering a call to battle. I quickly ranked my clothes from one to five in terms of sexual allure and picked the pyjamas that had once occupied the number one spot but which frequent high-temperature washes with biological detergent had relegated to number three. The tone I was aiming for was of subtle reminder rather than open invitation.

Newly fluffed and adorned in once-sexy-but-not-really-any-more pyjamas, I looked in on the girls. Phoebe was still awake, reading. Her face lit up when she saw me. 'What are you reading?' I whispered, not wanting to wake Claire who shared the room. Phoebe held up her book: *Philosophy Made Simple*. It was my subject and the significance of her choice made me want to weep with gratitude for her acceptance, her love. I blew her a kiss as usual, stifling my urge to take her in my arms and hug her to sleep as I'd done so often when she was smaller and troubled by nightmares.

We shared a conspiratorial smile as Claire produced a belch-like snorty snore that sounded exactly like Rob's. I always looked for Rob in his children. Every familiarity was a reinforcement of my fantasy that these girls were Rob's and Rob's alone. I'd seen pictures of Karen, of course, but I'd stopped myself from searching for bits of her in the girls.

Phoebe was absolutely her father's daughter with her sensitive nature and complicated face that couldn't decide whether to be plain or pretty. Claire, well, beautiful Claire snored like Rob and that was about it. There was nothing of Rob in her face although his mother insists that her eyebrows look like Rob's at the same age. I've learned that such batty, deluded observation is common with grandparents. It was much easier with the youngest two. If you cut up photographs of Jude and Ali, you could probably produce a spot-on photofit composite of a young Rob. Their personalities were very different. Ali had inherited Rob's quiet love of books and his gift for relating to animals whereas Jude harboured a wild core that was continually threatening to burst through when the appropriate opportunity came along. Any opportunity would do, she wasn't discerning.

I poked my head around the twins' door. They weren't identical but they both clung to their twinness, enjoying the specialness, the joint identity it bestowed upon them. Only twenty-seven months separated the four girls but Jude and Ali were still very much the youngest children. There's such a big difference between twelve and fourteen and they resented the exclusion from their older sisters' arcane initiations into teenage ritual.

My four girls. They defined my life and the fact scared me witless. I reluctantly dragged myself away and took myself to bed. I started to read something by a dyslexic Irish author nominated for the Booker Prize, gave up and moved on to a *Reader's Digest* omnibus of condensed classics. Now my headache had really come back. I took a couple more painkillers to knock me out and sank into blissful sleep.

Chapter Four

'What's happened to your hair?' I heard this five times before eight o'clock. Once from Rob and once from each of my four treacherous daughters who have not yet got enough experience in womanhood to know that this is a loaded comment to pass on to another of their sex. They all had a point, of course. I had slept terribly, turning on my pillow all night. The over-generous application of hair conditioner must have reacted with my pillowcase to produce an Afro effect which wouldn't have looked out of place in an episode of *Starsky and Hutch*.

'Am I the first person in this house to have a bad hair day?' I asked in frustration. Phoebe crumpled slightly over her Rice Krispies, fingering her own listless fringe miserably. I cursed my thoughtlessness. Awkward silence. As always, it was my job to defuse the tension. When in doubt, change the subject. 'So. What are we going to do about Dad's birthday?'

Everyone brightened up. 'Definitely a party,' Jude announced. 'We all want a party.'

'In a nightclub,' Claire suggested.

'Or a zoo. You can have parties in zoos. Dad would like that.' This was Ali's offering.

'Don't be stupid,' Claire scoffed. 'Dad spends half his life with animals. No, I think we should have it

28

somewhere really swish where we all have to get dressed up.' Since Claire would use a trip to the dentist as an excuse for a new top, it was reasonable to assume that the prospect of a shopping trip was the key motivation behind her idea.

'What about you, Phoebe? What do you think we should do?' I asked.

Phoebe let go of her hair at last and gave the question some thought.

'Don't ask her!' Claire said. 'She'll want to have a "nice quiet dinner with the family".' She mimicked Phoebe's gentle voice cruelly but accurately.

'There's nothing wrong with that!' Phoebe replied. 'Dad loves family dinners. He's always saying that. And it is *his* birthday, after all.'

She was absolutely right. There was nothing Rob liked more than a meal with his family, maybe a film first, or ten-pin bowling. Then on to the station to the pick-and-mix sweet stall. We'd all grab a bag and fill it to the brim with our personal favourites: Rob would have red liquorice laces and I'd have the pink candy shrimps and creamy, chewy milk bottles. The girls' choices varied according to their moods and fads. We'd eat them on the way home then collapse into armchairs, stuffed and overdosed on sugar.

It was how we always celebrated family birthdays. Occasionally one of the girls would invite a friend but, usually, it was just us lot. That was how we liked it.

'Phoebe's got a point. Your dad would enjoy a family dinner, but . . .' I quickly went on, predicting a riot among the younger girls, 'it *is* a special birthday and I think we ought to do something special.'

'Yes!' Claire hissed, clenching her fist in triumph,

already envisaging a Saturday spent rummaging through Top Shop.

Phoebe looked disappointed. 'I still think Dad would like things done the usual way.'

'Maybe, Phoebe. But all the family will be there. There'll just be some friends as well. And all the grandparents. It'll be lovely, you'll see.'

Actually, I had no idea what it would be like. I couldn't see beyond the present situation with Karen. Where would she be in a few months' time? What part would she be playing in our lives? With a bit of luck, she'd be back in the US, maybe with divorce papers in her suitcase. Maybe we could even use Rob's fortieth birthday as an excuse for a double celebration. I mean, he sounded quite enthusiastic about a divorce. And that must mean that he's thinking about . . . No. I won't say the words. If I even think it, then it won't happen. That's the rule.

I tried to blot thoughts of Karen from my head. 'So, what are we going to get Dad as a present?' That got them going.

'A set of golf clubs?' proposed Jude.

'But Dad doesn't even play golf.'

'No, but it's what you buy people when they're old.'

'Dad's not old!'

'He's going to be forty. That's ancient!'

'How about a book on dogs?'

'Oh, brilliant idea, Ali. He's only got fifteen million books on dogs already.'

'How about a watch?'

'Very original, Phoebe.'

'I know what Dad's always wanted.' Claire's pronouncement made us all stop short.

'Well. What?'

Claire smiled that beautiful slow smile that owed nothing to her father's genes. 'A trip to the Wolf Sanctuary in America.'

Of course. Why didn't I think of that? Many of his colleagues had visited the Wolf Sanctuary and he'd always said that he'd go there if we won the lottery. It was a huge enclosed area of land in the Midwest, where wolves could be studied in their natural environment. Rob loved wolves. He loved looking for the wild, instinctive behavioural patterns that he could interpret and control in the wolf's distant cousin, the dog. Wolves possessed all the beauty and intelligence of dogs but none of the accessibility. The wild wolf and the domesticated dog – so closely related and yet so distant in nature. I once asked Rob if he preferred wolves to dogs. He blushed as if I'd asked him a deeply intimate, revealing question. And he didn't answer. Yes. The Wolf Sanctuary. That was definitely the present of a lifetime.

I was childishly peeved that Claire should think of this rather than me. But it made sense that she should know instinctively what her father would like best. Just as Phoebe was my special girl, Claire was Rob's. Like me, he maintained the lie that he had no favourites, but it was clear that Claire and he had a rapport that the others could not replicate. All the girls knew it. And of course I couldn't criticise Rob for his show of favouritism when my own feelings for Phoebe were equally obvious to him.

I shook off my disloyal thoughts and hugged Claire. 'That's brilliant, you're a genius!' Claire blushed at the compliment. It wasn't often that she was praised for her mind. She took it as an incentive to assume control of the project. 'If you like, I'll look up their website after

31

school and find out how we go about arranging a trip there.'

'That would be great. Now we mustn't let your dad get wind of this idea. It'll be a fantastic surprise!'

I looked at the clock. It was eight thirty. 'Eight thirty! You're late! Quick! Out the door. You're all going to be late!'

'Stop stressing, Mum. There's plenty of time. We're usually early anyway.'

'Yes, maybe, but you can never tell what hold-ups there'll be.' They all laughed indulgently. My neurotic punctuality had long ago ceased to be an annoyance and now provided a source of familiar amusement.

They walked out of the door, deliberately strolling slowly to annoy me. Their kisses were all affectionate but something was different. It was me. My needs had changed. I wanted more. I wanted them to hug me, tell me they loved me. But how could they know that our life was under threat? I restrained myself from grabbing them and holding them tight. Let them enjoy the normality while they can. 'Bye,' I called from the door.

They were all chatting so excitedly that they didn't hear me. As I closed the door, I could only think of one thing. How could I ever find the money to send Rob to the Wolf Sanctuary?

The house was empty and I started to panic. I switched the television on but it just irritated me. I wished I smoked or had the lack of inhibition to start drinking before midday. Perhaps I should start compulsive eating. By all accounts, it was a distracting pastime and could even leave me with a weight problem that might prove an effective diversion from my current obsession.

32

How was I going to get through the day, imagining Rob's lunch with Karen? I had already drawn up mental storyboards for every conceivable outcome of their reunion. The possibilities ranged from the Walt Disney encounter where both actors struggled with awkward silences across a wobbly table waited upon by the comedy waiter with a funny walk, all the way up to the Sharon Stone version where they ended up in an Art Deco hotel room and rediscovered their marital rhythms to the pulsating accompaniment of Donna Summer's 'I Feel Love.'

This was sheer torture. I had no choice. I knew what I had to do. I called Andrea (again). The answering machine was on (again) and I left a desperate message (again). 'Hi, there. Me. Friday morning. Give me a call as soon as you get in. Planning to do something drastic. You can either dissuade me or join me.'

'This is a ridiculous idea.'

I knew Andrea would say that. 'So you're going to try and talk me out of it?'

'Did I say that? No, it's a ridiculous idea but I love it. Count me in.'

And so it was that two otherwise normal women with a high standing in South London mothering circles donned hats and macs and sidled towards Clapham Junction, trying and failing miserably to look unsuspicious. Yes, I know the clothes sound a little clichéd but how else is a woman supposed to follow someone who knows every item in her wardrobe? Besides, at least we didn't resort to sunglasses. Not in February. I may be deranged but I cling on to a minimal standard of fashion conformity.

'So tell me once more. What exactly is the plan?'

Andrea, a stickler for order and reason, always liked to have a concrete grasp on a situation.

I sighed. I thought I'd explained myself very clearly, albeit hysterically, when she turned up. 'As I said, we're going to follow Rob from the surgery to wherever he's meeting Karen.'

'I know that. It's what we do next that I don't quite understand.'

'Shoot a poison dart at her. I don't know,' I snapped. 'I haven't decided what we'll do next. I just want to see her.' I rubbed my head. Terrific. I was getting a headache and I hadn't even had a drink. Where was the cosmic justice in that?

When we stopped at the zebra crossing, I looked at Andrea more closely. 'God, Ange, where on earth did you get that coat and hat? You look like Danny De Vito.'

She was wearing a raincoat that was at least three sizes too big and formed a teepee over her tiny five-feet-nothing frame. Her striped hat, which didn't have a single shade of colour in common with the coat, was floppy and unflattering. It was as if she'd gone into a fancy dress hire shop and asked for a comic book disguise kit. All that was missing was the fake beard and moustache.

Andrea looked sheepish. 'I got it in the charity shop.'

I shook my head in admiration. 'How did you have time to get to the charity shop this morning before coming round to me? I mean, I'm impressed by your thoroughness and professionalism—'

She interrupted, 'I didn't buy it today. I bought it a while ago.'

I raised my eyebrows. 'What, just in case? What incredible foresight! I mean, I've got clothes that I bought in reserve for one-off occasions, unexpected funerals, lunches at the Savoy, that sort of thing. But you must be the only person I know who has a prepared outfit for short-notice spying expeditions.'

Before Andrea could answer, I grabbed her and yanked her into the newsagent. 'Quick, hide! Here comes Rob!' To her credit, Andrea went into conspiratorial mode with remarkable speed and efficiency. She immediately buried her head in a copy of *Woman's Own* while I faffed about in the ice cream cabinet muttering in a stage whisper about the desperate need for a tropical fruit-flavoured Calippo. Needless to say, it was me that the newsagent took to be showing ominous 'care in the community' tendencies.

Rob was too absorbed in his own thoughts to notice the two crazy women in the paper shop and walked on by to the station. We sneaked out of the shop before the police could be called and followed him into the station ticket hall.

A short lesson in following a subject effectively across all modes of transport: buy a Travelcard. Regrettably, Andrea and I had not been tutored in such basic rules. So it was that we fumbled frantically about in our purses and pockets, looking for enough change to buy two tickets from the machine since there was a queue at the ticket office. As we had no idea where we were going, we had to buy Travelcards that covered the entire Greater London network. Who could tell if Rob had chosen to celebrate his reunion with Karen in leafy Bromley or nearby Balham?

We got our tickets just in time to spot Rob heading up the stairs for the Victoria-bound platform. Typical, we buy tickets to carry us thirty miles into suburbia and Rob decides to go one station to central London. With quickly evolving cunning, we waited at the bottom of the stairs until we heard the train pull in. At that point, we dashed up the stairs and ran to the back of the train where we jumped on, concealed by two businessmen who were in urgent need of diet hints.

We noticed that the other passengers were staring at us strangely and, for a moment, couldn't understand why. Then we caught sight of our reflections – we looked seriously ridiculous. As the train began to move, we burst into girlish giggles. The journey to Victoria only takes seven minutes, just enough time for me to formulate the next part of our strategy.

'So, when he gets to the restaurant, we loiter on the other side of the street until Karen arrives. Then when she goes in, we take turns in walking past the window every few minutes to see what they're up to.' That was the plan. Not exactly John le Carré but then he wasn't a mother with half of his brain cells shot into the ether. Andrea couldn't think of anything better, so we agreed that this would have to do.

The train was crowded so it was easy to follow Rob from Victoria without being seen. We didn't have far to go. As he left the station, he crossed Victoria Street and went straight into Pizza Express.

'How could he?' I screamed at Andrea. 'Pizza Express is *our* restaurant. Our family's! How could he take *her* there?'

'But you don't go to this Pizza Express, do you? I thought you went to the Battersea one?' Andrea was tentative in her attempt to clarify this distinction. Mistake. I rounded on her, defending my right to take offence like a virago protecting her maidenhood.

'What difference does that make? If Pizza Express is our place, then surely that includes the whole chain, not just the one we frequent most often.'

36

Hah! Andrea couldn't argue with that! In fairness, she couldn't relate to the problem since her and Dan's restaurant was the Waterside Inn in Berkshire which didn't have a thousand franchises on high streets throughout middle England. This would certainly simplify matters should she or Dan ever need to take a former partner out for a reunion lunch without offending their present spouse – there would only be the one place to avoid rather than the thousand. If I ever have another relationship, I'll bear that in mind.

By now, Rob was in the restaurant and Andrea and I were loitering outside a souvenir shop, pretending to be engrossed in a display of T-shirts, all of which bore the slogan: 'My — went to London and all I got was this lousy T-shirt.'

We were both impressed at the extensive range of human types that were inserted in this basic phrase. The original 'mum', 'dad', 'brother', 'sister', 'boyfriend' and 'girlfriend' had been joined by 'stepsister', 'ex-husband', 'cellmate' and 'prayer group leader'. It was a veritable catalogue of relationships, most of which were inapplicable to my own life. (Memo to self: get out more.)

It was five to one. It seemed likely that the time of meeting was one. I looked up and down the street, scrutinising every female face for vague resemblances to ten-year-old photos. My eyes kept darting maniacally towards Andrea, searching for that first sign of recognition.

'There she is.' Andrea's words were quiet and full of foreboding. I knew then that Karen was going to be beautiful. She was.

Karen was floating down the street, taking no notice of her surroundings. She knew exactly where she was

37

going. I envied her ability to arrive somewhere new without struggling to hold on to an *A to Z*, a handbag and a mobile phone in case of emergency. She seemed not to have a worry in the world. Naturally calm. Serene, even. Cow. She was about my height and build but a zillion times glossier. She had that glow that all the women in *Friends* seem to exude. Maybe it's just down to better dentistry, I don't know, but it's real and palpable. Her hair wasn't big, as we'd imagined. It was cropped tightly to her head giving her the gamine look of a young Audrey Hepburn. She could have been twenty-eight instead of thirty-eight.

My resentment spilled out. 'We could all look twenty-eight if we didn't have four children to bring up.'

Andrea touched my arm. 'Don't let it get to you. I bet close up you'd see she's wearing an inch of fake tan and spot concealer.'

I wasn't reassured because I wasn't listening. As she turned into the restaurant, I had only one word ringing through my head. Claire. It could have been Claire walking by, the same face, even the same gait.

'She's the image of Claire,' I whispered.

'I think you mean that Claire's the image of Karen,' Andrea pointed out. In my next life, the one where I'm the first wife, the beautiful serene one with an 'our restaurant' that doesn't have subsidiaries, I'm going to make sure I choose unreasonable, irrational, ditsy friends who do not correct my sentence constructions.

'Why did she have to look like Claire?' I asked out loud. Andrea didn't answer, not daring to try and second-guess the point I was making. 'You know what this means, don't you?' I continued.

She didn't.

I sighed. 'Which of the girls is Rob's favourite? Come on, you've noticed it yourself. It's Claire.'

Andrea was beginning to look oppressed. She had caught up with my zig-zag train of thought and saw where it was leading. She pointed up to the sky like a madwoman. 'Oh look! Is that Concorde?' Since it was an easyJet plane with its garish orange bodypaint, I immediately interpreted Andrea's idiocy as a feeble but well-meaning attempt to change the subject.

I gave her one of my looks. It worked. She crumbled. 'OK, OK. So Claire is Rob's favourite. And Phoebe's your favourite and there's no hidden agenda there either. You feel something special for Phoebe because she needs you so much. That's natural. I'm exactly the same with Isabelle. And when the other girls need you as much, you'll feel the same for them. And Rob feels something special for Claire because . . .'

'Because she's the image of his ex-wife!' I exclaimed in triumph. I went on. 'All right, I mean wife, not ex-wife, before you point that out to me for the thousandth time.'

Andrea held up her hands in innocence. 'I wasn't going to say anything of the kind. What I was going to say before you interrupted me, was that Rob likes Claire for her independence, her feistiness, her confidence. All the opposite qualities you respond to in Phoebe. All children are different and they develop at different speeds. It's how nature ensures that all kids get their fair whack of special favour. Right now, the twins are still wrapped up in themselves but, eventually, they'll emerge as needy individuals and stake their own claims on your attentions.'

Before I had a chance to consider this possibility, Karen disappeared into the restaurant. 'Quick,' I yelled, 'across the road!' I grabbed Andrea's hand and pulled her across the four lanes of moving traffic, ignoring all the horns and screeching brakes that accompanied us. We reached the other side (alive) just in time to see Karen catching her first glimpse of Rob, who was using his breadsticks to drum on his side plate the atmospheric accompaniment to Phil Collins' 'In The Air Tonight'. I knew this because Rob has a limited repertoire of drum solos that he performs with Pizza Express breadsticks. I've seen and heard them so often that I can 'name that tune' even through a double glazed window. I bet Karen can't do that! One more victory chalked up to me.

Oh-oh! He's seen her. He's smiling. Which smile is that? Not 'our' smile, I don't think so anyway. But it's affectionate. What will he do now? I think he's going to kiss her. On the cheek, on the cheek, I prayed silently. He kissed her on the lips. Just briefly. But enough to hurt. He's holding her hands at arm's length and looking her up and down. Admiringly. I pull in my stomach unconsciously. I feel ... I feel ... I feel Andrea poking me roughly in the back.

'What!' I shout, spinning round, reluctant to miss a single moment of the encounter inside. Andrea was looking guilty and embarrassed. A man in a Pizza Express uniform stood in front of us.

'Excuse me, erm, ladies, but if you are not coming in, might I ask you move on? You're upsetting the customers.'

I was about to deliver my best 'I've never been so insulted in my life' line, when I caught sight of Andrea frantically looking up and down at me and I realised that we looked like mentally unbalanced vagrants. I tossed one last hopeful glance at Rob and Karen, who were now sitting down. Thankful that they weren't holding hands, I mumbled an apology, seized Andrea's elbow and pulled her back across to the other side of the road.

Again, we made it over in one piece. Andrea and I paused for a moment, exhausted by the stress of the episode. We each assembled our thoughts into a semblance of sanity before making our way back to Victoria. I only looked back once. Andrea looked at me kindly, full of concern. 'Are you OK, Lorn? Do you feel better now that you've seen her?'

I smiled my best smile. 'I'm fine now. I'm going to be just fine,' I lied.

Calm, calm, calm. Think calm thoughts and you'll fool your body into thinking that you really are calm. Another piece of women's magazine sophistry to upchuck into the spittoon of unwelcome and untrue advice. To be fair, it worked for twenty minutes, just enough for me to survive the train journey back to Clapham Junction and persuade Andrea that I was not going to do anything silly, or rather sillier, since the whole morning had been bonkers.

In fact, from the moment we left Victoria, I was planning my next phase of subterfuge and fully intended to head for the West End to one of those surveillance shops where you can buy spy cameras. It was Andrea who punctured this plan. Fooled into thinking that, inside, I was as calm, calm, calm as my face, she was relaxing into normal conversation. 'So what are you cooking tonight?'

I shrugged my shoulders. 'I don't know, something with oven chips and spaghetti hoops.'

Her puzzled expression made me think again. Oh God! The dinner party! I'd forgotten all about it. Calm,

calm, calm. I laughed, trying not to sound deranged. 'Sorry, I wasn't thinking straight. You mean for us. I was just thinking about the girls. You know me, always thinking of the girls!' That stalled her for a few seconds while I dredged my memory for the contents of the fridge and freezer. I was going to have to produce something impressive for six people, one of whom was a trained cook and another who had an encyclopaedic knowledge of Marks & Spencer's food hall and would spot a St Michael chicken cacciatore even if I turned it out into my own dish and drowned it in herbs.

I was in trouble. I was going to have think up a menu. I was going to have to go shopping. I was going to have to cook all afternoon. I was going to have to stay sober.

Andrea was still waiting for an answer. She is the M & S expert so is always impressed by anyone who would go to the bother of producing food of a similar standard to M & S without opening a single packet. But that's the status quo of our little circle. Andrea had bagsied the 'sluttish slave to expensive convenience food' position while Phillippa Jackson (or the boys' mum, as I still think of her) reigned supreme with her gourmet talents and utter disdain for anything that wasn't imported from Tuscany. I was left with the 'hardworking, barely competent reproducer of Delia Smith recipes' stance. I hadn't asked for this position, I had just moved into the wrong circle at the wrong time.

I made an executive decision. 'I'm going to do a pasta starter, then a beef . . . thingy and a chocolate . . . surprise.' I repeated it a few times silently to myself so that I wouldn't forget it when I got home.

'Mmm. Sounds yummy! What time do you want us there?'

'Is seven thirty all right? I don't want too late a night. Rob will probably want to talk about things.'

'Look, if you'd rather cancel, I'm sure Phillippa will understand.'

'Honestly, it's no problem. I've prepared all the food anyway.'

All couples have rainy-day funds that they only call upon in the direst emergency. I had no hesitation in declaring the dinner party an emergency and withdrawing £200 from the account. I took a taxi to a delicatessen in Belgravia where I bought ready-prepared meals that roughly answered to the description of pasta starter, beef thingy and chocolate surprise. The food came to £163 but I didn't care. It was fantastic. Sadly I would have to reheat it and overcook it all at home, otherwise it would be too obvious that someone other than me had cooked it. The chocolate ganache was covered in exquisitely formed white chocolate curls that I would have to replace with hundreds and thousands for the same reason.

But it meant that I could reclaim the afternoon. I transferred the contents of all the food cartons into pots and dishes so that the façade would be in place as soon as Rob and the girls got home. Then I did what I always do when I can't or don't want to cope with a situation. I went to bed. I lay there, thinking about my life and Karen's invasion of it. I wanted to cry, I longed for the peaceful catharsis that seems to follow the wallowing outbursts so often seen in American mini-series of Danielle Steel novels.

But I didn't. I'm not the crying sort. I just fell asleep.

Chapter Five

'Mum. It's half past six.' Phoebe's whisper penetrated the fog inside my head. It took all of five seconds before the significance of her words sank in. I leapt out of bed and looked blankly around me for some kind of divine prop that would support me through this crisis.

'Why didn't you wake me up earlier?' I yelled. Phoebe shrank. I knew that the girls would have been debating for the past hour who was going to be the miserable wretch that tried to rouse me. Poor Phoebe drew that short straw – the penalty for being maternal favourite. For a moment of happy distraction, I comforted myself with this new realisation that there *is* a penalty to being a favourite and that the other girls might actually be grateful rather than resentful that they were not the chosen ones. Thus bolstering my parental self-esteem, I dragged myself back to the present situation.

Half past six. Half past six. They'll all be getting here in an hour. Got to tidy up, sort out the food, set the table, have a shower and make myself look as if I was in control. I kissed Phoebe and we walked downstairs together. 'Sorry I shouted. I just can't believe I slept so long. You haven't forgotten that we've got the Jacksons and the Millers coming over?'

'Oh, sorry Mum, we had. We'd have woken you sooner if we'd remembered.'

'Don't worry. All the food's ready. It's not a disaster.' As I looked at the clock in the kitchen, another uncomfortable thought occurred to me. 'Isn't your dad home yet?'

Phoebe shook her head. 'Maybe he's stopped off to get wine or something,' she suggested.

No. It wouldn't be that. Even if he had, he would have been home by now. When Karen first left him, he had resolved that he would always leave work on time and always be home before six o'clock. It was a promise he made to his daughters, recognising that they needed all the security he could provide in the light of their mother's abandonment. If ever he was planning to go out after work or just popping to the shops, he made sure that we all knew about it in advance. Normally I would be worried about this lateness, but I had to sort out the dinner preparations before our guests arrived. I postponed my concerns accordingly, already planning some acid but witty comments to accuse and amuse him with when he finally turned up.

The hour passed in a whizz of frenetic activity. I even managed to feed the girls and clear up after them. OK, so they had Pot Noodles and all I had to wash up were four forks but they were thrilled. Pot Noodles were currently very cool among their circle of friends. Most parents were affronted by a foodstuff that required no more than the addition of boiling water and whose ingredients included little not prefixed by the letter E. Mums everywhere refused to succumb to this appalling attack on their earth-mother aspirations. For goodness' sake, they weren't even organic. Hence Pot Noodles were elevated to cult status in playgrounds across the country.

By the time seven thirty arrived, the girls were all

ensconced in their bedrooms with comics (if you can call the semi-pornographic magazines, masquerading as teenage fodder, comics). I poured myself a gin and tonic and calmed myself down. Then it came back to me. Rob was still not home. I checked that there were no messages on the answerphone. Then I called his mobile, which was switched off. I couldn't make up my mind whether I should be angry or concerned. The doorbell rang just as I'd settled for angry. It was Phillippa and Joe, as obsessive about punctuality as I am. The dogs rushed out to greet them first, jumping up and generously spreading a layer of hair all over their expensive clothes.

Phillippa looked immaculate as always. She was utterly, infuriatingly groomed. She was tall and slim and her clothes fit her in the way that only expensive clothes do. She had what I call upper-class hair, you know, that mid-length, natural blonde bob where every strand stays in place without any visible spray. And her face was perfect, angular and flawless. I always wonder if her astonishing bone structure is the result of expert make-up rather than natural assets but I will probably never know. I've never seen her without the full treatment, no matter how casual the occasion. If I dropped in unexpectedly at six o'clock in the morning, I suspect I would have to wait outside until she'd made herself up.

Joe wore his breeding like a brand across his sculpted face. He oozed that self-reliance that only men who had been sent away to boarding school at the age of four ever have the necessity to develop. I knew that there must be depths below the relentlessly amiable façade he presented, but I didn't know how to reach them. He didn't invite intimacy and our backgrounds were too different for me to find common ground that might lead to any kind of meaningful contact.

He looked as if he'd been selected from a catalogue to complement his wife in every respect. In a room containing a thousand people that you had never met before, you would be able to pair off Phillippa and Joe within minutes. I've never encountered that kind of perfect unison before and it makes me feel a little uneasy when I see how it doesn't apply to my own off-kilter, but happy, non-marriage.

Rob and I always laughed about how we felt a bit shabby and grubby in their presence. (This was before we lost our sense of humour yesterday.) We would never have chosen them as friends but the shared burdens of bringing up children had consigned our differences to the shadows, highlighting only the common bonds that now kept us in touch.

And we were true friends now. They had proven to be loyal and loving, supporting our whole family through those difficult early years. It was enough to make me forgive Phillippa for her current penchant for Country Casuals clothes, the fashion choice of Cirencester matrons and women who just want to look grown-up when they don't feel it.

We kissed affectionately and I happily relieved them of the two bottles of good champagne that they were carrying.

'How's it going, Lorna?' Joe asked. 'Something smells good!' He was married to someone who made her own filo pastry but he was always generous about my feeble attempts. Then I remembered that the food had been prepared by a Michelin-starred chef and had cost me £163. It really *did* smell good. I felt unashamedly proud, if not of my cooking skills, then of

47

my indisputable initiative in the face of challenging circumstances.

They made their way through to the living room. We'd all spent enough time in each other's houses over the years to feel comfortable about making ourselves at home. Joe went straight to our drinks cabinet and got the champagne glasses out.

'Shall I pour now or should we wait for the others?' he asked.

'Just pour it, sweetie,' Phillippa answered. I thought she sounded a bit abrupt and wondered if they'd had a row before they got here. I'd try and get her on her own later and find out what was going on.

'So where's the dogman himself?' Joe asked, as he played tug-of-war with JR while Kili lay on her back in front of Phillippa, waiting for her tummy to be tickled. I took my glass of champagne from him and swallowed a gulp.

'Cheers, everyone. Who knows where Rob is? Wherever he is, it is in a black hole where all communication has been rendered an utter impossibility.' There was an embarrassed silence and I tried to lighten my tone. 'Oh you know Rob. He'll be stuck in the off licence trying to get away from some old biddy who wants to know how to stop her fat Jack Russell from weeing on the postman's shoes.' Nobody was convinced and we all speeded up our drinking pace.

The doorbell rang again. The dogs jumped up and rushed to the door, ever-disloyal, always on the lookout for the better friend, always hoping that maybe the next visitors would have Maltesers in their pockets. It was Andrea and Dan and they did have Maltesers in their pockets. The dogs went berserk, leaping up with tongues stretching out to bestow drooly kisses on their benefactors.

Dan looked tired, I thought. He always had that rough-and-ready look that takes a lot of grooming for a man to achieve but tonight he simply looked as if he was too tired to make an effort. He looked less like Bruce Willis and more like Patrick Moore. Oh well, we all have our off moments. It took five minutes and two packets of Maltesers before Andrea and Dan could make it through the front door. Joe and Phillippa greeted them warmly and poured them some champagne. I went into the kitchen to check on dinner. I could hear Joe's loud whispers (men don't do whispers very well) as he explained dramatically that Rob had gone missing and I was in a mood. Andrea came straight out to see me.

'What's going on? Where's Rob?'

I stirred the pasta with a little more aggression than the instructions dictated. 'No idea.'

'You don't think he's still with Karen?' Andrea asked.

I dropped the spoon and almost collapsed at this possibility which, astonishingly, I hadn't considered. 'What is that supposed to mean?' I asked, trying to catch my breath. 'What are you suggesting? That they went to some hotel or something? That maybe they've run off together?' The calm, calm, calm thing wasn't working.

'Calm down, Lorna, I wasn't suggesting anything. It's just unusual for Rob to be unreliable . . .'

'Who says he's unreliable? Maybe he's been in an accident. We don't know what's happened.'

Andrea held up her hands. 'OK, OK. Take it easy.'

It was another of those occasions where it would have been useful if I could cry. Instead of showing my weakness and maybe even getting a hug for comfort, I just tensed all my facial muscles and appeared belligerent. Stubborn. Unlikeable.

49

A key turned in the lock. It was Rob's key. Andrea exhaled noisily in relief. 'Thank God for that.'

Rob walked in, all smiles and flowers. He kissed me causually and waggled the carnations before me. 'Special offer at the garage,' he announced proudly.

I would have killed him then and there but we had guests and there was £163 worth of food that had to be eaten and appreciated. I kept my voice as normal as I could. 'Where have you been?' I asked evenly, channelling my true feelings into a spatula attack on the innocent beef thingy that was now overcooked to the point where it genuinely looked like one of my own creations.

'Didn't you get my message?' Rob looked surprised.

'No I didn't get your message because there wasn't any message to get.'

'I left a message on your mobile. I was ringing here all afternoon but there was no reply and you hadn't switched the machine on. So I assumed you were out and left word on your mobile voicemail.'

I thought fast. I didn't want to tell him I'd been asleep all afternoon and wouldn't have heard the phone. I hadn't thought to check my mobile. I was confused. It's not easy to relinquish a sense of indignation once it's well established.

Andrea understood this instinctively and intervened smoothly. 'Well, you're here now and that's all that matters! Let me fetch you a glass of champagne before it's all gone.' She left a little more quickly than tact dictated and muted whispers soon drifted our way from the living room.

Rob was oblivious to the drama that had been unfolding on a continuous loop in my imagination since lunchtime. To him, I was the same me with the funny hair that he left this morning. He was wandering around the kitchen, tasting the food, making admiring comments, mumbling something about dogs. I don't know exactly what he was saying because I wasn't listening. 'So where exactly were you?' I asked.

'With Karen, I told you. This pasta sauce is amazing. Why haven't you made this for us before?'

'Don't change the subject. I'm not talking about lunchtime, I'm talking about this evening.'

Rob deliberately avoided looking at me. 'That's what I mean. I was with Karen. We got talking, you know what it's like when you're catching up with someone you haven't seen for years.'

'Well, not exactly,' I replied, no longer bothering to hide my anger. 'I mean, we're not talking about a "someone" here, are we, we're talking about your wife. You spent all afternoon with your wife. And I don't know what that's like. How would I? Marriage is an unknown place in my life. So what form, exactly, did this catching up take?'

'We just had lunch, that's all, Lorn. It dragged on. We had a bit too much wine so we drank coffee until we sobered up. I phoned to let you know I'd be a bit late. I forgot we were having people round. Sorry.' He was holding my hands at arm's length now, just as I saw him do to Karen in the restaurant. I pulled away roughly.

'Of course you forgot. You had other things on your mind.' I was getting loud. I always knew when I was getting loud because Rob lowered his voice in response. I carried on, not caring about my volume. 'So what did Karen have to say for herself that took all afternoon?'

'Shall we talk about this later when everyone's gone?' Rob asked.

I rounded on him. 'No, we shall not. We'll talk about it now. If my family is under threat, I want to know now.'

'Don't be so melodramatic. It's nothing like that. OK. Well, the long and short of it is that she would like to establish some form of contact with the girls. With our agreement, of course.'

'And if we don't agree?'

Rob didn't answer. I shook my head.

'I see. You've already agreed. Without even discussing it with me. But why should you? It's got nothing to do with me, has it? They're not my children.'

'Let's talk about this later. We've got guests.'

'I've got a better idea. Why not call up Karen and ask her to come round and host your dinner party? This is her house, after all. Her name is still on the deeds. How could we forget that? It's *your* name, isn't it? And you always said that she was a fantastic cook.'

Oh no. I've got my hand on my hip and a wooden spoon in my hand. I have turned into a soap opera harridan. I am Pauline Fowler with fluorescent silver hair yelling with dropped aitches at my delinquent son. I am Vera Duckworth screeching in my floral housecoat at my feckless husband. Rob never knows what to say to me at times like this. How could he when he doesn't watch television? He simply doesn't know the lines.

He closed his eyes in a blink of exasperation. He actually prefers my quiet, introspective sulks to one of my hysterical outbursts. Everything buried irretrievably below the surface, that's how Rob likes his life. 'Now you're just being silly. You have absolutely nothing to worry about. I understand why you're a bit cross but there's no need to be ridiculous. Besides, I think something's burning.'

*

I served cheese on toast as a starter and called it *pain surprise*. The surprise was that it wasn't pasta. The pasta (£28.49) had taken umbrage at being first ignored and then violently assaulted and had fused together in an unbreakable union with my nonstick pan. I cut the toast into little squares and put parsley all over it. Since every word of our row along with the loud and dramatic disposal of the ruined pasta had been heard in the living room, our friends were all tensely appreciative of my substitute offering.

'This is delicious, Lorna,' Dan said. Being married to Andrea, who only put things on toast to cover up burned bits, he was probably being honest. 'You'll have to give Angie the recipe.'

That was taking things too far, even by his standards. He winced, a good indicator that Andrea had just kicked him under the table. Actually it made me laugh for the first time since waking up that evening. 'You put cheese on top of toast and stick it under the grill as you well know. I think Andrea might just have that recipe already.'

'Not so you'd notice,' Dan mumbled, 'I can't remember the last time we had bread or cheese in the house that wasn't mouldy.'

Andrea's lips tightened. 'Well, darling, you could always go to that big place yourself, what is it called, oh yes, Sainsbury's. It's incredible how things have changed there. They allow men in now, you know.'

Dan put his knife and fork down noisily. 'And when do I get the chance to go shopping? I work twelve hours a day.'

'Supermarkets are open till ten o'clock at night now.'

'Oh well, that's all right then. I'll add that to my daily schedule, shall I? After all, I can't expect you to do the shopping while I'm at work. You're far too busy. Oh dear, I've forgotten ... what exactly is it that you do all day? Apart from having expensive lunches with your *chums*?'

That's the thing about old friends. They feel no need to conceal from you whatever irritations are currently dogging their personal lives. Just as a woman reaches a point in every relationship where she has to let her partner see her without mascara, so friends eventually drop the façade that theirs is the only perfect trouble-free marriage in the world and let all their troubles hang out cheerfully like shirt-tails.

I've never been able to get a real handle on Dan. Andrea and I are so close that we've effectively got rid of the need to talk about inconsequential matters and, for her, this led to the disappearance of Dan from her frame of reference. I always asked after him, the way you do, and got non-committal answers along the lines of 'fine', 'the usual', 'you know what Dan's like' and so on. But I don't know what Dan's like. When we all get together, I find myself interrogating him, extracting nuggets of solid information to fill in the silhouette that he still represents to me.

I do know that he was brought up in a council house, went to state schools and has an enormous chip on his shoulder about both facts. He always rips into Joe within minutes of seeing him, jokingly (although nobody ever laughs) mocking his public school background, constantly referring to the trust fund that got Joe started in life. The unspoken envy and resentment is obvious to us all.

But Dan's greater tragedy is that he was never really working class with all the kudos that currently holds in the so-called classless Britain. His parents insisted on

54

dragging their family towards middle-class frontiers that they straddled but never quite managed to cross. His dad was a taxi driver and his mum a shoe-shop manager. They may have lived in a council house but they were comfortably off and always had enough money to spend two weeks in Butlins each year. He was mortified when his parents started taking holidays abroad. It robbed him of a clear definition to his class. They didn't even have the foresight to bestow a Geordie accent on him which would provide him with true working-class credibility. People don't have much of an accent in Sidcup. What sort of identity is a man supposed to develop so close to the Blackwall Tunnel?

But he's a successful architect, a good dad and he always clears his plate when he eats here, no mean feat if you knew how hit-and-miss my cooking was. He has an encyclopaedic memory that guarantees he wins every time we play Trivial Pursuit, although he bows to my superior knowledge of the history of TV schedules 1963–present day. He can even do that $3-2-1$ thing with his fingers that Ted Rodgers used to do. In fact, Andrea says it was this skill that first won her over. She really is a girl after my own heart. My kids love Dan too, which is good enough for me.

So if his relationship with Andrea seems to be punctuated with an increasing level of bickering, I try not to be concerned. They've been together since they were students; maybe they're just so confident in the permanence of their partnership that they no longer feel the need to work at preserving it. I'd love that confidence.

But as things were getting a bit nasty, Rob quickly interrupted before matrimonial fists were raised. He frantically tried to think of something safe and non-controversial to say. 'So, Joe? How's work?'

Phillippa and Joe looked at each other. Wrong question, Rob, I thought. Joe cleared his throat nervously. 'Er, yes, work is fine. Well, not brilliant if I'm being honest. You know how things are. Everyone's having to tighten their belts a bit.'

Phillippa glared at him. 'They're not that bad. Don't exaggerate. Anyway, any small problems we have are your own fault. It's just you refusing to chase some of our clients for money. You're too understanding. Too soft. It's no wonder we're bottom of everyone's list when it comes to prioritising payments. You must be the only businessman who takes his clients out to lunch to ask them if they might possibly do us a huge favour and settle a six-month-old invoice.'

'We're a new business, Phil. Goodwill is essential. We can't put clients' backs up when they've had the faith to come with us in the first place.'

'Faith? They haven't come with us out of faith. They've come because you insisted on offering them terms that only a fool would refuse. Stupid terms. Three months to settle invoices. Fifty per cent discounts. Never mind the lavish lunches and dinners. And now we're paying the price.'

'Just give it time. The first year of a new small business is always a little hairy. Things will soon settle down. We're getting lots of interest from outside now. The phone doesn't stop ringing.'

'That's our creditors, darling. I know. It's me who answers the phone, remember? Because we can't afford a receptionist.'

Joe rubbed his temples. I know exactly how he feels. 'Darling, we agreed all this before we started. We

56

agreed the terms of business. We agreed that you would take on the office management in the short term until we stared showing a profit. You said you preferred to stay at home to be around for the boys.'

I ached for Phillippa. There's little worse than having some casual statement you've made in the past being dragged out as evidence of a lifetime statement of sacrificial intent or commitment. I mean, just because a woman has always said she's wanted a baby doesn't mean she's not entitled to moan about the child incessantly when it finally arrives. Why don't other people understand this?

Phillippa's response was to completely ignore Joe's admittedly reasonable point. 'What a true partnership of skills this has turned out to be. *I've* got the MBA but you've got the golf club membership so it's me who plays office skivvy while you do your would-be Richard Branson bit.' She drained her glass and immediately filled it up again, her over-enthusiasm causing the champagne to bubble over the rim and spill on the floor. The dogs rushed over to clear up the puddle. The best they normally get from the floor is Diet Coke with a sprinkling of crisp crumbs so a slurp of vintage champagne and cheesy crumbs proved a welcome treat.

There was a brief lull in hostilities. Definitely time to bring out the main course. 'Wow' was the unanimous reaction to the elaborate beef thingy. That had been mine as well until I came to serve it in the kitchen. It looked fabulous in the dish but, when distributed between six of my enormous dinner plates, the ragout formed tiny thick puddles that refused to spread to the plates' edges. It was supposed to serve six but, plainly, the chef was not like normal people who prefer a meal to satisfy their hunger rather than torment it. It hadn't helped that I'd overheated it and a lot of the gravy had evaporated. I hadn't prepared any vegetables because the ragout was supposed to be a complete dish. I carefully served three grape-sized chunks of beef, two rings of carrot and a comparatively generous four cubes of potato on to each of the six plates. Even when I tried to arrange the vegetables into something decorative and worthy of *Masterchef*, the plates still looked empty.

I rummaged through the cupboard, cursing myself for ignoring that article in *New Woman* about the few essentials you need in your larder with which you can produce a banquet for a hundred people at five minutes' notice. I had no rice, no pasta. Nothing. Saturday was our big shop day. And that was tomorrow. All I had was Pot Noodles.

'Wow!' they all said again. 'What exactly is it?'

'Beef ragout and noodles . . . Florentine.'

Phillippa examined the noodles with interest. 'I think your recipe must have got the name wrong. "Florentine" means that there's spinach in it and I can't see any spinach in here. Unless these green speckles . . . hang on, what are all these bits, Lorna? I've never seen herbs in these colours before.'

'They're special sun-tinged herbs that I got from a tiny family-run deli in Soho. Everything there is imported from Florence. *That's* why the dish is called Florentine.' That shut Phillippa up. Even I was impressed and it was my lie. I can be truly magnificent when I need to be.

The beef tasted wonderful although another ten or so pieces of it would have been nice. Phillippa had forgotten about her irritation with Joe, so intrigued was she by my culinary innovation. Every so often, her face furrowed and I knew she was biting down on some dehydrated colour-enhanced titbit. I always distracted her at that point with some complicated question about cooking that would force her to swallow her mouthful rather than spit it discreetly into her napkin and scrutinise it. Like I said, I am magnificent.

I was the hostess. It was my job to guide the conversation out of the tempest and into calm waters. This was tricky given the tension that was already hovering over each couple. Work was out. Home life was out. I was about to resort to that old faithful, the children, when Dan took it upon himself to break the silence. Now you can always guarantee one thing when a man, who has had a bit too much to drink, opens his mouth at a dinner party: he will either say something which is of no interest to fifty per cent of the guests or he will touch upon the subject most taboo on that particular occasion.

Dan went for the latter. Oh, if he'd only gone with his original plan to discuss Arsenal's latest abuse of the offside trap, what a happier evening we might all have enjoyed. But no.

'So, Rob, how did your lunch go?'

Andrea didn't bother kicking him. There was no point. The looks that both Rob and I flashed at him were perfectly adequate at communicating just how bad a question that was. To Rob's credit, he fielded it well. 'Fine,' he said. It was a good answer. One that I would not be able to drag back up when I had him in the witness box later that night.

One of those silences followed. Only dessert could defuse the tension. I started gathering plates. But Dan was on a roll. 'So where did you go?'

'Shut up, Dan,' Andrea suggested.

'I was only asking. I mean, there's no point in

pretending that nothing's going on. We all know that Rob met Karen today. And I don't see why I shouldn't ask about it. I bet you women will talk about nothing else when we're not around. Besides, I knew Karen as well, if you remember. I'm genuinely interested in how things turned out for her.'

Rob sighed. 'We went to an Italian restaurant in Victoria. Nothing special . . .'

Hah! I thought. He didn't say 'Pizza Express', he said 'an Italian restaurant'. That means he knows that I would be upset by his choice of our restaurant. That means his choice did have some significance. That means I was right to be offended. What a terrible, terrible shame that I was not going to be able to throw this at him later without revealing exactly how I knew where he'd met her.

He continued, 'It was just somewhere that we used to meet years ago when she worked in Victoria. It was the only place I could think of that she'd know after all this time.'

Oh my God. You know what that means, don't you? It means that Pizza Express was never 'our' restaurant at all. It was theirs, his and Karen's. He'd taken *me* to *their* restaurant. Is this worse or better than taking *her* to *our* restaurant? I wish Rob would stop talking so that I can work that one out.

'And to answer your other question, she's fine, Dan. She sends her love to you all, in fact.'

'That's nice,' Joe said. I don't think he was being facetious which makes his reaction all the more irritating.

Rob was encouraged by Joe's response and went on. 'By all accounts she's made a name for herself in the States. She's a child psychologist. Built up a big practice, written articles, even been on the telly, apparently.' He looked at me when he said that. I'm not certain how I was supposed to react. Oh how wonderful! Your estranged real wife has been on the TV and your current pretend-wife loves *watching* the TV! How delicious! Let's have her round to dinner! What a lot we'll have in common. What great friends we're all going to be.

Phillippa rescued me. 'Well, I think it's a bit rich. She ruins the lives of her own four children then sets herself up as some kind of expert on the other side of the world. I'd love to know what she says to the kids who've been damaged by their mothers' abandonment.'

Thank you, Phil. Rob interrupted her. 'I'm not being rude, Phil, but you don't know all the facts here. Today was the first time Karen and I really spoke about what happened ten years ago. In retrospect, it all makes a lot more sense. I think I finally understand why she did what she did. I think I can even forgive her although it will take a while for all the bitterness to disappear. There's a lot more talking that needs to be done. Anyway, the most important thing is, I believe, that the girls might be able to find it in their hearts to forgive her. And I also believe that it might be best for them if they do.'

'Forgive who what, Dad?'

It was Jude. We all stared at her with big phoney smiles stuck to our faces. 'Darling, what are you doing up? Are you not feeling well?' I asked, rushing over to her. She ignored me.

'Forgive who what, Dad?'

Rob cleared his throat. 'We'll talk about it tomorrow, sweetheart.'

'I want to talk about it now. I heard it all. It's her,

isn't it? That's who you're talking about. Mummy.' That single word hit me like a sucker punch. Jude's voice was shaking now. 'Tell me! Is it Mummy? Has she come back?'

It seemed ages before Rob answered. 'Yes, sweetie. Now don't—'

Jude didn't wait for him to finish. She turned around and screamed up the stairs, 'Ali! It's Mummy! She's come back!' Within minutes, all four girls were downstairs in various manifestations of shock. Ali and Jude were holding on to each other and crying. Claire was spouting a stream of questions that couldn't be heard over the din. Phoebe just stood there, looking from Rob to me, not wanting to ask questions, not wanting to hear answers. This was a girl who was being tortured by the physical changes wrought upon her by puberty. She didn't want any more upheavals. She wanted everything else in her life to stay the same. She needed her roots to be firmly grounded. I know, Phoebe. That's how I feel.

'Maybe it's time we were going.' Joe and Phillippa were standing awkwardly by the door. 'Thanks for a lovely evening,' Joe said enthusiastically.

'Oh don't be so stupid!' Phillippa snapped.

'I was just trying to be polite,' he hissed.

'We must be going too!' Andrea broke in brightly. She leaned over to kiss me, whispering as she did, 'I'll ring tomorrow.'

Dan tutted. 'I wish you'd stop whispering. I really hate it when you do that. We all know what you're talking about so why not say it out loud?'

'Because there are other people's feelings to consider here, in case you hadn't noticed.' Andrea swung her eyes round towards the girls who were getting more upset as Rob tried to calm them.

62

Dan and Andrea moved towards the door, their bickering rivalling that of Phillippa and Joe in volume, tone and content. I closed the door behind them, remembering suddenly my spectacular chocolate dessert which had been forgotten in the drama. It had cost £41.30, a costly coda to the whole appalling day. I walked past the living room and into the kitchen where the dessert sat on the worktop, blissfully unaware of the turmoil. I grabbed a spoon and plunged it into the chocolate ganache swirled around the side. I slurped it loudly, clinking the spoon against the plate as I worked my way through the whole creation, trying to drown out the noise from the other room.

What a swell party this is.

Chapter Six

I stumbled downstairs the next morning at eight o'clock, barely surviving the journey to the Alka Seltzer. Whose idea was it to keep it in the kitchen rather than right next to the bed where it's most needed? I can't remember so I'll assume it was Rob's idea and add it to the catalogue of grievances against him that I've been amassing throughout my restless night.

Jude was in the kitchen by herself eating cereal. First thought: oh no, am I going to be able to get the Alka Seltzer before I have to speak to her? Second thought: oh no, the girls are never up before midday on a Saturday. It's normally the day for a family lie-in punctuated only by forays to the kitchen for treats and nibbles. It hasn't even been forty-eight hours since Karen's letter and already the habits and quirks that define us as a family are being eroded.

Jude was reading the jokes on the cereal packet. Since she'd read them to us every day since the packet was opened a week ago, I took this to mean that she didn't want me to talk to her. You don't need to have carried the child in your womb to know this sort of thing, Karen, I thought bitterly. I made it to the Alka Seltzer just in time to stop the rising nausea from developing into something more visual.

Invigorated or, at least, passably human, I sat down

at the table. What do I say? Keep it neutral, I decided. 'Where's Ali?' I asked. Bad choice of question.

Jude flashed angry eyes at me. 'Why do you always do that?'

'Do what?' I asked wearily.

'Why do you always ask me where Ali is? You never ask Phoebe where Claire is. Just because we're twins, you expect us to be joined at the hip.'

I trod carefully. 'You do tend to spend most of your time together.'

'We don't have any choice in the matter. We share a room. And we share a room because we're twins so you seem to think that we wouldn't want to share with one of our other sisters.'

'Sweetie, you and Ali wanted to share a room, if you remember. If you're unhappy with the situation, you should have talked to us about it.'

'I do remember actually and I'm not saying that I don't want to share with Ali, I'm just sick of you all assuming that we do. And I'm sick of you calling us "twins" all the time instead of Ali and Jude.'

'But you always refer to yourselves as twins. I thought that was how you liked to be identified.'

'I do. But sometimes I don't and you should know when I do and when I don't and right now, I don't.'

I can't keep up with adolescent trains of thought when I'm at the peak of my mental abilities. With a hangover, I just wanted to slap her and go back to bed. I tried some controlled breathing exercises that I'd seen Nurse Hathaway advocating on a repeat of *ER* recently when Doug Ross was cheating on her with some over-acting trollop. Very effective it was too, which puts paid to theories from all those killjoys who claim that popular TV has no educational value.

It was lucky I was concentrating on my breathing because it distracted me from the panic I experienced when Jude delivered the question that she had clearly been harbouring since yesterday. 'Is Mummy back for good?'

I didn't really need to think about it. I'd been thinking about it and fighting with Rob about it for most of the night. I could have kept the fight going all night but Rob fell asleep. I hate that about him. No matter how wound up he is, he can just drop off into the deepest slumber. Even when I sigh and tut loudly right into his ear, he doesn't stir. This only serves to wind me up more and makes it even more difficult for me to go to sleep.

I'd made him tell me everything that Karen had said to him. I wish I hadn't. 'You should have seen her, Lorna,' he said, 'she was broken.' She hadn't looked broken when I saw her prancing into Pizza Express, *their* Pizza Express, she'd looked pretty pleased with herself.

'She cried. Actually, we both cried.' He said it so casually, perhaps he genuinely didn't know how personally I would take this. He's often laughed about my inability to cry, even at the sort of films that estate agents weep at. He puts it down to my inner strength, another of the qualities that he's always claimed to admire in me. I put it down to emotional constipation but I'm not one for parading my weaknesses unless it will serve a purpose. But now he was sounding all soppy, drooping at Karen's jelly-like vulnerability. Yes, he admired my strength. From a distance. At arm's length. But it didn't make him want to hug me. Or comfort me. It didn't make him cry.

I should have guessed that Karen would cry. But

66

Rob? I thought he was like me, private, repressed, civilised, English. Even in those early days when he was still in shock about Karen, he had maintained a façade of weary acceptance. Any turmoil that must surely have been haunting him was sublimated to the need to appear strong to his children. We held each other a lot after getting through the physical demands of each exhausting day and we left all the tricky bits unspoken. We bypassed a lot of the getting-to-know-you rituals of early courtship and proceeded directly to the laundry-basket-sharing stage.

It seems I mistook that premature intimacy for a union of souls. I thought we didn't need to say everything because so much was tacitly understood between us. Maybe all the time he was just waiting for my permission to cry. Oh God.

He wasn't crying now. He wasn't connecting with me at all. He was somewhere else. With her. 'We got it all out in the open. I knew she had a nervous breakdown, but I'd never truly appreciated that it was a direct follow-on from the postnatal depression after having the twins.'

Well, I certainly did. It seemed obvious to me. I didn't interrupt Rob.

'It was my fault to a certain extent. At the time, she'd tried to tell me how she felt, that she couldn't cope, that she was sinking into a black hole, but I just told her to cheer up, assured her that she just had the baby blues like she did with Phoebe and Claire. I bought her flowers and chocolates, told her I loved her, that sort of thing.'

I didn't want to hear this. I'd heard the story many times from Andrea and Phillippa. They both also carried residues of guilt from that time. They'd been too wrapped up in their own babies, tired and a bit down themselves, to recognise that Karen was genuinely and seriously sick. They remembered Rob coming to them, concerned about Karen, sensing that there was something different, darker about her state of mind this time. It was the two other mums, Karen's own friends, who'd told him not to worry. To his credit, he never blamed them for this.

'She left because she thought that she would probably harm them if she stayed for one more minute.'

'Rob, I know all this. It must have been terrible for her. But she got better. So why didn't she come back?'

'She got better but she didn't feel better. She was so ashamed. She already felt that she had failed as a mother by not being able to pull herself together and just cope like other mothers did. When she finally walked out, it compounded her sense of failure. She always wondered if she would do the same again, if she had some intrinsic weakness that made her incapable of being a competent mother. She couldn't take the risk. And then she heard about you and how the girls were settling down. For the girls' sake, she stayed away.'

His voice bore a mixture of admiration, sympathy and . . . could it be the hint of an old love resurfacing?

I lost all sense of caution. 'Listen to yourself, Rob. She's made you see her as the victim in all this. You've completely forgotten what she did to you and to her children.'

'Of course I haven't forgotten! But do you think she hasn't suffered? She's had to live without her daughters, daughters that she never stopped loving. She's had to accept that they were being brought up by another woman, that they neither loved nor needed their natural mother any more. All she ever had was occasional photos from her mum.'

I leapt on this. 'That's exactly my point. How could she live on the other side of the world like that if she really cared about them? She could have done the sacrificial bit, played the martyr, in London. She could have kept her distance and still seen the girls occasionally without them knowing.' I was really rolling now. 'She could have hidden behind trees and watched them in playgrounds. She could have sneaked into school plays in disguise. She could have stood in shop doorways and observed them coming out of school.'

Rob looked appalled. 'Is that what you would do?'

'Rather than never see them at all? Yes I would.'

'Not everyone is as devious as you, Lorna.' Thank you. 'And even if Karen had stayed in London, can you imagine how painful it would be to see the girls occasionally but not be able to hug them, not be able to be part of the family, not be able to talk to them whenever you wanted, watch every tiny development in their lives?'

Yes, I can. I've thought of little else since Karen came back into our lives and threatened me silently with the possibility of the same kind of exile that she imposed on herself. I couldn't bear it. But I didn't say any of this. And I didn't cry although I would have liked to do that too. No. I stumbled on in a true act of self-destruction. 'I'm sorry, Rob. I understand why you want to forgive Karen because it gives closure to a lot of issues that have tormented you since she left. And I know that eventually we would have had to confront the fact that the girls might want to see their mother again. But as for the rest? Karen setting herself up as somehow being a better mother because she didn't

69

come back? I don't buy it, Rob. And neither would any other mother.'

'Great. You're doing that "woman" thing again. I can't understand because I'm a man. Well I may be a man but I'm also a father and *you* may be a woman but you're not . . .'

He'd gone too far and he knew it. I finished his sentence painfully in my imagination. I walked out and went to the bathroom to compose myself. By the time I went back into the bedroom, he was asleep.

That stopped me from bringing up the subject of divorce and whether Karen's sense of failure extended to her role of wife as well as mother.

Is Mummy back for good, Jude? You bet she is. 'I honestly don't know, sweetheart. We'll have to see how things go. She'll need to talk to you, explain why things turned out the way they did.'

'Why she walked out on us, you mean?' she inter-rupted.

'You'll have to listen to what she has to say and then decide what you want.'

'I hate her and I never want to see her.' She sounded tired, all the fight quashed out of her by this unbearable new burden.

'I know you think that's how you feel . . .'

'I don't care what you say, I'm not going to see her and neither is Ali.'

'I'll tell you what. I'll make a deal with you. See her the once, hear what she has to say and then, if you don't want to see her after that, we won't insist.' I can't believe I'm doing this, persuading her to see this woman who holds all our futures in her bony hands.

Jude thought about this. 'And then I'll never have to see her again?'

'That's the deal.'

'Well I'm warning you. I'll still hate her. I'm not going to talk to her. None of us will.'

'That's fine,' I reassured her.

'So, when do we have to see her?'

I busied myself in the fridge hoping to appear engrossed in making a shopping list. I didn't trust my face not to betray my feelings. 'Tomorrow at Granny and Grandad M's. We were already going over for Sunday lunch. Now Karen, your mother, will be there.'

'It's funny. I always forget that Granny M is Mummy's mother.' I never forget. 'I suppose it won't be so bad if we're all together.'

'Actually, I won't be there.'

'Why not?'

Because Rob thought it would be better that way. 'We both thought it would be better if I wasn't there. Otherwise it might make things awkward.'

'I want you to be there, Mum.' She cleared her throat and we both pretended that she wasn't clearing away tears. I stroked her hair, rearranging strands to straighten her parting. I knew she wouldn't want a hug. We weren't like that, Jude and I.

'It'll be fine, Jude. Nothing's going to change. You'll probably feel better once you've seen your mother. I'm sure there are lots of things you want to say to her.'

Jude snorted. 'You bet I do!'

I congratulated myself on my maturity and selfless restraint. Jude picked up her spoon to continue with her now-soggy Frosties. 'Mum?'

'Yes darling?'

'Can I have my nose pierced?'

I was about to say: 'Why don't you ask your real mother when you see her?' which wouldn't have been very funny but which would have made me laugh in my rather confused state, when I was saved by the phone.

It was Phillippa. 'Hi there, me. Just phoning to say thanks for an interesting evening.'

'Do I detect a hint of irony in there, Phil, or is that a shamefully sadistic pleasure in someone else's misfortune?'

She laughed. The latter, then.

'Sorry, Lorn. I know it's not really funny. It was a bit of a shock, to be honest. We didn't even know Karen was back on the scene until Andrea told us last night.' A teensy trace of resentment filtered through.

'No. I tried to call you yesterday but I couldn't get through.'

A little lie, there. Once I'd spoken to Andrea and set our machinations in motion, I hadn't thought of calling Phil. Now here's a funny thing. Women pride themselves on the openness of their relationships, the willingness to talk about the most personal, private of subjects. But there's one subject that hovers, unspoken, over us all. The reason we don't talk about it is because we'd be too embarrassed to admit it. It's a problem that begins in primary school and continues in increasing complexity into adulthood: the fragile hierarchy of female friendship.

Your first 'best friendship' is very special indeed, an enclosed circle of total and utter intimacy. It excludes all others, promises everything and sometimes lasts no longer than a toffee. You share your sweets and ribbons and dreams and secrets. You develop your own language, invent games that no one else understands, form clubs with hundreds of membership rules that no one else can join. You are six years old.

Then interlopers make their advances. It could be the

new girl in Brownies, or the one next door or at school. You like them too but you can only have one 'best friend' so the others become 'other friends'. And then it happens. Maybe one of your 'other friends' has a birthday coming up. She can only invite one person to her birthday treat at the cinema. She invites you. You say 'yes'. And in the uncompromising eyes of your best friend, you have defected, you have chosen a new best friend at the expense of your old one. You declare that it is unfair, that you have betrayed nobody, that your feelings haven't changed. But it is too late. The unbroken circle of friendship has become just the first chipped link in a chain that stretches into your future.

And adulthood? When you put childish things behind you? Don't make me laugh. Take the three of us. Andrea is my best friend. When something happens, I call her first. Then I call Phillippa. Andrea and Phillippa are each other's best friend. They have been since those maternity ward days with Karen. Then I came on the scene. I slotted into the space left by Karen and we became a new threesome but the dynamic was not equally balanced. It couldn't be. I have never asked Andrea or Phillippa where Karen fitted in the triangle, as apex or merely the third point. I preferred not to know.

In the beginning, they didn't want anything to do with me. They felt that any acceptance of me would be a betrayal of Karen and they were still burning with guilt over not spotting Karen's psychosis. But slowly, they came to accept that Karen wasn't coming back. And their children and Karen's, mine, were established fixtures in each other's lives. They couldn't be excluded.

Eventually, they let me in. I lapped up their fellow-ship, their parenting advice and their support. I didn't have a clue about bringing up children and, once Rob had gone back to work, I was alone with four of them.

I was on the phone to them constantly, in and out of their houses and eventually joining their girls' nights out. And at some point, I found that I would always call Andrea first. Maybe it was discovering that Andrea shared my abhorrence of sugar-free organic rice cakes as the popular snack of choice imposed on fractious toddlers by humourless mums. Maybe it was because she was impressed by my philosophy degree even though she had been a biochemist before having kids. Probably it was because she'd been a *Magpie* devotee like me, wild and dangerous, rather than a *Blue Peter* fan making interminable sensible models. And her love of TV had grown until it almost rivalled my own. And everyone knows that there's no point in watching television if you've got nobody to share the postmortems with.

Andrea and I even went to Bingo together once, for a laugh. We really enjoyed ourselves – but we never admitted it to another person. And we didn't go twice. We both recognised the compulsion in our personalities for mass-market experiences and didn't trust ourselves not to become addicted.

You know those people who claim never to watch television apart from David Attenborough documentaries and Jane Austen dramatisations? And you never believe them? That's Phillippa. And she really never does watch television except for the rare series that merits a feature in the *Daily Telegraph*. And I'm sorry, I mean I love Phil to bits and her friendship is very important to me, but it's a bit weird, isn't it?

I've never quite worked out what she does with all the extra time that she must have. She doesn't read any more books than I do. With all that time, I'm frankly surprised she hasn't *written* any books. She doesn't darn socks or bake her own bread. I don't get it. How can I? There's a wall of mutual incomprehension between me and her that will never be completely breached.

But she and Andrea have gone through the whole childbirth thing together. Apparently it's a bond that transcends and outlasts all others. Amazing, but true. The bond is meaningful, with staying power. And I'm as jealous as hell about it.

An outsider would look at the three of us and never notice the subtle balance of relationships that our network supported, but we all knew. We never referred to it and we all maintained the equilateral triangle façade with a light sprinkling of occasional evasions.

And when I really grow up, when I'm fifty or sixty or something, I'll stop all this nonsense and divert my energies towards something useful like watching *Sunset Beach* which sounds gloriously tacky but which I can't yet slot into my viewing schedule.

So Phillippa didn't question the lie. 'You did us a favour, if I'm honest. Joe and I had been having a terrible row before we got to your house. But your problems really put ours into perspective. We both felt stupid for getting so worked up about money when you're watching your whole family fall apart.'

Now I remember why I always call Andrea first. 'So what's going on with the business?'

Phillippa's voice tensed. 'It's just cash flow. But it's quite serious. We've got quite a lot of bills mounting up, red ones and the threatening letters that follow the red ones, and we're having to choose which ones we pay and which ones we pretend not to have received. You must promise not to tell anyone this, not even Rob. Andrea knows, of course.'

75

Of course. 'What a rotten mess,' I said sympathetically. 'Still, it's not too difficult to establish your priorities. We all live beyond our means to a certain extent and we can all do without most of the stuff we buy. It's really only the mortgage and the utilities that you can't mess about with. And school fees.' No answer. 'Phil, you're not thinking of taking the boys out of Keaton House?'

'I'm not but Joe is. We're a term behind with the fees already and the headmaster is getting impatient with us. We've got to go and see him this week. That's what the row was about. Joe says the boys will have to leave, he thinks they'll easily get into Tooting Grammar and that will save us a fortune.'

I was stumped for something reassuring to say. Our children were all at Keaton House. They'd all been together at nursery and, subsequently, school since they were two. I couldn't imagine how difficult it would be for the boys to leave their friends, never mind the cushion and privilege of a private school with its small well-disciplined classes into the free-for-all of our local massive comprehensive. Because the fact was that the boys were simply not bright enough to get into a grammar school, however deluded Phillippa and Joe might be about their sons' academic ability.

Perhaps even more unthinkable was the prospect of Phillippa coming out of the PTA loop which filled her life. She was a stalwart of all the fundraising and social committees at Keaton House. She knew all the mothers and they all knew her. Her social life revolved entirely around the school. What would she do if that were taken away from her? I ached for her. 'Oh Phil, I'm so sorry. If there's anything we can do ...' I said.

Phillippa laughed nervously. 'Well if you happen to

have a spare thirty thousand pounds to tide us over, that might help. Only joking.'

We both knew that she wasn't joking. We were both embarrassed. However close our friendship, we never discussed money except in general moans about house price trends and school fee rises. I had an idea. 'Have you thought about doing away with your au pair?'

'Went three months ago,' Phillippa answered shortly.

I was stunned. I couldn't imagine Phillippa managing her family's lives without hired help. She'd had full-time nannies from the time that her first son, Elliott, was ten days old. She had Rupert eighteen months later. The timing was planned that way to streamline child-care arrangements. Once the boys were in full-time nursery, she switched to a sequence of au pairs. Andrea told me about those early days when the only time Phillippa actually did anything with Elliott was when she was meeting up with the other mums from their antenatal circle. She would probably rather have left him behind even then but realised that it would look somewhat remiss to turn up at a mother-and-baby group without a baby.

It wasn't that she didn't love her children as much as we did. She just didn't know what to do with them on a minute-to-minute basis. When she was forced to look after them, if the nanny was off sick for example, she would forget to feed them or change them. She'd wheel them to the park then read a magazine while occasionally rattling a toy into the buggy. If they weren't screaming, they must be happy, was the theory. She was the only mother we knew who went out without a huge suitcase of accessories. She relied on other mums to lend her nappies or bottles or entire meals when the need arose.

Astonishingly, for a mother we privately tended to regard as utterly neglectful, she had managed to end up with two of the most well-adjusted kids in our circle. It annoyed us like crazy that her children should not only have survived without twenty-four hour care from a mother, but actually thrived on it. What did that say abut the rest of us, sacrificing careers and leisure time to do what we thought was best?

Jude was now standing right next to the phone, pointing at her nose and looking impatient. 'Look, Phil, I have to go. Something's come up. But I want to talk to you about this. I don't suppose you could squeeze another body around your table for Sunday lunch tomorrow by any chance?'

'You know me, Lorn, I always over-cater. There's probably some heavy Freudian significance to that, something to do with over-compensation for perceived inadequacies. But I thought you always had lunch with the in-laws on Sundays?'

'Not tomorrow. Karen's going to be there.'

Phillippa whistled. 'Come at one, Lorn. Bring a bottle of something good. On second thoughts, bring two bottles of something cheap and nasty. I think we'll need them.'

I prolonged the farewells, not wishing to confront the nose-piercing dilemma that awaited me. Finally I put the phone down and turned to face Jude. For the first time in two days, my prayers were answered as Rob walked downstairs towards us.

Rob stroked Jude's face affectionately. 'Had your breakfast, Judie? Well done.'

I need to explain something about Rob. On the day he became a father, he resolved to apply only classic dog-training methods to the rearing of his children on the grounds that the basic rules were simple, logical and effective (for dogs, that is). There were two principles: ignore any undesirable behaviour and reward everything else. Therefore his praise for Jude simply for having eaten her breakfast is a throwback to toddler days when getting a spoonful in her mouth was a genuine achievement. But the praise still flows naturally from him, especially now when not that many praiseworthy actions occurred in his teenage daughters' lifestyles.

The resolve to ignore any bad behaviour was effective until he watched the girls manipulate themselves into countless life-threatening situations from which only a piercing parental scream would rescue them. But in general he was happy that his methods were producing some well-adjusted, socially acceptable offspring. I looked forward to seeing him test his philosophy with this new challenge.

I smiled sweetly at Jude and then at Rob. 'Good morning, darling. Nice sleep? Lovely. By the way, Jude wants to have her nose pierced. I'm off to have a bath.'

The rest of the day was horrible. Rob and I did our big shop as usual. No doubt we're just odd, but we generally enjoy shopping. We both share a childish pleasure in looking for new things to try, little treats, free gifts, great bargains, silly unnecessary products like toffee-flavoured porridge and gin and tonic ready-made in cans.

But today was different. We had barely spoken since meeting on the stairs. I didn't ask him how he'd handled the nose-piercing situation with Jude. I didn't need to. The slammed doors and poorly stifled mutterings emanating from the twins' bedroom said it all. Perhaps Rob should have tried dangling bits of chicken in front of her face. It works for the dogs.

Rob had apparently dealt with the girls' common reluctance to see their mother last night but the arguments had started up again. He wasn't impressed by the new compromise I had negotiated with Jude. He didn't say anything, I just knew.

Apparently, Jude was planning some kind of hunger strike in response to her father's refusal to permit the nose-piercing. The hunger strike lasted until she got hungry. She then sent Ali down to procure emergency rations (orange Kit-Kats and chocolate Nesquik) to sustain her in her misery.

Rob had retreated to his computer, evidently keen to avoid yet another confrontation with one of his newly difficult children. I was feeling pretty chirpy, all things considered. True, a domestic Armageddon was being visited upon my home, but I'd finally got rid of my headache and sick feeling that had been dogging me for two days. I can deal with Ali, I thought. I may have messed up with one twin but I won't make the same mistakes with the other. I knew exactly which question to ask first.

'How are *you* feeling today, Ali?' I asked.

'Jude is really upset,' she replied accusingly.

Karen's in for a real treat, I thought.

Between then and my shopping trip with Rob, I only had the briefest contact with the other two girls. Phoebe trudged around the house, three inches shorter from the worries that she'd heaped on to her already overladen shoulders. We exchanged sympathetic smiles, heavy with words that we didn't need to speak. I'd talk to her later.

Claire's sullenness had degenerated into petulance. Since I'd seen Karen for the first time, Claire's face had transformed in my imagination into a mirror image of her mother's. I'm ashamed to admit it but I was starting to feel something close to animosity towards her for possessing that face. It was wrong of me and, to compensate for my unfairness, I vowed to be even more loving towards her. 'Can I make you a cooked breakfast, sweetheart?' I asked. She was always asking me for one and I seldom had the time to prepare it.

'And make me even fatter than I am already?' she snapped and stormed off.

This never happens in *The Waltons*.

At Sainsbury's, Rob pushed the trolley and I piled essentials in without joy. Our sombre mood was encapsulated in our choice of digestive biscuits instead of chocolate Hob-Nobs. We didn't even stop at the cream cake counter. The queues were appalling and we had no alternative but to talk to each other.

I, of course, made the first move. 'So what's the plan of action tomorrow?'

'What do you mean by that?' he asked suspiciously.

I sighed. 'I wish you'd stop being so defensive. I'm just asking if you've thought about how you're going to introduce the girls to Karen. It's a big moment for them and it could be quite traumatic. They are all dreading it, you know.'

Rob softened his tone. 'Karen and I discussed that.' I bet you did. 'She expects some resentment. Her experience as a child psychologist has given her some useful insights into how to deal with situations that like this. She's been working with broken families for quite a while now and has had quite a lot of success in rebuilding longstanding rifts.'

'This is a bit different,' I suggested. 'This is her family. It might be a bit tricky for her to be so objective when it's her own children who have the rift that needs mending.'

'You're just being negative again. Look, you've got

81

to stop worrying about this. It isn't going to affect what the girls have with you. Nothing can take that away. In fact, things might get even better at home once they've resolved things with their mother.'

I hadn't realised that things needed to get better. 'So she's going to be in Mary's living room, arms open wide to greet them, is that the plan?'

Rob started loading the groceries on to the conveyor belt. 'No. She's going to be there but she won't make any moves towards them until she feels that they're ready. She just wants to talk to them.'

'And then?'

Rob didn't look up. 'Nothing's decided yet but she would like to see them a couple of times a week in the beginning and see how things go from there.'

I gasped. 'A couple of times a week? Does she have any idea what their schedules are like? What with ballet, guitar lessons, gym club, netball practice, never mind all the afternoons and evenings spent at their friends' houses, *we* barely see them a couple of times a week.'

'They'll just have to miss a couple of episodes of *Neighbours*, won't they?'

Pointed, or what? And he still hadn't mentioned divorce.

We didn't speak on the way home. When we got in there was a light flashing on the answering machine. Although all the girls were in, none of them had bothered answering the phone. Ah, the happy little rebellions of adolescents.

I pressed the button. It was my mum. 'Oh dear, I do hate these machines. Hello, Lorna dear. It's your mother here. Just phoning to see how you are. Can you phone me when you're not too busy? Bye bye.'

I sat down by the phone, suddenly struck by the enormity of the word she had chosen. 'Mother,' she'd said. Not 'mum' but 'mother'. I always called her 'Mum' and yet she always referred to herself as my mother. I had cruelly mocked her for this apparent affectation. But for the first time in my life, I understood exactly why she did it.

She had been a good mum, devoted, warm, affectionate, encouraging. She had made sacrifices without martyrdom, supported me in all the right, knowing ways. She had done the best she could and I am now paying her the highest compliment by emulating her mothering skills with my own daughters. She was my mum. That's how I thought of her, how I introduced her to other people. But she wasn't my natural mother. And although she never mentioned it, it must always have bothered her, hence her use of the word and the unspoken plea it carried.

Not my real mother. Of course, I'd throw that at her when I was a child. Children will always use any weapon at their disposal to hurt their parents. I'd never apologised for it, though, and I now see that I should have. The girls have said it to me on countless occasions, but they haven't for a long while, and it always hurt even when I understood that they were only trying to offload their own pain.

It's two days since my daughters' own real mother has come back on the scene. And I hate to admit it, hate to open up a chest of such enormous potential hurt, but I'm starting to think about my own mother. Not my mum, my mother. For the first time in thirty-six years, I want to see her.

Chapter Seven

My mum brewed tea. It was what she did and who she was. It was her own alternative medicine which, tested over the course of her life, she had found to be more effective against the diseases of modern life than homeopathy. The English compulsion to make tea has been mocked but it has its practical uses. It enables a person to leave the scene of a confrontation for a good ten minutes (unless you use tea bags, which don't count, or you have one of those kitchens which encourage guests to follow you). That gives you plenty of time either to think carefully about what you are going to say, plan some clever ripostes, that sort of thing, or come up with a solid method of changing the subject.

My mum always changed the subject. She only liked subjects that she initiated. She needed more than ten minutes to think through challenging situations and this situation in particular was one she was totally unprepared to meet.

It hadn't helped that I'd sprung my visit on her without advance warning on a Thursday morning when I always visited on a Monday afternoon. After she'd established that no one had died or been struck with a terrible illness or had an accident, she began berating me for not giving her enough notice to bake a cake. She started to flap and ended up defrosting a Sara Lee chocolate gateau that she kept in the freezer for when the girls came round. I wasn't the least bit hungry but knew that to refuse cake would start her accusing me of anorexia or ingratitude depending on her mood.

I tried to lead up to my request gently but it was impossible. She knew that something big was up and she insisted on knowing what it was. She even refused to put the kettle on until I told her exactly why I was there. I took a deep breath. 'Mum, I want to trace my birth mother.'

Then she went and made the tea.

I followed her. I didn't want her to come back with an endless monologue of somebody who'd died or had a baby or got four numbers on the lottery and only won £52.45. It was hard enough to say what I had to say the first time, I didn't fancy having to do it again.

I watched her as she went into tea-making mode. She was wearing one of her five dresses, all of the same cut but in different materials. She was not the greatest needlewoman but she could sew an A-line dress with a big zip down the front. So she made a job lot of them. It wasn't that she was hard up. Dad had left her a decent pension when he died and the mortgage had been paid off ages ago but she couldn't get out of the habit of thinking that she was poor. She'd had a very tough upbringing and refused to be convinced that another depression was not around the corner. She had a larder full of tinned and packet goods just in case of emergency. Most of them were way past their sell-by dates but I didn't like to tell her. It would be like wrenching the dummy from a fretful baby's mouth.

Her hair was permed, and coloured into submission every Friday, her one indulgence. The severity of the style which was superglued into place with industrial-strength hairspray contrasted disconcertingly with the softness of her features. Her face was tired and most of the lines reflected a life of frowns rather than smiles. But when she did smile, she was lovely.

She was filling the kettle and fussing about with the rituals, warming the teapot, wrenching the lid off the antiquated tea jar, getting the good china out. I waited until she had satisfied her own rigorous standards before speaking. 'Mum, did you hear what I said?'

She turned quickly and, to my astonishment, I saw tears in her eyes. I think they were tears of anger but I was stunned nonetheless. We're not big on tears in our family. We find them a bit embarrassing. Even when my dad died, we didn't cry that much, not in front of other people. We just made a lot more tea than usual.

'Of course I heard what you said,' she snapped. 'So what's brought all this on? After thirty-six years? You always said you had no interest in tracing your birth mother. We went through everything when you turned eighteen. Is it me? Have I done something wrong and you're trying to punish me?' She was holding on to the worktop for support.

'Oh Mum, it's nothing like that. Please don't get upset. Please.' I poured out the tea for her. I knew that would calm her down.

I told her about Karen. She visibly relaxed. This was something she understood. A pain she could relate to. She was my mum once more and I needed her. She cut the cake into alarmingly big slices as if the size of the slice was proof of the extent of her love for me. Big portions are her way of saying 'I love you' without having to speak.

'When did all this happen?' she asked.

'Three weeks ago,' I replied.

She put her cake down in surprise. 'And this is the first I hear of it?'

'Mum, I needed to get everything clear in my head first. I didn't want to burden you with it until I knew what was going to happen. There was always the possibility that Karen wouldn't stick around and that it would all blow over so there was no point in worrying you over nothing.'

'And I presume that she is still around?'

Still around? Bit of an understatement, that. She has become the focal point of our lives. She has her own column on the family calendar headed 'Karen/Mum 2'. The Sunday lunch was a great success apparently. Even Jude grudgingly admitted that Karen was 'nice'.

By all accounts Karen had handled that first meeting masterfully. She had ignored the initial sullen glances, the ugly replies that greeted her first tentative questions. She'd sat back, waiting until she judged each child ready to be drawn out. Rob must have primed her carefully. She knew that she had to win Jude over first if she was to break Ali's resolve. I was soon to find out how she wooed the normally intractable Jude. Claire, by all accounts, was most impressed by her mother's full-on make-up. As for Phoebe ... Sweet Phoebe just wants a quiet life and quickly fell in with her turncoat sisters.

Karen's timing had been spot on, the legacy of her training as a psychologist, Rob pointed out. I took this as a jibe at my philosophy degree. 'Well do forgive me for having chosen a non-vocational discipline,' I said. 'I may not have a certificate in talking to children from the University of Gobbledegook in California but ten years of child-rearing have given *me* some quite good insights into *our* children.

'And I'm sorry if my teaching doesn't impress you as having any humanitarian applications but it has paid half of the mortgage for ten years. Karen's half, incidentally. And I'd like to see Karen prepare and deliver a lecture on Aristotle after being up all night nursing the girls through an attack of croup. Oh, I've just remembered, she won't have to do that, will she? The croup days are long gone, she missed them.'

I hated myself for being like this, for going on and on about Karen. I was overflowing with self-pity and I just didn't know how to stop. I needed Rob to hold me and reassure me over and over again. But instead, he ignored my rambling bitterness. He was getting used to it. He walked away rather than keep the row going.

I heard the rest from the girls. 'She was so beautiful,' gushed Claire. I wonder if she was aware of the astonishing resemblance between herself and her mother.

Ali was excited by the new extension to her family. 'She's going to get a dog and a cat when she's moved into her new house. And some mice. And I can give them names.'

'That's nice,' I said, trying to sound happy for her. New house? Pets. Sounds permanent to me. Even if the house is just rented, it implies long-term intentions. What if it didn't work out for her? But of course it will work out for her. She's trained for it.

Jude had a quietly triumphant look on her face. 'What about you, Jude? How do you feel about all this?'

'Well, *she* thinks that I shouldn't have my nose pierced just yet because my nose hasn't stopped growing yet and it could damage the shape of it. So she suggested I have my ears pierced while I'm waiting.'

I had to control my anger because Rob was there and I'd vowed to try and appear unthreatened since that annoyed him so much. 'And did you point out that you are not allowed to wear earrings at your school until you're sixteen?'

Jude sighed that horrible adolescent sigh that judges and condemns a parent as being the worst, most stupid person in the world. 'The teachers don't notice if you cover them up with your hair. Everyone wears them except me.' This was not the occasion for me to list the girls in her class who I knew didn't have pierced ears. She'd really hate me then. Thank you, Karen.

'Is everything all right, Phoebe?' Phoebe didn't look up when she answered. 'She said that the next time she goes to the States, she'll bring me back some fantastic new cream that gets rid of spots in five days.'

I stifled my indignation as best I could. 'But you said you didn't want to try any creams. I've been trying to get you to come to the doctor with me for months. I've heard he can prescribe tablets as well as creams that might sort your skin out. He may well even have the same cream that is used in America.'

'I don't want to go to the doctor. He'll ask all sorts of questions. It'll be horrible. I'll just wait for ... my mother to get them for me.'

There. She'd said it. My mother.

I shouldn't have been surprised. They were children. Of course they would want to forgive their mother. They all had holes in their lives that needed to be filled, spaces that I could paper over but never truly seal. They couldn't hate her and they shouldn't. God knows they would find enough reasons for hating other people when they grew up, let them enjoy the gift of easy forgiveness while they could.

I hadn't intended to tell my mum all this but it just came out. Phoebe's defection was the hardest to take. Over the past three weeks, I imagined I could feel her slipping away. Maybe it was my fault for trying too hard to compete with Karen, but I felt I was losing Phoebe. I resented every second she spent with Karen, every piece of advice she took from her, every casual comment she spoke to her. Yes, I know how childish and possessive I sound. Perhaps you could be big about sharing your kids but I can't.

'Oh, love, I'm so sorry.' My mum was pouring me another cup of tea and cutting me another huge slice of cake.

'The thing is, Mum, I think I understand what they're going through. I tried to imagine myself in their position, what it would have been like for me, for us all, if my mother had come back on the scene when I was the same age as the girls.'

My mum got up. 'I'll put the kettle on again, shall I?'

'No, Mum. I don't want another cup of tea. Please sit down. We need to sort this out.' She sat down reluctantly. I went on. 'If she'd come back when I was a teenager, I would have felt torn between the two of you. I'd have been confused, wanting to hate her, needing to know her and all the time thinking of you and your feelings. Because you are my mum and always will be. I want to spare the girls this struggle. I don't want to make them choose between us. I hope it won't come to that. So I'm trying to stand back, just be there for them, keep life as normal as possible.'

'It must be tough for you.'

I shook my head. 'Almost unbearable. I just can't believe how quickly they've all accepted her after what she did to them. Whenever they have talked about her in the past, they've always said that they hate her. Then the minute she comes back, all is forgiven and forgotten. It makes no sense.'

'They're just children, sweetheart. They're confused and needy. And look at yourself. You want to trace your own mother, who abandoned you every bit as much as Karen did her children. And you're prepared to put it all behind you and greet her with open arms. There's something about children and mothers . . .'

I shrugged. 'Maybe you're right. Maybe I just want to occupy myself. Maybe I just need to go through what the girls are going through. I haven't been able to stop thinking about it for the last three weeks. But I need to do this. Please, Mum. Say you're OK about it.'

She sniffed. 'There's not a lot I can do if you're determined to go ahead with this.'

'Oh thanks Mum! I promise that nothing will change between us, no matter what happens. I just have to get this out of my system, that's all.' I was about to give her a hug when she anticipated the unwelcome display of emotion and stood up. 'Now can I put the kettle on?'

As she began the tea ritual once more, my mobile rang. It was the hospital. I panicked immediately and wouldn't let the nurse finish her message. 'Is it one of my daughters? Or my husband Rob? Are they OK? What's happened? I'm sorry. I'm listening . . . Isabelle Miller? But she's not my . . . I see. I'll be there as soon as I can.'

'What was it? What's happened?' My mum's voice was shaking. She'd only heard the word 'hospital' and had aged five years.

'It's all right, Mum. It's Isabelle, Andrea's daughter. She's had quite a bad accident and the hospital can't contact either Andrea or Dan. I suppose I was the only person Isabelle could think of although I can't imagine how she'd know my mobile number. I'll have to dash. Sorry. And thanks. I'll let you know what happens. About the other thing, that is.' We both knew what I referring to.

She shook her head at this. 'That won't be necessary.'

I sighed. She wasn't going to make this easy. 'But Mum . . .'

She struggled to hold up her hand as if it was heavy. 'No, you don't understand. What I'm saying is that you don't need to go through the agency.'

She was right. I didn't understand. 'But there are procedures,' I began.

My mum's voice was different. Older. 'You won't need them. I know who your mother is.'

I couldn't believe what she was saying. 'How can you? I thought it was all supposed to be anonymous.'

'When we brought you home that first day, there was a little note hidden inside your vest. It was against the rules, of course, but I couldn't blame the poor woman.'

'What did it say?' I whispered, trying not to resent my mum for keeping this from me.

'Just that she wanted us to look after you. And then she wrote her name and address. Just, you know, in case of anything.'

'Why didn't you say so?'

'Because there was no need. You didn't want to know. Until today.'

'So where is it, this note?' I asked weakly, wanting it and not wanting it, desperate for it and not ready at the same time.

Mum sighed. 'It's upstairs somewhere. I'll get it all

out for you. Actually there's more than a note. There's a letter she wrote a few years back.'

This was too much. Too many secrets. Too much news. 'How could she? How did she know where to find you, us?'

Mum shrugged. 'Things weren't quite so strict when you were born. There were no computers, no security codes. Apparently, your mother knew one of the nurses on the ward where you were born, it was the nurse who gave you to me. They both lived in the same street.' She shrugged to convey the ease at which the rest of the story, my story, unfolded.

There was nothing to say. I gathered up my coat and bag like an automaton, trying to concentrate on getting through the next couple of hours in the knowledge that so much was going to change for me.

I could see my mum suffering on my behalf, utterly unable to take my pain away. She cleared her throat. 'I'll sort that out, then. Just one thing. Don't get your hopes up.'

Too late for that. 'I won't, Mum. And thanks again.' I'm not sure what I was thanking her for. I kissed her and left.

'Are you Isabelle's mother?' the nurse asked.

'No. But I've known Isabelle for most of her life. And I'm close friends with her mother.'

The nurse looked concerned. 'We've tried the home number, her father's work, both parents' mobile phones and all the contact numbers Isabelle could give us. The school are quite angry, especially given the circumstances. Isabelle's teacher is on her way now. At least one parent should be contactable during school hours precisely for such eventualities as this.'

I couldn't explain it myself. Andrea was always so meticulous about keeping her mobile switched on so that she could be contacted. We both were. Even Phillippa ensured that the school was kept up-to-date with her complicated business schedule, although I have no idea what she'd do if she was summoned in an emergency now that she had no au pair.

'How's Isabelle doing?' I asked.

The nurse was unsure of how much she should tell me since I wasn't a relative. 'I can't go into all the details but she fell off a bus in Oxford Street.'

'She can't have been in Oxford Street. It's a school day.'

The nurse raised her eyebrows. 'Have you got children of your own?'

I bristled. 'Four actually.'

'Then you should know that you can't always rely on them being where you think they are.'

'I can assure you that from Monday to Friday, I always know that my daughters are at school.'

'Hi, Mum.'

It was Jude. 'What are you doing here, Jude? Why aren't you at school?'

She had the good sense to look sheepish. 'Sorry.'

That was all she needed to say. I filled in the rest of the story for myself. She and Isabelle had bunked off school to go to the West End. Knowing both girls as I do, I guessed that it was probably Jude's idea. Now I understood how my mobile came to be called.

'We'll talk about this later. Are you OK?'

Jude nodded. 'Isabelle's really hurt her leg, Mum. It was all my fault. I was messing around and she fell off. I'm sorry.'

Her voice was breaking and I took her in my arms. It

94

was rare for Jude and me to hold each other like this. Come to think of it, physical contact in general has been thin on the ground recently. I forgave her instantly and completely. Something scratched against my hand. I looked down and saw them. Two gold sleeper earrings. That's why she had wanted to go up to the West End. I'd refused to allow her to have her ears pierced despite Karen's eloquent recommendation so she'd decided to go ahead and do it behind my back.

She sensed the tightening of my grip and pulled away, her hands flying to her ears defensively. 'Sorry, Mum. But you wouldn't let me have it done. And it's not fair. My other mum said—'

'That's enough,' I snapped. 'We'll talk about this later.'

The nurse was waiting patiently for us to follow her through to Isabelle's cubicle. The poor little thing looked terrified. Despite the fact that she was two years older than Jude, she had always been easily led by her. Isabelle and Phoebe had both been born on the same day but it didn't take long for the two girls to discover that they had nothing in common. Then came Claire, all girly and flirty. When Jude came along with her free spirit and thirst for rebellious adventure, Isabelle found her soul sister. And Jude found her acolyte.

The two earrings glimmering from beneath a bandage around Isabelle's head completed the picture. I sat down next to her and stroked her hand and face. 'It's all going to be fine, poppet,' I whispered soothingly. 'You'll be as right as rain.'

Her eyes filled with tears. 'Where's my mum?' she sobbed.

I cursed Andrea for putting me in this position. I shushed her to calm her down. 'She'll be here soon. I expect her mobile's not working.'

It was another hour before Andrea turned up, during which time I'd had to sign a consent form for surgery on Isabelle's broken leg to begin. The doctors simply couldn't wait any longer.

Miss Brownlow arrived and I immediately quaked with fear at her imposing presence. The fact that she was only about twenty-five and delicately beautiful was outweighed by her terrifying reputation. She'd evidently decided long ago that her fragile appearance could be a disadvantage in the world of teaching. She had dealt with this by adopting the persona of Margaret Thatcher. Even her impeccably applied make-up seemed aggressive in its clinical precision. She was so utterly obnoxious that you quickly forgot how gorgeous she was. I dreaded having to explain my daughter's aberrant behaviour to this scary woman. But she went into one of the relatives' rooms, probably to wait for Andrea and Dan. Thank you God.

A minute or two later, Andrea came tearing into the hospital. Her hysterical appearance was compounded by the Danny De Vito raincoat and stripy hat that she'd worn on our espionage mission. 'Lorna! Thank God you're here! What's happened? Where's Isabelle? Is she OK?'

'She's in surgery. We waited as long as we could for you but they were a bit concerned about the possibility of internal bleeding so they went ahead. Where were you? Why didn't you have your phone switched on?'

She looked flustered. 'I thought I did. The battery must have gone or maybe I accidentally switched it off, sat on it or something. So what happened? How can she have fallen off a bus?'

I told her the story, trying to play down Jude's role in the escapade. My attempt to protect Jude didn't work. Andrea decided to focus her anger on her. 'So because Jude wanted her ears pierced, she had to drag Isabelle along as well?'

'Hang on a second,' I protested, rising to defend my daughter who didn't deserve it. 'Isabelle is older than Jude.' This was a little feeble because we both knew who called the shots in the partnership. But I had to say something. 'Besides, Isabelle has had her ears pierced too.'

'Yes, because Jude talked her into it, no doubt. Isabelle hasn't even mentioned having her ears pierced recently. She knew she could have it done any time she wanted.'

'But they're not allowed to wear earrings at school until they're sixteen,' I pointed out.

Andrea snorted. 'They all wear them. As long as they cover them up with their hair, the teachers don't mind. Didn't you know that? All this has happened just because you wouldn't let Jude have her ears pierced?'

Now *I'm* the bad mother again. Everything has turned out to be my fault once more. Why don't I just run off to California and renew my maternal kudos like Karen did? I could watch reruns of *Dallas* and *Dynasty* all day while studying for a degree in past-life regression or something.

Engrossed in this ludicrous but appealing fantasy, I hadn't noticed Dan arrive. Immediately, he and Andrea began laying into each other. 'Where the hell were you when all this happened?' Dan hissed. 'The hospital told me that they'd been trying to contact you for two hours.'

'*Us*. They've been trying to contact *us* for two hours. Isabelle has two parents in case you'd forgotten. Where the hell were you?' Andrea hissed back.

'I was in meetings. I work in case *you'd* forgotten.'

'Well your secretary didn't know anything about any meetings.'

I was rather enjoying this. It had been a long time since I'd been able to watch another family in crisis. It wasn't saying much but at least I always knew where Rob was. I clung to that small triumph with sad desperation.

When I returned to my eavesdropping, Dan and Andrea had moved on to more specific accusations. 'Don't think I don't know where you were or who you were with,' Andrea said. 'I've known for ages. And frankly I don't care but when it puts our daughter at risk . . .'

Dan laughed without humour. 'That's rich coming from you. Don't think I don't know the significance of that coat and hat.' Well, I hadn't known the significance of the coat and hat and I was looking forward to hearing what it was although I now had a good idea. Unfortunately a nurse turned up at that moment. Spoilsport.

'Mr and Mrs Miller?' she asked.

'Yes,' they both replied.

'Your daughter is doing fine. She's out of theatre and a doctor will come and talk to you soon. It's lucky that your friend was able to come and be with her. She was very distressed that you weren't here.' The abruptness of her tone made her feelings very plain and Andrea and Dan looked appropriately guilty. The admonishment delivered, the nurse took them both to the relatives' room where I'd been taken earlier. An ersatz relative was no longer required now that the real ones had turned up and, boy, was I grateful. Little did they know that the fearsome Miss Brownlow awaited them in that chamber of doom. I could almost hear the theme to *Jaws* as they got closer to their fate.

I called after them. 'I'll see you later then. I've got to get Jude back to school to face the music.'

Andrea turned. 'OK. And thanks, Lorna. For coming and everything. And sorry about what I said. I didn't mean it, I was just upset about Isabelle, that's all.'

It was gracious enough under the circumstances and I had to accept the apology. Because we both knew that she'd been right. It *had* been Jude's fault. As always, I was the one left to deal with the fallout. And without the benefit of a degree in child psychology.

My resentment towards Rob was cranked up a further notch when he couldn't make it to Keaton House in time for a humiliating lecture from the head teacher on parental responsibilities. He confirmed Andrea's suspicions that the whole episode was ultimately my fault. Apparently it was also my fault that Rob didn't turn up. I plainly hadn't communicated the seriousness of the matter to Jude's father. No doubt, if I'd stayed longer, he would have found some way to attribute responsibility for Third World debt to my fast-rounding shoulders. I took it like the trouper I am, all the while imagining the hideous revenge I would visit upon Rob and Karen in the future. One of the more bloody images must have made me smile.

'It's not funny, Mrs Danson.' Mr Walters' disapproval brought me up short. I wasn't shocked by his calling me Mrs Danson. Rob and I had decided to let the school believe we were married for the girls' sake.

I cleared my throat and tried to sound humble. 'I'm sorry, Mr Walters. I'm just still in shock from all the business at the hospital. Isabelle is like another daughter to me.' I thought this would sound better than telling him why I was really smiling.

This appeased him. Wow, I'm getting good at this deception stuff. I can't think why I ever bothered being honest and open all the time. Life's so much easier when you lie.

'In many ways, it's fortuitous that Judith's truancy should bring you here. I've been meaning to invite you and your husband in for a few days now.' I suspect he's not talking about a social cup of tea here. He continued. 'I've been receiving reports from all your daughters' teachers, but from Miss Brownlow in particular, about a marked deterioration in academic and disciplinary standards over the last few weeks. Apart from Phoebe, of course.'

Of course.

'When this happens, we generally ask the parents in the first instance if there is any change of circumstances at home that might explain the change.'

He stopped talking. I think this meant that he wanted me to speak. Rob, Rob, where are you? I shouldn't be having to do this by myself. I shuffled awkwardly in my seat. 'There has been a bit of upheaval recently.'

Mr Walters nodded but didn't say anything. He wanted to hear more. But I'm damned if I'm going to tell him that the girls are not actually my children and that I'm not actually their father's wife. Call me a snob but I do value my status which is precarious enough in the absence of any legal substantiation. My acceptance and acknowledgement in the eyes of this school mean something to me. I'm not letting them go without a fight.

'Perhaps my husband and I can make an appointment to come and see you together early next week?' I suggested. I won't turn up. See how Rob likes it. I'm beginning to think that maturity is overrated, I'm thoroughly enjoying my more childish flights of fancy.

'I suppose it can wait until then,' he grudgingly conceded. 'But in the meanwhile, we have to decide what to do about Judith. I have no alternative but to impose a two-week suspension. Any further episodes of this nature and expulsion will be considered. It is a harsh punishment but a necessary one in the light of Isabelle Miller's serious injuries.'

I couldn't argue with him on this. I didn't have the energy, anyway.

Jude and I didn't speak on the way home. Jude was immersed in an Oscar-worthy sulk and I was mentally preparing a lecture on Kant for that evening. When we got home, she went straight to her room and slammed the door. I went and put the kettle on – yes, I realise I'm turning into my mother – and shoved thoughts of my fragmenting family from my tired mind.

Before I could collapse, the phone rang again. I wished I could be the sort of person who lets it ring but my instinctive curiosity coupled with a maternal terror of bad news always makes me succumb.

'Hello, is that Lorna?'

'Speaking,' I replied.

'It's Simon. Simon Flynn. From your class.' He didn't need to add all the qualifiers. I'd recognised his voice and was surprised at the flutter I felt when I realised who it was. I'm not being disloyal to Rob but it's a long time since I've had any attention from an attractive young man, even if the intentions were entirely innocent.

'I'm really sorry to call you at home but you did give

me your number in case I got stuck on something,' he continued.

Did I? I had no recollection of doing so but it was the sort of thing I would have done to bring a conversation to a close when I was too tired to think of anything else to say.

'Oh yes,' I said inanely. 'But I'll be seeing you in a few hours. If you're stuck on your homework at this late stage, then there's not much I can do for you.'

'It's nothing to do with the course, actually. What I was wondering was if we could have a quick chat after class tonight. I know you have family commitments so I thought if I fixed it with you in advance you might be able to get a late pass or something.'

'I'm not sure. Things are a bit complicated at home right now.'

'I sensed that.' He sensed that. What does it mean when a (single, young) man starts intuiting things about a (married, older) woman? Discuss in no more than 500 words. 'Look if it's impossible, I'll understand. It's just that I have a business proposition for you.'

'What sort of business proposition?' I asked, intrigued by the prospect of any sort of proposition from him.

'It would take too long to explain on the phone. But if you can spare half an hour . . .?'

I considered it for about one second. A further thirty minutes away from this domestic cauldron. 'Sounds intriguing. Half an hour it is.'

'Fantastic! Great!' He sounded really pleased. I liked having that effect on someone after the veil of misery I seemed to be casting over my family with every passing day PK (Post Karen).

When I'd put the phone down, I reevaluated my life

102

in the light of this new possibility. A business proposition. Half an hour with a man who was not under Karen's all-encompassing spell.

Even the fact that the daytime TV schedule had been usurped by golf and snooker couldn't ruin my good mood. And that's a first.

Chapter Eight

'Oooh, get you, all glammed up!' Ali looked me up and down with obvious surprise. She was the only one in the kitchen as I prepared to leave. I was disappointed that none of the others could see me looking like this. I could have gone into their bedrooms to say goodbye but this would have been too contrived. It's not what I did on college nights.

I puffed up inside at Ali's praise. I suppose I had made a bit of an effort. Not for Simon, you understand. No. It was because I didn't know where we would be going after class. It might be a grotty old pub or it might be that swishy new bar near the college that served snacks made from the most endangered species on the planet. I'd noticed that it had very tall tables and stools and all the women in it looked as if they had just told *Hello*! magazine about their latest romance with an Italian footballer.

So if I wear a skirt with glossy tights instead of my usual jeans and tatty grey socks, you'll understand why.

Rob arrived at that moment and looked at me approvingly.

'You do look nice, actually. Going somewhere special?' Rob asked.

'Just college. And then I'd promised to join everyone for a quick drink afterwards. Thought I'd make a bit of an effort.' That 'everyone' slid out smoothly. Maybe I too am just one step away from the Danny De Vito coat and hat brigade.

Rob looked thoughtful. 'I can't remember the last time I saw you in a skirt.'

I took this as an accusation. 'I can't remember the last time we went anywhere that I needed to wear a skirt.' The image of Karen going into Pizza Express (Rob's and her Pizza Express, not mine) in a shortish skirt, showing off almost-perfect legs, suddenly hit me in the face. I stifled it. I'm getting better at curbing my lapses into self-pity and confused jealousy. Or rather, I'm getting better at hoarding them away until I can talk to Andrea or Phil and unleash it on to them.

Rob nodded. 'You're right, you know. It's been a long time since the two of us went out. Why don't we do something Saturday night? Maybe try out that new place in Balham, the one that does Thai fusion or something?'

'Like a date, you mean?' I found myself saying.

Rob smiled. 'It could be like a date. As long as you wear that top I always liked, with the hearts and the see-through sleeves.'

'Only if you promise to wear your lucky tie,' I replied. When Rob and I had first met, he'd been wearing a tie covered in German Shepherds in various poses. He was not an instinctively romantic man but he decided that I might be pleased if he wore this tie on special occasions, to show that the little details of our first meeting had never left him.

Over the years, the tie had accumulated some rather unpleasant stains along with the memories and, despite all the family's efforts to replace it, he absolutely refused to swap it. We teased him ruthlessly, especially when he insisted on wearing it with his best suit. But now I clung to any residual references to our shared history, hoping that our family could stay glued together with the cement of sheer commonality.

He smiled our smile. Everything was going to be all right, after all.

Then it struck me. 'Hang on a sec. What about the girls? They've got to get their project work finished this weekend. We said we'd help them and they've only got the evenings free. We can't just leave them.'

Rob picked up his newspaper and hid behind it. 'That's all right. Karen can come round.'

I froze. Not in a million years was I ever going to allow Karen back into this house, my house, even if it was technically half her house. I didn't say this, of course, because the new, calm me now thinks before she says the wrong thing. I still end up saying the wrong thing but with more structured eloquence.

'Here?' I find that one-word answers are the safest.

Rob lowered his paper. 'Why not? She can help out with the girls' work, if necessary, and be here when they go to bed' – I don't like this at all – 'or they could go and stay in her house. She's got beds ready for all of them if they ever want to stay with her.'

I like this even less. I consider the possibility of locating her landlords and asking them if she mentioned the existence of four marauding adolescents when she filled in her tenancy agreement.

Think, think, think. I smiled brightly. 'I'll tell you what. Let's forget this Saturday and do dinner another night. I'd promised Phoebe I'd go through her essay with her. Karen can't possibly know what exactly is required from each girl's year group.'

'I'm sure she can work it out. I'd really like us to go out *this* Saturday.'

'Why this Saturday in particular?'

Rob raised his paper again. 'No special reason. Only I've already told Karen she could have the girls for the night. She never has more than the odd hour with them and she wanted a whole evening so she could really be...' He couldn't find the word to complete this contentious sentence.

'And you didn't think to ask me?' Oh, oh! Now I'm sounding like Pat Butcher. I'm even folding my arms like she does, except I don't have the brick-solid chest to rest them on so I just look floppy and round-shouldered.

'It was only arranged today. I tried to call you at lunchtime but you'd switched your mobile off.'

'That's because I was in the hospital dealing with a crisis.' One ultimately caused by your wife, if you're interested.

'Anyway, I didn't think you'd mind. I thought we'd agreed that the more time Karen spent with the girls, the sooner we'll all be able to put the upheaval behind us and settle down again. Get back to normal.'

I liked the old normal. I don't like the new normal. One horrible thought occurred to me. I was going to have to meet her. If she was coming to this house, I would have to meet her twice, once when she arrived and once when she left. And this was twice too often.

I was learning to cope with the image I had of Karen arriving at Pizza Express that day. I'd consoled myself by giving her a shrill voice and hairy armpits and bad skin close up. I didn't want to find out for myself that she was even more perfect than I had first suspected. And now I'm going to be late for college. I hate being late. I can't think of clever ripostes when I'm running late as Rob well knows. Damn him for being so cunning as to choose now to deliver a *fait accompli*.

I quickly brushed my hair and topped up my lipstick in the hall mirror. I called out goodbye to the girls upstairs and gave Ali an affectionate kiss for boosting my confidence. Rob saved me the dilemma of whether to deliver a Judas kiss or storm out in a strop by retiring to the downstairs loo with his paper. Why do men do this? Surely it can't be comfortable, I mean there are no armrests and your legs must get chilly. And is it hygienic?

I tapped on the door as I hurried past. 'I'm off now, Rob. Don't forget I'm going to be a bit late tonight.'

'Oh, by the way . . .'

I hate Rob's 'by the ways' from the loo. They're always big issues that he is too cowardly to bring up in my presence. I said nothing, made no encouraging sounds, making him summon up the courage to complete this particular gem.

'You know that symposium in New York I was invited to?'

I did but I still said nothing.

He cleared his throat. 'Well, amazingly I'm going to be able to go.'

I couldn't stay silent any longer. 'How can you? I thought you said we couldn't afford it.'

He cleared his throat again. 'It's a stroke of luck. Because Karen has been flying all over the States for her job in the last few years, she's amassed a load of Frequent Flyer points or something and she's offered them to me.'

Rob once explained to me that there is no point shouting at dogs because they will simply extract the key words that they understand, their name, certain commands etc. and disregard the rest. I finally understand what he was getting at. All I heard was 'Karen' and 'me'.

'Isn't that great?' Rob asked in desperation.

I didn't slam the door on my way out. I hope that didn't go unnoticed. It took quite an effort.

It was the grotty old pub, not the buffalo couscous place. I was pleased with my choice of skirt. It was black (classy) but not velvet (showy) and not too short (pushy). I didn't feel overdressed and nobody was staring at me. I'd completely forgotten that, in the world outside of the family, normal women dressed in clean co-ordinating clothes to go to grotty pubs as well as smart wine bars.

Simon carried our drinks over. I'd ordered a half-pint of cider and, when Simon went back to the bar to collect his change, I quickly swallowed three aspirins, hoping to forestall the hangover that cider always gave me. Maybe it was my clothes, maybe it was the pub atmosphere, I don't know, but I felt that I was stepping way outside of the tutor/student circle that had previously defined and limited my relationship with this man.

'Cheers!' he said. We clinked glasses a little too enthusiastically and our drinks spilled on to the table. We both grabbed beer mats to try and absorb the liquid and our fingers met in the mopping frenzy. We both apologised a little too profusely and finally we reached that peak of embarrassment when you can either laugh and ease the tension or sink into an abyss of misery where you long for a natural or unnatural disaster to remove you from the situation.

Simon laughed. I sank. Clearly he was a laugher while I was a sinker. This was a good sign. Normally I laugh and Rob sinks. It's a form of complementary compatibility that works well in a couple. Ah ha, you're thinking! She's already considering the possibility of being a couple with Simon. Sorry, you're wrong. I'm not that sort of girl. No, honestly, I'm not. I'm terminally prim and uptight. I could no more be unfaithful to Rob than I could hitch up my pants in public. Even though the thread that links me to Rob appears to be fraying and shredding, I'm still holding on tight to it.

I know that Andrea and Phillippa both find me a bit of an anachronism with my unforgiving views on fidelity within marriage, especially in the light of the fact that Rob and I aren't actually married. It's like everything else in my life, I suppose. I find something good, something that works for me and I want to freeze the moment, the emotion, the comfort, the security and carry it with me unchanged through the rest of my life. I don't want to threaten it and I don't want it threatened.

So while I find myself automatically evaluating potential futures with the man sitting opposite me, it is just a game, like doing one of those *Cosmopolitan* quizzes to find out if you should leave or stay with your man.

Where was I? Oh yes, he was laughing, I was sinking. He expertly ignored my descent and got down to business. 'Before anything else goes wrong, let me quickly tell you what I have in mind.'

I stopped sinking and clawed my way back up to congeniality with a smile. 'I must say I'm intrigued,' I said.

'I think I've told you about my company,' Simon went on. 'I build websites for companies, advise people on how to make money from the Net, that sort of thing. I don't know how much you know about the Internet.'

I laughed. 'I have four children plus a husband who are all addicts, I never get near the computer.'

'That's OK. It doesn't really matter. Anyway, one of my clients is compiling a revision site for college students. You know that schoolchildren can now log on to revision sites for all their GCSE and A level subjects and get extra help and coaching?'

I didn't know but I pretended I did.

'Well, up until now, there's been nothing similar for degree students. So this client of mine is going to bridge that gap. Eventually he plans to build sites for all the major degree courses in the UK, covering all the major topics in each subject.'

'I think I understand,' I said. 'It's a bit like a crammer's guide with all the basic facts expressed in the simplest form.'

'Exactly!' Simon exclaimed. 'And you'd be great at it. I mean I'm a complete moron but you've made me understand more about philosophy than I could ever have learned from the original books.'

I was ridiculously pleased to hear this. While I have dedicated the last ten years of my life to being a good mother first and foremost, it's a wonderful bonus to be told that the part-time job I slot in among my main responsibilities is having an impact on other people.

'So are you in?' Simon asked.

'In what?'

'Will you do it? Head up the philosophy website? You have to let me know straight away because the whole project has to be completed in six months.'

Six months to translate the entire history of the thinking world into comprehensible soundbites. 'That's impossible.'

'What if I tell you that you'll be paid ten thousand pounds?'

I thought of Rob's forthcoming birthday and the trip

111

to the Wolf Sanctuary. Then I remembered his announcement that he was going to New York, courtesy of Karen. I was tempted to forget the lavish birthday present in the light of his new betrayal, but I realised that I couldn't. The girls would be devastated, they were so looking forward to seeing their dad's face when they surprised him with the gift of a lifetime. That's that, then.

'I'll do it.'

'Fantastic!' Simon said. 'Let me get you another drink to celebrate. Unless you're in a hurry to get home, that is?'

'No hurry at all,' I replied, not even bothering to look at my watch. Just because I was mortgaging my free time for six months to pay for Rob's damn trip of a lifetime didn't mean I had to go home on time and be nice to him as well.

While Simon was at the bar, I looked around at the other people in the pub. It was a fairly young and fairly affluent crowd as was common in this part of South London. I played my favourite game of guessing the life histories of all the punters until I was stopped short by the sight of a familiar face. And then another familiar face.

I wasn't too surprised to see Joe in this pub. He and Phillippa lived nearby and I knew he often went to the pub to watch sport on satellite TV since Phillippa refused to have it in the house. What did surprise me was his drinking companion.

There is one rule to friendships within couples in my book. This states that the first point of contact becomes the defining point. If the wives meet up first then the husbands become secondary members of this friendship circle. The wives' friendship is sacred. If it is the husband of one couple and the wife of another that become friends first then the same rules hold fast.

So although I like Andrea's and Phillippa's husbands a lot, I wouldn't expect to go out alone with them. Nor would I ever phone them in preference to their wives. I just wouldn't. And we've talked about this on our many nights out and they've agreed.

So although I tried really, really hard to find an innocent explanation, I could not think of a single legitimate reason why Joe would be sitting at a corner table with Andrea, her Danny De Vito coat draped behind her chair.

'There you go.' Simon interrupted my line of vision with a pint glass. 'I decided to get you a pint since we're celebrating.'

I knew that I should object, remind him that I was driving, but I didn't. I needed the drink and I took it willingly. It was suddenly very important that Andrea and Joe didn't see me. I had to work out how I was going to handle this new situation before I faced them. I looked around the pub. 'Why don't we go and sit over there?' I suggested to Simon, gesturing to a snug table in a poorly lit corner. He looked a little surprised but, since I was already halfway across the room, he had no choice but to follow me.

It was perfect. Even when the faithless pair left, they wouldn't see me. 'That's better.'

Simon looked at me curiously. 'Is everything all right? You seem a bit . . . edgy.'

I took a few heavy gulps from my glass. 'I'm fine. Absolutely fine. Well I'm not, actually. I've just seen one of my two married best friends with my other best friend's husband.'

I could see Simon's eyes narrowing as he tried to work

out the complex web of relationships that I was describing. 'Perhaps they're just having a drink together.'

'They're both married,' I repeated. 'To other people.' Am I the only sane person in a crazy universe? Does nobody but me recognise that rules and boundaries offer our only foundation for security in a fluctuating world?

Simon looked at me thoughtfully. 'What I mean was, perhaps there is an innocent explanation for it. Perhaps they are planning a surprise party or present for his wife or her husband. Perhaps they bumped into each other on the street and decided to pop in for a quick drink and perhaps they'll tell their respective partners who won't feel remotely betrayed by a shared pint and bag of crisps.'

'If it had been any other day, I might, just *might* have gone along with that. But her daughter had a serious accident today. She's in hospital.' I told him the whole story, elaborating the facts, the way one does with an episode that isn't as dramatic as it seemed when it was actually happening. 'No mother would just go out for a casual drink when her child was in hospital. Even you must see that.'

He looked amused. 'Even me? Because I'm just a man, not even a father?'

I blushed. 'Sorry. I didn't mean it like that.'

'Don't worry, I didn't take it personally. I take your point but, under the circumstances, maybe your friend is even *more* likely to jump at the first friendly face she sees and grab the excuse to have a drink. It sounds as if she might need one after her day.'

I wasn't convinced. I tried to explain Andrea's recent strange behaviour and the Danny De Vito outfit. Admittedly, it sounded weak when I laid out all the evidence but I still felt certain I was right in my suspicions.

'What do you think they'd have to say if they saw you with me here?' Simon's question pulled me up short.

I bristled uncomfortably. 'They wouldn't have to say anything. I'd just explain that you are one of my students.'

'There! My point exactly!' His point was lost on me. I shook my head to indicate my complete lack of comprehension.

He went on. 'You said that you would just explain ... You are assuming that they would come up and speak to you. What if they just hid away in a corner and conjured up wild imaginings, like you've been doing? You haven't even given them the chance to explain themselves.'

Now I was in a bad mood. If I wanted to spend an evening with a man who constantly pointed out how illogical I was, I could have just sat outside the loo where Rob was posted with his paper and let him harangue me. This was supposed to be an escape from all that.

Simon seemed to sense my growing frustration and changed the subject. 'I've got a confession. When you moved over to this table, I thought you wanted us to have a bit more privacy.'

I realised what he was saying. 'You mean . . .?'

He laughed. 'Yes. I know that makes me sound stupid but I suppose I'd been thinking about you for a while and I was looking for any kind of sign that you might have some feelings for me. Not just looking. Hoping.'

If the object of this admission was to distract me from what he considered my delusions, it worked. At this point I decided that I would not be driving home.

115

Only a serious intake of alcohol was going to get me through this testing evening. (I have to confess that I was rather enjoying this new part of the challenge, though.) I emptied my glass. 'My round, I think.' I stood up to walk over to the bar, then remembered Joe and Andrea. I sat down again.

Simon smiled. He picked up the empty glasses and gallantly humoured me by getting the drinks.

'Now I've embarrassed you,' he said when he returned.

'Of course you haven't,' I reassured him. He raised his eyebrows. I backtracked. 'Well, all right then, I might be a little embarrassed but I'm more flattered than anything. I mean, I'm a middle-aged married mum.'

'You are not middle-aged and you're not married.'

'I'm practically married.' I was getting defensive now.

Simon shook his head. 'No you're not. You're either married or you're not. There's no in-between. If you're not married, it's because you don't want to be married, you don't want to make that absolute commitment. Or, at least, one of you doesn't want to.'

I don't like this at all. I want to get back to Andrea and Joe. I know where I am with that one, basking in self-righteousness, in black-and-white indignation as they break, or contemplate breaking, solemn marriage vows, vows that I would never break . . .

I become all schoolteacherly. 'Like I said, I'm not that embarrassed. So tell me more about this project. It looks as if I'm going to have get started on it quite quickly.'

Simon looked at me thoughtfully for a couple of seconds before tacitly agreeing with my pleading eyes to go back into safer waters.

116

I don't recall exactly what we talked about for the rest of the evening as we both got progressively drunker. I think I delivered a garbled monologue on the sanctity of marriage or the non-marriage status that we not-quite-marrieds enjoy. I think Simon might have made a quiet declaration of his feelings for me to which I graciously responded by knocking a bottle of lager over him as I stumbled to the loo where I intended to compose myself. I vaguely remember being helped into a cab and touching Simon's hand gently in acknowledgement of the fact that our relationship had changed but not to the extent that he had hoped.

Then I remember spending the night in the bathroom throwing up.

'What happened to you last night?' Rob asked with that smug indulgence of one who doesn't have a hangover talking to one who does. The nausea had finally passed leaving me weak, tired, drained and headachey. I stirred my tea slowly and methodically, hoping I could stir my jumbled thoughts into a semblance of sense.

'Just had a bit too much to drink, that's all. You know what it's like when you're in a big group, everyone gets a round in and you end up having a dozen drinks before you realise it.' The lie seemed worse in the light of my awareness of Simon's feelings. I felt as if I was having an affair even though I had made it perfectly clear to Simon (at least I think I did, I hope I did) that I would never be unfaithful to Rob.

Which reminded me. 'Guess who I saw in the pub last night?'

I knew Rob wouldn't say the Dalai Lama or David Ginola or anything like that, he's not one for the ridiculous retort. Suddenly I was irrationally irritated by his solidness. The very down-to-earth reliability, the dry, gentle wit that had first attracted me to him, now annoyed me.

When I first announced that I was moving in with Rob, all my friends and family were surprised. They'd met him and liked him of course. What was there not to like? But they all found him ... safe. And it was generally agreed that I had no need to settle for somebody safe. I had enough security in my own life that surely I ought to be taking a chance on someone more challenging when choosing my life partner. That was the prevailing theory.

They'd all missed the point. It was because of my secure upbringing that I was able to choose someone simply because I loved him. He didn't need to meet a checklist of emotional qualifications necessary to complement my own particular stable of hang-ups. I was a whole person and I saw and respected that same wholeness in him. And this was despite the appalling predicament that was testing him. I know some people find complex characters interesting but I've always considered neurosis something of an affectation, promoted by utterly unneurotic individuals who believe it will compensate for an absence of personality.

I remember telling my best friend at that time something I'd learned from Rob's mum. Apparently Rob, as a teenager, had plastered his bedroom walls with pop and football posters just like everyone else – only he'd put his up with the help of a spirit level. I'd found this desperately funny. My friend had just found it desperate. 'Good God, he was middle-aged when he was sixteen! What's he going to be like when he's forty!'

Pretty much the same, I now know. And very grateful I've been. When you have four children soaring towards adolescence, you don't need surprises from your partner as well. It was our concrete normality that had kept this family together and kept Rob's and my love strong. It was what I'd hoped would allow us to get through this current crisis.

But now, right now, I see Rob through others' eyes. I imagine Simon finding him dull, maybe even not good enough for me. I see our relationship playing itself out on a detached screen, Rob and I as Percy Sugden and Emily Bishop killing each other with courtesy in a suburban hell when all of a sudden I want us to be Angie and Den killing each other with passion or Dempsey and Makepeace just trying not to get killed by unlikely assassins. And I feel foolish for letting a student crush have this insidious affect on me.

It's just I'd laughed a lot last night, once we'd got all that awkward stuff out of the way. With Rob, it was more shared smiles than laughs. And it was good to laugh big belly laughs sometimes. And Simon was attracted to me. So much so that according to him he was unable to get involved with any other women. And he was undeniably attractive. What was I doing? I was comparing Rob with Simon and the implication took my breath away. Is this a form of infidelity, I wonder? Because you can't undo doubts. You can't push thoughts out of your mind, however damaging. I can't, anyway.

Rob had no idea that I was deconstructing our entire life together during this short pause. He simply shook his head and looked blank. 'No idea. Who did you see in the pub last night?'

'Andrea and Joe.' I sat back, waiting for gasps and oohs. There were none. Rob started buttering another piece of toast.

'That's nice. How were they?'

Now I know that everyone else is mad. 'Andrea and Joe. Did you hear me. Just the two of them. Not with Dan and Phillippa.'

'So?'

I was exasperated. 'Don't you think that's strange?'

'Not really.'

Something occurred to me. 'Why, have you ever been for a drink with Andrea or Phillippa without me?'

'Of course I haven't.'

'Ah ha! See! You said "of course" because you know that it would be a suspicious thing to do.'

Rob sighed. 'I said "of course" because you know everything I do and everywhere I go. If I did go for a drink with anyone, then I would tell you. It wouldn't be a secret. The same way that you would tell me if you were going out with another man.'

Oh oh. I don't like where this is going. I refuse to feel guilty for bending the truth about last night. I know that nothing happened nor *will* anything happen. It's just easier all round to keep the facts simple.

Something amazing has occurred. I haven't thought about Karen all morning – OK it's only half past seven but it's progress. It must be one of the pleasant side-effects of deception, this focusing of the mind on the thread of untruth that leaves no room for other concerns. My headache is getting worse.

I remembered what my mum did at moments like these and immediately went to the kettle.

Rob cleared his throat. 'I spoke to Karen last night.' Oh well, it was good while it lasted. 'I said that it was OK about Saturday night. That she could come here, as we agreed.'

'Fine,' I said wearily.

'Really?' Rob asked, stunned by my acquiescence.

I turned to him. 'Yes, really. You were right. It will be good for us to go out, the two of us.'

'And you really don't mind about Karen coming here?'

'Rob. I've just said yes. Don't push your luck. You're not going to get me to say that I'm happy about things, but I am tired of fighting.'

He jumped up and came over to me. He put his arms around my waist. I melted into the contact, trying to squash the sense of betrayal that was tormenting me as I remembered Simon's steadying arm helping me into the taxi last night.

Chapter Nine

'Are you sure you're all right about this?' Rob asked for the tenth time as I applied mascara with a shaky hand. As it got nearer to the allotted hour, my nerves were beginning to let me down.

I tried not to snap but it didn't work. 'I've already told you, I'm fine.'

'There's no need to snap at me. I'm just concerned about you.'

This time, I didn't even bother trying not to snap. 'The only reason I snapped is because you keep asking me the same question. We've flogged the subject to death already and you keep on resurrecting it. We're going out. Karen's coming here to help the girls with their homework. I've agreed. That's the end of it.'

Rob managed to stop himself from trying the kiss of life on the subject one more time. He came over to my dressing table and watched as I tried to turn my face into somebody else's. He began to massage my shoulders. 'You're probably just tired, that's why you're so irritable. You were on the computer till gone midnight.'

Don't you just hate it when someone tells you that you're tired when you are so clearly in the throes of a fully justified strop? And it's always the person who has caused your strop in the first place. Maybe it's a defence mechanism, avoiding the need for any self-analysis by just blaming all your partner's problems on tiredness. Or maybe it's a male thing. Most women are so used to being assigned the blame for all problems, both practical and personal, whatever their provenance that we automatically assume initial responsibility for each new crisis whatever the cause.

In this case, Rob was half right. That makes me even more irritable. I had been making a start on Simon's project and was struggling with the computer. Rob had been thrilled when I asked for his help to show me how to access the Internet. I'd never shown much interest in the computer before and he immediately saw the potential for a new shared interest which was blessedly free of conflict. Once he got me started, I was hooked. I admired Simon's foresight in glimpsing the possibilities of the Web for academic use. I completely forgot my assignment and lost myself in arcane websites across the world devoted to obscure philosophers and their bizarre theories. I could see how useful it would be for a student to have access to one website which gave clear direction to the more meaningful sites along with some helpful guidelines and pointers to approaching each branch of the subject.

I explained to Rob what I was trying to do, mentioning Simon as casually as I could. Not that I needed to worry. Rob's first concern was how much I was being paid. 'Five thousand pounds,' I mumbled. The lie was necessary in the light of my plans. I needed the other five thousand for Rob's birthday, now that I was organising a party as well as the trip to the Wolf Sanctuary.

Rob looked doubtful. 'It seems an awful lot of work for just five thousand pounds.'

This is what happens when you're planning surprises. You end up embroiled in lies, wide open to carping judgements and snipey criticisms from which you can only defend yourself with more lies. Still, I comforted myself with the knowledge that Rob would feel really guilty when he found out that I'd done all this for him.

'That's my business,' I replied tetchily.

He went to bed at that point, leaving me to explore the twilight world of virtual life. It was gone two o'clock before I could tear myself away.

So yes, I'm tired but that doesn't mean that I'm not also entitled to feel aggravated by an irritating man asking me continuously if I'm happy to have his estranged wife come into my/her house and spend quality time with her/my children.

The doorbell rang. I jumped up, brushing Rob's hands away from my rock-hard shoulders that refused to be soothed. In all the hours I'd spent imagining this moment, I hadn't thought about who would open the door. And it was not an insignificant decision to make. If Rob opened the door, I would not be able to see the first interaction between them, wouldn't be able to read their expressions or prevent some kind of intimate collusion as Rob guided his wife back into the marital home. The game would be in their control.

On the other hand, if I opened the door, how could I stand it? How could I drag a plastic smile to my unyielding face and let her into my world? How could I be pleasant, civil, to someone who had declared her intent to upset my life? What if she was more beautiful than I'd remembered? What if I couldn't restrain myself and punched her in the face?

'Darling! Karen's here!' Oh no. While I was trapped in a paralysis of what-ifs, Rob had just gone and let her

124

in. How could he be so thoughtless? I took a deep breath, checked my face and hair in the mirror and sashayed downstairs like Gloria Swanson in *Sunset Boulevard*. Or I would have if I hadn't been wearing slippers. You really need heels to sashay. In the end, I just walked slowly as if I was wobbly on my feet. It was only when I reached the bottom that I finally came face-to-face, person-to-person, with Karen.

She looked at me and I looked at her. We both tried to avoid an obvious top-to-toe appraisal of each other. We both failed. But I saw enough. I saw her move a couple of inches closer towards Rob, pretending to avoid being caught by the closing door. I knew she was just pretending. Rob didn't. He should have moved a couple of inches further away from her out of loyalty towards me. But he didn't. He didn't have a clue what Karen was doing.

He didn't see her take a swift inventory of all the pieces of her life that had left their roots in my life, mine and Rob's. I watched her eyes take in the telephone seat with its cushion imprinted by fifteen years of confession and gossip, the battered address book that we'd, I'd, never got round to replacing, the skirting board which was still dented from Karen's aggressive hoovering. She hadn't been here a minute, she hadn't got more than a foot inside this house and she'd spilled the first blood just by her presence.

It's hard to explain how so many thoughts can go through your head in one second. In the second between reaching Karen and extending my hand to her, I had absorbed every element of her being. I suppose all the groundwork was in place. I knew what I was looking for.

I covered her face first. She had no spots or lines, but her make-up was heavy which made me suspect she had something to hide. Probably under-eye dark circles. And I detected the subtle presence of that green stuff people put on under their foundation when they have a tendency to red patches.

Her figure appeared perfect on first glance but she'd chosen those clothes with care. The Donna Karan jacket skimmed over her waist, perhaps because she didn't actually have a waist. I remembered that this woman had borne four children in quick succession. I suddenly envied her loss of waist. I would willingly have sacrificed my figure for the right to be undisputed mother to four wonderful children. Or any children.

Her jeans were also by Donna Karan and they were of that shape recommended for women with less-than-skinny hips and thighs. They work, of course, the wide bottoms and high waist giving her legs an elongated shape. Her shoes were exactly the same blue as the jeans. She must have spent weeks searching for that exact shade. And I know why. She's read that it will continue the illusion of length started by those oh-so-carefully-selected trousers. Yes! I know all the tricks. All those years of watching makeovers on GMTV have finally paid off. This woman may look as if she has pulled those clothes out of her wardrobe and chucked them on with a cavalier confidence in her own natural elegance, but she can't fool another woman.

She wears her vulnerability, her neuroses, like a designer label. True, to the casual observer (i.e. any man), she looks fantastic, effortlessly slim and gorgeous. But inside she's a mess of insecurities. She will have spent hours in front of mirrors, standing in different poses at different angles, trying to see what makes her look the slimmest. She will have an entire drawer overflowing with expensive lipsticks applied once and then discarded when they didn't make her look like Gwyneth Paltrow. She will be holding her stomach in right now until the muscles hurt. All the admiration and wolf-whistles in the world will never make Karen feel beautiful. I know all this in one second. So would any other woman. And it makes me feel a million times better.

My smile is almost sincere. 'Hello, Karen. It's nice to meet you.' There. That wasn't too difficult. I'd rehearsed the line, selected it for its absence of undertones or controversy. I was surprised at how easy it all was.

Karen's response seemed equally unstrained. 'Likewise.'

My, we are civilised. We all stood awkwardly for a couple of seconds, wondering at the protocol of decamping from the hall. Rob took control masterfully and led us all through to the living room where the girls were watching television with desperate concentration, none wishing to say or do the wrong thing. I'm ashamed to admit that I hadn't given much thought to the girls' reactions to this evening. They must have been dreading it, not wanting to look too pleased to see Karen in case it upset me, terrified that there would be a scene or that they would be called upon to make some kind of stand in one court or the other.

I could have wept for them. They didn't deserve this. They didn't need it. It was all difficult enough for them without me making things even more complicated. I resolved that Rob and I would talk about the situation from the girls' point of view when we were out. We hadn't thrashed out the situation with the girls' declining marks at school yet. We just didn't know what to do.

Well, at least I could make this easier for them. 'Your mother's here,' I announced cheerfully, hoping that they wouldn't notice how much effort went into the words.

The girls all exchanged nervous looks. Karen followed my cue and tried to ease the strain in the room. 'So what are you all watching?'

I detected a faint American twang to her voice that I found strangely reassuring. It made her sound more foreign, less familiar. She was no longer my South London predecessor who had once lived my life and was now angling to move back from understudy to starring role. She had not just moved on and evolved. She had become a totally different person. One who spoke differently. I think this is good.

Claire was the first to speak. 'It's *Blind Date*. We always watch this.'

Ali piped up. 'We all take votes on who's going to get picked and the one who guesses right the most times in a month gets to pick the pizza topping next time we phone out for one.'

Jude tutted without looking away from the screen. 'Yes but it's not fair because Mum nearly always wins so we always end up with ham and pineapple which everyone knows is Phoebe's favourite.'

'And Dad's,' Phoebe interjected quickly, anxious to avoid being the cause of an argument.

It was Karen who resolved the issue. 'It's my favourite too. I'll tell you what, have you guys eaten yet?'

'Mum's made us a shepherd's pie for after *Blind Date*. It's in the oven. Yuk.'

Thank you, Claire, you little turncoat, you always said that you loved my shepherd's pie.

Karen looked disappointed. 'Oh. It's just I was going to suggest we send out for pizza. I know this little place in Hampstead where they do giant pizzas divided into sections so everyone can have whatever they like. Oh well. Maybe some other time . . .'

The girls all looked to me with pleading eyes. What could I say? 'I suppose we can have the shepherd's pie tomorrow. I'll go and take it out of the oven.'

As I went into the kitchen, an explosion of excited chatter broke out behind me. They were all laughing together with Karen, shouting out their pizza orders while Rob cheerfully tried to get them to talk one at a time. They'd waited for me to leave the room before they felt allowed to start enjoying themselves with Karen.

When I came back in, they all stopped laughing. I wanted to say something witty, something to make them all laugh with me, to remind them that *I* had once been the source of fun in this house until I became the Grim Reaper. But I didn't dare take the risk. Because if they didn't laugh, I would die. I produced a cheery, uncontroversial smile instead. 'Right you lot. Now you've got your supper sorted out, your dad and I can go off and enjoy ourselves in peace.'

They all smiled politely and awkwardly, including Karen. Once more, she was the one to defuse the tension. 'Don't worry about us. Once we've had our pizza, I'll work them like a slavedriver.'

The girls laughed, confident that she would do no such thing. That their new mother would find some way of turning their dull, demanding projects into some glorious fun-filled adventure. She'd probably take them all out and have them jumping through chalk drawings on the pavement.

Rob rescued me before I said something unfunny that I couldn't unsay. He gently took my arm and pulled me towards the door. 'Come on sweetie, I'm starving.'

I let myself be propelled out of my home like an automaton, pulling on shoes as I went, hoping I'd get a chance to sashay before I got in the car.

The girls followed. They all kissed me extra-affectionately, before they kissed their dad. Normally, Rob gets the first kisses and I knew that this was the girls' way of bolstering me. If I was ever going to cry, this would be the time. Karen followed behind, looking awkward in the face of this excluding ritual. If Rob kisses her, that's it. I'm punching her and nobody is going to stop me. And him too. But even Rob is not that insensitive. He delivers a swift dispassionate 'Bye' towards her and turns away quickly. Too quickly? What am I saying? I must stop this excruciating analysis of every inflection and movement. It will kill me in the end.

Rob holds my hand down the path. We look at each other. The love is still there. I can feel it. I can see it. I exhale in relief. As we leave, I turn back to see Karen standing in the doorway, our doorway, her doorway, watching our closeness. Rob does the same. She has her arms folded tightly in front of her, hugging herself against the cold, or some other invasive force. And I see something in her face. Something behind the thin smile. It's not a grasping, conniving resolve to win her husband back. It's not a bitter, self-destructive envy. It's not self-pity. It's utter isolation. Desolation. Defeat.

I know what she's thinking. She's looking at me and seeing everything that could have been hers and now can't be. She knows that she's lost and I've won. Whatever happens in the future, she will never be able to get back the last ten years of family life, of married life, the fullest years for us and the emptiest for her. I now have a longer history with her husband and family than she has. She is broken and temporarily glued together with make-up and expensive clothes.

For God's sake, I hate the woman yet I want to go and comfort her. What on earth must Rob be feeling? I glance at him in the hope that he will not have seen her in the same way. Maybe I'm over-empathising. Maybe it's just me in my fragile emotional state, transferring my insecurities on to her. And Rob's not renowned for reading between the lines. But I'm out of luck. I can tell by his expression that he is aching for her too. Of course he is. He's a decent man and doesn't like to see anyone suffer.

This is not the same woman I watched walking into Pizza Express with all the confidence of Leonardo DiCaprio perched on the prow of the *Titanic*. This is the real Karen I am now seeing.

And when I notice how Rob is responding to her raw pain, to the circles under her eyes defeating the best efforts of her concealing cream, to her quivering mouth struggling to keep the smile going, I fall apart inside. For this real Karen is a million times more of a threat to me than the imagined one.

Let me see. At what point did we realise that the evening was going to be a disaster? It started with the traditional argument about who was drinking and who was driving. Rob waited until we were actually at the restaurant, looking at the wine list, before he started. This argument was entirely his fault. I'd suggested a taxi from the outset. But Rob has this thing about his car. He can't see the point of having an expensive car if you don't use it at every opportunity. This is how the argument went:

Rob: I drove last time. So it's your turn.
Me: But if I'd known it was my turn, I'd have insisted on a taxi.
Rob: What's the point in getting a taxi when we've got the car?
Me: The point is that now I can't have a drink.
Rob: Yes, but last time, I didn't have a drink and I didn't complain.
Me: That's because you knew it was your turn before we left so you made an informed decision not to go by taxi.
Rob: You should have known it was your turn this time. I knew.
Me: That's because you have nothing else to think about. I have four children who are on the road to becoming juvenile delinquents.
Rob: They're not just your children.
(Getting on to very, very dangerous ground here)
Me: What's that supposed to mean?
Rob: Just that they're my children too.
Me: Then why didn't you make it to the headmaster's office on Thursday?
Rob: I've already told you, I was out visiting a disabled client with her dog. I had the mobile switched off. By the time I got the message, it was too late.
Me: I'm not allowed to have *my* mobile switched off. I have four children who might need me at any time.
Rob: I need a drink.

Me: So do I but I can't have one.

Rob (not very nicely): Have a drink. We'll get a taxi home and pick up the car tomorrow.

Me: Why didn't you just say so in the beginning?

We'd been in the restaurant for precisely five minutes by the time this delightful exchange ended. By the time the waiter arrived to take our orders, we both had our elbows on the table, chins in hands, staring past each other, sinking into a gloomy abyss. With monumental effort, I ignored my total lack of appetite and found something I thought I could swallow. I was going to rescue this evening. I had to. We had important things to clear up and it would be tricky if we weren't speaking.

'Can we talk about the girls?' I asked, using my friendly voice, the one that doesn't hold over any rancorous undertones from a previous row.

Rob looked at me coldly. 'Do you mean *your* girls?'

Calm, calm, calm. Even though everything is Rob's fault, I decide to be big and absorb this negative energy.

'Whatever,' I say levelly. 'Anyway. We've got a big problem. The girls are obviously finding this whole situation with Karen more difficult that we thought. Perhaps we were asking too much to expect them just to accept their mother back into their lives after ten years. Perhaps we should have done it all more gradually.'

Do you like all those 'we's' I used? It was a nice touch, I feel. Since none of this was my idea and I would happily have told Karen what she could do with her born-again maternal instincts, I could easily be smug and do that I-told-you-so look that we women deliver with such skill. But I don't. I share the

133

responsibility. Watching those poor kids sitting terrified in the living room as their two mothers limbered up for the first round of emotional tug-of-war was a shock. I might not have visited all this on them but I could certainly have made things easier than I did.

Rob acknowledged the concession in my voice and relaxed accordingly. 'Maybe you're right. I don't think there are any hard-and-fast rules for these things. The girls are clearly getting something out of their time with Karen. They want to see her. And they are not showing any hostility towards you. So that's good, isn't it?'

I swallowed the sarcasm that was rising up inside me like heartburn. 'Yes, that's good,' I agreed.

Rob smiled for the first time since we left the house. 'So we just need to ease them through this period of readjustment. I'm sure they'll settle down soon enough.'

I chose my next words very, very carefully. 'Rob, I think the reason they're not readjusting, is that they don't know what's happening here.'

Rob looked baffled, as I knew he would. 'What does that mean?'

'It means that they don't know where things with Karen are going to end.' I couldn't say the words I needed to say. They were too loaded. But Rob's blank expression meant that I had no choice. He was going to force me to spell it out. So I did.

'Rob, the girls are wondering if you're ever going to get back together with their mother. That's why they are so insecure at the moment. They don't know.' And neither do I.

Rob was stunned by this. I can't believe that he hadn't considered the possibility of getting back with Karen, especially since I'd assaulted him with my suspicions since that very first lunch he'd had with her.

134

He was shaking his head, more to himself than to me.

'I can't believe this. I made it clear to you from the start. I told you that I loved you. I'm doing all this for the children's sake.' He could sense that I was about to interrupt and went on quickly. 'I grant you that I did feel sorry for Karen. I still do. You can see how much she's suffered and is still suffering. And, I'm sorry Lorna, but I once loved her and I get no pleasure from seeing her in such pain. But that's it.'

My voice was shaky now. 'That's all fine, Rob. But maybe you should be telling the girls all this. It's only natural for them to think about the possibility of you getting back with their mother. Especially . . .' I stopped abruptly.

'Especially what?'

'Nothing,' I said, praying for the waiter to come and interrupt us.

'There must be something,' Rob said impatiently.

I gave the waiter another few seconds then gave up. 'Especially since we're not married.' There. I've said it now. And it's quite a relief to get it out.

Now Rob was looking around for a waiter. I could tell. He was crossing his legs, which he only does when he needs to go to the loo and is forced to wait or when he's extremely tense. He too eventually gave up on the waiter. 'I thought we'd cleared this one up,' he said obliquely, trying to avoid direct reference to the subject as if we were talking about cancer or wombs or something.

'When did we clear it up?' I asked, genuinely interested in this imaginary resolution he believed we'd achieved somewhere in our shared past.

He was playing with the condiments now. 'Well, I

135

remember you said that you weren't religious but that you would definitely get married if you had children.'

I waited for more. There was no more. 'That's it?' I asked.

Rob tried to think of something else. I wish he hadn't bothered. 'I thought we'd agreed that it didn't matter if we were married or not. We loved each other. I'd already been married and that hadn't guaranteed any permanence so there seemed no point in going through it all again.'

'I never agreed that. You agreed that all by yourself,' I replied. Calm, calm, calm.

Rob shrugged. 'Well, we *did* agree that we couldn't have more children while the girls were still so young and so close to each other in age. It would be too much for you to handle. And the girls had enough problems of their own, trying to understand what had happened to their mother. So if you weren't going to have children of your own, there seemed no point in getting married.'

I couldn't believe what I was hearing. 'Rob, this is a conversation we had about nine years ago. I assumed that you would be divorcing Karen in the foreseeable future and that we would reassess our plans at that point. I didn't envisage waiting until the girls were all halfway towards menopause before we were entitled to some life of our own.'

'So what are you saying?' Rob's volume was rising now. This is all going horribly wrong. The waiter was on his way to our table, heard the tone of Rob's voice and made a swift U-turn. Rob continued. 'You want to get married, do you? You want children of your own? Which is a bit rich when you've spent the last half-hour banging on about *your* daughters whose lives I am now ruining by daring to introduce them to their mother. But that's what you want, is it?'

136

Yes, yes yes! I want to shout. But I don't. I don't say anything. Because Rob is unstoppable. 'You want me to divorce Karen, marry you, get you pregnant and subject the girls to yet more upheaval when they are barely coping with what's going on already?' He waited for an answer which didn't come. 'Fine. Let's do that then. Of course we'll have to move. Buy a bigger house. But that's OK, isn't it? I mean, you'll want to give up work when the baby arrives but that doesn't matter. Because the money fairy will wave her wand and provide one for us.'

I have never seen Rob like this. While he has always had mood swings like everyone else, they've tended to erupt in minor peaks and troughs along a basically steady threshold. He's never been angry enough to shout or miserable enough to comfort-eat. That was fortunate really. I have sufficient excessive tendencies for us both.

That's why this outburst was so disturbing. Not just because it was an unfamiliar experience but because it proved that Rob has not been unaffected by Karen's reappearance. I'd been trying to convince myself that it was just my paranoia making me sense Karen's presence gradually overwhelming us all. He must have been bottling up his own reactions until they frothed over on to me tonight. It was up to me to put the lid back on the froth before it stained us permanently.

'Stop it,' I say quietly. Everyone in the restaurant is now listening to us. Rob either doesn't notice or doesn't care.

'So let's not waste any time. Let's go home and give them all the good news. I think we've got some champagne somewhere. I'm sure Karen will want to toast us. This will make her day. A good divorce, that's

137

what she needs at this difficult juncture in her life. And the girls will be thrilled. Another baby! When their needs are getting bigger all the time and we have so little time for them that they're all going off the rails. Fantastic! Perhaps all four of them can move into one bedroom so that your baby can have a bedroom to herself. That's a good idea, isn't it?'

'Stop it! Stop it!' I scream.

Rob stops it. We both sit ominously still, hyperventilating, avoiding each other's eyes. I have so much anger inside me that I know I have to hold it in or else Rob and I will never survive the fallout. I want to mention that his divorce could have been arranged painlessly and invisibly years ago when the girls were unaware of the drama being played out in the background. That if we'd had a baby, it might have united us all as a family. That maybe the girls didn't understand the subtle difference between their father marrying their real mother but not their stepmother. I certainly didn't, so why should they, unless the true difference was that Rob always intended to spend his whole life with Karen whereas . . .

'I think we should go.' Rob was standing up. There was no need to get the bill because we hadn't ordered anything. The management was not going to make a fuss about us leaving. Despite the impromptu floor show with which we'd entertained their other customers, they were very happy to see us depart, despite the loss of revenue. While raised voices can be amusing, they always have the potential to lead to uglier scenes.

We went outside and walked towards the car, Rob automatically taking the driving seat. How ironic that, after the drinking/driving debate which had laid the foundations for the vitriolic fight that followed, neither of us had had a drink and the whole subject was now irrelevant.

We both sat in the car, wondering what to do next. I broke the silence. 'We can't go home now. They'll know that something is wrong.' The truth is, I couldn't bear Karen to discover that she had caused this rift between us. While I felt sorry for her and all that, I had no intention of giving her any opportunity for feeling sorry for me. I was clinging to that sense of pity I felt for her because it meant that I was in the stronger position. If *she* envied me, I must have a life worth envying, something like that.

Rob looked at me as if I were a stranger. 'Maybe that's not such a bad thing. I thought you were all in favour of honesty and openness.'

I closed my eyes, hoping things would be different when I opened them. They weren't. 'Please, Rob. No more. I can't take any more of this.'

We sat there for what seemed like hours but which was probably only a couple of minutes. 'What do you suggest?' Rob asked. 'That we drive around for a few hours just for the sake of appearances?'

Actually, that was exactly what I was thinking, but it sounded rather foolish the way Rob said it. 'We could always go to a pub. Just have a drink or something?' I was sounding pathetic now, I knew it, but I couldn't help myself.

Rob relented. 'OK,' he said.

And so we ended up in the same pub where I'd seen Andrea and Joe. Where I'd spent a confusing drunken evening with Simon two nights earlier. Hey ho.

We left the car outside the pub and got a taxi home. We'd spent a tense but unexplosive couple of hours talking about dogs, philosophy, Tony Blair, everything except the state of our lives. It was in the cab that Rob mentioned, as an aside, that his trip to New York was scheduled for four days' time.

Chapter Ten

'How long will you be gone, Daddy?' Ali hadn't called Rob 'Daddy' since she was five. The other girls just looked down mournfully into their cereal. He'd been away before on courses, seminars and the like, but things had been different then. Despite our best efforts, Rob and I hadn't made a very good job of hiding the difficulties between us and the children hated it.

When we got home that Saturday night, they were all still up, tired but excited from their evening. 'Look what we've done, Mum!' Phoebe cried as we turned the key in the door. I was disproportionately pleased that it was me she chose to share her achievements with before her father. I didn't have a chance to take my coat off before I was dragged over to the computer. Claire, Ali and Jude were all huddled around Karen who sat in front of the screen, pumping the keys like Liberace.

As elaborate images flashed before us, Rob patted each of the girls affectionately and gave them each a word or two of praise. 'Good work, Phoebe, well done Claire, did you do this as well Ali? Fantastic! Good stuff, Jude, I knew you could do it if you tried.'

Karen laughed and watched Rob with undisguised affection. 'Still using your dog-training techniques to reward the puppies, I see!'

I died a little inside. In a distant area of my memory, I remembered Rob once telling me how he and Karen had called the girls his puppies in those early days. This easy intimacy was torture to witness.

She pressed one last key with a flamboyant gesture and sat back as we all watched twenty illustrated, professionally typeset pages scroll colourfully from our printer. This was not so much a schoolgirl's project as the Bayeux Tapestry.

I thought back to all the projects I'd helped the girls with. The hours I'd spent poring over encyclopaedias with them, the endless graphs we'd drawn together, all the pictures we'd cut out and carefully mounted. Yes, I always knew that the computer had the capacity to produce amazing graphics and eventually I fully intended to learn how to use it. But when did I have the time? I was a working mum, muddling my way through, keeping the mechanics of a sprawling household ticking over. I'm only getting to grips with the technology now because it's a job and I need the money. For Rob.

I look at their faces. They are desperate for my approval. And I'm such a selfish cow that all I can think of is how if I give them my approval, I will be giving it to Karen as well. Maybe if I'd had a less disastrous evening, I could have been bigger about it. But I hadn't and I couldn't. I smiled and oohed and wowed as best I could but the girls were too attuned to my moods to be fooled by that. Only Phoebe was brave enough to ask what they were all thinking. 'What's wrong, Mum?' She only asked because she didn't suspect that anything serious was up. She was probably anticipating some story of parking problems or bad service at the restaurant that would become funny as I told it.

They were all looking at me expectantly. I was tired, very tired and a bit drunk. I did what any sensible person would do under the circumstances. I went to bed. My parting words were, 'Ask your father.'

Of course I felt terrible the next morning and not just because of my hangover. After all, they are almost a daily occurrence these days and I'm getting used to waking up with a headache. But I felt guilty for imposing my mood on the girls so I tried to make up for it by apologising at breakfast. I vowed that I would buy them all a treat – yes, thank you, I am aware that is not considered good parenting to try and buy children's favour. But since most children are brought up on a basic reward system, it is a language they understand.

Anyway the poor things were so eager for a semblance of normality to return that they insisted there was nothing to forgive. I made a big thing of reading their entire project, making sure that they each got praise for their individual contributions. And that was that.

But when they heard that Rob was going to New York, they were distraught in a way that I'd never seen before. They weren't clingy or weepy, just withdrawn and sullen. They all lost their appetite and stopped speaking apart from the essentials needed to get through the day. It was like living in a modern opera, all surreal and minimalist, with discordant tones making you feel uneasy and a plot that made no sense.

Rob had tried to explain that it would only be for five nights but they refused to listen.

'I don't know what I'm supposed to do, Lorna,' he told me. We were speaking again, just avoiding all contentious issues. 'I can't cancel the trip now. I've agreed to lead one of the seminars. Besides which, it's a great chance to make some contacts over there. Now we're linked to the Internet, I could get some really lucrative consultancy work going. I know things are a bit difficult at the moment' – understatement of the year – 'but I just can't turn this down. You understand, don't you?'

I did understand, as it happens, now that I was emotionally detached from the situation. The shock of our vicious row the other night had shaken me badly. It was what I'd needed to force me to pull myself together. I'd resolved to become a source of mature, quiet strength for the whole family. I would allocate time to each girl to try and resolve their problems at school and at home. I would be civil and pleasant to Karen and I would renew the passion and affection that had been missing with Rob for a long time. When he got back from New York, that is.

In the meantime, we all had to get through this short, enforced separation. I tried to get the girls to kiss Rob goodbye before he flew off. I knew they'd regret it if they didn't. Phoebe went to the other extreme and hugged him as if he was going off to war and might never return. This was even worse for Rob who, by now, was tormented by the certainty that he was the worst father who ever lived (apart from Terry Duckworth, of course, who sold his own son in a seminal *Coronation Street* storyline).

As he left, I was Krystle Carrington, sending Blake off to another boardroom meeting with Joan Collins. Boo, hiss! you all shout gleefully, ruing the glory days of glamorous American soaps where the shoulder pads were wider than the field of probability and villains always died a horrible death. (Horrible, but never facially disfiguring, since soap icons have to look fabulous right up to and including the coffin scene. After all this is a world where physical perfection is a prerequisite of saint and sinner alike. Even the should-have-been-canonised Pam Ewing did a runner when she contracted a disease which, we were reliably informed, would leave her looking like Michael Crawford in *Phantom Of The Opera*.)

No, I wanted Rob to carry the image of me as the fragrant Krystle, all soft focus and floral. I was beautiful and soft-spoken and understanding, delicate and strong at the same time, the sort of woman who brooked no prospect of betrayal. I'm not sure how successful my performance was but I was convinced.

And then he was gone.

He was probably somewhere over the Atlantic when the phone calls started. Phillippa was first. She sounded frantic. 'Lorna, are you free for lunch today? Please say that you are.'

Before I could stop myself, I found myself saying exactly what I was thinking. 'What about Andrea, isn't she free?' It was an obvious question given our respective positions in the friendship hierarchy.

Phillippa recognised this immediately and didn't bother lying to make me feel less of a second choice. 'No. She went all mysterious on me. Said she had something urgent that couldn't be cancelled.'

'Maybe she did,' I suggested.

'I don't think so. Because then she said it was a doctor's appointment.'

I love the shorthand that develops between friends. It removes the need to amplify every trivial statement and frees up time to talk about more interesting things like why nobody remembered the rules for that game on

Crackerjack ('Crackerjack!') where the contestants had boxes of cornflakes and cabbages piled into their arms. In this instance, the shorthand was straightforward. If Andrea genuinely had a doctor's appointment, she would have said so right away. But since she only offered this explanation after using the old *something urgent* excuse, it was patently an afterthought.

I acknowledged my appreciation of Phillippa's justified pique by tutting and murmuring.

'Precisely!' she replied to my mumbles, knowing exactly what I was trying to convey with my Robert De Niro impersonation. 'I don't know what's going on but it's something she doesn't want to tell me about.'

I hate this. I really hate this. I know exactly what Andrea is hiding and why she is hiding it from Phillippa and I can't say a word. If Phillippa were here rather than on the phone, I would go and make tea right now and prepare an elaborate detour to a safer subject. In the end, I just pretend to be batty and ignore her transparent need to discuss all the possibilities. 'So how are the boys?' I ask cheerfully, careful not to include Joe in the question in case that leads us somewhere risky as well.

'What? The boys? Fine, fine. Playing up a bit, in truth. But nothing too serious.' Not like Jude's suspension, was the silent footnote to this comment. 'Sorry, Lorn, I'm not being rude. I've got to dash out. The bank manager wants to see us and I'm meeting Joe there.' My heart was reassured by the possibility of somebody else's life being in trouble as well as mine. Does that make me a bitch? I don't care. 'So can you make lunch?'

Damn. I should have used the time when she wittering on about the boys to come up with a preemptive strike to get out of this invitation. At any other time, I would have loved to go out with Phil. We seldom spent much time together without Andrea and I would have enjoyed seeing how we got on together. But I knew what she would want to talk about and I didn't think I could trust myself to remain cool and objective. In other words, I wasn't sure I could lie and pretend that I didn't know anything about Joe and Andrea.

Too late. After her initial gripe about Andrea's feeble attempts to get out of meeting her, I couldn't do the same. It would be too cruel. I had to go along with it. I'd just have to drink a lot. No, I'd have to stay completely sober to keep a hold on my tongue. 'That'll be lovely, Phil. I'll look forward to it.'

'Oh that's great, Lorna. I'm really grateful. It'll have to be somewhere cheap, money things are a bit you know . . .'

I felt deeply for her embarrassment. 'Don't even think about it. McDonalds it is!'

Phillippa gasped. 'No I couldn't possibly. Things aren't that bad.'

I laughed. 'Phil, there's nothing wrong with McDonalds. Rob and I often go there after shopping. There's something decadent about eating there without children. It makes you feel somehow . . . reckless.'

Phil wasn't convinced. 'What if someone sees me?'

'We'll wear macs and dark glasses.' I suddenly think of Andrea meeting Joe in her Danny De Vito outfit and feel sick. 'I'll meet you at one o'clock outside Marks and Sparks. It's just down the road from McDonalds and, that way, if you meet anyone you know, you need feel no shame.'

Phillippa sighed. 'I'm too tired to argue. Thanks a lot for this, Lorn. I really need to talk to someone or I'll go mad.'

147

'It'll all be fine, I'm sure,' I say before saying goodbye. When I put the phone down, I cursed myself for that last bit. What right did I have to say that everything would be fine when it probably wouldn't. I was dreading this lunch. What Phillippa didn't realise was that I chose McDonalds because it would keep lunch short and wouldn't allow much scope for intimate chat in the frenetic lunchtime maelstrom.

As I congratulated myself on this optimal solution, the phone rang again.

'Lorna, it's me. Who were you talking to? I've been trying to get through for ages!'

'I'm sorry about that, Andrea, had I known it was you, I would have hung up immediately.'

The sarcasm was lost on her. She sounded more desperate than even Phillippa. 'Why can't you get Call Waiting like everyone else?'

'If you had *four* teenage daughters, instead of just the one, you'd know the answer to that,' I replied dryly. 'So what's the problem?'

'I must meet you for lunch. I've *got* to talk to you.'

Now I'm confused. 'I can't do lunch today. I'm meeting Phillippa. Who, incidentally, only called me because you told her you had an urgent doctor's appointment, something neither of us believed, if you're interested.'

'You'll have to cancel Phillippa. This is more important. I only told her I had a doctor's appointment because I didn't want her to know that I was having lunch with you.'

'I didn't know we were supposed to be having lunch today.'

Andrea was sounding exasperated. 'That's because I was just about to ring you when Phillippa rang me. And

148

I couldn't say anything in case you couldn't meet me and then Phillippa might find out and know that I'd lied.'

This is worse than having a conversation with Jude at her most recalcitrant. 'I don't know what you're going on about, Angie. But I can't cancel Phillippa. She sounded terrible and really needed someone to talk to.' OK, I know it looks as if I'm trying to make Andrea feel guilty. 'Whatever's going on with you will just have to wait until tomorrow unless you want to tell me on the phone.'

If I sound smug, it's because I am so convinced that I know what she's going to say. I believe I have all the facts and can predict every possible outcome. I am wrong.

For a while I can only hear Andrea breathing until it occurs to me that she is crying. 'God, Ange, what's happened?' I can only guess that something has gone horribly wrong with Joe. He's broken it off or Dan has found out or perhaps Joe's got her pregnant or something appalling like that. When she finally chokes it out, I learn what the phrase 'lost for words' truly means.

'It's Dan. He's having an affair!'

It was while I was walking down to McDonalds to meet Phillippa that I mused on how badly I'd handled the conversation with Andrea. I swore an oath to myself that this would be the last time I ever made the assumption that I was in complete possession of the facts of a situation before relying on my pre-prepared responses.

I had no responses for Andrea's particular announcement. I'd been struggling with the knowledge of Andrea's affair with Joe for days and had covered all possible approaches to the subject for when I finally broached it with Andrea.

I had considered the sympathetic-but-firm exhortation to desist in this insanity before anyone got hurt. This was the common sense approach, the New Labour voice of reason. I had also worked out a moral lecture which would crush her with my perceptive insights into her descent towards depravity. All my own work except I sounded suspiciously like Anne Robinson on *Watchdog* berating British Rail. I even found myself mentally replicating her trademark wink when I got to the stern bit. And of course I'd constructed a balanced argument where I encouraged her to look at the inevitable consequences of continuing the liaison i.e. divorce, custody battles, damage to Joe's and her children, being ostracised by the PTA cake-baking committee, that sort of thing. Too dull to outweigh the probable thrills of passion she was currently enjoying, I concluded.

I'd intended to gauge her mood when she finally confessed the affair to me, as I assumed she eventually would, and deliver the appropriate set piece. But there was no set piece for this hysterical pronouncement that Dan was having an affair.

I managed to stop myself from saying 'Hah! Serves you right, you scheming Jezebel! Now you know how it feels!' Because of course Andrea had no idea that I knew about *her* affair.

Perhaps this is a suitable moment to tell you something about myself. One of the reasons I refuse to get cable television, even though I know it will soon be practically compulsory, is my terrible fear that somewhere in the television ether I will accidentally stumble on one of those Brian Rix farces that used to torment us seasonally. I hate farce. Loathe it. I cannot bear the tension of watching all those doors opening and shutting with split-second timing. I just want the whole set to collapse, everyone to pull their trousers up or do up their blouses and crack on with the dénouement. I can't even laugh, I'm just too stressed by the whole setup.

And this is getting the teensiest bit farcical with Andrea not knowing that I know something and Phillippa probably suspecting the something that I know and Andrea avoiding her so that Phillippa won't find out that Andrea is the cause of the something that she suspects and I know. If you follow me.

'Oh dear.' That was my response. 'Oh dear.' As if she'd snagged her tights. As if it wasn't that big a deal. Fortunately Andrea chose to put my understatement down to shock. Which indeed it was. But from a different direction.

If we'd had this conversation a couple of weeks earlier, before my discovery, then I would certainly have been palpitating indignation down the phone line before rushing round with wine and cake so that we could work out exactly what she should be feeling and doing. I would have been seething with resentment at the hurt being dealt to my long-suffering soul sister. But everything was different now. Andrea was no victim and her marriage was a reference point that had shifted to a place I couldn't see. Her own infidelity had coloured all my judgements on this situation grey, like clean white linen washed with one grubby dark sock.

I mean, who was unfaithful first? If Dan was unfaithful first, then maybe it's understandable if Andrea also looks elsewhere. On the other hand, this justification is completely obliterated by the choice of best friend's husband.

I needed time to sort this out and I had the perfect excuse. 'Look Ange, I'm really sorry but I can't let Phil down now.' Unlike you, I said to myself, willing her to read my mind.

My words seemed to have an impact on her. She was definitely more subdued when she spoke again. 'You're right. Well, can't you come round after you've seen her?'

Sure. But I'll need a drink first. I can't see myself getting much fortification from a Filet-o-Fish and a strawberry shake. Perhaps I could join the winos on the High Street corner for a couple of cans of Special Brew. I try and convey a smile in my voice. 'Of course I will. It'll all be fine, I'm sure,' I added. It didn't sound convincing when I said it to Phillippa but I think repetition has given it more resonance. Or am I just desperate to find something positive in the terrible way I'm handling this mess?

And why can't I stop thinking about Simon?

Phillippa was standing outside M & S looking furtive. To a casual bystander, she would have looked like an impeccably groomed middle-class woman of indeterminate age. To anyone who really knew her, she was a mess. Her hair hung straight, clean and lovely, but betraying its natural shape rather than the attentions of the chief stylist at Harvey Nichols beauty salon. She had no make-up on, by which I mean she only wore tinted moisturiser, lipstick and mascara – this is her emergency face which I've only seen once, when Elliott was in hospital with appendicitis. I don't know what it would take for Phil to show a completely bare face to the world but I was reassured that her misery was not yet on a level with nuclear apocalypse.

'Thank God you're here!' she whispered, grabbing my arm and dragging me down the street towards Starbucks.

'I thought we were going to McDonalds?' I asked.

'Don't be ridiculous. I knew you were only joking. I may be in a state but I'm not so befuddled that I'd believe you actually intended for us to go in there.'

That told me. Still, Starbucks was fine. It encouraged a fast turnover of customers by whisking away your cup as soon as you'd finished your last surreptitious finger-slurp of frothed milk from the bottom of your caffè latte. There was a jostling queue which prevented all but the most superficial of chit-chat, mainly provided by me in my newly appointed role of peacebringer. I was trying to lay a soothing foundation to the tricky conversation that was to follow. It just annoyed her.

When we finally sat down, Phillipa nursing her de-caf espresso, me with my capuccino (extra chocolate) and a brownie, I switched tack by offering my own problems in an attempt to add some perspective to Phil's growing sense of impending doom. Wrong.

'The girls are all upset,' I said, 'Rob's gone away to New York for a few days and it couldn't have happened at a worse time.'

'At least you know where he is,' she answered gloomily.

Here it comes. 'What do you mean?' I asked, pretending I didn't have a clue.

'He's having an affair.'

'Oh dear,' I said. Not for the first time that day. Phillippa looked at me in astonishment.

'Did you hear what I said? Joe's having an affair. You're supposed to laugh and tell me not to be so absurd.'

'Sorry. It was a shock, that's all. I didn't know what else to say. I don't know what one is *supposed* to say in such situations.' That pacified her. 'It wasn't what I expected,' I added weakly.

Phillippa took a ladylike sip of her coffee which prompted me to stop shovelling the chocolatey froth into my mouth with my fingernail. 'It wasn't what I expected either. Actually that's not true. I've had my suspicions for some time but it was only yesterday that I found out for sure.'

I donned my serious expression. It's the one I use when teaching symbolic logic, my weakest subject requiring all my presentation skills to cover up my near-inadequacy. 'Tell me exactly what you know,' I said.

Phil sighed. 'I know he's been having lunches and dinners with someone and saying that he's been meeting clients. But it all started to sound a bit strange. We work together, you see, so it's hard for him to be vague with me. I know all the clients, they're my clients too. And even the potential clients will have spoken to me on the phone at some point. Joe's been quite clever. He's always met up with the person he claims to be meeting but recently they've all been mentioning, in passing conversation, how he left early for some urgent appointment. And there haven't been any urgent appointments. I know because I'm the unpaid secretary saddled with making all of them.'

I clutched for a hole in her reasoning. 'Perhaps he's working on something that he doesn't want to tell you about until it's all settled. It must be difficult for the two of you to be working so closely all the time. Maybe he's having a go at something ambitious and doesn't want to tell you in case it all falls through. Something like that?' *I'm* convinced and I know it's a lie.

154

I looked for a sliver of hope digging in behind Phillippa's dead eyes. There's none.

'I suppose it's possible,' she said grudgingly. 'I might even have gone along with that. Until today. Joe got a mysterious phone call last Thursday morning. He said it was some new business lead that he'd tell me about if it came off.' I didn't bother restating my premise that this was a plausible explanation. I knew where this was going. To be precise, I knew where Joe was going last Thursday. 'He was out all afternoon, came home for about an hour then he got another phone call and disappeared again. And this morning I found this in his pocket.'

She pulled out a phone bill with an inky scrawl defacing the payment instructions. It took a while for me to decipher. The writing looked as if it had been scribbled in a storm. It was smudged and veered off towards the corner of the paper like a dying insect. There was nothing particularly exciting about it, no declarations of undying love, no coded references to sweaty assignations, just a name and a phone number.

'Do you see what I mean?' Phillippa asked impatiently. I didn't actually. 'This is Joe's writing. The phone bill only came yesterday. So you tell me what he's doing writing that name and phone number on it?'

And I couldn't or rather I could but not in any way that would alleviate her suspicions. Because the name and phone number were of Tara Brownlow, gorgeous, scary teacher.

I could see how it had all happened. Andrea and Joe had been together (I'm trying not to think of what they were doing – I'll give them the benefit of the doubt and imagine that they were having anguished discussions about the futility of their relationship, like in *Brief*

Encounter). When Andrea finally switches on her mobile, she finds the stern message from Isabelle's teacher. She yells at Joe to get a pen and paper and write down Miss Brownlow's mobile phone number (I never knew her name was Tara, she was the sort of teacher you felt was born with the Christian name 'Miss'). In the midst of all the drama, he stuffs the phone bill back in his pocket, forgetting to destroy the evidence.

There. That's that mystery solved. Now all I have to do is find an innocent explanation. Too late.

'See! And he's underlined it three times. You can't think of a good reason why he'd have that woman's name and number, can you?'

'I can, Phil. The obvious reason is that Miss Brownlow is not a woman, she's an android, a monstrous representation of a woman created by demonic forces who've misinterpreted our society's bizarre enslavement to the power of conventional beauty. No normal man would ever be attracted to her or it or whatever she is.'

'Don't be so absurd, Lorna. She's stunning. Any normal man would throw himself at her feet if he thought she would allow him to lick her shoes.'

Oh yes, I've just remembered. Phillippa also inhabits that parallel universe where the price you are prepared to pay for moisturiser determines your intrinsic value to society. Miss Brownlow's undisputed commitment to personal grooming immediately sets her apart from mere mortals such as I and admits her to the *Übermensch* class where folk such as Phillippa and Joe can confidently crossbreed and socialise. It was a world from which I exclude myself every time I apply Vaseline to my lips.

Miss Brownlow was the worst kind of rival in Phillippa's eyes, someone to be admired and emulated, someone like herself.

I'm amazingly calm, all things considered. Phillippa believes that Joe is having an affair with her son's teacher. I have to decide whether this is better than an affair with her best friend. I don't have time to wonder for long.

'Anyway, I know what I'm going to do,' Phil announced decisively. Oh God. What is the mad, deluded woman going to do? She tells me. 'I'm going to the school to report her to the headmaster.'

I wonder when Brian Rix is going to burst out of the toilets with his pants around his ankles.

I tried to dissuade her from this action. It was pointless. She was deranged and closed to reasoned argument. 'But Phil, shouldn't you speak to Joe first?'

She snorted. 'What's the point? He'll just deny it.'

I was clutching at straws now. 'Then how about talking to Miss Brownlow? Get her side of the story. Maybe there really is an innocent explanation. Don't forget, she is Elliott's teacher. Perhaps he needed to speak to her about something.'

I could tell by the look she gave me that I'd said something ridiculous. 'Joe doesn't even know who the boys' teachers are. He's not like Rob. I've always looked after that side of things.'

I seize my chance. 'There you are then! How can Joe be having an affair with one of the teachers if he never has any contact with them?'

This finally penetrated Phillippa's certainty. 'I don't know, I suppose. But I can't think of any other reason.' She sounded less sure.

I hastily finish the last remnants of my chocolate brownie and gulp down my coffee, burning my tongue and forcing myself not to cry out in pain. I really, *really* want to get out of here before I say the wrong thing. 'Well, there you go. Ask Joe about it before you do anything silly. Please!'

'All right.'

A result! Now all I have to do is warn Joe and Andrea and possibly Miss Brownlow so that they are all prepared for the fallout. All I'm interested in at this juncture is protecting Phillippa. I'll sort out the others later. And then, I'll be ready to deal with all those silly squabbles over global nuclear disarmament.

I pulled my coat on and made one of those tutting/sighing noises that is generally understood to mean that a person has had a lovely time but now has to leave. Phillippa didn't notice. She screwed up her eyebrows as if she'd suddenly thought of something puzzling. 'Did you say that Rob was in New York?'

Safe ground. 'Yes, a doggie symposium. It was all arranged at the last minute.'

Phil nodded thoughtfully but didn't say anything. This is really irritating. I *have* to ask her. 'Why are you nodding like that?'

She smiled awkwardly. 'Oh nothing. It's just a coincidence, that's all.'

Is she doing this just to annoy me? 'What's just a coincidence?'

She started pulling on her own coat, probably hoping that this would distract me from the import of her words. 'Nothing, honestly, nothing. It's just that I tried to call Karen this morning and there was a message on her machine . . .'

OK. This is her last chance. If she doesn't spit it out this time, I'll slap her. 'And?'

'It just said that she was going to be away for a few days but could be contacted on her mobile. She said that she would be in New York.'

Chapter Eleven

Did you know that, when given two completely devastating bits of information, your brain deals with them by processing the less important one first? I do.

With impressive aplomb, I'd managed to extricate myself from Starbucks with my dignity intact. I'd laughed about the 'coincidence' with Phillippa and even been so mean as to direct her attention back to the domain of her own problems to get her away from mine. 'Now I come to think about it, Rob did say something about Karen being in New York,' I lied smoothly. 'I didn't pay much attention. I won't worry until I start finding phone numbers in his pocket!' Now that wasn't very nice. Phillippa's face dropped and I immediately felt guilty. But I longed to find Miss Brownlow's phone number in Rob's pocket. Or anyone's phone number as long as it wasn't Karen's.

After Phil and I had said some uncomfortable good-byes, I started off on the walk to Andrea's, allowing these searing new facts to weave their way into my consciousness.

Resentment and self-pity began jostling for pole position. I couldn't believe how casually Phil had mentioned that she'd phoned Karen that morning. There were two implications here: firstly, that she was in regular contact with Karen and hadn't mentioned it before. Did this mean that Andrea was also in touch with her? Secondly, it meant that she'd tried to call Karen *before* she called me. I wasn't second choice for supporting shoulder after Andrea, I was third. And yes, I do mind. Karen was back in the loop. How did this happen?

I would have liked to brood on this for longer. I wanted to sort it out in my head before I met Andrea. But there was a bigger issue to face.

Perhaps it was my fault for being so dim. When Rob explained about Karen's Frequent Flyer points or whatever they were called, maybe I was supposed to ask how they worked, if he could use them by himself or if he had to fly with Karen. I've never been on an aeroplane before. Don't look so surprised, it's not that uncommon. I've always had dogs and therefore I've always had holidays in the UK where you could take dogs with you. So Frequent Flyer programmes are things I've seen on TV commercials without ever bothering to take in the details.

But I had a vague recollection of seeing promotions where you could take another passenger anywhere you wanted free of charge if you went round the world a zillion times first or some such nonsense. Perhaps this was what Rob meant and he could only go with Karen.

But I do know something. He didn't tell me this. I can remember every single occasion when Karen's name has been mentioned. I've absorbed every tiny little fact about her involvement in our lives, using any knowledge as a necessary counterbalance to all the imagined horrors that have tortured me since she came back. If Rob had mentioned that Karen was also going to New York, I would have remembered. I would have collapsed inwardly at the prospect of them going away together. I would have hyperventilated or thrown a tantrum. It would have been a big deal.

I'm not stupid. I know that the reason Rob 'forgot' this little addendum was out of terror of my reaction. He knew I would go berserk and he was sensitive enough to understand why. So he just didn't say anything. And I may be paranoid where Karen is concerned but I don't automatically assume that this is evidence that Rob's relationship with Karen is developing in some sinister fashion. I mean, perhaps it is, but I doubt that's why Rob lied. He would know that eventually I was going to find out and that a monstrous row would ensue. He just couldn't face it before he went, especially when things were so strained between us.

No, what worried me was not the intention but the actuality of the two of them in New York. I could only hope that contact between them was restricted to the flights there and back. In general, these symposia tended to be very time-intensive with a schedule covering every hour from breakfast through to post-dinner talks. And they also tended to take over an entire hotel. So there would probably not be any spare rooms for Karen. And she probably had friends in New York, maybe even still had her apartment.

Now you're impressed, aren't you? By my optimism. My positive thinking. Looking on the bright side. It's not like me at all. And this would be the one time when I would be entitled to feel hysterical with betrayal and jealousy. No normal woman could be happy about her husband going away with his sort-of ex-wife. So what's going on here with me doing a convincing impression of a little ray of sunshine? I don't know what's the matter with me. I think, though, it might be a kind of insanity. Today has obviously been too much for my overloaded psyche. It's still trying to cope with all the deceit that Phillippa and Andrea are squeezing out of me. There's simply not enough energy left for dealing with personal trauma on top.

Yes, that must be it. I've gone crazy. And I'm manifesting my madness by emanating a calm acceptance of all the personal attacks life is now dealing me. While I recognise that this is a totally unnatural calm that will inevitably shatter in time. I'm quite enjoying the novel experience.

So this is the me I take to Andrea's. My serene façade forms its first hairline fracture within seconds.

'You're late,' is her greeting. Thank you. I suppose I'm third choice after Phillippa and Karen, you disloyal cow, I think. Calm, calm, calm. I follow her into the kitchen where her Danny De Vito coat is draped over a stool like an implausible prop in one of those *Generation Game* playlets. I fully expect to find my lines stapled to the sleeve.

She puts the kettle on. Unlike my mother who makes tea at the first sign of crisis, Andrea holds the brewing process in reserve for only the most serious situations. For the general challenges of modern life, a gin and tonic and a tube of Pringles is usually sufficient. When Andrea needed her faculties to be thoroughly unimpaired, she made tea. Like now.

'Aren't you going to ask me how Phillippa is?' I asked her, a little cruelly, I suppose.

She didn't look me in the eyes. 'I was just about to. So how is she?'

'Terrible. She was hardly wearing any make-up.' That shocked her. I didn't stop there, determined that she would bear in mind the other side of the story when she pleaded for sympathy. 'Joe's having an affair.'

163

I stated this baldly, then waited for her to come up with an appropriate reaction. She became my mother, or everyone's mother, and started opening cupboards randomly, using the search for non-existent foodstuffs as an excuse to postpone her response. 'Who with?'

This was the moment, the completely unplanned moment, when I took the spontaneous decision to mislead Andrea. Since it was unplanned, I don't know what my long-term intentions were other than to deliver a swift, well-aimed kick up her emotional backside. 'Tara Brownlow,' I replied.

It worked. She recoiled with a satisfying gasp. 'What?' she asked. 'What are you talking about?'

I got up to help her with the tea, playing along with her pretence that she was the victim of some dastardly marital wrongdoing. 'Joe's having an affair with Tara Brownlow. Miss Brownlow, Isabelle's teacher,' I elaborated.

'I know who she is,' Andrea snapped. 'But I also know that Joe isn't having an affair with her.' Ah ha! Now we're getting to it! She's going to come clean. But not just yet, it transpired. 'So what on earth makes Phil think Joe's having an affair with her?'

I feigned confidence. 'She doesn't think, she knows. She's got proof. I saw it myself.'

'What sort of proof? Compromising photos?' Andrea asked half-jokingly, her voice decidedly shaky.

'I think you should ask Phil that yourself. She was speaking to me in confidence.' What a beautiful, wicked sign-off that was. I wondered if Andrea would have the nerve to bring the matter up with Phillippa. I'm not a natural bitch and I was beginning to get twinges of guilt. Before I could decide whether to proceed with my teasing deception or put her out of her misery, I needed to find out something.

164

'Andrea, have you been in touch with Karen since she got back?'

The hesitation before she answered told me all I needed to know. And don't bother reminding me that there was nothing wrong with this, that she was entitled to contact an old friend who she hadn't seen for ten years. I know and accept all that. It's the fact that she didn't tell me. And neither did Phillippa. And it makes me think of those car stickers, you know the ones that say: 'Just because you're paranoid doesn't mean they're NOT out to get you'.

Andrea had the good grace to look sheepish. 'I'm sorry, Lorn. I was going to tell you, but the timing was never right. I knew how you felt about her, I'd have felt the same in your position. But she phoned me. And, well, what was I supposed to say?'

You were supposed to say that you didn't want to be her friend any more, that I was your friend now. I manage to stop myself from saying this, aware even as I think it, that this would sound ludicrous coming from anyone over the age of six. 'You do understand, don't you?'

What am I supposed to say? Because I *do* understand. It's probably the insane me that understands rather than the real me, but that's who I am at the moment. 'Yes, I do. I just wish you'd told me.'

Andrea's face brightened at my unexpected acknowledgement of her difficult position. 'Anyway, I've only seen her a couple of times and it was all a bit awkward, really.'

I didn't want to ask but I did anyway. 'What did you talk about?'

'I don't know. General stuff. Reminiscing over old times, baby things.'

Things that I could never understand or join in with.

165

'And what did you think of her?'

Andrea answered this cautiously as she was right to do under the circumstances. 'She's changed. A lot. She seems to have had all the stuffing knocked out of her. It can't have been easy for her, even you must appreciate that.'

'I do appreciate it, Ange. It just sticks in my craw to watch her reinventing herself as a martyr who is somehow a better mother for having walked out on her kids.'

'I don't think she's trying to do that at all. She asked lots of questions about you.'

I don't know why I was surprised to hear this since it was an obvious subject but I was. 'What sort of questions?'

'She wanted to know everything about you. How you were with the girls, what sort of person you were.'

'And what did you tell her?'

'Don't worry, Lorn. I'm on your side here, as far as there are sides to take. You and I have been friends for ten years now and Karen knows that.'

I smiled with difficulty. 'So you left out the bits about me beating them with sticks and locking them in the cellar when they were naughty.'

Andrea returned the smile. 'She's so jealous of you, it was painful to witness.' Good. 'But I won't deny that I was pleased to see her. I never had the opportunity to apologise all those years ago for letting her down. Now I have.'

'And what next? I mean, are you back to being bosom buddies again?' Now I'm rooting through cupboards myself, trying to sound nonchalant.

'That won't happen. We've both moved on. I expect we'll meet up occasionally but we won't be on the phone ten times a day like we used to.'

'So she's definitely back for good, then?'

166

Andrea looked confused. 'Didn't you know?'

Terrific. Something else I didn't know. And doubtless it will be something I didn't want to know. 'Know what?'

'She's got a new job here. Presenting a daytime chat show. Something more serious than the normal *Kilroy*-type trash' – the sort of trash that Andrea and I always loved in the pre-Karen days – 'dealing with emotional problems, resolving family disputes, that sort of thing.'

Now I believe in God. Not a particularly benevolent one, but a definite supreme being. There's too much symmetry in all this to discount the probability of an outside manipulator. She had to get a job on daytime television, didn't she? My area. The field where I have been exposed to constant mockery for years. And somehow, she's managed to do it in a way that makes her look sophisticated, accomplished and successful.

Another little confession. This is one that even Andrea doesn't know about. I once prepared a proposal for the head of daytime television at the BBC suggesting that they produce a series of short educational programmes for adults explaining the great milestones in the history of science in simple, fun, accessible terms. Rather like the project I am now working on with Simon. I've never held with the belief that women at home are, by definition, brain-dead imbeciles whose only interest in science is whether detergent tablets fizz in the drawer or in the washing machine.

True, they are mainly fed a diet of pap from the beginning of GMTV until children's TV takes over the airwaves in the afternoon and they might even enjoy it (OK I know I do), but this is not necessarily their choice. I believe that women are as open to mind-stretching as anyone else.

I got a letter back two months later along the following lines:

Dear Ms Fitzwilliam (I didn't bother with the married-name pretence in this instance. Is this significant? Discuss in 500 words)

Thank you for your proposal outlining a series based around science and philosophy. While we have, of course, given your idea a great deal of thought, we have concluded that it would not be in keeping with the ethos of daytime television at the BBC as it currently stands. Viewer research consistently proves that daytime viewers prefer a schedule of programming that delivers a pleasant antidote to the challenges of household life. For those viewers interested in furthering their education, our late-night Open University scheduling is incomparable.

Of course, this is not to say that we promote 'dumbing down', a charge that is so often levelled at us. Indeed, I would like to direct your attention to the *Around And About With Ulrika* show, where Ulrika Jonsson was recently invited into Ann Widdecombe's home to discuss politics and feminism (as well as being give a rare private viewing of the MP's famed teddy bear collection).

Thank you for your interest. We are always happy to hear from our viewers.

Yours etc. etc.

Nigel Blah-de-Blah-Nephew-To-a-Labour-Peer

That told me then. I immediately realised my mistake. I should have centred my idea around an appropriate personality. Maybe even a series of personalities. The potential was limitless: Lorraine

Kelly presenting recipes that might have been popular at the time of Wittgenstein; Carol Vorderman wearing unflattering trousers in front of a blackboard and explaining Einstein; Richard arguing with Judy about Jean-Paul Sartre; and, of course, Rosemary Conley presenting the pre-Socratic Hip and Thigh Diet.

Yes, so now I'm just filling up with bitterness. I don't care, I'm entitled to feel bitter. Karen just waltzes into the country after years away, not knowing the first thing about daytime television, and gets a dream job presenting to people like me, my sort of people, not hers. She hasn't paid her dues. I bet she's never even heard of *Going For Gold*, let alone struggled through five series of it. How can she possibly expect to find a point of communication with viewers who have all taken completely different journeys to her to get to this point in their – our – commonly-shared lives?

'You're annoyed about that, aren't you?' Andrea observes with an understatement that makes me question the basis of our entire relationship. Since every other aspect of my life seems to be under threat, I decide to hold on to whatever friendship is still available to me and so I refrain from answering her. 'It makes sense, though,' Andrea went on. 'Apparently, it's exactly the same format of programme that she once presented in the States, so it was quite easy for her to sell.' She had, falsely interpreted my silence as encouragement to continue.

'I'm sure,' I agreed, hoping that my abruptness would persuade her to drop this subject. 'Anyway, enough about Karen.' Please. *Enough* about Karen. 'What's going on with you and Dan?'

Andrea looked confused as if she'd forgotten her original reason for calling me round. She swiftly got back on to the right track, the track where her life is a complete mess and I am the well-balanced, well-adjusted friend whose orderly existence qualifies me to apply my sword of reason. 'Oh yes. Sorry. It's you talking about Joe and Phillippa and . . . Tara Brownlow. It threw me off course for a moment.' I could see her brain computing this new, unwelcome piece of information, trying to make sense of it while not looking as if it mattered that much.

'It's Dan.' Yes, I know that much already. I'm tired and drained and I'd appreciate *somebody* just delivering a straightforward, lucid account of their problems without my having to fill in all the gaps with blindingly obvious questions. But that's not going to happen today so I play along. 'You said that you think he's having an affair,' I prompt.

'I know he's having an affair,' she corrected. 'I've known for some time but it's only recently that I found out conclusively who the other woman is.' She paused here for dramatic effect, oblivious to the fact that I would prefer this conversation to be driven along by anything, hyperbole, rhyming couplets, whatever, anything except dramatic pauses where I have to feed the drama. I'm tired, I told you.

Andrea finally gave up waiting for me to deliver my line. 'Aren't you going to ask me who Dan's other woman is?' She said this with a malicious glint in her eyes, leading me to surmise that I know the woman in question. So now I *have* to ask.

'Go on then. Who is it?'

'Tara Brownlow.'

All I need now is to learn that Phillippa is conducting a secret affair with Rob and is expecting his love-child for this mini-series to be complete. I tried to work out when I last took paracetamol and when I could take some more. I gave up worrying, thinking that a mild overdose might not be such a bad thing, offering, as it would, some much-needed thinking time in bed. While I rooted around in my handbag for any kind of painkiller, I began the requisite interrogation.

'You're joking, of course?'

Andrea looked indignant. 'Do you think this is funny?'

Yes, actually, in a *Schadenfreude* kind of way, which is the only *Freude* available to me these days. 'No, of course not. I'm just having difficulty keeping up with all this.' A ludicrous thought occurs to me. 'This isn't some kind of practical joke that you and Phillippa have cobbled together to distract me from my problems, is it?'

Andrea glared at me. No, it wasn't then. Whoops. 'Sorry, Ange. Look, you're going to have help me out here. I've had Phillippa give me some pretty plausible evidence that Joe is having an affair with Miss Brownlow.' I cross my fingers behind my back at this. 'And now you're saying that you've got evidence that Dan is having an affair with her too. I mean, what's going on here? Is she at it with both of them?'

'Don't be ridiculous.' I wish my friends would stop calling me ridiculous. 'Joe isn't having an affair with her.'

'How can you be so certain?' I ask her quickly.

Andrea breathed in sharply and then looked at me astutely before crumbling. 'Oh my God, you know, don't you?'

I considered lying but her distress was so palpable that I couldn't watch her struggling any more. 'Sorry, Ange. Yes, I've known for a few days now.'

'Why didn't you say something instead of letting me make a fool of myself?'

'Oh, so now I'm the bad guy here? Why didn't you tell *me* instead of letting me find out in some sordid way?'

'Because I knew you'd be shocked. And I was right, wasn't I? You are shocked.'

I laughed without humour. 'You make it sound as if that's a bizarre reaction, as if I'm some kind of quaint throwback to Victorian values. Phil's your best friend! By anybody's standards, this is the lowest of the low. How could you do this to her?'

She slumped on to a stool in front of the breakfast bar, stirring the tea in the pot in a dulled rhythm. 'I don't know. It just happened.'

'Oh come off it, Ange. It's only on telly that these things *just happen*. And even then it's only because the scriptwriters can't think of a better justification. Earthquakes just happen. Women jump into bed with their best friends' husbands as the consequence of some really bad decisions.'

Her shoulders rounded even further. 'I know. There's no excuse for it. Except I've been so lonely. And scared.'

'What are you talking about? This is the first I've heard of it. We talk a dozen times a day. I tell you everything,' apart from details of my thwarted attempts to get a show on daytime television, 'and you tell me everything. When did you ever say anything about being lonely and scared? Scared of what?' It's like talking to a stranger. I'm angry with her for having held back so much from me. I thought that our friendship had been deep, authentic, all-encompassing, but it now turns out that we were little more than schoolgate

172

acquaintances, exchanging factual information and inconsequential revelations.

'Since when have you told me everything?' Andrea asked harshly.

I was stung by her tone and it forced me to think carefully before defending myself too eagerly. Before I could answer, Andrea did it for me. 'When have you ever talked to me about how badly you want to be married to Rob? And how deeply you resent his refusal to divorce Karen? And how desperately you want, need, children of your own?'

I don't like this. I don't like this at all. This isn't about me. I get all this when I'm by myself with my thoughts. I come to my friends to rubberstamp my current reality, not to force them to gaze with me through broken windows on to impossible futures.

Andrea stopped stirring the tea which was now stewed into undrinkableness and placed her hand gently over mine. 'Sorry, Lorn, I shouldn't have said that. But it's all true, isn't it?'

'What if it is? There's no point in talking about it so I don't bother. It's not that I'm holding things back, I simply don't see any reason in churning up feelings that can't be resolved. It would just be futile and depressing.'

Andrea went to the fridge to pull out a bottle of white wine. She was obviously feeling better. That was only fitting since I felt a lot worse. 'Well, it's the same for me, Lorna. What is the point of me telling you how miserable my marriage is making me, when we both know it's a subject that torments you? And you have this incredible, unrealistic idea of marriage. Because you want it so badly, you've created a myth around it, seeing it as an unassailable fortress. You think that, if

173

only Rob would marry you, you'd be secure for the rest of your life, that nothing could touch you.'

I don't recall ever saying such a thing and I'm struck by her perceptivity at instinctively understanding that about me. It makes me feel inadequate for lacking such insights into her own inner life. 'Well, you have to admit that being married gives you some security, don't you?' I point out.

Andrea shook her head. 'It gives you a contract like any other job contract. And just like in the rest of the world, there are no guaranteed jobs for life any more.'

'But you and Dan seem so happy all the time.'

Andrea poured two generous glasses of wine and laughed out loud, this time genuinely amused. 'How can you say that? We are at each other's throats all the time. We don't even bother pretending to get on in public.'

'Yes but that's just the way you are, surely? You've been together such a long time, it doesn't mean anything, does it?'

'Lorna, you and Rob have been together for ten years. You don't fight all the time, do you?'

We do at the moment. But I don't tell her this. I realise that there is a lot I don't tell her. I'm reevaluating our friendship and I'm uncomfortable with what I'm discovering. 'But how did Joe come into it? Even if you were really miserable, surely you could have found someone else, anyone else?'

Andrea swallowed a gulp of wine. 'You mustn't be mad when I tell you this?'

'Why should I?'

Andrea didn't look convinced. 'When I said it just happened, I meant it. But it wasn't complete chance. We bumped into each other outside a pub one day. If it had been any other day, we'd have just said hello and

174

walked on but something astonishing had happened. Karen had phoned me that morning.'

I almost passed out with this new information. 'When was this?' I asked, my voice strained.

Andrea looked sheepish. 'A couple of months ago. She just said that she was coming for a job interview in London and wanted to know if we could meet up. I was knocked for six! I hadn't heard from her in ten years!'

'What did you say?' I asked.

'Not much really, I had to pick up the girls so I waffled something about giving me a call and that was the end of it.'

'And then?' I asked, too, too calmly.

'Nothing. I didn't hear from her until you told me she was back. But when I bumped into Joe, I had to talk to him about it.'

I filled in the gaps. 'Because of course you couldn't talk to me about it?'

'Obviously I couldn't. I'm sorry but I was trying to protect you. There was no point in getting you all worked up about something that might turn out to be nothing.'

'You could have told me later, when Karen came back.'

'You'd have gone mad at me for not telling you sooner, whenever I told you.'

She was right. Cow. 'I suppose Phil knew all about it?'

'I tried to call her that day but she was at her health club all day. So when I bumped into Joe . . .'

I can't breathe. This is all too much. 'So one thing led to another and you and Joe thought that, if you were going to have a chat about Karen, you might as well have it in bed?' I summed up.

175

'There was more to it than that. We were both unhappy, fed up. I knew that Dan had been seeing someone for months and I just couldn't handle it.'

'Why didn't you tell me? I could have listened or helped or something,' I asked.

'Because I was embarrassed. Ashamed even. As if it must have been my fault in some way that our marriage wasn't working. I know it sounds crazy but that's how I felt. Now I understand how women can stay with men who beat them.' I must have looked shocked because she went on, 'No, I'm not saying that. Of course Dan didn't do anything like that. But when I first found out, it was like being punched. It hurt, a real physical pain.' I knew what that pain was like and I wished that aspirin worked on it.

'Joe was really down because of the business and money problems. I know Phil is my best friend but frankly, she'd been a right cow with Joe this past year.'

'Come off it, Angie. It's been just as hard on her. She's had to let the au pair go.' As soon as I said it, I could hear how feeble it sounded on the general scale of personal suffering.

'How will she manage?' Andrea observed sarcastically. 'I expect like the rest of us.'

'It's still no reason to cheat on her,' I said.

'He didn't plan to,' Andrea replied. 'It—'

'Just happened,' I interrupted wearily.

Neither of us spoke for a while. Andrea broke the silence. 'I was hoping that, even if you didn't understand, you wouldn't judge me. Friends shouldn't really judge each other, should they?'

'I'm sorry, but sometimes I think they have to. There are still absolutes. I wouldn't condemn you for having an affair, even if I disapproved. There are choices that

176

we each make as to how we live our lives and I will support you even when I don't approve of your choices. But sleeping with a best friend's husband? Sorry, Ange. That's wrong and I refuse to endorse it whatever the circumstances. It also undermines our friendship because I now see that your concept of loyalty to a friend is a whole lot weaker than mine. And if you could do this to your best friend . . .' I didn't bother finishing the sentence. It wasn't necessary.

Andrea nodded sadly. 'You're even more shocked than I'd anticipated. At least now you can understand why I didn't dare tell you.'

'Sorry.'

That's all I could say. I was sorry. I understood it all very clearly. I just didn't like it. Our friendships, mine, Andrea's and Phillippa's, they were all changed for good. There would forever be lies that must be maintained and truths that must stay buried. We would never be able to get drunk together in case our inhibitions were too loosened. The balance had shifted, loyalties subtly altered and we would never again feel totally at ease with each other. But the worst thing of all was that Phillippa had no idea what was happening around her. She was trying to cope with a marriage that was falling apart, a comfortable way of life that was being chipped away and she would soon notice her two closest friends distancing themselves from her for reasons she couldn't fathom. At least I hoped that she would never find out the reasons.

Still, at least she'd have Karen. Hooray for Karen, riding into the film on her white charger. Now I come to think about it, maybe I'll develop a friendship with Karen too. After all, we have so much in common.

I wanted to ask Andrea if she loved Joe, if he loved her. But I didn't. That stuff about us telling each other

177

everything was just gas. We never talked about love. In fact I've never talked about love to anyone. I tell Rob I love him and he says he loves me. But talking about it? No. It's just too risky, too revealing. I'll talk about sex with the cleaner but I won't ask Andrea if she loves another man. And I think she feels the same. And Phil. Maybe it's the mutual respect we each have for the others' repressions that binds us together. Still, I wish I knew if she and Joe were in love. I'd quite like to find a reliable touchstone for love because my own concept of it is becoming hazy and blurred. I miss the confidence I once had in my own emotions.

Andrea and I sat in an almost-companionable silence, drinking our wine, reappraising each other in the light of our revelations. Andrea smiled at me. 'So all that stuff about Phillippa suspecting Joe and Tara Brownlow, you were just saying that to wind me up?'

I smiled back, relieved that we seemed to be back on a less shaky footing, however artificial, even if the ground had shifted below our feet. Although I hated what she was doing, I wasn't going to walk out on her. We needed each other. 'Sorry, that was wicked of me. I was just annoyed with you for not telling me about Joe yourself. Still, it got you going!'

'But you didn't tell me what gave Phil the idea in the first place.'

I told her the whole saga of the phone number on the phone bill. I also confessed that I'd seen her and Joe that night in the pub. I didn't add that I'd been with Simon. There seemed little point in clouding the issue with superfluous information. Honestly, that's the only reason.

Andrea shook her head in amazement. 'You won't believe it, but it's the exact same phone number that put me on to Dan and Tara Brownlow. I'd seen Dan's mobile phone bill and the same phone number appeared continuously over the last few months. Every time I rang it, I got a recorded message with no clue as to whose number it was. But I learned the number by heart. When I saw it written down like that . . .'

Hence the three underlines. How satisfying to tie up the loose ends even on a messy parcel. I wondered what had gone on in the relatives' room at the hospital between Andrea, Dan and Miss Brownlow. I presumed that concern for Isabelle had overcome any more primitive urges and that civilised discussion was the order of the hour. I made a mental note to ask her when we were less tense.

Then something occurred to me. 'Hang on a second. If Dan is having an affair with Miss Brownlow, then where was he on the day of Isabelle's accident? He can't have been with her because she was at school. And apparently he was unobtainable like you.'

'He was following me,' Andrea said flatly. 'And he found me.'

'You're kidding! So he knows about you and Joe?'

'He certainly does. That's why I had to see Joe that night. Dan had stormed off somewhere and I had to warn Joe that Dan knew about us. I had no idea what he might do.'

'And what has he done?'

Andrea shrugged. 'Nothing yet. Dan's sleeping in the study at the moment and we're not talking. It's easy while Isabelle's still in hospital but she's coming home tomorrow and I don't know what Dan's planning.'

'Have you confronted him about Tara Brownlow?'

'Of course I have but, as he's not talking to me, we didn't get very far. It's hard arguing with someone who doesn't answer.' I stored that gem away for future reference.

It was my turn to take her hand. 'What a mess. I wish I could do something to help.'

Andrea tried her best not to cry. I pretended not to notice. 'Well, I'm glad you know now, at least. I've really needed someone to talk to during all this.'

And while I felt very awkward about my perceived collusion in something that I condemned, I let her talk. What else could I do?

In retrospect, I shouldn't have finished that third glass of wine. I'd only had a brownie in Starbucks and a handful of aspirin. When my mobile phone rang, my first thought was relief that Jude was still suspended. It couldn't be the school with more problems, at least.

'Hallo, is that Mrs Danson?'

I giggled completely inappropriately. 'Yes it is. Who's that?'

'It's Mr Walters at Keaton House.'

I sobered up instantly. 'Is anything wrong? Is it one of the girls?'

Mr Walters sighed. 'I wonder if you could come over here right away. It's Claire.'

Chapter Twelve

'Oh well, two down, two to go,' I announced cheerfully as I frogmarched Claire towards the bus stop to join Jude at home on a two-week suspension. 'That just leaves Phoebe to burn down the science lab and Ali to liberate the class rabbit and I'll have all four of my precious babies home with me once more.'

'There's no need to be sarcastic, Mum, it wasn't my fault.'

'Oh silly me! Of course it wasn't your fault. It must have been that body double of yours, half-undressed in the sports cupboard with Elliott Jackson.'

Claire was having trouble keeping up with my marching pace. Unfortunately, I couldn't slow down because I felt sick and needed to get home quickly. (Note to self: too many painkillers plus alcohol minus substantial food = nausea.) 'I *wasn't* half-undressed, I had a couple of buttons undone and that was just because it was so hot and there was no air.' Claire's adolescent pedantry was impressive.

'Cupboards do tend to be hot and airless, that's why most people tend not to shut themselves in them,' I pointed out.

Claire became more petulant. 'We didn't shut ourselves in. Somebody else did.'

I rounded on her. 'Who? Come on then, who? And

how did they entice two robust teenagers into the cupboard in the first place? With food titbits? And why didn't you simply open the door with the inside handle when you somehow found yourself forced inside this cupboard against your will? And why, when Miss Brownlow found you, were the two of you quote flushed and dishevelled unquote?'

I don't know why I bothered. It's not as if I don't remember being a teenager. I never minded being yelled at, in fact it rather appealed to my enjoyable feeling of being misunderstood and victimised. But I always hated it when my mum (it's always the mums who do it) threw a sequence of unanswerable questions at me. It always forced me into a corner from which the only escape was a very long period of sulking broken only by bedtime or mealtime, whichever came first.

And now I was doing it to Claire. I was flinging incontrovertible evidence of her crimes at her, crimes that we both knew she'd committed. But because she insisted on keeping up this charade of innocence, I was compelled to keep up my onslaught of logical argument until she either admitted defeat (never happened yet, unlikely ever to happen) or she retreated to sulksworld which would at least give us both a bit of peace. If only Claire had watched *The Bill* more often, she would realise that confessing your crime usually led to a softer sentence (and sometimes an invitation to a well-paid position as policeman's nark).

But she was too entrenched in her futile defence to backtrack. Fortunately, she chose to begin her sulk at this point. I say that it was fortunate because I had a strong feeling that I would be sick if I had to open my mouth once more. In fact I'm inspired right now to send another letter to my new best friend Nigel Blah-de-Blah-Nephew-To-a-Labour-Peer at the BBC with a new idea.

'Dear Nigel,' I would write, 'I have watched every single human interest story being flogged to death by your audiences of sad lonely people whose empty lives are only made complete by appearing on TV and being patronised by your presenter-of-the-moment. I have watched self-confessed adulterers, mistresses, bigamists, compulsive eaters, drug addicts, wife beaters, kleptomaniacs and every other kind of maniac spilling their hearts into your studio microphones. Yet there is one topic that is been sadly neglected throughout your history.

'I refer you to the commonly experienced but woefully neglected theme of physical sickness caused by taking too many painkillers in response to an increase in hangovers following extended drinking sessions made necessary by your partner, your partner's estranged wife and your friends insistent on upsetting the happy equilibrium of your life with their unacceptable behaviour.

'I grant it is not as catchy as "I SLEPT WITH MY STEP-FATHER'S BANK MANAGER!" or "I AM A BISEXUAL BURGLAR", but I believe it would strike a chord. Yours subserviently etc. etc.'

Maybe I'll suggest it to Karen. After all, she works in daytime television.

I felt fine until I arrived at Mr Walters' office. Mr Walters hadn't given me any details but I was reassured that, since police stations and hospitals were not mentioned, things couldn't be too bad. I was wrong. When I got there, it was like walking on to the set of a Miss Marple mystery. The suspects had been convened and the guilty party was about to be announced.

There was Tara Brownlow, beautiful and cold with her perfect, lifeless face and lithe, expensively clothed body. There was Joe, looking ten years older than when I'd seen him a week earlier. The circles under his eyes told the story of a man waiting for his executioner to bang on the cell door. For this man was in prison, for certain. And there was Phillippa, transmitting murderous glances alternately at Joe and Tara.

I didn't know what they were doing here. I knew that Tara Brownlow was Elliott's teacher (as well as Phoebe's and Isabelle's) but Claire only had her for English. I had a feeling that this meeting was going to fall under the heading of 'Other Things You'd Prefer Not to Have Happened Today of All Days'. I wished I could be alone, live alone, not have friends with interlocking lives and husbands, not have children interlocking even further until we all melded into a metallic, clangy tangle.

Please don't let this be Claire's fault, I thought.

It was Claire's fault. Or, to be more precise, it was her idea. While Elliott might have been an unwitting accomplice, he turned out to be less than unwilling. It seems that Claire had suggested a twenty-pound bet to a cartel in her class (remarkably not including any other of my daughters on this occasion) that she couldn't lure Elliott Jackson into the sports cupboard and get his trousers off him. The big joke here was that everyone knew that Elliott had an almighty crush on Claire but that he was too repressed to do anything about it.

Yes, it was cruel, teenagers are cruel, why are you so surprised? Then Claire proved to be more resourceful and perceptive than I had ever given her credit for. Rather than sidle up, Lolita-like, to the unsuspecting Elliott and tantalise him with looks and promises into the said cupboard, she took him to one side, apprised him of the bet and offered to split the money with him if he played along. I grudgingly admitted to myself that this was a very lateral solution to the challenge and one that acknowledged the particular sensitivity of the chosen stooge.

But of course the sweaty confines of the cupboard with all its heady overtones of physical exertion cast its spell on the hapless pair. And once Elliott's trousers were off, the bet was forgotten and the pair got down to some serious communication. Miss Brownlow was alerted to the covert operation by the crowd huddling outside the sports cupboard, giggling and squealing. Luckily, she opened the door before any further clothes were removed, preventing any lasting damage to the teenagers' education while guaranteeing their place in school mythology.

Maybe it was because I was drained of reaction by the day's other dramas, but the whole incident didn't strike me as being that big a deal. Obviously I played the game, tutting, looking disappointedly at my errant daughter, stating my intention to deal with the matter seriously but I wasn't overly concerned. Claire was a little young to be getting involved in any kind of physical relationship but I didn't think this was a typical act. Knowing Claire as I do, I think she was probably motivated purely by the money on offer. She'd sell her soul for a Nike vest.

I could have done without more trouble at the school especially since, yet again, I was having to deal with it without Rob but I didn't see this as a sign that Claire was beginning a moral decline. And if this had happened a month earlier, I think Phillippa would have felt the same. But everything was different now.

Everything was coloured by the consequences of her husband's infidelity.

I let Mr Walters deliver another of his sermons on parenting and the need to instil moral values. I reiterated my promise to come and see him with Rob to discuss wider issues. I gratefully accepted the two-week suspension passed on to Claire even though I thought it was a bit harsh. And at that point I would have got up and left. But Phillippa had been filling up with anger like a hot-air balloon. I knew instantly that I should have allowed Phillippa to get all her anguish and frustration out of her system earlier, in a more neutral environment. But it was difficult in Starbucks.

I've never yet been in a Starbucks where there isn't at least one table of breastfeeding mothers and lunchtime in Clapham was no exception. If you're in the mood to scream and rant about your husband's sexual proclivities, it is probably best to avoid any establishment that includes provision of crayons in its mission statement. And ever mindful of social conventions, Phillippa swallowed her emotions with her bitter espresso.

She must have gone home and paced the floor, fuelling the flames of her misery with endless rehearsals of all the devastating things she would say to Joe when she saw him. And then, when she finally did get to see him, who should be there as well but his concubine! Knowing the dreadful but exact synchronicity that was infecting this sequence of events, I hazarded a guess that when Phil arrived, Joe and Tara were already there.

Only her breeding (and perhaps a feeling of responsibility towards her nails) would have prevented her from attacking them, then and there, and punching them to the ground. Instead, while the headmaster was droning on about Elliott's misadventure, her fury must have been simmering away deep inside until it rose and finally erupted like acid bile.

'Can I ask something?' she asked sweetly.

Please don't, Phil. I swiftly intervened. 'Let's all go home and calm down, Phillippa. It's been a bit of a shock and I think we all need some time to think things through.' I pleaded with her silently not to take this any further.

I was wasting my time. 'Don't worry, Lorna. I won't cause a scene, if that's what you're worried about. No, I just want to clarify an issue of school policy with Mr Walters.'

'Of course you can, Mrs Jackson,' Mr Walters said, blissfully unaware of the rocket he was lighting. 'Ask anything you wish. I've always had an open-door policy at Keaton House.' It serves him right that he's about to have his day ruined. Anyone who uses the phrase 'open-door policy' deserves all he gets, in my book.

Phillippa was wearing the broadest smile ever seen on a miserable face. Only I (and possibly Joe) could tell what was going on under it. 'Thank you. You recently wrote to us concerning our overdue fees for both Elliott and Rupert.'

Mr Walters looked confused. Joe looked uncomfortable. Tara looked bored. I looked at the floor.

'It's just that I noticed that children of staff members were entitled to a fifty per cent discount on fees. Is that right?'

'Ye-es,' Mr Walters replied, very cautiously.

Phillippa's smile didn't budge. 'Only I was just wondering if this also applied to the children of parents who just happened to be *sleeping* with staff members.'

187

This is the first time I have ever seen Miss Brownlow's face show anything apart from a supercilious disregard for everyone with conspicuously lower spending power. She looks sick. Now you know how I feel, lady. Joe looks baffled. Hang on in there, Joe, you'll catch on soon enough. It's confusing, I'll admit, but you'll work it out.

Phillippa was at full flow. 'You can see my point. In today's world of extended families, broken homes, open marriages, distinctions have become blurred. It seems that just sleeping with someone for more than a couple of weeks confers a certain respectability on a couple. Marriage or any exchange of solemn vows no longer seems a prerequisite for commitment.' Ouch, Phil. I know you're too wrapped up in your own obsessions to think carefully about what you're saying, but this is getting rather close to home.

'What exactly do you mean, Mrs Jackson?'

You shouldn't have asked that, Mr Walters. There are some things that are better left unclarified. I know.

'What do I mean? I don't think I'm the one who needs to answer that. Take a look at your teacher's face and tell me what you think it means.'

We all looked at Miss Brownlow whose face had turned a very unattractive shade of crimson. I should introduce her to Karen. Karen could tell her the brand of under-foundation concealer that she uses to tone down her skin redness. Women should help other women.

'Why are you all looking at me like that?' she said defensively.

Phillippa answered without dropping her smile, which was becoming ever more maniacal. 'We're all interested in your thoughts on this matter, Miss Brownlow. How do you feel about the children of parents with whom you're sleeping? I use the plural because, if you've done it once, you've obviously got no qualms about the principle involved and may well have worked your way through quite a few husbands during your time here.'

Tara Brownlow was struggling to find something, anything, appropriate to say. Phillippa helped her out. 'Are you saying that you are not having an affair with the father of one of your pupils?'

Tara's flustered lack of response led Mr Walters to step in. 'That's enough. Some serious allegations are being made here and I would like this to be handled professionally and sensitively.'

'What about you Joe? Would you like to add something?' Phillippa had turned her smile on to him. Joe had no idea what he was expected to say. He knew what Phillippa was talking about. Or at least he thought he did. I knew that Andrea had told him about Dan and Tara Brownlow so he probably thought that Phillippa was making an ill-timed stand in defence of a friend. On the other hand, he wasn't sure what it had to do with him or with school fees or Elliott or anything else, for that matter.

He cleared his throat. 'I think Mr Walters is right. I think we should leave this to the professionals to sort out.' He sat back, satisfied at his non-committal assessment of things as they stood. Like most men, he hated getting involved in emotional situations that didn't directly involve him. And he still thought that this didn't involve him. I longed for a director to burst on to the scene and shout 'Freeze!' to all the other protagonists, so that I could fill Joe in on the recent plot developments before he unknowingly killed off his own character.

Phillippa looked at him curiously. 'Do you, Joe? Do you really think we should leave this to professionals?'

Her tone finally got through to Joe that he was missing something very significant here. He didn't know what it was and needed another cue.

Phil duly fed it to him. 'We've been called here to discuss the aberrant behaviour of our son, your son. We've never had anything like this happen before. You heard what Mr Walters said to Lorna.' *Please don't bring me into this. I want to go home.* 'He said that, in his experience, when a pupil starts displaying anti-social behaviour which is completely out of character, he looks to upheavals in the family for some possible explanation. So why don't we think about any possible upheavals in our family. Frequent, unexplained absences by one parent, for example, followed by lies and excuses.'

Now Joe had caught on. He hadn't yet made the connection with Tara Brownlow but he was aware that his infidelity was in the open and being made very public. He jumped to his feet. 'Let's go home, Phil. We'll discuss it there.'

Phillippa refused to budge. 'I want to discuss it here. Now. I want you to admit in front of everyone that all this is your fault because you're having an affair. Or are you going to try and deny it?'

He didn't say anything.

'You see!' Phillippa exclaimed with a rather pointless gesture of triumph. 'He's admitted it!'

Joe's eyes pleaded with me. I put my arm around Phil's rigid shoulders. I noticed her body shaking and felt for her. 'Come on Phil. Just go home now. Go and sort it out. Don't make a scene here. It's not fair on Elliott.'

It was this reference to her son that finally broke her resistance. She'd completely forgotten that he was waiting outside for her along with Claire. She immediately lowered her voice. 'Sorry. Yes. Right. Of course. Elliott.'

She allowed me to help her into her coat like an invalid and she took a few deep breaths to return her face to its normal mask for her son's sake. She even held out her hand to Mr Walters as if they'd just enjoyed a pleasant tea party together. He took it warily, saying nothing, terrified of sparking off another irrational outburst from this deranged mother. Joe also shook his hand and then went to shake Miss Brownlow's hand as well. While Phillippa was looking the other way, I slapped his hand down and glared at him warningly. He took the hint and although he didn't understand why, he stopped himself from approaching Tara. He'd find out soon enough, I thought. I just hoped he'd have the good sense not to tell Phillippa who he was *really* having an affair with when he eventually persuaded her it was not Elliott's teacher.

I detected a note of warmth in Mr Walters' handshake when he said goodbye to me. I think he appreciated that I had rescued him from a potentially explosive encounter. Whether he had made any assumptions about the complicated relationships being alluded to in Phillippa's oblique comments, I don't know. And whether this cancels out my poor showing as a mother in other respects, I also don't know but I'm optimistic. But I do know with absolute certainty that he will be abandoning his open-door policy as of this afternoon.

Claire and Elliott were both subdued when we picked them up outside the head's office. They must have heard some of what went on. Knowing kids, they were probably listening at the keyhole. Elliott appeared closed in on himself. He was a shy, introspective boy at the best of times. The business with Claire would have mortified him and then, to hear your mother and father talking about, shouting about ... No, I didn't want to think about it. I must stop adding everyone else's pain to my own. I haven't got enough room. Or time.

I gave him what I hoped was a comforting pat on the back. 'Don't worry, Elli, everything will be fine. Honestly.' He stared right into my eyes, searching for some kind of proof that I knew it would be so. He was still young enough to hope that grown-ups had access to solutions from which children were restricted. He wanted to believe me and I felt a fraud.

I grabbed Claire a little more roughly than I'd intended and guided her out of the door. 'Where's the car?' she asked.

'I came in a taxi,' I replied, annoyed by her lack of concern at the trouble she'd caused.

'Are we getting a taxi home then?'

I started to walk more quickly, spurred on my irritation. 'No we're not getting a taxi home. It cost me eight pounds fifty to get here. We can get a bus home.'

She moaned that horrible teenage moan that signifies a hideous injustice had been wreaked on her by an unfeeling universe. 'But it's miles to the bus stop and miles at the other end.'

'Then we'll both be very fit when we get home, won't we?'

I'm not sure how I did it but I succeeded in conveying that I had been pushed to the limit and she stopped protesting forthwith. By the time we got to the bus stop, we were both out of breath. Endorphins had kicked in (unless it was one of the ingredients in my cocktail of proprietary painkillers) and I felt reasonably positive that I had handled things as best as I was able. I decided not to punish Claire any further.

'What did you hear when you were outside Mr Walters' office?'

'Nothing,' Claire replied too fast.

'Come on. I know you were listening at the door. I'm just concerned about Elliott. Did he hear everything his mother said?'

Claire nodded miserably. 'It was awful, Mum. I thought he was going to cry. I mean, when she was going on about Miss Brownlow, we were laughing. We thought she was just having a go because Miss Brownlow's a bit of a slapper.'

'Claire!' I think I managed to sound indignant even though I agreed with the sentiments entirely. As a mother, it was my duty to perpetuate the conviction that all teachers, even slappers, should be treated with respect by pupils. I, however, am not her pupil, and I can call her anything I choose, even slapper. I love being a grown-up.

'Sorry,' Claire muttered, not meaning it for a second. Good for her. 'But when when she started on Elliott's dad, it was horrible. Is it true? About him having an affair?'

'I don't know, Claire. It's nothing to do with us. We have to let Elliott's mum and dad sort it out between them. You just have to be a good friend to Elliott. He'll need his friends, whatever happens.'

Claire's eyes widened. 'You don't mean that they might get a divorce?'

I exhaled loudly. 'I don't know, Claire, I really don't know. Let's just drop it. And you mustn't talk to anyone else about this. I'm sure Elliott is embarrassed enough about this as it is.'

But Claire didn't hear me. She was brooding on her last thought. 'That would be the worst thing, if they got divorced. Everyone says that. It's worse even than if your mum or dad dies.'

I shuddered at the direction this conversation was taking. 'You mustn't worry about it, sweetheart. I'm sure everything will be fine in the end.' I must stop saying this. It sounds less plausible with every outing.

'You and Dad won't get divorced, will you?' Claire asked anxiously.

'We're not even married, how can we get divorced?' I answered gently.

'You know what I mean.'

I planned my words carefully. 'Claire, are you worried about something?'

She looked down at her feet, around at the walls we passed, anywhere except in my eyes. 'You and Dad have been fighting a lot. We hear you.'

I injected a cheerful note into my voice. 'All parents fight. It's normal. Ask your friends at school, they'll all say the same thing.'

'But it's different now. It's because of our other mum, isn't it?'

'It's made things a bit difficult, I won't pretend it hasn't. But it hasn't changed the love I feel for you and your sisters.'

'But has it changed how you feel about Dad?'

Of course it has. 'Of course it hasn't! Your dad and I are just adjusting to having your mother back in our lives. And when he gets back from New York, we'll all sit down together and sort out how things are going to work so there are no more rows. Would you like that?'

'What, you mean with you and our other mum?'

That wasn't what I meant. 'If that's what you want. If that'll help, then yes.' Wow, haven't I become Miss Maturity? 'I can't promise that there won't be a few grumbles along the way, but it will be better, that I can promise.' I meant that. I've seen both of my best friends take the first steps towards the destruction of their marriage. Those poor children. That isn't going to happen to my children. Whatever happens, I'm keeping this family together.

That evening, we all had Pot Noodles and tinned ravioli followed by Angel Delight topped with crushed Crunchie bars. We ate off our laps in front of the television and drank Coke out of a big bottle which we passed around, all suppressing belches with diminishing levels of success. When Rob phoned, he was astonished to hear shrieks of laughter in the background and a chorus of 'Hi Dad!' accompanied by burps in four-part harmony. 'I can hear you're all pining away without me,' he observed dryly.

'We're lost without you but we're struggling through,' I replied.

'I'm glad you're all enjoying yourselves. I really am. It's good to hear people laughing in that house again.'

'Well the girls and I have had a long chat and we've decided that there are to be no more rows and everyone has to tell at least one terrible joke before they're allowed to leave the house each morning.'

'That sounds fine by me.' I could hear all the tension evaporate from his voice.

'So how is it all going?' I asked.

'Oh you know, the same old crowd, same old speakers. But I'm making some good new contacts.'

And then that silence came back. And I remembered Karen. But I didn't ask. And I didn't ask loaded questions that would force him to lie or prevaricate or evade. Because I could hear my daughters laughing in the living room and that was too important to jeopardise for the sake of another argument that nobody could win. When he came back, he'd tell me all about it. And I would be prepared. I'd be calm and understanding and he would know that everything was going to be all right. We'd both know.

'I love you,' I said to him awkwardly.

'Love you too,' Rob replied softly.

We'd never said this easily and I liked that. I meant that the word had significance to us both and would only be brought out on significant occasions. We hadn't said it for a while and it was like an infusion of strength that would see me through the coming days. I would try and remember how important it was to reaffirm my feelings like this whenever I felt unsure of Rob in the future. When I put the phone down, I felt better, happier than I'd done since Karen turned up.

A huge scream brought me running back into the living room. The girls were all on the floor, doubled up with laughter and holding their noses. It didn't take me long to work out what had happened. The dogs had been in the corner guzzling the remainder of the Coke and polishing off the rest of the Crunchie multipack. Their subsequent contribution to the family windbreaking outbreak sent us all rushing into the kitchen to escape the smell. It was a crazy, wonderful, stupid little incident but it patched us back together. The damage had been done, the scars were still there but running repairs would keep us going. We were going to survive.

Chapter Thirteen

We survived for four more days. It was like living out an Enid Blyton novel. Jude and Claire were at home and we'd turned their suspension into an unofficial holiday with biscuit binges and computer game marathons. We tried to hide this from the other two girls who might have felt tempted to join their sisters in this glorious fun-filled purdah by whatever dastardly deeds necessary. I insisted that, as soon as Phoebe and Ali got home from school, they must find Jude and Claire sitting in their bedrooms studying. Nobody was fooled by the pretence but it all added to the prevailing atmosphere of end-of-term tomfoolery.

Claire had devoted the first two days to sorting out Rob's Wolf Sanctuary trip. It had turned out to be more complex that we first thought. There were no direct flights and the Sanctuary was only open to visitors at certain times of the year. I'd managed to cajole Rob's receptionist into relinquishing his diary in his absence. Claire and I found a ten-day slot in November and provisionally booked this through the website.

Claire contacted the airlines and worked out an itinerary that would get Rob there and back on the required dates. It was a labour of love and I was very proud of her for organising everything by herself. I knew that Rob would be touched by her efforts. That would mean more to him than the money involved which was actually proving quite fun to earn.

Once the girls were in bed, I was staying up until very late, working on Simon's website project. It was stretching my capabilities but I found it enormously satisfying. I had become adept at sorting through the morass of useful and useless information available over the Internet, filtering the most recent academic developments, interpreting and restating the data in an accessible format.

I was meeting Simon for lunch most days. It seemed easier than making twenty phone calls a day trying to track him down with all my technical queries. Since I'd settled things with Rob over the phone, I felt more comfortable about spending time with Simon. My resolve was stronger, my life was moving on along level tracks once more. I was unshakeable. His feelings for me, while always perfuming the atmosphere between us, were no longer disturbing me.

And do you know what? Having an attractive man so clearly besotted with you, when you are secure and committed in a good relationship, is nice. More than nice. Reassuring. Like having a world-class player as first reserve on your world-class team.

Besides, I've needed a friend these past days. He found this amusing.

'Glad to be of use. In whatever capacity you need me.' He put down the glasses on the table. We'd found a pub halfway between our homes that was quiet, served great steak and kidney pie and had exclusive selling rights to a fabulous cider from a family-run orchard in Devon.

I was appalled. 'You don't really think I'm using you, do you?'

He laughed. 'You take everything so seriously. Don't.

I'm happy to be your friend. But I think you're wrong to cut Andrea and Phillippa off like this.'

I bristled at the implied criticism. 'I'm not cutting them off. I'm just giving them some space. I don't think I'd be much help to either of them with what they're going through.'

Simon appraised me with amusement. 'That's not why you're not calling them and we both know it. You just don't want to know what's going on in case it's bad.'

I wasn't amused. 'We have lunch a few times and suddenly you know me better than I know myself. What a cliché.' I didn't like this intrusion into my motives, I had enough difficulty explaining them to myself.

On the day after Black Wednesday, as it became in my mind, I woke up to a stark reality. I only had two friends in the world and I couldn't call either of them.

There are people who have friends and people who have acquaintances. The distinction can usually be spotted in terms of number. You can't have a hundred friends. I don't believe you can even have twenty. There simply isn't enough time in a life to give and take enough of twenty people's existences to constitute twenty true friendships. You can meet them all a few times a year, catch up on the essential comings and goings, fill in the big gaps, but you can't prop each other up or just link arms and saunter through the day-to-day minutiae that truly define you.

I'd always had acquaintances until I met Rob. I knew dozens of good types, mates for every situation. I had drinking friends, dancing friends, friends to go to the cinema with (subdivided into foreign, arty films and mindless blockbusters), friends to eat pizza with, friends to go on holiday with, friends to get depressed with. Of course I wasn't that calculating about it but that's how it panned out.

It was a while after I moved in with Rob before I truly knew that he was the man for me. And then I did what countless other women have done before me and will continue to do to universal condemnation: I stopped seeing my old friends. Not straight away of course. Nobody does that. But my life became wrapped up in Rob and the girls. I became discerning about how I wanted to spend my time. If there was a film I wanted to see, I wanted to see it with Rob. I wanted to eat with him, drink with him, get to know him. And then there were the girls. They didn't know what was happening to them. Their mummy had gone away and now a new lady was always in the house. It wouldn't have been fair to flit in and out of their world. They needed security and stability and I had my part to play in that.

So I initially just kept in touch with the friends I felt closest to. But I could see their eyes glaze over when I regaled them with interminable stories about one child or another. And when it became evident that I was settling down, it was as if I was emigrating. I could feel myself drifting away from old ties as I entered the new country of family life. The occasional drink became the occasional Christmas card and eventually fizzled away to nothing.

As I immersed myself in instant motherhood, I found myself reaching out for help to Andrea and Phillippa. I needed them, needed their practical advice, their knowledge and experience. I spent hours with them, on the phone to them, at the park with them, shopping with them, in their houses, in my house. And out of this grew my first real friendships. For as my practical dependence lessened, I began to accept them as gloriously unexpected fixtures and fittings in my new life.

I loved getting to know them, establishing histories, laying the foundations of shared memories and private jokes, telling them (almost) everything and learning (almost) everything about them. I became scathing of those who settled for superficial acquaintances and missed out on the experience of deep, involving, encompassing friendship.

But now I feel a bit silly. A bit precious. A bit pretentious. A bit up myself. Because when you only have two friends apart from your partner, the time will inevitably come when you have to face your foolishness for not setting up contingency plans.

Rob is away. Phillippa is sorting out her marriage and I dare not call her in case I say the wrong thing. I know too much to be an outside observer in that home. And I don't know what Andrea is doing. She hasn't called me since Wednesday. Perhaps she's waiting for me to call her. Perhaps my refusal to endorse her affair with Joe has tarnished things between us. Whatever. I don't know what to say to her so I don't say anything. If she needs me, she will phone.

Everything is blurry. I can't quite remember how I left matters with Andrea. I thought we were OK but I left in a hurry when I got the call from the school about Claire. I have this unpleasant suspicion that I might have tossed out some twee little homily about marriage and friendship before I left. That would have annoyed the hell out of her and would explain why she hadn't called me.

And although I still feel strongly that her affair with Joe is about as low an act as it's possible to imagine, I'm feeling a bit queasy about my self-righteousness as I sit here with Simon, wearing my favourite purple jumper that everyone says suits my colouring. And wearing make-up.

It's funny really. The aftershocks from the tumultuous events in my friends' marriages are shaking the foundations of my own life and forcing me to question all my values and goals. I'm changing too. I'm desperate to share my thoughts with someone, talk them over and try to find a thread of reason that will hold all the madness together. But there's no one to talk to. Because those very relationships which have, up till now, offered me refuge are the areas where the conflict is greatest and my presence is prohibited.

There was no one but Simon. Truly, that's the only reason I turned to him. I suppose there are some other mums at the school that I'm quite chatty with but none that I'm close to. And I could hardly talk to them about Andrea and Phillippa's marriages, could I? Not when they know them as well. And I suppose there's my mum. But we're not that kind of mother and daughter. My mum stores every piece of information that I give her, however casually I may mention it. Anything that so much as hints at dissatisfaction in my life will take root in her and grow epically until she can't sleep for worrying about my future happiness.

Mum knows Phillippa and Andrea and likes them both, although she finds Phil a bit uppity for her liking. If she knew any of the crises they were currently going through, she would never again be able to sit in a kitchen with them without passing a hopelessly indiscreet comment on their lives. She would feel obliged to lecture Andrea on the sanctity of marriage (with me in earshot, of course, because my lack of marriage was an ongoing sore point for her) and insist on making a lot of tea for Phillippa.

It would be uncomfortable. And if everything sorted itself out, as I prayed it would, then our status quo would have been disrupted for nothing.

But this still left me with the problem of who I could turn to. Simon is the first male friend I've ever had, proper friend, that is. I suppose Rob is my friend but in a different way. For example, I can't talk to Rob about any problems I am having with the most important relationship in my life, i.e. my relationship with Rob. I know that some couples talk about everything but I don't know if that's healthy. I'm always aware that anything said can never be unsaid and therefore I think it's better to say some things outside the marriage where they won't do any lasting damage.

I've never understood why women value male friends so highly until now. Simon is completely different to Andrea. OK, OK, don't laugh, I know that's obvious. But he brings a completely different viewpoint to all my experiences. He doesn't automatically empathise and follow my train of thought through the same processes. He takes me round unexplored corners, asks difficult questions, plays devil's advocate without worrying about upsetting or annoying me.

But there is one important difference between Simon and any other male friend. He appears to love me. There. I've said it. And so has he. Only once, over lunch on Thursday. And it wasn't the most romantic of declarations.

'I've just got to get one thing out of the way before we start,' he said, as he slooshed brown sauce on to his chips. 'I'll only say this once and then you can forget all about it, but I have to say it. I love you. There. I've said it. I know you don't feel the same. At the moment anyway. So you don't have to say anything just to sound kind. But it's how I feel. So when or if you do start feeling something similar, there will be no misunderstandings. You will know that I feel the same and you can just come right out and tell me without fear of being rebuffed. So that's that done.' Then he ate a chip. 'Now tell me about your mad friends.'

It wasn't exactly Shelley but it was the most moving

thing anyone had ever said to me. We didn't discuss it further. He was right, we didn't need to. Strangely I didn't feel embarrassed or confused or cornered. I felt different, as indeed I should. Love *should* make you feel different even if it's one-sided. Which it is. I'm almost sure of it.

Simon's sense of fair play is breathtaking. He is always quick to defend Rob's position since he acknowledges that he and Rob are both coming from the same direction – that of loving me. He never runs Rob down or puffs himself up. He just listens, observes, gives advice, makes me laugh and changes the subject at exactly the right moment.

Within four days, he has successfully filled in all the gaps left by Rob, Andrea and Phillippa. I'm a little alarmed with how easily that happened. It suggests that I'm more shallow than I thought. Or maybe there was already a space going vacant that only he could fill, a space that I'd been clearing for him. No, that would be too premeditated, I won't accept that. But as soon as I start thinking along these lines, Simon seems to spot my digression and my discomfort with it and redirects me back to the neutral territory of our project.

'I'm really pleased with how it's going,' he said today. 'You're way ahead of schedule.'

'I've got a lot of time on my hands at the moment. Once Rob's home, he'll start monopolising the computer again and I'll drop behind.'

'When's he due back?' Simon asked politely, knowing full well that it was today.

I looked at my watch. 'He's due to land at about five o'clock.'

'Are you going to meet him at Gatwick?'

I shook my head. 'No. It's too complicated with Phoebe and Ali's school run and keeping an eye on Claire and

Jude, making sure they're up to date with their work, that sort of thing.'

'I don't know how you keep up with everything,' Simon said admiringly.

'Neither do I. The secret is never to think about what you have to do or the sheer enormity of it all will paralyse you. You just have to get on and do everything as it come up. Sometimes it all goes wrong and I simply muddle my way through.'

'Do you always pick up your kids from school?'

I laughed. 'You mean, am I one of those neurotic mothers who won't let her children out alone, who sees child molesters and drug dealers everywhere?'

Simon held up his hands in self-defence. 'I was just interested, that's all. I know that kids at my secondary school who were picked up by their parents got quite a lot of stick for it.'

'That's OK. You're right. But things are different now. It's nothing to do with protection and everything to do with chauffeuring. When school ends, the whirl of extracurricular activity begins. It's a neverending journey from music lesson to dance class to sports practice to sleepover. All the parents share the ferrying duties so it's not every day but, right now, it seems to be down to me most of the time. I expect, when you were a kid, you came straight home from school and went straight out to play football.'

Simon raised his eyebrows. 'Sat straight down at the computer actually. I wasn't the most physical of kids.'

I looked him up and down shamelessly. 'You surprise me.' I surprised myself with that comment. I think I was flirting.

Simon was amused. 'Why, Lorna, if I didn't know you better, I'd say you were flirting.'

'Don't be ridiculous.' It felt good saying that to somebody else after being on the receiving end of the comment so often myself.

Simon inclined his head to look at me from a different angle. 'If you say so. But this hunk of prime masculinity that you are appraising so slyly was not always so hunky.'

'Now you're making fun of me.'

He touched my hand lightly and briefly. He didn't do this often. I was glad because his touch opened too many doors inside me. 'Sorry. You're easy to tease. I'll spare your blushes by getting back to me. I was an early nerd when the word didn't exist. Computer boffs were not so common a breed at that point so we tended to keep ourselves to ourselves. I didn't care, I was only interested in computers, not people.'

'You're lucky,' I said. 'You saved yourself a lot of heartache by keeping people out of the equation.'

'Oh I don't know. Eventually they find their way in however high you build your particular barricade. The earlier you learn how to deal with other people, how to live with wanting what you can't have, the sooner you will develop mechanisms to defend yourself against heartache. Whether you go looking for it or not, the heartache will come and find you. And it's no less painful if it happens for the first time when you're sixteen, twenty-six or fifty-six.'

And then I did it. I touched his hand. OK, I know that this is not up there with William Hurt hurling Jessica Lange across the kitchen table and ravishing her in *The Postman Always Rings Twice*, but it was a step in another direction for me. A forward direction. I don't take many forward steps, being a great one for treading water, resisting tides, maintaining my current position against all onslaught. So when I do move, it involves enormous

206

momentum. And emotional momentum is hard to predict and control. I don't know where I'm going with this but I'm already nervous. I wonder if the pub staff would mind me popping into their kitchen to make tea?

Infidelity's a funny old thing. There are people who have strings of affairs or countless one-night flings but insist that they were never actually unfaithful to their partners because it was only physical. That only what is going on in your head matters. I never understood that distinction until now. Because even though I have just stroked Simon's hand, something much more involving is going on inside me. I am not a touchy-feely, huggy sort of woman, I can't spontaneously emote. So for me to reach out to Simon in a way that I have only previously done to Rob is as total a betrayal in my eyes as a quick, sordid coupling in a Travelodge would be to someone else.

Do you know this, Simon? I wonder.

Simon saw how stressed I was becoming and rescued me. He deftly moved up back into safe waters. 'What you were saying about your kids, I just wanted to say that you're a good mother, the best, in my opinion.'

This was the right thing to say. I needed to be told this more often.

I held on to his words when I got home and found an envelope addressed to me on the kitchen table. It was Phoebe's handwriting. She must have come home from school at lunchtime just to deliver it. I went very cold. In our household, notes consist of torn pieces of envelope attached to the fridge door with a Wallace and Gromit magnet saying something like 'Dairylea Dunkers, yogurt and that orange juice with bits in' or 'Gone to B's' when we don't know anyone whose name begins with B.

But this was a proper letter in an envelope. We never leave these for each other. They belong in Mike Leigh films with suicide notes or abusive confessions inside. I didn't want to know what was in this one but I ripped it open as fast as I could. Please, no more problems. I've got more than I handle already. The small sheet of paper fell to the floor and I couldn't catch hold of it immediately. As it flit-floated down, I could see there were only a couple of words on it and neither of them appeared to say 'die' or 'goodbye'. I calmed down slightly and managed to pick it up. I was puzzled by what Phoebe had written. And then I thought back to our conversation this morning.

'You seem quiet, this morning Phoebe, is everything all right?'

She smiled a strange smile at me. It wasn't sad but it was reflective. She had something on her mind and I was worried that it might be serious. Remembering what Mr Walters had said about all the girls manifesting behavioural changes in recent weeks, I was on the lookout for any warning signs in Phoebe and Ali.

So far, Ali had displayed nothing more sinister than a growing obsession with animal rights. She was going to become a vegan, she insisted, as soon as she could find out how strict their rules were. I took this to mean that she was going to find out if Jammie Dodgers and Cheesy Wotsits were acceptable before making the final commitment. So far, her protest had extended to refusing anything that didn't have Linda McCartney's name on it and tutting loudly when we walked past Dewhursts, the Master Butchers. I think what swung it for her was when she heard a prominent animal liberationist announcing that he never washed because no soap products were completely free of links with animal cruelty. I'm just waiting for her to start dropping hints about me buying her some military fatigues and a beret.

Phoebe, on the other hand, is quieter than ever. She has been keeping up the high standards we'd come to expect in her school work, working as hard as ever but, in an odd way, she seems to be more relaxed. She is holding her head a little higher, pulling her hair back from her face with a little more confidence, smiling more often. This gentle but happy metamorphosis has caused me to wonder if she might be taking drugs. But I soon realised how stupid an idea that was. Drugs would have completely the opposite effect on such a sensitive girl.

But something is having a positive effect on her and I can only come to one ghastly conclusion. Karen. Karen must have used her expertise as a psychologist to bring about this change in Phoebe and it makes me furious. I have spent years coaxing Phoebe to the point where she could face the world without crumbling under the pressure. I've never expected to turn her into Bonnie Langford but I was happy that she was making friends, coping with schoolwork and getting through adolescence without too many tears. That was all I hoped for at this stage.

But Karen steps in and my favourite daughter (there, I've said it again) starts projecting a new serenity. While the rest of us are gibbering about, not knowing how to react to the New Order imposed by Karen's arrival, Phoebe has blossomed. That's simply not on.

Anyway, that was how I was thinking this morning. Then Phoebe looked at me with concern in her eyes. 'I'm all right, Mum. But are you?'

The girls have all been asking me this quite a lot recently, reflecting their worries about the stability of Rob's and my relationship. I was doing a lot of reassuring and thought I was finally seeing a relaxation of tension in them all. But Phoebe seemed to need more persuading.

'Phoebe, I'm fine, sweetie. Your dad will be home this afternoon and you'll see that everything's been sorted out. We're all going to be fine. Don't worry.'

Phoebe wrinkled her brow as if she was facing a silly child babbling in baby-talk. 'That wasn't what I meant. I wanted to know if *you* were all right. You.'

I wasn't sure what she was getting at. 'I'm fine. Honestly, I am.' I couldn't mask my impatience. I didn't mean to snap, I just had so many things churning up inside.

Phoebe looked at me sadly. 'But I don't think you are.'

I wanted to ask her what she meant but there was no time. Our morning routine was disrupted by Claire and Jude's suspension. We had all got up late and we had to rush if we were going to make it to school on time. I didn't need any more calls to Mr Walters' office. I was languishing in the pleasure of knowing that only fifty per cent of my children were currently suspended, not bad statistics if you compare them with your average inner-city family and retain your sense of humour. But I was anxious that, when Rob returned, I could at least claim to have kept Phoebe and Ali out of trouble. It's a challenge but there you go.

So I didn't get a chance to talk further with Phoebe about what was on her mind. But now I've seen her note, I know exactly what it is. It's not even a note as such. It's a reference. A Bible reference. It just says: 'Dear Mum, 1 Peter 5 : 7, love Phoebe.'

Terrific. She's got religion. All that worry about drugs and she's actually got religion. I suppose religion is better than drugs but I'm not absolutely sure. I mean, if your child has a drugs problem, there are leaflets you can get. Do they have leaflets for parents of children who leave Bible references on kitchen tables? If not, they should.

She certainly seems happy so that's a good thing. But I don't feel comfortable about it. I've never been one for religion and, as far as I know, neither has Rob. I've just thought of something astonishing. I have no idea whether Rob even believes in God. I mean, I know what he thinks about politics, money, sex, education. But I don't think we've ever mentioned the word 'God'. After ten years, you'd think we'd have spent some time finding out how we each see the Big Picture. In fact, I don't know what any of my family or friends believe. I can ask a complete stranger at a dinner party how much he earns but I'd never dream of inquiring if he believes in heaven. It would be like throwing up on the carpet. Just not on. I'll have to ask Rob when he gets back. Or maybe I won't. Not while we're still slightly on edge.

But I'll certainly want to know what Rob thinks of Phoebe's new dalliance with the church. And no doubt Karen will have an opinion too. Or does Karen know already? If there's some way I can blame Karen for this, I will be pleased to do so.

And I wonder what the relevance of this particular Bible reference is. I try to think if there's a Bible in the house. There must be, mustn't there? Isn't there a copy in every house? I had an old school one but I left that at home when I moved out. The girls must have Bibles from school. I decide to go and root one out to look up the quote. Just for curiosity's sake. But I don't get the chance. The phone rings.

'It's me, love.' It was my mum. She sounded ill or tired or just different.

'What is it?' I asked anxiously. 'Has something happened? Are you all right?' Oh no, listen to me panicking. I've become my mum. It's finally happened like they all say it will. I'll start stockpiling tins of corned beef next.

211

She dutifully took on my role of reassuring appeaser. 'Nothing's wrong. I just thought you'd want to know that I found it.'

She didn't need to tell me what the 'it' was. I hadn't forgotten about the note. Not exactly. I'd shoved it to a less prominent part of my consciousness where it wouldn't interfere with all the other pressing questions demanding my attention on an hourly basis. She'd found it. It was real. My mother was real. At last I could allow myself to let the actuality of this person, this stranger, surface and take shape.

Now I know what people mean when they talk about their lives flashing before them. Except, in my case, it's just the first week of my life. I've tried to imagine my real mother in those first days following my birth, what she was like, what she must have gone through, why she gave me up. And then I fast-forward thirty-six years to an imagined meeting. She's different each time I picture her. But she's always beautiful. I'm not beautiful but she will look like me, a beautiful version of me. And she will smile at me. And a line of mutual understanding and love will instantly be sparked between us. That's how it always is.

'Oh,' I say.

'Anyway, just to let you know that I'll put it in the post to you. I thought you'd want to know.'

'Right,' I say dumbly. 'Thanks a lot.' I'm amazed that I can even get monosyllables out. My body has frozen and I'm astonished that any other part of my being is capable of sensible response to this news.

'Everything all right, love?' Mum asked, obviously concerned at my reaction.

'Yes, fine. Just a bit tired, that's all,' I manage. I'm getting positively articulate now. 'Thank you,' I repeat in case I haven't sounded grateful enough. I'm not sure if I said goodbye before putting the phone down. It wasn't at the forefront of my priorities. If this were a film, I'd sink into a chair or even down to the floor. But I am my mother's daughter so I go and put the kettle on. I must remember to ask my birth mother if she makes tea compulsively in times of stress. It will be an interesting litmus test for the 'nature vs nurture' debate. I am calm. Really I am. Not inside where my thoughts are wobbling and whizzing like a tangled cassette. But my hands aren't shaking and my head isn't throbbing. This is a whole new experience for me.

And then the phone rings again. I thought I was ready for anything now. That's what I thought. Things must surely have gone as far as they could for me. Surely. I had a not-quite-marriage that had been severely tested but seemed to have made it through to the next round. I had two children who teetered on the edge of apparent delinquency, and two others, one with urban terrorist aspirations and one who had got religion. I had two friends intent on destroying their own or each other's marriages. I had two mothers, a real one and one I was about to meet. I'd got Karen, an uninvited guest in my life who was making me question and defend all of my roles. And then there was Simon. No, I'm not ready to categorise Simon. Too tricky.

Isn't that enough?

It's Rob on the phone. I sigh with relief. He obviously hasn't been killed in a plane crash which was always a possibility while I remained at the epicentre of malevolent forces which I seem to have been occupying for a while.

'Are you OK?' I ask breathlessly.

'I'm fine. Couldn't be better!' He sounds slightly hysterical. 'Guess where I am?'

I look at the clock. 'Gatwick airport, I hope,' I answer

nervously. There's something not quite right with this. I know with a certainty that I've come to recognise as reliable that I'm not going to like this.

'Guess again!' Rob says, laughing.

Bad. Very bad. I'm getting a very, very, bad feeling about this. I try and sound cheerful, just in case I'm wrong and I don't have anything to worry about. Ha ha. 'I can't guess. Tell me. Now.'

'Where have I always wanted to go? More than anywhere else in the world?'

No. Please, no.

'Can't you guess? I can't believe it myself but it's true. It's an early birthday present from Karen, but don't be cross. I said you wouldn't mind because you always said you wanted me to go here one day. And this was such a once-in-a-lifetime opportunity, I couldn't turn it down. I knew you wouldn't want me to. Have you guessed yet?'

No. Please, no.

'I'm at the Wolf Sanctuary!'

214

Intermission

Me and Barry Manilow

There is no love as transitory and fickle as that of a teenager for a pop icon. Once I loved David Cassidy. I mean, I really loved him. I used to cut pictures of his face and stick them on to my family snapshots so that he'd seem a real part of my life. Look, there's me and David at Colwyn Bay! And there he is at Auntie Iris's sixtieth birthday party!

But overnight he was usurped. I heard my first Barry Manilow record when I was fifteen, twenty-one years ago. I'd heard it on Radio One (yes, he used to be played on Radio One) and bought it the next day. I dumped David Cassidy immediately. He had terrible skin anyway.

As soon as I got home I rushed upstairs, yanking the record from its sleeve as I ran, not wanting to waste a single moment. I pulled my curtains across, lit a cheap white candle which I'd pilfered from my mum's emergency cupboard (already at the halfway stage of readiness between postwar and possible pre-nuclear holocaust), delicately placed the stylus into that first groove and lost myself in another place.

Yes, I know, well I was fifteen, OK?

Fifteen. I reached a peak of self-awareness at that age, locked into the futility of my own hopeless existence.

215

Never had a boyfriend. Never been kissed. My life had no meaning. There was no point in trying to instil any sense of perspective in me because teenagers have no concept of other viewpoints; they each occupy the central position of their own one-dimensional universe.

It was just me and Barry from then on. Even then, he understood. His songs, thankfully devoid of scary sexual allusion but packed full of pathos, lessened my isolation. He sang of things that other pop stars didn't touch. He sang of the courageous acceptance of abandonment, the pride in survival, the generosity of unselfish love. True, he also sang of Lola, she was a showgirl, but if he hadn't, we'd all have slit our wrists.

Of course, he was never cool. But I liked that. (I still do.) When I was fifteen, I was clever, chubby and didn't have any brothers. In a girly peer group, that made me social death. In other words, born to be a Barry Manilow fan. At the exact time I went looking for my voice, my style and my direction, I found Him. Well, it could have been drugs. Or religion. So my parents got off quite lightly.

But this was no passing phase. The seeds of my one-and-only lifelong commitment were sown that first time I heard 'Trying To Get The Feeling.' What was great about Barry was that he didn't just sing of unrequited love or no love at all. He sang of love that ran a rugged course, went wrong, left scars and demanded heroic acts of unselfishness to resolve. It appealed to my desire for complexity and complications. That life might actually turn out to be a bit of a breeze was inconceivable and unwelcome to a teenage girl reading Albert Camus and Barbara Cartland alternately.

Even when I finally experienced the love as an adult that I'd yearned for as a dreamy teenager, I still found myself

216

drifting back, craving that muted pain of being fifteen. Because when I did grow up, I learned that perceived misery was much more bearable than the real thing. And right now, I long for the days when my deepest worry was that I might never taste the joys of holding hands with a boy over a Bender Brunch in the Wimpy Bar.

And those of us who grew up with Barry have become a club, a network of sisters who outlasted the Greenham Common women. I went to my first concert when I was eighteen. We were more subdued then, more thoughtful, humming along quietly, not wanting to appear rude or unappreciative by drowning him out with our tuneless singing.

So it developed. One night we joined in with the songs. And he seemed to like that. I can't remember when they started waving candles. I never waved candles, of course. I'm not a candle-waver. Or a whooper or screamer. I'm not even much of a clapper-alonger. I just tap my leg with a tense finger, hoping nobody will notice and have me thrown out for neglecting my duty to enjoy myself in a conspicuous manner. And when Barry sings 'Can't Smile Without You' and everyone holds up banners begging him to ask them up on stage to join him a duet, I shrink back into my seat and smile nervously. I'd rather drink Fairy Liquid than have a microphone and a spotlight on me.

But I'm eaten up with envy at the gift of spontaneity, the complete lack of repression that my fellow fans all seem to possess. I would love to be able to stretch up my arms and wave a candle and sing at full volume. I would love to scream, 'Choose me!' But I don't. I can't.

I've been going to concerts for seventeen years and each time it's like coming home. Those of us in the know get priority on booking tickets and always sit near the front. We see each other and greet each other as if we were old friends, even though we don't know each other's names. And I expect we would have nothing else in common if we did ever try and strike up a contact outside of this closed world. All we share is this single point of constancy and continuity in our lives.

But things change. They don't wave candles any more, they wave flashing fibre optic wands that dodgy vendors sell outside the theatre. They wear diamanté brooches spelling out the name BARRY. They drink dry white wine from plastic cups. And they're getting older. We all are.

Right now, I'm struggling to find my balance and I'm reaching out for something to steady me. I remember a concert about eleven years ago. It was the interval and I was looking around at the audience, interested in the small number of men present. There were a few real male fans who kept themselves to themselves. There were a few who seemed as if they'd stumbled into the wrong venue and just looked bemused. You always get some of them. And then there were the rest.

They had come to support their partners who were all real Barry devotees. The men wore bewildered expressions, carried coats and held handbags while their wives queued in the overstretched loos. During the concert, they watched on and tried to do the right thing. They stood up when it would have been churlish to remain seated, clapped and laughed at the appropriate moments and stifled yawns invisibly.

But what I noticed most was when their partners turned to them in moments of pure pleasure. Because each man returned each woman's smile in an act of love, sharing and total mutual incomprehension. They had no idea why this funny little singer should make their wives so happy but happy they were. These men derived *their* pure pleasure from seeing this. And the women had the bonus of some-one to share that with, someone all of their own.

When I watched them leaving at the end, holding hands, I knew I wanted a man like that. I didn't need to be understood, that was asking the impossible, I just wanted someone to keep me company, who wanted to see me smile even if he didn't understand why I was smiling.

And when I met Rob, I found that man. It was his idea to accompany me to the next concert and I was apprehensive because I knew that he found the music bland and cheesy. But it was a magical evening. He bought me chocolate brazils and a ludicrous programme that cost ten pounds.

I wondered if the other women were watching me, if they'd noticed that I'd moved into a new category, a good one, and got myself one of those rare men who slot painlessly into our dream worlds. Although I was concentrating on the show, I could still feel his eyes smiling at me every time I smiled. When everyone else clapped along and I was doing my restrained leg-tapping, he laughed and nudged me until I joined in properly. And when we were all standing up and swinging in time to 'Could It Be Magic', he swung along. Unfortunately, we never managed to synchronise our swinging and we spent the whole song trying not to bump hips. In ten years, he's never got the timing right. But he still comes with me. And he keeps trying to adjust his timing to mine.

It was on that night, at that first concert, that I knew I loved Rob. And don't tut and groan and say that's pathetic because I bet your truth is no less bizarre. When did *you* first *know* that you loved someone? Was it when you saw the fading sun highlighting his brow in front of the Taj Mahal? Was it when he swam the Zambezi to bring you a single gardenia? Of course it wasn't. It was when he laughed at your dad's jokes or gave you the Flake from his 99 or put your pyjamas on the radiator to warm. It was something like that, I know it was. Something that meant something to you. That's how proper love works.

I love Rob. That I know. I have a man worth holding on to. But deep inside me, I can feel him slipping away from me. That's scary. Perhaps even more frighteningly I can feel me slipping away from him. Towards Simon.

I'm a stupid, foolish, childish, obsessive, silly, silly woman who is losing her way through a refusal to countenance change. I'm trying to hold on to Rob by chaining us both to our past. I'm throwing nervous, sideways glances at Simon, reaching out, pulling back, reaching out, pulling back. There's no plan, I'm just drifting. The future, Karen, is pulling us all forward and I can't resist her any longer. I'm going to have to move on if I'm to fight for whatever position I decide I want.

The old songs are great but they're stifling me, restraining me. It's time to learn some new ones, songs where we both know the rhythm. Not love songs, but battle songs.

Chapter Fourteen

My resolution to make radical changes to my entire outlook on life ended with a marathon wallow in old records. As do the majority of my attempts to break free of the past. Tell me I'm not the only one. I lugged the old record player from the attic and played all my scratchy singles at top volume.

Claire and Jude swore never to put another foot wrong as long as I promised never to play my Barry Manilow records within their earshot again. If only I'd known that aversion therapy was the ultimate key to motivating them. It blows Rob's reward method approach to child-rearing out of the water. Hah!

I then undid my achievement by giving them money to go to the pictures. They were now fervently wishing they'd arranged to get themselves suspended before and will doubtless insult my taste in music at every opportunity in the future to see what prize they receive. They will probably try it on their father as well. In my vindictive state, I look forward to watching Rob try and work out why his well-trained offspring are expecting to be patted on the head for disparaging his cherished Status Quo CDs.

There was an awkward moment. At first, they didn't want to go out. 'We want to be here when Dad gets back.' It was Claire who said this. Claire. Who had invested so much of herself in the surprise present for her father. I coughed quietly. 'That was your father on the phone earlier. He's not going to be back today.'

Both Claire and Jude groaned at the news. They suddenly looked like the helpless, needy children I'd first met ten years earlier. Jude was having difficulty in holding back tears. 'Why not? He promised!'

'Something came up. He's going to be staying in the States for a few more days. He'll tell you everything when he gets back at the weekend. He's really sorry.' But not sorry enough.

I know I'm being a coward but there is no way that I am going to be the one to tell them where their father is. I made that clear to Rob immediately before slamming the phone down on him. I didn't tell him why I was so incensed. Let him think it's just me being jealous over Karen. I don't care. He'll find out soon enough what he's done. And just because this devastating blow to his daughters has not been intentionally planned doesn't make it any more forgivable. If Karen had spoken to any of us first, then this could have been avoided. But she plainly has her own agenda in motion. And, right now, it's the least of my concerns.

I ached as I watched the girls leave the house in silence. But I needed time to myself to think things through. For all our sakes. And I only had half an hour before the other two girls would have to be picked up from school. It was time to call in a favour. I had no choice. I had to phone Andrea.

'Hello?' Her voice sounded suspicious and tired. I should have ring before. Damn.

I became a little ray of sunshine, hoping a cheery voice might shake her out of her mood. 'Hi there, it's me.'

'Oh hello.' Now she sounded bitter. It's going to be

down to me to salvage this, I can tell. 'How are you?' she asks, not really caring.

'Fine,' I say, pretending that I don't know that she doesn't care.

'Good,' she says, aware that I am pretending that I don't know that she doesn't care.

This is hopeless. 'Oh for God's sake, Ange, this is stupid. I don't even know why we're not talking. But since everything else is my fault, then I'll assume this is as well. So whatever it is I've done, I'm sorry. Now will you please tell me how it's all going.'

She didn't let me off the hook easily, which is a bit rich since I still don't think I'm the one in the wrong. But what do I know? All I know is that I need a friend right now and if that means swallowing some pride and letting Andrea indulge in some mind games, then so be it.

So I cajoled and wheedled and Andrea sniffed and grunted. She finally ran out of reasons to continue punishing me. 'Oh what the hell, Lorn. I've really missed you. I haven't had anyone to talk to.'

'Not even Joe?' I couldn't stop that from slipping out. But I wish I'd tried harder.

'If you've phoned up to have a go at me about that again, then you're wasting your time,' Andrea snapped.

'I'm sorry, Ange, I'm sorry. I suppose I just wanted to know how things stood. You know.'

She knew. 'You want to know if I'm still seeing Joe. And just what Phil knows.' That's exactly what I want to know.

'No, I want to know how *you* are. And Dan. How you're both coping. If you don't want to talk about Joe, I'll understand entirely.'

Andrea laughed. 'I've missed your hopeless inability to lie. It was one of your most endearing qualities.' In the

223

light of my recent mild subterfuge, this goes to show that she knows me less well than we both thought. 'Let me put you out of your misery.' She stopped laughing abruptly. 'I haven't seen Joe since last Wednesday. We've spoken on the phone but he's keeping his head down. He told me about what happened in the headmaster's office.'

'It was awful, Ange.'

'How was she?'

'Devastated. She was so torn apart, I thought she was going to start throwing chairs. It was only when I mentioned Elliott that she calmed down and then . . .'

'Sorry, are you talking about Phillippa?'

I was taken aback by her interruption. 'Of course, I was. Why? Who did you . . .?' Of course. She wanted to know about Tara Brownlow. She wasn't remotely interested in how her best friend was holding up as her world fell apart. Whatever guilt Andrea felt about destroying her friend's marriage, it wasn't as strong as the desire to know everything about her own rival. I didn't recognise this person on the phone at all. When Angie made the decision to betray Phillippa, she didn't just taint our friendship along with the whole concept of friendship but she began living by rules that baffled me. It was like a gangrene, insidiously invading and spoiling everything that was once healthy.

Not only was she no longer bothered about the implications of what she'd done, but she had the temerity to be simultaneously incensed with indignation about Dan's treachery. The two states didn't strike her as being incompatible. In her mind she was the wronged woman, the woman scorned, defending her nest against invasion. She was entitled to do whatever was necessary to fight her corner. Quite what perverse logic convinced her that this justified starting an affair with Joe, I can't imagine.

Andrea must have sensed that she had overstepped the

mark. 'You must think I'm terrible,' she said quickly. 'It's not that I don't care about Phil. I just can't afford to think about her too much. It's only Joe who makes the situation with Dan bearable. If I had to give him up, I'd have no one.'

'So what you're saying is that you're holding on to Joe just in case Dan goes for good?'

Andrea's voice betrayed her distaste at this suggestion. 'You make me sound so manipulative. It's not like that at all. I . . . have feelings for Joe. But also I don't want to give up on my marriage if there's still a chance it might be saved.'

'So you're hedging your bets?' I summed up incredulously. This wasn't the sort of passion I expected from the woman who'd seen *Truly Madly Deeply* eleven times. The conversation wasn't going well. I'd phoned Andrea primarily to beg her to pick up Phoebe and Ali and transport them to piano classes in a godforsaken part of Streatham unserved by buses. I was going to have to be nice to her and I wasn't feeling nice.

'You're doing it again,' she answered.

'Doing what again?'

'Judging me. And you are in no position to judge.'

Now *I'm* bristling. 'What's that supposed to mean?'

'Just forget it.' Andrea sounded as if she regretted opening this new gate.

'I don't want to forget it.'

Andrea sighed. 'Just that Phil and I both saw you yesterday walking down the street with a *very* attractive man, looking *very* cosy.'

'You and Phil? You went out together?' I was playing for time here, hoping I didn't sound defensive. Why should I? There was nothing untoward going on, after all. I could hardly see the *News of the World* printing a front

225

page headline: 'DOG TRAINER'S GIRLFRIEND IN HAND-STROKING SCANDAL WITH COLLEAGUE!' But I didn't want to discuss this with her. I mean I did. Of course I did, but I couldn't. I'd painted myself into a moral corner with my condemnation of Andrea and I was no longer entitled to declare myself beset by a similarly dubious situation. Note to self: even when you know you're right, keep your big mouth shut when dealing with friends' ethical choices in the future – you haven't got enough friends to risk losing even one and you're going to look really hypocritical when you next put a foot wrong.

The distraction worked. Andrea became flustered. 'I had to. She kept phoning me, leaving messages on the machine. In the end, it would have been more suspicious if I didn't meet up with her. I'm still her best friend.'

Don't say it, Lorna. You've managed to lure her off the topic of you and Simon, just stay cool. 'So how was she? What's going on with her and Joe?' This is too weird for words. I have to draw a mental line separating Andrea from Joe when talking about Phillippa, and a line between Phil and Joe when talking about Andrea. Where the drama ends and the reality begins, who knows? Still at least I now know why Andrea didn't enquire after Phil. She already knew. This redeems her and makes me feel a whole lot better.

'She's not doing very well. The only way Joe could persuade her he wasn't having an affair with Tara Brownlow was by telling her that Dan was. He's insisting to her that he's not having an affair at all, that all the sneaking around has been to have heart-to-hearts with Dan and that Dan swore him to secrecy knowing that Phil and I were friends.'

Phew. This is only one tiny step away from 'the pellet with the poison's in the chalice from the palace while the

226

vessel with the pestle holds the brew that is true.' How does Andrea keep up with the catalogue of big and little deceits that have punctuated her affair? I'm having trouble with my teensy-weensy omissions that don't even count since I'm not doing anything wrong. 'And does Phil buy this?'

'I don't think so,' Andrea answered miserably. 'She wants to. But her gut instinct tells her that Joe is lying.' As well it should. 'That wasn't even why she insisted on seeing me. She wanted to sympathise with me over Dan and Tara, give me some support and a shoulder to cry on. She played down her suspicions about Joe because she thought my problems were greater. How terrible do you think that made me feel?'

As bad as it gets, I surmise. 'What did you say to her?'

'It was an impossible situation, Lorn. I could hardly look her in the eye. But I have to admit I was really grateful to have someone to talk to about Dan's affair. I know you don't believe this but I *am* bothered by him and Tara. And don't forget, Dan was the first to be unfaithful. And, yes, that does make a difference.'

If only Dan hadn't been unfaithful ... And if Karen hadn't phoned that one time ... And if Phillippa hadn't been at her health club ...

'That's not to say that we weren't both unhappy for a long time before that but I wasn't planning to do anything about it. I suppose I thought if we could just stick it out, things would right themselves or at least we'd be able to hold out until we'd got Isabelle through school so that she wasn't disrupted by anything happening to us.'

'But?' I prompted, genuinely wanting to understand how this all came about now we'd finally dropped the pretence that this had 'just happened'.

'But it was too hard, Lorn. By myself. Knowing that

Dan was with *her*. Isabelle didn't need me, I hardly ever see her with her social life, you know how that is.' I do. 'And I know it shouldn't have been Joe. But it's not as if I have such a great circle of friends and acquaintances myself, that I can pick and choose a man to get me through this. Where do married mums like us meet men?' A wicked note of humour crept into her voice. 'Now I come to think about it, I should have asked you.'

Whoops, she's getting back to me again. 'You're barking up the wrong tree there. That was just one of my students that I'm helping out with a project. There's nothing going on between us.'

'So Rob knows all about him?' Andrea asked. Very astute, Angie. You're getting good at this.

'Not exactly. But only because there's nothing to know. I don't talk about my students much. And these past weeks, we've had bigger things on our minds, if you recall.'

'If you say so.' She didn't believe me and I don't blame her. I don't believe me either. There was a short silence that I was determined not to be the one to break. I won.

'OK, so you're not going to tell me about him. Fair enough. But I won't forget. Where was I?'

'You and Phil,' I reminded her, relieved to have postponed the inevitable interrogation.

'Oh yes. Well that's about it. I felt gutted. She was so sympathetic about me and Dan, told me what a complete bitch she thought Tara Brownlow was and how she hoped Dan would catch some disease or something. And every so often she'd casually drop something in about Joe, desperate for me to reassure her that she was wrong about her suspicions, that all his excuses made sense.'

'And did you?' I asked.

'I think so, although God knows how I managed.'

'You did the right thing, Ange. Phil needs protecting until you can sort out what's going to happen long-term. I'm not getting at you, honest I'm not, but she's the real victim in all this.'

Andrea swallowed tearfully. 'I want to be protected too. I don't want to get divorced. I don't want everything to change. I want everything to get back to how it was when Isabelle was little. We were really happy then.'

Then it hit me. I'd solved one of the mysteries of life. Now I knew why time never went in reverse, why God, whoever he was, never turned back the clocks. Because every single person would turn time back to a completely different moment. There was probably not a single second in the history of mankind when more than one person was experiencing absolute happiness. Every time a baby was born, somebody was dying somewhere else. For each first kiss there was a corresponding slap and for every moment of stolen pleasure there was someone suffering betrayal. There's no commonly shared optimal time pocket to zoom in on. So onward time plods as we all scramble about looking for one more cherished moment to hold on to. That's not to say that there's no comfort to be had in contemplating the past, in dreaming and wishing.

'You need to get all your old records out,' I suggested wistfully.

'Sorry?'

'Never mind. So what are you all doing?' I meant 'all' in the widest sense: Andrea, Dan, Phil, Joe and the pivotal Tara.

Andrea saw what I was getting at. She took a deep breath. 'Phil and Joe are trying to act normally, Dan and I are sleeping in separate bedrooms but Isabelle doesn't know that, Dan doesn't even bother with excuses for sneaking out to see *her*, and Joe and I, well, we're keeping a low profile.' I could almost hear her struggle as she felt her comfort blanket being tugged from under her.

One more thing occurred to me. 'Didn't you say that Dan had found out about you and Joe? Has he done anything about that?'

'I managed to stop him from going round there and causing a scene. I persuaded him to think of Phillippa and that stopped him in his tracks.'

'That was decent of him,' I suggested.

Andrea snorted. 'Do you think?'

'What do you mean?' I asked.

'Think about it, Lorn.'

I thought about it. I got nowhere. Even though Dan apparently started off the chain of events by embarking upon an affair with his daughter's teacher, I could still imagine how he would be incensed to learn about Andrea and Joe. We all knew how Dan felt about Joe, his deep-rooted resentment at Joe's privileged background. He would probably have interpreted Andrea's choice as a direct dig at himself. And he too had been betrayed – by someone in their small circle of friends, what's more. It would have been perfectly understandable – cruel, but understandable – if he'd gone straight round to the Jacksons to confront Joe in front of his wife and family.

But he didn't. And yes, I think that was decent. Andrea became impatient with me. 'Think about Phillippa, Lorn.'

'I am thinking about her. What's your point?'

'Who does she remind you of?'

Then I got it. The light went on. Tara Brownlow and Phillippa. They were practically identical twins all the way down to their camel pashminas. I can't believe I didn't spot it myself. I mean, I did make the connection, I'd seen the similarities between them but I hadn't grasped the possible relevance of that in the light of Dan's choice of Tara Brownlow. Andrea was right. Absolutely right.

'Andrea, you're wrong. Absolutely wrong.'

'No I'm not and I tell by your voice that you agree with me. Dan must always have fancied Phil, that's why he went for someone who was just like her.'

I didn't have the energy to argue this one all the way. This suggestion was almost incestuous and it bothered me. Why couldn't they all just go to wife-swapping parties in Yorkshire, get whatever it is out of their systems and then come back here with the dynamics of our circle left intact? Am I being unreasonable? I don't think so. 'Even if you are right . . .'

'Ah ha! You see, I was right! You do agree!'

'. . . even *if* you're right, at least he didn't do anything about it. He had enough respect for your friendship with Phil *not* to do anything about it.'

'Unlike me with Joe, I suppose is what you're saying.'

Here it comes again, the headache, like a stalker who refuses to obey the injunction served against him. By now, I should have enough painkillers in my system to have paralysed all my nerve endings into submission. But still the pain comes back. Calm, calm, calm.

'We're going round in circles, Ange. Look, I'm sorry to land this on you but can you do me a huge favour?' Please don't say no.

'I suppose so,' she muttered sulkily. You can sulk all you like, Andrea. I have four daughters, I am the Supreme Champion of ignoring sulks. If you're not going to refuse me flatly, I'll take that as a willing acceptance.

'I know it was my turn to take the girls to piano this afternoon, but something urgent's come up. Can you do it just this once? Please?'

Big, sulky sigh worthy of Jude (Undisputed Queen of

the Sulky Sigh). 'OK.' Curiosity then got the better of her. 'What's come up that's so urgent?'

I only convey the full content of our conversation so that you have an accurate feel for Andrea's hostility to me. So that you will sense how troubled I was that relations with my friends were no closer to resolution. So that you will understand why I didn't feel happy about confiding my latest troubles in her. So that you will see why I couldn't bother Phillippa in her preoccupied state. So that you'll know straight away why I was so churned up that I had to scrap my plan to spend time alone thinking things through. So that you will empathise with my urgent need to share my mounting problems with someone out of the loop. So that you won't judge me for going to see Simon. Or for everything that took place when I got there. I wasn't my fault, it just happened

Chapter Fifteen

'I'm sorry.'

'No, I'm sorry.'

'You don't have to be sorry, nothing happened.'

'If that were the case, then you wouldn't have to be sorry either, and you said it first.'

He had a point. I stopped apologising and so did he. Then we went back to the excruciating embarrassment which was where we'd got to when we started apologising.

I should point out that no clothes had been removed although we'd come close. We were probably guilty of getting up to no more and no less than Claire and Elliott Jackson in the sports cupboard and, in my defence, it was I who stopped things before they went any further. I didn't need Miss Brownlow's intervention to curb my excesses. I possessed self-control.

Who am I kidding? We stopped – I stopped – because I was terrified. Terrified of getting hurt. Terrified of getting caught. Terrified of the consequences. Terrified of going so far down an unmarked road that I wouldn't be able to find my way back.

And yes, it did 'just happen'. I can prove it. I can prove that I went to Simon's flat without any intention of luring him into a sports cupboard. Look at me. I'm wearing leggings. You see? I rest my case. Now you understand. All women will understand immediately.

'You've changed, what on earth *are* you wearing?' Simon looked me up and down in amusement.

'What are you talking about?' I looked down at my clothes. Nothing out of the ordinary there. Or rather, nothing out of the ordinary for a woman who was planning to spend the afternoon doing the housework and then pick up her kids from school. As soon as I got home from lunch with Simon, I changed out of my best jumper and skirt into leggings and one of Rob's old jumpers.

Question for you. Two questions actually. No, three. When did you buy your last pair of leggings? Where did you buy them? What were you thinking of? You can't answer any of them, can you? That's because you didn't buy them in the first place. Because leggings arrive in all our wardrobes by some supernatural osmosis that mortals cannot comprehend.

Take these, my navy blue favourites. I couldn't possibly have bought these. I think the Leggings Fairy left them in my tumble dryer one day, already baggy at the knee and splitting at the crotch, the Lycra long ago departed to elastic heaven. I would never have chosen them. No sensible, rational woman with an ounce of self-esteem would knowingly choose a garment that was designed to highlight her flaws and minimise her assets.

It is commonly accepted that nobody looks good in leggings. They make a woman with perfect legs look bandy, the average woman look elephantine and, if you happen to be a woman of ampler proportions who thinks the stretchy fit gives you a sleek silhouette, I'll tell you what, take a stroll past a building site and see what the cheeky chappies there have to say about it.

I have no doubt whatsoever that a legal precedent

somewhere in the system rules that the wearing of leggings is conclusive evidence of innocence of any crime of passion. Quite right too.

But before you consign your own shameful, tatty collection to a skip in a street where no one knows you, let me pass on something to you. Leggings have a unique, reliable application that will aid you in your pursuit of true love. I may even patent it.

Now you might be fortunate enough to have a partner who gave you a convertible sports car or a kidney as proof of his boundless, selfless love. But for the rest of us, a more practical testing kit would be invaluable, wouldn't it? At no expense whatsoever, I bring you the if-he-really-loves-you-he'll-still-find-you-attractive-when-he-sees-you-in-old-leggings leggings.

Most of us can can transform ourselves into something approximating OK when we devote six hours to the preparation. At the beginning of a relationship, we give it all we've got: face pack, leg wax, manic flossing, mouthwash, nose-hair tweezing, toenail cuticle removal, total body exfoliation, cellulite cream, that black skirt that makes your backside look flat, your hair blow-dried until it defies the laws of physics, make-up applied with a precision worthy of open-heart surgery and a thong. He falls at your feet. Of course he does.

Six months later, it's a flannel under your armpits and you're wearing your Ibiza '79 faded T-shirt in bed.

If he's still around, it's decision time. You need to find out if the reason he's stuck it out is because he can't face going back to individual steak and kidney puddings in the microwave or because he loves you and is in for the duration. You've pushed him just about as far you can without offering him your placenta pan-fried in an omelette and he hasn't left you yet, but you can't help wondering what would happen if you were maimed in a freak windsurfing accident or put on ten stone.

Now you no longer need to mutilate yourself to test his level of aesthetic endurance. Just grab your courage in your hands, take a deep breath and slip into that appalling thing at the bottom of your sock drawer which you last wore when you did Legs, Bums 'n' Tums down at the Methodist Church Hall. Don't even bother calling them leggings any more since their warped shape no longer comes close to resembling any legs known to orthopaedic specialists in this solar system.

When you next see him, just walk in coolly as if nothing out of the ordinary is happening. Maybe cover yourself with a coat or something so that there's a real sense of revelation as you peel off the outer layer and the full horror of your bottom half seeps into the marrow of his being. If he doesn't run screaming from your life, then basically you've got yourself a winner.

'What on earth are you wearing?' It was the tone of amusement rather than repulsion that confirmed what I already guessed. It was the real thing for Simon. As it was, is, for Rob, I hastily reminded myself.

I sat down quickly and pulled the jumper over my knees to conceal my shame. 'Sorry, I didn't have time to change,' I muttered.

Simon tried unsuccessfully to suppress his glee. 'I'm not being rude, well actually I am being rude, but did you look in the mirror when you changed into that?'

That was it. I stood up, flaunting my poorly conceived fashion statement. 'For your information, these are practically compulsory for mothers. If you're wearing these, it doesn't matter whether you've got stretch marks or not, your maternal identity is assured. Genealogists don't need to go to libraries to trace family connections, they just need to examine the stains of the matriarch's clothes.

'Each garment carries the history of the family that nurtured it. Look.' I point to a washed-out blob on the knee. 'That's where Phoebe was sick after eating beetroot when she was six and I tried to scrub it out with Jif. And that one, there?' I showed him a badly sewn rip on the well-rounded rear. 'That's where I fell over doing the hokey-cokey in playgroup about a year later.'

'And you were so poor that you couldn't ever afford to simply buy new trousers?' Bless him for paying me the ultimate respect of calling them trousers. It must be love.

'You don't replace leggings! It would be like putting down the family dog just because he's muddy. These clothes are a testament to years of sacrifice at the altar of motherhood.' Now we were both laughing. It was good to laugh again. And somehow I didn't feel I was doing anything wrong by being here dressed like this.

'Tea or coffee?' he offered, beckoning me to follow him into the kitchen.

'Tea, please,' I answered, interested in how he made it, with or without neurotic tendencies.

I sat at the breakfast bar, wondering why I felt so at ease in this man's kitchen. I hadn't been in a man's kitchen since I first met Rob. And even then it wasn't his kitchen, it was Karen's. But this was definitely Simon's. I drank in the incongruous juxtapositions of Coco Pops and state-of-the-art espresso maker, electric wok and Sunny Delight ice-lolly moulds, American Express Gold Card bills stuck to the fridge with Teletubbies magnets.

He saw me taking stock and raised an eyebrow. 'Caught in the act. If I'd known you were coming round, I'd have rearranged things to present a more sophisticated picture of my lifestyle.'

'No you wouldn't,' I said decisively.

'You're right, I wouldn't. It's quite clever of you to realise that.'

I thought about it. 'Not really. You don't hide your true self away like most people I know. What you see is what you get, isn't that the way you like to be?'

He dropped tea bags into mugs. I was relieved that he did this so casually. It meant that he was comfortable with this situation. So was I. 'I've never given it much thought. Being honest just makes life so much simpler. I've always wanted things to be simple, no complications, no stress, none of the syndromes that everyone seems to boast of as if their life only has meaning when you stop being able to cope with it.'

'I think that's a bit harsh. Most of us want the same as you. It's just that events take over, pulling us where we don't want to go and we just have to deal with whatever's thrown at us.'

Simon looked doubtful. 'Are you telling me that you never envisaged all your current problems? You must have known that you were in for some pretty stormy times moving in with a man and his four small children. Especially when the wife was always in the background threatening to drop back in at the most inappropriate moment.'

I was feeling got at. 'Of course I didn't think it would be easy. But you can't choose who you love.' I can't believe I'm talking about love. I've never done it before apart from during *very* occasional soppy moments with Rob in our early days.

Simon looked straight at me. 'Of course you can.

238

You can choose who you love and you can choose who not to love. I'm not saying it's easy but it's absolutely essential for survival.'

What is he talking about? He must be thinking of some completely different kind of love. He can't mean the woozy, stomach-fluttering kind that the rest of us know as love. You can't switch that on and off. It creeps up on you, grips you, takes over every aspect of your being until you're lost. But I didn't say that. I didn't need to. He knew what I was thinking.

'Let me prove it to you. Did you fall in love with Rob at first sight?'

'No. He was sorting out a problem with my dog. I thought he was attractive but there was nothing earth-moving.'

'And did you know about his family situation from the beginning?'

I thought back. 'Yes. I had to go to his house for the appointment because he hadn't decided to get anyone in to help with the kids at that time. Karen had only left him a few days earlier and he still hoped that she'd come back. It was chaos there.'

'So when did he ask you out?'

'About a month later. He accepted then that Karen had gone for good and he was crawling up the wall trying to juggle childcare with his work. Actually . . .' Suddenly I caught my breath.

'Actually what?' Simon asked.

Could that be right? How could I possibly have forgotten that? 'Actually I think I asked him out. I took pity on him, he was under so much pressure. I think I suggested he get a babysitter and come out with me for a pizza or something. Not a date or anything. Just to get him out of the house.'

This is unbelievable. Surely everyone remembers all the details of meeting their partner, don't they? Whenever I play out the scene in my memory, Rob always asks me out, just to get out of the house, not a date. But now it's right there in front of me. I asked him first. How strange that it should come back to me now.

'Well there you go then,' Simon declared.

'What's your point?' I asked irritably, still coming to terms with the fact that my memory had tricked me over something so important for all these years.

'My point is that you *chose* to start a possible relationship with someone in the most convoluted situation, someone you might or might not fall in love with somewhere down the line. Anybody could see that a person getting seriously involved with this man was heading for some major crises. But you went ahead anyway.'

He sat back, happy that he'd made his point.

'But how was I to know that I was going to fall in love with him? It was just a pizza. I didn't know anything would develop.'

'Now you're lying to yourself. I don't believe that you hadn't considered the possibility of this being more than a pizza. I bet you played the what-if game. I bet you thought of those four poor little motherless girls and that poor abandoned man. I bet you pictured yourself flying in and saving them all. Cooking wholesome meals for the family, healing the children's open wounds, filling the terrible gap in Rob's broken life . . .'

I think I prefer my friends to be less perceptive. (I'd also prefer ones that didn't sleep with each other's husbands but maybe I'm being too picky.) I don't believe I had any of these thoughts but my selective memory might well be tricking me again. 'Even if I did, what's wrong with that? They did need me. Or maybe not me, but they needed someone. And I'm sorry if it sounds as if I'm blowing my own trumpet, but I did rescue them. The reason those girls didn't fall apart, the reason they grew up so intact, is down to the solid framework that Rob and I gave them. Together. Are you suggesting I should have anticipated that things might get hairy at some unknown hour and left them to stumble through?'

'That's what I'm suggesting, yes. And do you know what would have happened?'

'No. What?'

'I don't know. And neither do you. No one knows. But Rob might have met somebody else. Or made monumental efforts to win Karen back. Or he might have coped by himself until Karen finally decided to come back herself. Didn't you say that Karen told Rob one of the reasons she stayed away so long was because she knew the girls were happy and settled with you?'

I couldn't take this all in. 'So you're saying that the family might have sorted things out for themselves if it hadn't been for me? That Karen might have come back and they might all have lived happily ever after?'

Simon shrugged. 'I'm just trying to get you to face up to your *choosing* this ending to your particular love story. Because this was always how it was going to turn out. Anyone could see that, you included.'

By now I was standing close to him, squishing the tea bags against the side of the mugs while he poured in the milk. We'd silently established a working rhythm, slotting in with each other smoothly. It was some time later that I considered how we'd managed to make tea together in a small kitchen without bumping hips or even spoons.

I jabbed my finger teasingly at his white T-shirt. 'Now *you've* missed the point. I did fall in love with Rob. And he fell in love with me. It was no easygoing little fling. This was a ten-year epic voyage with kids and troubles and the rest. We've proved that this was for real. And you're saying that I should have stopped it all happening before I started? Because I knew that it might get bumpy? And then what? How many chances at the real thing does a person get?'

'As many as you like.' He said it just like that, as if he was talking about buying new wallpaper for the same old house you'd always lived in. He was gently holding my finger, the one I'd been jabbing him with. I didn't pull away, engrossed in what he was saying.

I narrowed my eyes sceptically. 'You can't just decide to go and find love. It's not that easy.'

Simon now had my whole left hand in his and he was playing with my fingers, teasing the ring on my finger that I pretended was a wedding ring. 'Yes it is. I think you decided to fall in love with Rob. And then you did. Just as I decided to fall in love with you. And I did.'

He was now stroking the inside of my wrist. I couldn't move. I didn't want to. 'Ah, you see that's where your argument falls down! By your own thinking, you have *chosen* to fall in love with someone who's inevitably going to cause you a degree of grief. I mean I'm married . . .'

'No you're not.'

'As good as married, with four children . . .'

'Who have another mother.'

I pulled my hand away. 'That was uncalled for. I'm still their mother.'

242

Simon took my hand again, this time more firmly. 'And always will be. Leaving them won't change that. But it won't kill them either.'

How did we get on to leaving? Who said anything about leaving? I let him touch my wrist and suddenly I'm leaving my family? This is batty. I tried to bring him back to this planet. But I left my hand in his. 'I don't want to leave them. I'm not even sure I want to leave Rob.'

Simon's got his wry look back. 'That doesn't sound very committed.'

'I mean I know I don't want to leave Rob. It's just that with Karen and everything ... Anyway, this is not about what's happening in my life.' For a change. 'It's about you breaking your rules and choosing someone who, whatever happens, is guaranteed to bring a heap of baggage into any relationship with you. If there is any relationship, that is.'

'I can deal with baggage. Baggage doesn't bother me. It's the ending that matters. Just as your story with Rob was always going to have an unhappy ending, I always felt, still do, that you and I could be going for the big chorus-line finale, standing ovations, bouquets, rave reviews, the lot. It may not look like that right now but the long-term prospects are still good.'

Now I was stroking his hand. 'What on earth makes you say that? What have I done to give you the impression that I'm looking for someone else or something else?'

'Because we're the same, you and I. We want the same things. Marriage, real marriage that is, not the pretend sort, children, real children that is, not somebody else's although I'm not belittling what you feel for your daughters, but you want your own, don't you?

You want the normal, simple stuff like me. You want to introduce somebody as your husband not your partner. You want to hold a newborn baby while your husband takes your picture. You want the same name as your children. You want an exclusive family where nobody else has claim, where there are no loose ends that constantly threaten to unravel and cause pain in your future. You don't want all this mess.'

For years, I'd got used to burying all these secret desires, feeling that they were a silly girl's dreams detached from the harsh complexities of modern existence. No intelligent girl can hope to build a clean, seamfree life with an unscarred man. It's not like that any more.

Couples live together unmarried for all sorts of reasons, none of which appear very convincing to me and all of which seem to be due to a lack of commitment. Family groups are sprawling and untidy, incorporating children from any number of previous entanglements and necessitating continued contact between former partners chained inexorably together by the accident of children. Rings are put on and taken off with or without corresponding vows. Ex-step-grand-mothers send birthday cards and children change their surnames like socks.

This life was never what I wanted and yet, Simon was right. I chose it and embraced it when I was in full possession of all the messy facts. I was hardly a spin-sterish hag with no prospect of ever meeting a decent man. I was twenty-six when I met Rob, for God's sake. I'd met other men. None who'd offered to come to Barry Manilow concerts, granted, but nice, single men without too much history. I could probably have loved them too.

But it's too late. Whatever Simon thinks about Rob and the girls surviving without me now that Karen is back in the picture, my life is unequivocally bound up with my family. *My* family. However much I may prevaricate about Rob and I admit I'm confused about the two of us, the love I have for the girls is unshakeable and unbreakable. I love them utterly and all the agony I've ever experienced is nothing compared to the agony I feel for them.

Those poor, poor girls have no idea what is going on right now. The three people who control their lives are toying with decisions that will affect them all based almost entirely on selfish desires and needs. I cannot exclude them from the equation when I evaluate my options. They are the most important part of my life, the only indisposable part, the one essential.

My love for them is physical and absolute and won't fade whether I stay there or not. And as well as the emotions, I have responsibilities and I don't intend to walk out on them just because something more straightforward has come along. I still believe they need me more than they need Karen. My birth mother may not have taken commitment to a child seriously but I do.

I disentangled myself from Simon but didn't move away. 'You're wrong and you're not being fair on yourself or on me. Nothing's going to change in the immediate future. If at all. I don't know what will happen when Rob gets back from the bloody Wolf Sanctuary but I do know that I will be there waiting for him, trying to work things through.'

Somehow, my hands were back in his, as if they had an independent life of their own. 'Lorna, I know all that and it's one more thing I love about you, your sense of duty, of what's right and wrong, your loyalty.'

I looked frankly into his eyes. 'I don't feel very loyal.'

'You'll do what you have to do. But you've already begun to distance yourself from Rob.'

'That wasn't my choice. He's the one having the experience of a lifetime with his ex-wife, his wife.'

Simon returned my gaze. 'And you're the one here with me.'

'You know why I came round. I told you on the phone. I needed someone to talk to.'

'You wanted to be with me.'

And that's how it happened. I'm so embarrassed. I don't know what came over me. We were like fifteen-year-olds, all gangly and nose-squashing and hands not knowing where to go. He was breathing when I was kissing and I was breathing when he was kissing. We made all those squelchy noises that are supposed to be drowned out by sultry music. We should have been in a sports cupboard with a bunch of schoolkids sniggering outside. There was nothing remotely adult or significant about the groping. It was my leggings that stopped things before they got irretrievable.

His fingers were poised just above the waistband and all I could think of were the fraying edges of the seam from which the elastic was poking at numerous intervals. It wasn't just that this shamed me into wanting to hide my cavalier, sluttish attitude to personal couture. It was more that I was shocked back into an awareness of who I was, all bound up in this standard piece of uniform: it told everyone who knew the rules that I was a wife and mother, that I was safe and stable, that I was not looking for change, that I was staying where I was.

I leapt up from the sofa (I'm not certain how we got

246

into the living room – by the same process of osmosis that originally conjured the leggings into my possession, I expect) and pulled myself together. I was slightly out of breath and not because we hadn't managed to synchronise our breathing during our short kissing session. My head had been spinning with a crazy jumble of conflicting thoughts, and regular breathing had been relegated to lowest priority.

Simon's last tentative touch had been like switching on a tap in my head and sluicing away all the conflicting debris leaving behind a flawless picture of a perilously close escape.

My hand rushed to my throat, which I could tell was deep red. My thinking was returning to normal but I couldn't form sensible words yet. Simon started to laugh then so did I. That's when we started apologising to each other.

'What are you going to do?' Simon asked, making more tea.

This was the funniest thing anyone had said to me for a long time. I did a brief recap of the hundred or so serious predicaments squabbling for attention in my increasingly Byzantine set of personal storylines. 'About what in particular?'

Simon saw what I was getting at and had the grace to look sheepish. 'Sorry. That was a little vague of me,' he said without going on to clarify.

I'm going to start editing the 'sorrys'. I think you've got the picture. He said it a lot more and so did I. And then we had a period of apologising for saying sorry. We were both flustered and finding it difficult to extricate ourselves from this tortuous scene.

I drank my tea while it was still scalding hot,

wanting to get out of there as swiftly and tactfully as possible. 'What am I going to do? Let me see. I'm going to contact my birth mother, prepare the four girls to have their plans for Rob's birthday surprise shattered, decide if I want to save my marr—my relationship and then work out how I do it if the answer is "yes", try and help Phillippa and Joe patch . . .'

Simon softly restrained me by touching my hand. Here we go with the hand-touching again. 'I get the picture!' he said.

It is *definitely* time for me to leave now. This time, when I pull my hand away, I fold my arms firmly so that they won't sneak their way back the way they did before. If I had been wearing a proper pair of trousers, I could have put my hands in my pockets. Back to the drawing board with the Multi-Purpose-Love-Testing-Garment concept.

I start walking backwards towards the door, wishing I had a coat and handbag to pick up to break the long journey through Simon's flat. 'Must go' I mumble, avoiding all eye contact.

He followed me to the door looking tired. 'See you tomorrow?' he suggested.

Is he mad? We needed time apart to calm things down. I had to let him down softly. Of course I couldn't see him tomorrow.

'Of course I'll see you tomorrow.'

Chapter Sixteen

the thing that they were to do, be possible. "How can we go to the sense

If the first four days of Rob's absence were like living in an Enid Blyton novel, then the last four were like *Gormenghast*. And if the girls had been younger, I would have been looking to E-numbers to absorb some of the blame. They had all been abducted by aliens and replaced by identical replica bodies inhabited by hideous mutant forms with no knowledge of social or family conventions.

Our lovely, bright Edwardian house had become a gloomy baroque sepulchre, every room overcast with each girl's particular take on the state of play. Phoebe's skin had erupted into angry spots and she was less communicative than ever. 'Did you look up that quote, Mum?' she asked me accusingly this morning.

I coughed self-consciously. 'I meant to, but I didn't know where my old Bible was. Why don't you just tell me what the quote is?' I asked cheerfully.

She retreated inside herself at that. I'd hurt her feelings, as if she wasn't under enough attack already. 'I wanted you to read it for yourself,' she whispered. And then I got it. She wanted me to know, to feel, that we could still reach each other through our private, exclusive communication. I didn't know what the content of the quote would be but I knew what it would say to me: Phoebe understood how I felt. And my failure to acknowledge her gesture told her just one thing: I no longer cared how she felt. Terrific.

Jude had a different communication problem. She'd varnished the letters b-i-t-c-h on her fingernails. The 'b' hadn't come out very well and looked like a 'd' rendering the statement somewhat meaningless. She'd also dyed her hair black. I had not passed any comment on any of this. This infuriated her even more and I wondered how far she would go to get my attention. Ali had stopped washing and refused to eat meals with us on the grounds that all food prepared by me was tainted by my meat-eating tendencies. Claire had stopped curling her eyelashes and tucking her tops into her jeans. This was her version of letting herself go without causing permanent damage to her status within her crowd. They were all furious with their father even though none of them yet knew how bad it really was.

I'd told Rob about the 'surprise' present that Claire had planned for him. He was distraught as I'd known he would be. I must be insane because I felt very sorry for him. To know that he was going to be the cause of a huge disappointment to his children must have been gut-wrenching. Whatever pleasure he derived from finding himself at the Wolf Sanctuary was conclusively snuffed out by the prospect of the confrontation awaiting him back at home.

We discussed the possibility of lying about his trip, saying that he went to visit some dog trainer in Idaho or something. But we weren't convinced it would work. Everyone at the symposium in New York knew that Rob had flown to the Wolf Sanctuary and many of them dropped by the house on occasions. There was far too great a risk of the truth slipping out. And for children as insecure as these four were during this period of transition, being lied to by their parents was the worst thing that could happen.

No, we had to tell them the truth and try and help them get over the blow as best we could. We'd tried to come up with something to take their minds off the let-down. After some very expensive transatlantic phone time, we jointly arrived at one distinct possibility: Disneyworld, Florida.

It was something we'd often discussed as a family when planning holidays, always before settling on the Norfolk Broads. The girls never thought we meant it. They knew that money was on the tight side while they were all at private school. And they weren't resentful about it. They were good kids.

But it was an ongoing fantasy and a constant source of 'one day we will . . .' daydreams. We could afford it with my money from Simon's project, especially since we wouldn't be spending it on Rob's birthday present any more. We'd tell them when Rob got home tonight.

It was only the prospect of delivering this fantastic surprise to them that made these days (just about) bearable. For Rob as well as me. That's a lie. The only thing that *really* made the days bearable was Simon. That rather murky afternoon of fumbling in his flat proved to be a turning point for us both. I finally acknowledged to myself that I had growing feelings for him, not love or at least I don't think it was love, but something tangible. And something illicit.

I met up with him every day for lunch as I'd done before but now I dropped the pretence that this was a business arrangement. I dressed carefully for each meeting as I'd done before but now I was conscious that I was dressing for him. When I put on my make-up, I watched my face in the mirror, imagining how it would look to Simon's eyes. I wore my shoes with the highest heels to bring myself closer to his six-foot height. I didn't eat breakfast because my stomach was knotted up with excitement.

If this had been Claire describing a date, I would have had a solemn talk with her about the dangers of getting too involved with a boy too soon. But I'm a grown-up and there's no one to stop me. I know how foolish I'm being. I'm like a teenager, worse than a teenager since I should know better. I'm displaying all the hallmarks of a fourteen-year-old in the throes of a major pash.

I haven't lost my objectivity. I have one eye on the facts even while my emotions are regressing to those of a hormonally overcharged pubescence. We've shared a few drinks, a few lunches, a few classes, a few hand-holds and one clumsy grope. Even I can calculate that any feelings I derive on the basis of such a thin history are going to be unreliable. Powerful but unreliable.

And, in a way, I'm happy to look at it that way. By regarding myself as a stupid woman indulging in a harmless flirtation, provoking tuts and wagging fingers from the chorus, I stop myself from facing the potential seriousness of what I might be doing.

If I ever thought for one second that I might genuinely be falling in love with Simon, I would have to start weighing up the consequences. I've got too many other issues to weigh up without throwing more consequences into the pot so I put them to one side. Perhaps I'm deluding myself but until Rob comes back and I find out how things stand between us, I don't intend to make any firm decisions or take any action that could be construed as commitment. Andrea would throw back my 'bet-hedging' accusation at me if she knew what was going on. I wish I could talk to her.

Anyway I haven't gone back to Simon's flat and he hasn't pushed the matter. After that, I haven't touched him although I've been quite incapable of pulling away from him when he holds my hand. I haven't talked about love and he hasn't talked about Rob. The website project hit a few stumbling blocks and we've spent a lot of time talking about practical problems. Until today.

I'd promised myself that I wouldn't take things with Simon any further for the time being but there was one question that I wanted cleared up. I hoped he wouldn't misinterpret any interest in the most personal side of his personal life as an indication that I was thinking of him as a future partner.

I hate that word. Partner. Simon was right about that. While I have no beliefs about marriage holding any sacred significance, one of my reasons for wanting to be married is certainly so that I can call Rob my husband. I hate introducing him as my partner. I always have to stop myself from justifying and explaining our unmarried state. I'm sure I'm just over-sensitive but I always imagine that other people are feeling sorry for me. 'Poor cow. He's got her where he wants her. Doesn't have to marry her. And when he finally meets someone he *really* loves and wants to marry, he can just shake hands with this one and chuck her out, nothing to sign, no lawyers.' OK, you've got me bang to rights, that's what *I* think when *I* meet unmarried couples. I'm probably the only person who thinks like this so ignore me.

I was curious about Simon's last girlfriend. They must have separated about seven months ago because that's when he joined my class. It occurred to me that he hadn't seemed very traumatised by the split.

'I'm not being personal here . . .' I started.

'Which means you're about to ask something outrageously personal,' Simon translated accurately.

No point in arguing. 'I was wondering about when you joined the class last term.'

'You were wondering about Sophie and what led to our split. You want all the gory details and want to know why I never talk about her while you talk about nothing except Rob and the girls.'

Hang on a second! 'No! I mean, yes, I was curious but I didn't want to pry. If you don't want to talk about it, I'd understand entirely.'

'But?' Simon prompted dryly.

I gave up the pretence. 'All right. *But* I remember you saying that you started my course because you'd just separated from a girlfriend and that it had all been very heavy.'

Simon nodded. 'That's right. She left me on the Tuesday and I enrolled in your class on the Wednesday.'

I was amazed. 'But you seemed so cheerful. How come you just got over it immediately and moved on? And when did you decide that I was going to be your next . . . whatever I am? You can't have had anything that special with this Sophie, surely?'

Simon withdrew his hand to top his wineglass up and I noticed that he didn't put it back in my hand when he was done. I'm getting observant with these little gestures. The paranoia of those early days in a new relationship, I suppose, when you're always waiting for things to go wrong, for him to look at you and realise that he's made a dreadful mistake and goes off to find someone much prettier than you. Or is that just me as well? Is everyone else out there really cool and self-assured? And what am I saying about a relationship? This isn't a relationship.

Simon started playing with his upper lip, the only indicator of stress that I've yet spotted in him. 'You're wrong all the way down the line.'

Thank you. I've always been proud of my intuitiveness. It's lovely to discover that I've been deluding myself all this time. I really needed to hear this when my own self-awareness is telling me so many things about myself that I didn't want to hear.

'Firstly, I loved Sophie. The big one. The real thing as you mentioned the other day. She was beautiful, clever, funny, kind, gentle and sensitive. She was the first girl I've ever loved and I wanted to spend the rest of my life with her.'

Is it too late for me to tell him that I've changed my mind, that I don't want to hear all this, only the bits where she is cruel, dishonest, insincere and rather ugly as well?

'We were together for twelve years,' gulp, 'and then she told me that she wanted to be sterilised.'

I was horrified. 'What for? Did she hate children that much?'

Simon was now pinching his upper lip so hard that his fingers were going white. 'Nothing so dramatic. She had no interest in children one way or the other. She was always good with friends' kids and nieces and nephews but she didn't want any of her own.'

'Yes, but to be sterilised? What if she changed her mind, when the old biological clock kicked in?'

'That was why it all came to a head. She'd always insisted that she'd never want children. And I'd always said that I would. But we were young when we met and I assumed that she'd change, like you said. I know loads of women who hated the idea of kids in their twenties then became the most devoted of earth mothers in their thirties. And I thought that's how it would be with Sophie.'

I gently teased his hand away from his lip which was starting to bleed. I wasn't supposed to be holding hands with him, it was against my self-imposed rules, but this was an emergency. He needed me and I'd never yet in my life been able to ignore someone needing me.

'So what led her into making the final decision?' I asked.

'I asked her to marry me. I mean, I'd asked her tons of times before. I'd always wanted to get married. She never did. Said she was happy living together, that it wouldn't make any difference being married. We used to have fights about it all the time.'

'So what was different the last time?'

'We both knew that it was an ultimatum. It was a turning point and we had to decide finally which way we wanted to go. She was beginning to make plans. Talking about travelling, maybe working abroad, setting up her own business. The way she told it, it sounded as if she had the next thirty years tied up.'

'And you played no part in her plans?'

'On the contrary. She'd planned my life for me too. My website company was taking off and I could run that from anywhere. So we'd live off my income for basic living expenses and she'd work for our fun money. She even had an itinerary worked out.'

He had detached his hand and was pulling on his lip again. I pulled it back. 'It wasn't what you wanted?'

He looked angry. 'Of course it wasn't! We had a

huge row. I asked her where babies fitted into this round-the-world extravaganza. She just stared at me as if I was stupid. Said that I knew she didn't want kids, she'd told me often enough. That's when I suggested that she might change in time. She went berserk. Said she would never change. That she'd always known what she wanted to do with her life and that a family would only get in her way.

'But even then I wasn't listening. I got down on one knee. Begged her to marry me. Said we could travel for a couple of years then see how she felt after that.'

'She wasn't interested?'

Simon's eyes widened in disbelief. 'Are you kidding? Have you ever heard of a woman who responded to a proposal of marriage by announcing that she was going to get her tubes tied the next day if it was possible?'

'She can't have meant it.'

'She meant it. She said it was the only way of making me accept that her decision was final. Then she asked me if I would marry her if she had the operation.'

'And?'

'And I said no. That marriage to me meant family. Without the family, you might just as well skip around the world, swapping partners, constantly reinventing yourself. But when you married, you stopped the role-play games and settled for the person you were and the person you'd decided to commit yourself to. You have kids. That's what it's always meant for me.'

'Was she upset?' I asked, curious as to the reaction of this uniquely focused woman whom I would never meet.

'Hysterical. She said I obviously didn't love her or I would marry her and accept her as she was, rather than trying to make her change to fit my needs.'

'Let me guess, you said that it worked both ways and she obviously didn't love you for the same reasons?'

Simon smiled wryly. 'Seen this film before, eh? Yes, we had a shouting contest about who loved the other the most then she stormed out. Two hours later, her brother came round with a van to pack up all her stuff. And that was the end of that.'

'After twelve years?' I was appalled. I didn't even want to think of the implications of my moving out after ten years with Rob. Putting the stuff in a van was the least of it. 'And the next day, you walk into my lecture hall as if you're the happiest man alive and start something new? Was that just an act? Were you in shock?'

Simon smiled. 'Not at all. It was twelve years but it wasn't love, I knew that. It can't have been. So I had to put it behind me and go out and find the real thing.'

I was astounded at his detachment. 'But you must have grieved? It may not have been real love for her but it was for you. You said so. You can't just switch off that feeling.'

'Yes you can. And you have to. It's perfectly clearcut. According to my definition, it's only real love if it's reciprocal. If the feeling is not returned then it was never real at all. I was deceived into thinking I was in love. Then I was enlightened. So I moved on.'

I'd never heard anyone talk like this before. It was ... foreign to me. Defining love and then adjusting the emotions to fit the definition? 'So you just got over it in a day?'

Simon found the question droll. 'Why? How long is it supposed to take? A week? A month? Three days for each year of involvement?'

'I don't know.'

'There you go, then. Neither did I. But I would have

felt really silly wasting one more single day on a love that never was, that had already taken up a massive percentage of my life.'

'I couldn't do that.'

'You could if you wanted to.' He stared out into the distance. 'And now shall I tell you the postscript, the frightfully amusing, wonderfully ironic punchline to the whole sorry joke?'

'Go on,' I answered, not sure I wanted to hear it.

'Five months later, she got engaged and now she's pregnant.'

He said it so matter-of-factly that he could have been talking about a change of job rather than a complete reversal of lifeplan. I was shocked. Not just by the bizarre actions of this woman but by Simon's ability to assimilate the news without losing his mind.

'That's unbelievable!' I said. 'You must have been stunned.'

I could feel Simon's hand relax in mine. The story was reaching its conclusion and he appeared to be calming down. I couldn't see why. I would have been murderous in his position.

'Not at all. I wasn't even surprised.'

'But you must have been. After all she said about not wanting babies. And after twelve years with you, suddenly to settle down with somebody else! How could she just change like that?'

'Don't you see? I was right all along. As I knew I was. She didn't love me. Not enough. If Sophie had loved me, she would have married me, would have had kids with me. After twelve years, we'd run our course. We'd grown and given as much as we could. She wasn't going to feel any differently even if we stuck it out for another twelve.

'Then she met someone else whom she *did* love enough. All the way apparently. Enough to want children with him. She didn't change. She was the same person that she was with me. But now she was in love. It made a difference to how she viewed her life but it didn't *change* her in any fundamental way.'

'I still don't see how she can just switch off her feelings for you after all that time and then turn on this new improved love for a stranger a couple of months later.'

'That's because you're desperately clinging on to this picture of you and Rob as two people destined to be together, lovers in every true sense of the word, hindered in your attempt to find absolute fulfilment by circumstances outside your control. You think that sheer persistence and bloody-minded stubbornness will get you what you want in the end. And you think everyone is like that. But I'm not and you shouldn't be. Not if you want to be happy.'

Now it was my turn to pull my hand away and Simon's turn to pull it back. 'It's what I've been trying to get you to see. I hate saying it because it sounds so cruel but it has to be said. You want to get married. After ten years you are not married. There is only one reason for that. It's because Rob doesn't want to marry you. He doesn't love you enough. I know you prefer to see it as all melodramatic, you and him against the world, but that doesn't hold water and, deep down, I think you know it. He doesn't love you enough, Lorna. Face it. Then decide what you're going to do about it.'

I waited for the tears. Because I wanted to cry. He was breaking my heart, tearing down all the walls of excuses that had protected me from seeing the truth for so many years. My life was based on a lie, a self-

260

inflicted one at that. I now recall with a blinding clarity that Rob never once talked concretely about marrying me. Not as such. He'd always waffled around the subject, made obscure comments about difficulties and complications and left it for me to interpret as I wished. It was I who read vague promises between the lines.

All those conversations I imagined had taken place where he swore that he would marry me as soon as he divorced Karen, none of them happened at all. Except in my imagination. And the divorce that he convinced me was impossible. It was never impossible. Just inconceivable.

Rob had all the answers. He said that divorce would hurt the girls, that its finality might unsettle them at a time they were perfectly secure with the way things stood. He said it would stir up old memories, that Karen might cause trouble, that the girls would be forced to relive the rejection of their mother all over again, that it might end up in the papers, especially since Karen was a (very) minor celebrity in the States. I allowed it to make sense at the time because I was too scared to analyse the arguments too deeply.

I'd heard it many times but the message had never sunk through until now. He doesn't love me enough to marry me. That's all there is to it. After ten years, my world should be falling around me. At the very least I should be crying. But of course I don't.

That was just one and a half hours ago and I'm still bruised. When I got home, I picked up the afternoon post and then carried out a quick inventory of the house to make sure that there was no major damage, no teenagers in states of undress in any of the bedrooms, no knotted sheets hanging from windows, no children lying unconscious on bathroom floors. That sort of thing.

Everything was ominously calm. Then I realised that they had all gone to their grandparents' house for tea. In Rob's absence, I've lost my normally instinctive grip on household routines. I don't have to look at a calendar to work out where everyone in the household is at any time of the day, seven days a week. I just know. It must be a hormonal thing because all women will tell you the same whereas men have trouble keeping up with their own appointments.

I've lost track of everything because I've dared to venture having a life outside the family calendar. I've been meeting another man for lunch. I've been to his flat. I've done things that can't be written on the official Danson Family organiser and now the whole system is collapsing. My old routine used to be so predictable that I formed the centre of a self-contained galaxy. Rob and the girls, even the dogs, all revolved around me, relying on me to stay put so that their orbits had a stable point of reference.

If it's Wednesday, I'm washing the pet blankets and it's netball practice. If I'm here, they must be there. That's how it went. But I don't know where I am any more. I know where I'm supposed to be but I ignore the call of duty and go off and do my own thing. I'm romping on the floor with a man who wants me to abandon my family so it must be ...? I'm back from lunch where I've just been informed that Rob doesn't love me, so it must be ...? God knows. I wish I didn't care that the lines are all wobbling. But I do. I feel a failure if I lower my standards. And yes, I know it serves me right for setting them high.

It's just the dependency they all have on me grinds me down sometimes. Most of the time I love being needed with such an urgency. Then there are other occasions when continuous deadlines strangle or stifle me. Like now. At this precise second, I want to sit on a beach all by myself and make a list of my own that doesn't have any headings on except 'Me'. What *I* want. What *I* need. What *I* have to do.

I'm so tired. The calendar, the demands, everyone's problems, everyone's needs, the tangles. Like most women, I am the linchpin in my family, the bit that holds all the other bits together. If I don't keep things moving on, then everything stops. But if it stopped now, I'm not sure I'd mind. And I should mind.

Frankly, I don't know why I've allowed myself to get so sucked in. Phillippa has brought up two perfectly well-adjusted sons with benign neglect. Even when she fired the au pair she still found time for manicures. But I have to put all of myself into the family. Leaving nothing over for me. What sort of return did I ever imagine receiving from such a total investment of my whole self?

Then I see it. On the kitchen table. It's another of Phoebe's little missives. She must have left it for me after our little exchange this morning. Damn! I'd meant to look that first reference up. But I was in a hurry. It's on my list, honestly it is.

I opened the note with only slightly less foreboding than the first time. It's another reference.

Dear Mum,
2 Corinthians 9: 6–7.
Love, Phoebe

I had a slight panic when I wondered if this was spiralling in some way that mirrored her own despair. The first might have been a gentle communication. But when I let her down by ignoring it, perhaps she decided to go further. Perhaps this was about death or something. Or the Devil. Perhaps it was a cry for help. It would be typical of her not to want to draw attention to herself too obviously.

We don't have our chats any more. I've tried. When she comes home from school, I sit down encouraging her to join me the way she used to. But she's always got somewhere else to go. Upstairs, out, anywhere where she can be alone. I don't know what she feels. All I have is these notes, two of them now. I really must find a Bible.

And I would have looked for one, really I would, if I hadn't glanced through the post and seen the package. It was from my mum. I ripped it open, scattering the contents everywhere. The first thing I saw was the envelope that had fallen out. Now I'm a complete sceptic when it comes to anyone claiming psychic powers. I don't believe in any of that New Age stuff or any of the supernatural mumbo jumbo (apart from the Leggings Fairy – I *know* she exists). So if you'd told me that I would be able to look at an envelope and know instantly who it came from, just by the writing, I would be mocking you remorselessly.

But this letter was from my mother. I knew it. I absolutely knew it. Not just because I don't get many handwritten letters apart from thank-you letters from various children forced against their will to write to me after birthdays and Christmas. And not just because it was glaringly plain to anybody that this was bound to be a letter from my birth mother, especially since my mum had told me she was sending it to me. Actually, she hadn't said that the letter was addressed to *me*. I'm sure she hadn't.

Anyway, none of this mattered now. I refuse to diminish the validity of my intuition. I just knew this was from her. I looked at the handwriting. Touched it. Smelled it. It was something of an anti-climax. She'd used a Biro of poor quality that left inky blobs in the middle of words. And her writing was – now don't jump down my throat, I'm just telling it how I saw it, first impressions and all that – a bit scrappy. Now you think I'm a terrible snob. It's only that I had formed a comprehensive picture of my mother and the picture included bold, looped handwriting, maybe using a coloured ink, full of personality and grace. Something special. And this? Well, it was the writing of a woman of a certain age. Someone ordinary.

I didn't want to open it. It was too important. Too much was riding on it. But this isn't a soap opera where otherwise sensible characters leave letters on tables to open later. Who does that? I've just thought – I haven't watched the telly for over a week. I haven't had the time with everything else going on. I wonder what's going on in Summer Bay? And Erinsborough? And Albert Square and Weatherfield. No I don't. I'm not wondering at all. I'm truthfully not bothered about catching up. How alarming.

I'll have to think about what this means after I've read this letter. Oh no, I'm supposed to be finding a Bible first and finding out if Phoebe is tinkering with Satanism. That's right. *Then* I'll ponder my casual desertion of my soap opera obligations.

The paper doesn't match the envelope. She couldn't even buy proper writing paper for me. This isn't starting well.

I unfold the plain white sheet. It's not long and seems to have been written in a rush. Or possibly that's the way her writing always looks. The address is in Essex. Not far, then. I read on.

16th March, 1995
Dear Nancy,

I know that's not your name now, but you will always be Nancy to me. I am writing this letter in the hope that one day you will want to find me. I'm sending this to you via your mum. From what I've heard, she's a nice lady so I'm sure she'll know what to do with this.

I'll keep it short in this first letter. If you get in touch, I'll write a longer letter next time. Or maybe we could meet.

I've never stopped thinking about you and hope you were happy with your family. I'm sorry I gave you up. I had no choice. We had no money. Your father was out of work and we were about to lose our flat. We thought it was for the best. Your dad passed on twenty years ago but I know he was always sorry that he didn't get to meet up with you again.

If you can forgive me, I'd like the chance to get to know you, tell you about why we had you adopted. You might like to know about your other family as well. After you, things picked up for your dad and me and we had four more children, two boys and two girls.

I'll send you some pictures, if you like.

Sorry again.

Love,

Betty Speck

Nancy Speck? Who the hell is Nancy Speck? Someone with a stupid name. Someone with two brothers and two sisters. Someone who came along when finances were on the tight side and so was given away. Someone whose mother waited over thirty years before bothering to try and make contact. Nancy Speck?

She's not me. No way. I screw up the piece of paper and throw it into the bin. I'm finding it difficult to breathe, I'm so consumed with hatred for *Betty Speck*, whoever she is. She can rot in hell with her four other children who were fortunate enough to be born in a more favourable economic climate. Then I retrieve the letter and smooth it out on the table and reread it. Again and again and again.

Chapter Seventeen

You'd think I'd watched enough poorly scripted drama on TV, overrun with clichés and stereotypes, to know that a spontaneous plan to surprise a loved one always ends in disaster. Simon would probably say that I guessed it would end in tears and subconsciously wanted to accelerate the asteroid of doom that was falling unstoppably towards all our heads.

He's right about everything else, so I'll bow to his judgement. Anyway, I thought it would be nice to meet Rob off his flight at Gatwick. What a brilliant idea. Or, at least, it seemed a good idea at the time. The letter from Betty Speck had unnerved me considerably and I was way off-kilter when it came to sound reasoning. By the time the girls got home from their grandmother's, I was drinking tea and talking to myself.

'Are you OK, Mum?' Phoebe asked. She looked concerned and put her arms around me in a rather oppressive hug. She didn't look as if she was in league with the Devil and I decided that I probably shouldn't worry too much about this religious flirtation. Still, if she could avoid any more notes for the foreseeable future, I'd be very grateful.

'I'm fine! Never been better!' I replied loudly. Whoops. Turn it down.

Even Claire, not famed for her perceptivity outside of

the subjects of clothes and boys, looked bothered. 'Has something happened? Is it Dad? Has something happened to his plane? He is coming home tonight, isn't he Mum?'

Ali and Jude joined in. 'What's happened to Dad?' 'Why isn't he coming home? He promised!'

The noise was unbearable. 'Will you all shut up!' I yelled. They were instantly silent. I rarely shouted and it always scared them. I took a couple of calming breaths and composed my face back to the motherly mask they all clung to. 'Sorry. But you wouldn't let me get a word in. Your dad's fine as far as I know. I checked with the airport earlier and there are no delays. His flight took off on time and should be landing in,' I checked my watch, 'about two hours.'

'Will our other mum be with him?' Ali asked.

The other three girls threw accusing glares and audible hisses at her. Ali went bright red. I rescued her. 'It's all right. I know that Karen went with your dad. She had to, it was part of the deal for your dad's free ticket.'

'See, I told you she'd know!' Ali shouted at Jude.

'No you didn't, you just blurted it out.' Claire and Phoebe looked as if they might faint with relief.

'You don't mind, do you Mum?' Phoebe asked anxiously.

Those poor wretched girls, burdened with secrets for reasons they didn't fully understand. How could I even consider leaving them for Simon? Not that I have. Not seriously. Not really. I mean, they are barely coping with the rifts caused by Karen's reappearance. And I hardly know Simon. It would be rash, stupid. And if I left at all, for any reason? Me, the stable influence in their life for as long as they could remember, the one at home twenty-four hours a day. Always available, always around. If I left?

How could I leave?

So I did what I do best. I reassured them that everything was the same as it's always been, as it should be. 'Of course I don't mind. I'm getting used to Karen being around. I was a bit iffy in the beginning, I know, but I think it's all working out just fine. I'm glad you're getting to know your mother. Honestly I am. And I don't ever want you to think you have to choose between us. Or that you have to protect me in some way.' The way they all exhaled told me I'd got it right. They were protecting me. Damn Karen for imposing this on them! She was planting wedges that didn't need to be there. If only she and Rob had been upfront about this trip, we'd all have been spared this anguish. No wonder the girls have been so difficult.

'Do you want to know a secret?' I asked them.

They all shouted 'Yeah!' as if they were children once more and not wizened old Buddhas struggling with too much knowledge. It was a split-second decision but I felt intuitively that it was the right one.

'The reason I understand how difficult all this has been for you and how you're feeling your loyalties tugged is because I'm in the same boat.'

That had them all puzzled and intrigued. 'Do you feel loyal to our other mum as well then?' asked Jude, misunderstanding entirely.

I laughed. And they laughed. Not because they got the joke but because recently they had seized on any reason for laughing, however inappropriate or unfunny the occasion might be. That's how miserable this house had become. 'No. I'm in *exactly* the same position as you.'

I left it to them to work out. They all know that I'm

adopted but we don't talk about it much. Not for any particular reason, it just hasn't been of great interest to the girls. Phoebe twigged first. 'You've found your real mother!'

I nodded, pleased that Phoebe was still intuitively bound to me. The other girls all began talking at once. 'You're kidding! What's she like? Is she rich?' Claire asked.

'That's a terrible thing to say, Claire!' Phoebe exclaimed.

'She must be really old,' Ali pointed out.

Jude seemed to be following a different line. She had a serious expression on her face when she finally spoke her piece. 'What does Granny F think about all this?' Jude asked.

That deflated the balloon of excitement pretty effectively. I tried to bluff it out. 'Oh you know Granny F. Made a lot of tea, blustered about. She's fine about it. Not bothered at all. Why should she be? She's my real mother and always will be.'

But I don't think my act was convincing. My heart wasn't in it. It was too busy beating too fast as I thought about what I was going to tell my mum. She knew that I was thinking about my birth mother but that was a wholly separate matter from making direct contact with the woman.

I appreciate this only too well. I always knew that Karen was out there. I always knew that she would come back into the girls' lives at some stage in the future. I dealt with that without any difficulty. But when she became a flesh-and-blood person, talking to my children, having input in their development, touching them, it was another issue.

She posed a threat, pure and simple, to everything I'd achieved and was holding on to. She would be diluting my relationship with my daughters, influencing their life choices, guiding them in other directions. That's the official line. Then there are the unmentionables, the worries that I can't voice because they reveal me in a poor light.

Worries that the girls might like Karen more than me. That they might find her advice more useful. That they might play us off against each other. That they might see me as the stopgap that it turns out I always was and pack me off to carry out my stand-in duties in another abandoned family. Bye-bye, you've been swell but we don't need you any more.

It may not be quite like that for my mum. I'm an adult for one thing, the bulk of the mothering process is complete and we're just in the maintenance phase. I'm also supposedly mature enough to be able to analyse the situation dispassionately and be cautious in how I handle the sharing of information with both women so that nobody is offended or hurt. There shouldn't be secrets or taking of sides.

So if it's all that easy, then why am I dreading breaking the news to her?

Which is why I'm going to meet Rob off his plane. So that I can put off calling my mum. I'll do that tomorrow. And also because I want to see Rob's face as soon as possible to see if it's changed. Or if it's stayed the same but I've changed. To see where I was going wrong in believing I saw love in his eyes when it transpires I was misled.

And the girls thought it was a good idea. First of all they wanted to come with me. And they wanted to bring the dogs. I saw this as a need to see the family together in every sense of the word. I dissuaded them on practical grounds. There was no room in the car for us all and their dad's cases and document bags, since none of knew how to put the roof rack on.

Then they thought that two of them might go. You can guess how that discussion went. Each girl declared that she should go for a very good reason: because she was the oldest, youngest, smallest, Dad's favourite (very dangerous ground, Claire), hadn't been suspended etc. The list went on and tempers began to spark.

'Right, that's it! I'm going by myself.' I grabbed the car keys and headed for the door.

The girls all groaned. 'Oh Mum! It's not fair.' It was Jude who came out with that classic. You don't know the half of it, I thought.

I'm not sure when it first hit me. Certainly not during the drive to Gatwick. I spent most of that time alternating between thinking about Simon and then pushing the thoughts aside guiltily. So it wasn't until I was approaching the airport that I remembered Karen.

I'd been far too bogged down with more pressing concerns to think about her before. As a general survival tactic, I've been trying to shove her out of my mind whenever I could. But it struck me like a slap that she was going to be at the airport too. Obviously. She and Rob were travelling together as a matter of necessity so they would be arriving together. I wanted to turn round and go straight home but I couldn't. It would be too awkward to explain to the girls. Besides I'm a grown woman. I can handle this.

The traffic was heavy and I got there just as the plane was landing. I parked the car and went to the arrivals lounge. I wondered what I looked like since I'd left the house in a hurry. I gave myself a quick once-over in the ladies' loos. Rob won't recognise me, I thought. I've got a new dress on which I wore to meet Simon for lunch. Didn't I mention that? I'm sure I did. And I'm wearing make-up which I never usually wear during the day. I look like another woman. Which I am. I wonder what Rob will think. I'm more intrigued than worried. Another bad sign.

But the biggest change is in my eyes. He must surely notice it because I can feel it emanating from me like lasers. The love I felt for him has gone. Vanished. Died. Or the old love has. The one that I thought was reciprocated.

It's been replaced by something more tentative, more suspicious, more exploratory. I think I still love him. But I can't shake off Simon's definition of love only being love if it's returned. Because I believe that too. And try as I might to reproduce the feeling of love I felt for Rob when he got on the plane last week, I can't. It's gone. And I don't know what's in its place yet.

I made my way to the gate where he was scheduled to arrive and watched as the first trickle of passengers started to emerge. I scrutinised every face, pondering the ludicrous possibility that Rob's appearance might have altered dramatically over the last eight days. Every so often, a group would turn the corner, huddled together, so that I couldn't see all the faces in the centre of the group hidden behind backpacks and foolish hats. Left and right I looked, avoiding eye contact as one does. The crowds dwindled until the stragglers filtered through in ones and twos.

Then I saw them. Long before they saw me. They were together, properly together, anyone could see that.

Well, not anyone. You'd have to know Rob, to know how he detested casual intimacy, how he reserved his limited quota of physical affection for his daughters and for me. And for dogs. It was something we shared in common, the dislike of hugging or being hugged or kissed by almost-strangers on the strength of a ten-minute acquaintance.

Rob and I had both been horrified at the last PTA meeting when the teachers all greeted us with mwah-mwah air kisses and strokes of the arm. We managed to dodge the worst of excesses by waving from a distance. This unwillingness to conform apparently condemns us as social pariahs. Can't say we've lost much sleep over it.

So if you bear that in mind, you'll know why my stomach sank when I saw Karen holding Rob's arm. Rob allowing Karen to hold his arm. They seemed so . . . at ease, at peace with each other. They were talking companionably and even though they didn't look happy, they were fully attuned to each other. The looks they exchanged were full of shared experience and they were speaking in conversational shorthand, not needing superfluous gestures to animate their talk. There wasn't much laughter. Whatever they were discussing was serious.

They looked like a couple. They looked like a married couple. You could read it on his face. On both of their faces. There was no urgency there, no sense of desperation to recapture something that had long passed beyond their reach. Whatever was in the past was there no longer. It was back in the land of the living. My living.

Just before they came though the barrier, something happened that confirmed my suspicions beyond all doubt. They were both carrying bags but he stopped and

275

put down one of his carriers. He then brought her to a
halt, turned her face towards him and tenderly flicked
back a strand of hair that was draping over her eyes and
annoying her. He tucked the strand behind her ear
without apologising, without speaking at all. It wasn't
Rob's action that told me that he had slept with his wife.
I mean recently, it was her lack of surprise or gratitude.
She accepted it. She expected it. Then they saw me.

Their faces dropped with one fluid, perfectly synchro-
nised movement. I bet he wouldn't bump *her* hips at a
Barry Manilow concert, I thought. I bet they'd sway in
perfect harmony like a fused human metronome. They
recovered reasonably quickly, all things considered. I
watched with sadistic pleasure as they did a quick recce
of their stuff to make sure that nothing incriminating
was on display. Nope, no tights dangling from his
jacket pocket, no Y-fronts twisted round her coat
button. Their hair was in place and Rob's mouth was
not smeared with her (expensive) lipstick.

I wasn't going to confront Rob here and now. I
needed to think before I said anything that committed
us to a plan of action we would both regret. More
importantly I needed to discover how I felt. Nothing
was clear any more.

I had the upper hand because they assumed that this
absence of physical evidence let them off the hook. Sad
deluded creatures that they were, they had no idea that
an intimacy as absolute as theirs would glow through
even if there was a brick wall between them. So many
things were rushing through my head that I said nothing
and Rob beat me to the first word.

'Hi! You look ... amazing! What a surprise! We
weren't expecting you.'

Oh, Rob, listen to the way that 'we' tripped off your tongue. You don't know what you're saying but unless you shut up right now, there will be no way of back-tracking from your self-incrimination. Funnily enough, Karen spotted this as soon as he said it. She would. She's married to him.

She and I had not yet found a level of communication that we were both fluent with. We hadn't made much effort, if you want to know the truth. We were both content to keep all our meetings restricted to civil, factual exchanges. If we managed to avoid snide digs or defensive insults, then we both adjudged it a result.

Consequently we were a bit lost as to how we should behave towards each other in this unplanned encounter. She must have been petrified that I was going to hit her as indeed I might have if I hadn't been too repressed to cause a scene in public. She knew that I knew. I could sense that. She saw in the way I looked at Rob and then at her. Rob hadn't got a clue. Bless him, he's got none of the necessary qualities for a serial philanderer. He will sleep well, secure in the knowledge that, unless there are videotapes of his adultery (now I come to think of it, since he is still married to Karen, it's only adultery when it's with me), then he can't be accused of any wrongdoing.

But Karen and I know better. We know how pupils dilate when a lover is in visual range, how a voice modulates when a lie has been told, how a man can't hide his past from any woman who cares enough to look for the proof.

There's nothing to say on the subject that won't set off a sequence of explosions that none of us are ready for. Yet.

Karen takes the initiative and skilfully swerves all the

mines. 'Rob had to wait for me at passport control. There was a problem with my having been working in the States for so long then coming back to live. The computers had me down as a possible illegal immigrant.'

This was supposed to be funny, I believe. We all laughed with such a loud, mirthless roar that the security officers manning the gates appeared alarmed.

Then we were silent. It was apparently my turn to say something vacuous. 'I thought I'd surprise you by meeting you,' I said. Yes. As vacuous as it gets.

Rob leapt on the cue like a dog with a sausage. 'It is a surprise. A wonderful surprise.'

'I thought you'd appreciate a lift,' I continued, looking at all the bags. Then I noticed that none of the bags were Rob's. 'Where are your cases, Rob?' I asked. My God, Karen had three suitcases for an eight-day trip, she must have changed every two hours.

Rob looked gloomy. 'They put them on the wrong flight. Someone from the airline alerted me while we were in the air. They're on the next flight out of JFK. Won't be here for another five hours.'

He looked at me for an answer to this dilemma. As if I was his mother. He gave up waiting when he saw my face hardening. 'So it's a bit of a pickle, really. I've got to hang around here till the bags turn up. But the airline are paying for a taxi to get me home. Which is good of them, isn't it?'

'Why can't you come home with me now, Rob, and the airline can send the bags on to you in the taxi? Why do you have to sit in the taxi with the bags?'

'Airline policy. I have to claim the baggage myself.'

I was growing impatient with him. 'For God's sake, Rob, this is their fault and they have to sort it out. They

278

can bring the bags to our home and you can claim them there.'

He was avoiding my glare. 'The thing is, I said I'd wait here. It was the girl on the desk who made the mistake. She phoned me in tears. She's asked one of the stewardesses on the next flight to check the baggage through and just hand it over to me so there's no official note made of the mistake. I didn't want to get her in trouble.'

Welcome back headache, my old friend. 'So if it's not official, how are they organising a taxi for you?'

He didn't answer. I slapped the side of my head as the penny dropped. 'I get it. There is no organised taxi. You just made that up so I wouldn't think you were a complete idiot. You're quite happy to ruin the girls' homecoming dinner, when they are already about to be dealt a massive blow by you, and you're quite happy for me to have wasted three hours on a futile journey. But some incompetent girl on a desk on the other side of the world *cries*, and you drop all your responsibilities to accommodate her.'

He said nothing. Karen was about to say something, in his defence I expect, and then wisely thought better of it. She started rummaging around in her handbag. It's what women do in these challenging situations when tea-making facilities are not available.

Rob held out his hand weakly to touch mine. It was supposed to be conciliatory but it enraged me. I shook it off irritably. 'That's what it all boils down to, isn't it? The tears. You can't stand it, so you buckle under every time. Like your *wife* here crying in Pizza Express, *our* Pizza Express, or is it *your* Pizza Express? She cries so that's it. All is forgiven! Never mind the last ten years when she left your children without a mother. Never mind all the things you said about her when she didn't get in touch.'

Karen looked up sharply at Rob when she heard that. She would have interrupted but she wasn't quick enough. I had months of unspoken resentments that I had to get out in the open and where better than the arrivals lounge at Gatwick airport before an audience of fascinated strangers? Anywhere, now I come to think about it. Still, too late to worry about that now.

'So is that what you want from me? Is that what I have to do? Cry? Go all weepy and gooey and fall on your manly shoulder? Because I thought you loved me for my strength. That's what you've always said. Well maybe you've never said it as such but it's what you led me to believe. But if it's crying that gets your attention then I'll start doing that. Will you come back to me then?'

'I haven't left you,' Rob said softly.

An ear-piercing shriek followed by an unintelligible announcement deafened what he said next. I can't be sure, I think he might have said 'I love you' or 'I need you' or perhaps it was 'I'm leaving you.' I should have said 'pardon' but I didn't. I wasn't ready for big truths. I can't tell if he knew that I hadn't heard him but he didn't repeat whatever he said.

'So what do you want to do?' he asked wearily.

Back to me again. I want someone else to make the decisions, that's what I want, what I really, really want. I sighed. 'I suppose you've got to wait for the bags now you've made the arrangements. I can't hang around and wait with you though. I've got to get back to the girls.' The girls. I'm going to have to be the one to tell them that their dad will be late. Great.

'And what about you?' Me? What's that supposed to

280

mean? But he wasn't talking to me. He was talking to Karen. I'd forgotten she was there for a glorious five seconds. Who cares what she's going to do? As long as she doesn't cry, she might just get out of here without a vicious physical assault.

Karen started dithering. I didn't have her down as a ditherer and I was pleased to add another flaw to my list. 'I don't know. I haven't got any cash on me. I'll have to wait and share your taxi, I suppose.'

I felt Rob's questioning gaze on me. This is priceless. This is worse than *Take Your Pick*. At least in that show, some of the choices turn out to be good. It's all down to me. I know exactly what this means. I can either give Karen a lift home and expose myself to an hour or so trapped in a one-to-one showdown with her or I can leave her to spend another five hours with Rob. The two of them alone. With airport hotels a breath away.

I choked out the words. 'I suppose I could give Karen a lift.' Karen looked as if she would rather spend a month with a Jehovah's Witness than an hour with me. That cheered me up considerably. If it made Karen suffer, it might not be so bad.

I let her grope for an excuse, an alternative solution to her dilemma. 'Couldn't you lend me the money for a taxi?' she asked Rob pleadingly.

He scratched his head. 'Sorry, I haven't got any cash on me. I was going to use a hire firm I know where you can pay by credit card.'

'Then I can do the same!' she exclaimed in joy.

Rob shook his head. 'You've only got an American Express card. They don't take that.'

For one insane second I watched her brain debate whether or not she could ask me for a loan. Don't even think of going there, Karen. She was smart enough to dismiss the idea swiftly.

How cruel am I? Could I stand there for another hour while she worked her way through a catalogue of ever more impracticable possibilities until she resorted to selling her body or hitch-hiking?

I looked at my watch. It was no use. I couldn't hang around any longer. I had to get back to the girls. I made up Karen's mind for her. 'Oh for goodness' sake, I'm leaving now and you may as well come with me. You can see the girls, explain why their father's been held up. You might be able to pacify them.'

Karen hesitated. She shot one last worried glance at Rob. Probably wondering if it was worth turning on the waterworks. Don't try it, sister. I'm not in the mood. Rob didn't respond. Smart move, Rob.

'Right then,' Karen said with as much grace as she could muster, which wasn't a lot. 'Off we go.'

The three of us stood there like characters in a Bergman film, our inaction substanceless and stultifying. We couldn't settle on a goodbye protocol that satisfied our unhappy triangle of interconnections. Since I was the only one in a hurry, I took the initiative.

'See you later, Rob,' I said. 'Give me a call if you're going to be delayed any longer. You know the girls will want to wait up for you.'

I didn't kiss him. I bustled about with Karen's trolley to hurry her along. 'Are you coming?' I asked her impatiently.

Karen jumped. 'Right. Thank you. Right. Erm, bye Rob. I'll . . . be in touch.'

I watched Rob closely to see how he let her go. He wore his guilt like a badge and averted his face, pretending to look for something in his jacket. 'Absolutely. Bye.'

Karen waited but Rob didn't say anything more. She pulled her coat around her and began following me towards the exit.

'Karen!' We both turned round at Rob's shout. He looked lost. 'Thanks. For everything. You know.'

She knew. I knew. We all knew. When Karen got into my car, we both knew exactly where we stood.

Chapter Eighteen

'Did you start sleeping with him before the trip or during it?' I asked. We hadn't even left the car park but it seemed foolish to waste time on niceties. I was stuck with her, I might as well get a few things sorted.

Karen stared at me in disbelief. 'What are you talking about?'

I sighed, bored already. 'I'll tell you what, Karen, let me whizz through the preliminaries so that this journey isn't any longer than in needs to be. You'll say you're not sleeping with Rob and I'll say that I know you are. Then you'll work your way through the standard responses from indignant through defensive through to qualified confession all the way to reasonable and unreasonable excuses and a promise that it won't happen again.'

Karen sat up to start the indignant bit but slumped straight back down. 'It's not what you think.'

'Of course it's what I think. I think you're sleeping with Rob. That's all I think and that's true.'

'It's more . . .'

I helped her out. 'Complicated? Involved? Sordid? Banal?'

'If you're going to be like this, then we're not going to get very far.' I got the impression that this was the professional tone she assumed with her crazy clients.

'I'm not under any illusion that we'll get anywhere. I didn't offer to give you this lift, I was conned into it. I'm hoping that I never have to spend such an uninterrupted time in your exclusive presence again. But since I have been forced into this, I may as get the unpleasant business out if the way so that we've got no misunderstandings between us. Now, did you start sleeping with him before the trip or during it?'

'You don't want to know all this,' she said gloomily.

I spotted the speedometer climbing fast and slowed down. Unless I can selectively kill my passenger, I would rather not crash the car. 'Yes I do and I'm going to keep asking the question until you answer it.'

'It was only once.'

'Before or during?' I asked for the hundredth time.

'During.' There. That wasn't too hard, was it? I feel sick.

'When during?' I asked.

'What do you mean when?'

She is a very irritating woman with all these counter-questions. 'I mean, was it in New York, or was it at the Wolf Sanctuary?'

She shifted uncomfortably in her seat. 'It was at the Wolf Sanctuary.'

I slap the steering wheel with aggression I didn't know I had in me. 'I *knew* it! I knew it. You knew it would work, didn't you? Even after all these years, you knew which button to press. Please, *please*, don't insult me now by saying that it just happened, that you didn't plan it. We both know that's a lie. What other purpose could you have for booking the trip for him?'

'He told you, didn't he? It was an early birthday present.'

'Yeah, right. A five-thousand-dollar trip. I'm not

285

strong on the etiquette of present-buying between estranged spouses but I think a keyring might have been more suitable.'

'Think what you like,' she said sulkily. Ding! That's where Jude gets her sulking talent from.

'Well, we'll ignore your protestations that it wasn't planned because we both know it was. Next question. What do you want?'

'What do you mean?'

'I wish you'd stop asking me what I mean. If I want a shrink, I'll find someone in the Yellow Pages who analyses inkblots. You know exactly what I mean. So answer my question. Please.'

She started fiddling with her nails. 'I presume that you want to know if I want Rob back?'

'Exactly,' I said, hoping that my one-word answers would dissuade her from waffley pronouncements that gave me nothing.

'Yes,' she said. Just like that.

Her bluntness was absolutely unexpected and I was stunned.

'Aren't you going to ask me if *he* wants *me* back?' Karen enquired. I wasn't planning on it. I hadn't thought that far ahead. But I couldn't back down now.

'Well, does he?' I asked, failing in my attempt at nonchalance.

'No,' she said. Just like that.

We left it at that. It was too much information for me to filter and react to. I didn't have enough tablets for it. I merely summed up my response with a judgemental tut that I thought was quite expressive. I suppressed my anger because I didn't think I'd be able to drive home if I unleashed it. I needed to stay in control at least while

I was in the car. I wanted her to be quiet so I could think. But she kept on talking.

'I can't predict the outcome and neither can you, but you have to believe that my main concern will always be the girls. I know how much you love them and how worried you must be about the effect all this is having on them. Well it's the same for me. It always has been,' Karen said quietly.

'*Hah*! So concerned that you didn't even want to see them for ten years?'

'Of course I saw them,' she retorted. 'I came back half a dozen times a year, every year. It was sheer torment but I couldn't stay away. I spent hours standing behind trees watching you playing in the park with *my* children. I put on stupid wigs and sneaked into school plays. I watched sports days with binoculars in an adjoining field. I even hid in the bushes on their birthdays so that I could peer through the windows and watch them blowing out the candles on their cakes. I was always there. How do you think I amassed so many Air Miles?'

I almost swerved off the road. I thought of Rob's words to me when I told him that this was what I would have done. 'Not everyone is as devious as you,' he had said. This woman was becoming more real with every revelation. She was getting fleshier, harder to dismiss. She had done exactly what I predicted a real mother would do. She wasn't crazy and detached. She was sane and normal and focused.

I had to reassess everything now. It was as if Rob had come back with a complete stranger and I'd found out that *she* was my rival after all. I wasn't equipped for this particular battle. I'd need new tactics, new weapons.

Karen was still waiting for my response to her confession. 'Are you surprised?'

I raised my eyebrows. 'I'm shocked. I can't believe you got away with it. We never had any idea that you were there. And your parents never let on.'

She turned to face the road again. 'That's because they didn't know. They would have been petrified that I was having a breakdown again. I couldn't put them through it. So I came over without telling them and stayed in hotels. It became a routine part of my life.'

It didn't make sense to me. 'So why didn't you try and get in touch properly? Why did you wait all this time before contacting Rob?'

'You didn't believe it when I said it before, but maybe you will now. At the time, I sincerely believed it was best for the girls that I stay out of the picture. I could tell that they were settled and happy with Rob. And with you. I've learned a lot about how children's minds work in the past years. Although they seemed stable and secure from quite early on after you moved in, it would have been a long long time before they truly began to be healed. Any more upheaval and the damage could have been irreversible.'

'But you could have stayed in contact with Rob. Found out how the girls were doing. Let him tell you all the things you can't find out by sneaking around bushes. He might have understood.'

'And what would have happened to the two of you?'

'What do you mean?' Oh no, now I'm saying it. Still I have an excuse. I don't claim to be a professional mindreader and inquisitor. I'm allowed to ask stupid questions.

'Think about it. If I'd been on the phone to Rob

288

every five minutes, he would always have wondered if I was planning to come back. And you . . .'

And I would have realised that he was incapable of committing to me while his wife was always hovering over us. I wouldn't have hung around for long. I recalled Simon's theory and had to put it to her.

'If I hadn't been in the picture, would you have gone back to Rob?'

Karen acted as if she needed to give the question some thought even though she must have flogged the subject to death over the years. 'Maybe. Eventually. I was sick, you know. Mentally ill. It was a genuine illness. And although after a couple of months, I recovered sufficiently that I could more or less function, I couldn't have been a mother to my girls for quite a long time more.'

'That wasn't what I asked you.' I was less aggressive now.

'No it wasn't. You may not like this but the answer is yes. I probably would have gone back, certainly during the first year when the babies were all still so little. I even discussed it with my doctors. They were satisfied that I would never harm them, that my problem was one of coping. They felt that I might recover better at home. I could have had help for the children and continued treatment for me. Then as my strength returned, I would gradually take over some of the child-care until I was able to cope with the whole scenario.'

Great plan. I'm not a psychiatrist but even I can see that this was the most obvious way of getting this troubled mother back to health. What sort of healthcare professional would ever say to a mother: 'Here's a good idea. Go away for ten years. Don't have any contact with your husband or small children. Deny all your maternal impulses. Stop loving your husband. You'll feel heaps better in no time at all.'

So why did we all just accept that it was for the best for Karen and for ourselves if we just forgot all about her and planned our long-term futures without her? Because it was best for us, that's why. We didn't care about Karen, we just pretended that we did to make ourselves feel less selfish. She was the villain of the piece after all, neglectful abandoning mother, runaway wife. Even knowing she was ill didn't absolve her from blame because her illness was misunderstood. Mental illness never gets the same level of sympathy or attention as a physiological one. She'd have got a better press if she'd hurled herself down the stairs and exploited a full complement of broken bones.

'I'm lost. I don't know where I'm going,' I said edgily.

Karen touched my hand on the gear stick. I changed gear hurriedly and removed my hand. What is it about my hand that makes everyone want to touch it? I can go for days, years even without needing to stroke anybody's hand. If Karen and I ever get over this agonising awkwardness, I must ask her professional opinion on the psychological undercurrent of this impulse I inspire in everybody I meet.

She assumed her most empathetic voice. 'Of course you feel lost. Anyone in your position would be. I can guess what you're going through. You want to hate me. You probably do hate me. You need to hate me if you're going to fight me. And it's easier if you see me as some unfeeling monster with hideously fiendish motives. You've built me up in your imagination as someone undeserving of the slightest acknowledgement, let alone the love, of four sensitive adolescent girls that you are justifiably proud of nurturing.'

290

'You're right about that,' I was about to say. But she hadn't finished. I was trundling along in third gear, unable to change up for fear of encouraging further hand contact. I'm developing quite a complex about it, actually.

'But now you've learned something that you didn't want to know,' she continued.

'Yes, that you're sleeping with my husband,' I said, defying her to correct my use of the word 'husband'.

'You could handle that if it wasn't for the fact that you've just learned how like you I am.'

And with that staggering pronouncement, I braked the car to a screeching halt (without changing gear).

'I beg your pardon?'

'That's why you're feeling lost, Lorna. You've lost your balance, lost your way. You were over here and I was over there and now we're both in the same place. You thought you had your bearings and then I swept them away from under you. And you don't know where to go from here.'

I spoke as clearly as I could. 'Karen. The reason I said I was lost is that I *am* lost. Lost as in, I don't know what this road is except it's not the A217. As in, missed my turning and haven't seen a signpost for five miles. As in, going to have to turn back and look for the right road.'

I did a gear-scrunching U-turn, confident that Karen wouldn't dare touch my hand again. 'Sorry,' she said, abashed. 'I misunderstood you.'

'Yes you did. But that's all right. Because I didn't misunderstand you, Karen. To give you credit, you weren't far off in that assessment of me. I was a bit taken aback that you're not the person I thought you would be. It's been very enlightening. You've had a

291

tough time of it. But I've always known that. Ever when I was petrified that you'd come back, I still thought of you, of your pain. I pitied you, any feeling woman would do the same.

'And I believe a lot of what you said about why you stayed away. It must have been a long time before you truthfully felt that you could offer something to your daughters again. And by then, I had moved in. And very happy we all were too. So you watched from a distance, played for time.'

Karen gasped. 'Are you saying that I stayed away because I didn't think I could win them back from you at that point? Because I wasn't good enough?'

'That's what I'm saying, yes. And I think you've come back now because you think the climate is right for the odds to shift in your favour. And you're probably right. Your masterful ploy with the Wolf Sanctuary proves that Rob is weak.'

'Well if you are insinuating that any of my behaviour has *not* been motivated out of love for my daughters you are very much mistaken.'

We were approaching a red light. I slowed down and took a second to stare at her face. There were tears on her cheeks. I hadn't been wrong, she was crying. Doubtless, I shouldn't have said what I said but it was at the front of my mind today and it was pertinent. 'I know you love your daughters. But you didn't come back and fight for them before. And that means only one thing to me – you didn't love them enough. Well I do.'

The girls came rushing to the door to meet us. They were surprised to see Karen and unsure how to behave towards her. But their uncertainty was outweighed by their attempts to spot their dad on the path. 'Don't panic, kids, your dad's been delayed ...' The girls began remonstrating and I held up my hand to calm them down. 'Listen to me. He's got to wait at the airport to pick up his luggage that was put on the wrong plane.'

Ali chirped up, 'That happened to Sandra Cross's dad and the airline sent the cases to his house in a limousine the next day *and* gave him fifty pounds. Why does Dad have to hang around and get it himself?'

I put on my Julie Andrews no-nonsense face. 'You'll have to ask him that when he gets home. But it won't be until very late, I'm afraid.' They all groaned again. By this time, we'd all moved into the living room, Karen following behind like a double-glazing salesman unsure of the welcome she'll get.

'So you might be better off going to bed and seeing Dad in the morning,' I ventured.

Further howls of protest greeted this as I knew they would. 'OK, OK, you win, you can stay up.' Cheers at last. I'm the good guy once more. 'So shall we order the pizza now?' They were less enthusiastic than they would have been if their dad had been here, but their teenage appetite won over in the end and we ordered an absurd amount of pizza, garlic bread and ice cream.

While we waited, Karen opened one of her bags. 'I expect you're all waiting for your presents,' she announced, handing them all small packages. The girls yelped with delight and I watched with interest as they unwrapped their presents. I couldn't see immediately what they were. They looked like radios or computer games.

Phoebe came rushing over. 'Look Mum. It's a miniature telly! Isn't it fantastic!' There was a small compensation in the relief I felt that Phoebe could still be so excited by a telly. It was wonderfully normal. Religion can't be having too negative an impact on her after all. (I must look up those Bible quotes.) Then all the girls rushed up to their rooms to see if they worked up there as of course they would.

I thought about what Karen had done. I was careful with my choice of words. 'You bought them each their own television set?'

Karen thought I was overwhelmed with her generosity. 'They are only little. They cost next to nothing in the States. And I know how mad you all are about TV in this house. They're always talking about it!'

I nodded slowly. 'So you thought I would approve of them all having their own sets?'

She was looking nervous now. 'As I said, they're only little sets. Have I offended you in some way?'

She'd never get it, not in a million years. People of my generation who have grown up loving TV see things differently. Television used to be a member of the family with personality and rights. There was only ever one in each family. And no video, of course. They didn't come for years.

Families watched television together. They negotiated their own rules for selecting programmes. It was usually your mum who had the final say on what you all watched. Unless there was sport on and your dad always got to watch that. And because of this, children absorbed their parents' culture. Which became the family TV-watching culture. They watched the films their parents liked and so classics were established. Programmes were made for the whole family, the whole nation, that's why sitcoms were ageless and classless.

It forged a unifying thread across generations.

Brought the country together. And if you think I'm just being sentimental, then maybe I am. But my daughters know more about world cinema than any of their contemporaries, because they watch it with me. And I know more about *Hollyoaks* than any of my contemporaries because I watch it with them.

It's part of our life as a family and the minute you break up the family routine in any way, the whole fabric becomes threatened. It sounds crazy but it holds true for us. They now have their own little sets. They will stay in their rooms, watching an undiluted diet of teentrash. They won't bother with that documentary on suffragettes next week even though I know they'd enjoy it if they watched it with me. They'll watch the soaps alone and so will I and they won't be funny any more.

Have you offended me, Karen? You have no idea. And there's not a thing I can do about it because I could never take the sets away from the girls now they have them. But even though it's a big deal to me, I can't get excited about it. It's one more thing but it's not the biggest thing. If the worst hurdle we face as a family is a surplus of TVs, we should be OK. Look at me, I can even smile about it.

Because, do you know what's really funny? It's that Karen *actually* chose this present thinking that I would be as pleased as the girls, that I would appreciate her contribution to the defining leisure pursuit of this family. And it's wonderful how wrong she's got it! Denise Robertson would *never* have made that mistake. Richard and Judy wouldn't stand for it. Call yourself a daytime TV shrink? Hah!

'It's fine, honestly. I was surprised, that's all. It's a lovely present, Karen.' I walked away to the kitchen, took tablets and calmed down.

When the food arrived I took pity on her. The girls were showing her something on their mini TVs but she was very ill at ease. The conversation in the car had not resolved any of the conflict between us, it had churned up even more. We talked all the way home but only one thing stuck in my head – the bit where she said that she wanted Rob but he didn't want her. She sounded beaten. And even if I didn't know what this all meant, I was top dog once more in her eyes and could afford to be generous.

Besides, she was my daughters' mother and she was going to be around for good. I'd promised myself that I wouldn't expose the girls to the fallout of our problems and I meant it. Also, it was too exhausting and I wasn't as cruel as I liked to think I was.

I asked her to come and help me in the kitchen. She looked as tired as I felt and appeared to be psyching herself up for another attack on her motivations.

'Don't worry,' I said, 'I'm not starting it all up again.'

She exhaled in relief. 'Thank God,' she said, 'I couldn't take any more. I've got such a headache.' She rubbed her temples.

'Do you want to take something for that?' I asked.

'What have you got?' she asked. I opened my hangover cupboard and Karen burst out laughing. 'A girl after my own heart!'

She saw my eyes widen and slapped her hand over her mouth. 'I didn't mean that! You are nothing like me! Is that better?'

'Much,' I replied, grateful for the relaxation in hostilities. (This woman has slept with my husband – have I forgotten that? Why am I not beating her with her my tenderising mallet?) 'Help yourself,' I ordered her.

She examined all the various proprietary brands until she found the one with the highest dose of active ingredients and took four. She's a girl after *my* own heart. (*I* can say that because I am the woman scorned in this little triangle. *She* can't because she is the scorner. Those are the rules.)

After she'd swallowed the tablets, she livened up. It was the prospect of the tablets working that generated the most benefit, in my opinion and in Karen's too, it seems.

'Better?' I asked.

'Much. Can I do anything to help?'

'You can. But not in the kitchen.' I swallowed all the resentment I harboured against her and told her what I was thinking. She was the only person I could share it with. 'I'm worried about Phillippa. Andrea too, although for different reasons.'

Karen nodded. 'I called them both from the States.' My surprise must have been evident. 'I may be the worst mother in the world as well as the worst friend but I'm doing my best to make amends.' I noted her gently self-mocking tone.

'How were they?' I asked, unsure of how much she knew.

She faltered. I got it. 'You're not sure how much I know,' I surmised.

Karen screwed up her face in acknowledgement that she'd been found out.

'It's OK,' I said, 'I was wondering the same about you.'

'Shall we both assume that the other knows everything? It'll make things easier,' Karen proposed.

'Good idea,' I agreed. 'Anything that makes anything easier is fine by me. So what was going on with them both?'

'They were both in a mess. I spoke to Andrea first to find out how much, if anything, Philly knows about her and Joe.'

Philly?

'Is Phil still in the dark?' I asked.

'Thankfully, yes. But I don't know how long that will last. Dan's the loose cannon in all this. He is burning up with jealousy about Andrea and Joe. I can't see him managing to keep it buried for much longer.'

I agreed. 'Our only hope is that he and Andrea work out their differences and try and patch things up. Then there would be no mileage in having it out with Joe.'

'Do you think that's feasible?' Karen asked glumly.

'Not really,' I replied.

'I agree. What really upset Andrea was that she found out that Dan's affair with the teacher was cooling. But of course, when he found out about Andrea and Joe, that just made him ten times worse. He hardly ever comes home now. Mind you, even if there was a miracle and they all sorted out their differences, the couples won't be able to stay friends. And I don't see how they're all going to explain that to Phillippa.'

'How was Phil when you spoke to her?' I was cutting the pizza slowly, ignoring the screams for food from the living room. I didn't want the girls to hear any of this.

'Dreadful,' Karen answered. 'She knows Joe is seeing someone and that it's not the teacher. But she's pretending to go along with Joe's protestations of innocence, hoping that it will all blow over somehow.'

I could sense her sadness at these ruined lives. This is bizarre. I ought to hate her, I mean I do hate her. She's slept with Rob. She's *told* me that she wants him back. She's vulnerable and devious and flawed and real and she's the girls' natural mother. Of course I hate her.

298

Except I don't. I don't hate Rob either. I'm furious with them both for tangling the chains even further and giving me another headache. I'm more mad with them for messing up the girls' birthday surprise, if I'm truthful. The thought of them together? Yes, there's a frisson of pain, but one which I'd anticipated for too long, for ten years. Because Rob has never been mine, I know that now. And you can't miss what has never been yours.

Rob finally arrived home at four thirty a.m. Don't even ask. I didn't. A crying cabbie, I expect. I was in bed asleep. He woke me up, which was not a sensible thing to do. I was exhausted and I had indigestion. I was not in the correct frame of mind to absorb his announcement. I decided not to encourage him by speaking. I kept my eyes closed and hoped he'd take the hint.

'It's OK, sweetheart,' he whispered. 'Go back to sleep. We can talk in the morning. I just had to tell you something.' Then hurry up so I *can* get back to sleep. 'I just wanted you to know that everything is going to be different from now on.' Surprise, surprise. 'I learned something when I was away.' Me too. 'I learned that whatever I've felt for you in the past, it wasn't real, not a hundred per cent, not like the hundred per cent you've had for me. I thought I loved you but there was something missing.' I know. I worked it out for myself. Can I go to sleep now? 'But that's not all I learned.' Isn't that enough? Can't the rest wait until the morning?

'I've changed. I see things clearly now. I love you. Isn't that amazing? I love you. Can you hear how different it sounds now? That's because I really mean it finally. That's what I learned. I love you. It won't be easy. I've got a confession to make and I'm praying

299

you'll forgive me. But it will be so much better from now on. You'll see. It's all going to change. I love you. I can't stop saying it.'

I wish you would.

Chapter Nineteen

'Haven't you been here recently?' the nurse asked, trying to place my face.

'Yes, a couple of weeks ago. It was a friend of my daughter, she fell off a bus.'

The nurse didn't laugh. I don't know why I did. I didn't find any of this funny. I was just a bit hysterical and laughing inappropriately was preferable to screaming. I wanted to see Claire. She'd been there for three hours before Karen finally got through to me. Karen phoning *me* to tell me that *my* daughter had sprained a finger in a fight with Elliott Jackson and Isabelle, Andrea's daughter! I would make sure that Tara Brownlow was fired for contacting her in the first place.

The nurse nodded as she recalled the incident with Isabelle. 'Oh well, at least you're here now,' she said as she led me towards Claire's cubicle.

What's that supposed to mean? Is it supposed to be some subtle criticism of my parenting? Some dig at my arriving *after* her real mother? Maybe I'm being a tad over-sensitive here, but who could blame me? Just being here in this hospital again reminds me that I'm not anyone's real mother, not Isabelle's and, now, not Claire's. That much is becoming more apparent with each day.

I was doing OK. I was coping. Just. But this incident

was one too many. And none of it would have happened if it wasn't for my mobile phone.

I was at my mum's watching her make the fourth pot of tea. My bladder was screaming out in protest and I was no closer to breaking my news to her. But there was other news of equal import.

When I was lying in bed last night, seething with rage that Rob was going to be even later back from the airport for some absurd reason, I tried to clarify the jumble of interwoven threads cluttering my consciousness, keeping me from the restorative sleep I craved.

The big one: I thought of Rob and Karen sleeping together. If it happened once or a dozen times wasn't relevant. It happened. And I was still alive. Worse, I wasn't prostrate with grief, which I certainly would have been had it happened the week Karen came back.

This meant one of three things. I might no longer love Rob, that's possibility number one. Number two is that I am in love with Simon, daft but still ominously possible. Number three was that sensory overload had rendered me incapable of normal human reaction. I might have one of those syndromes where you can't stop yourself blurting out bizarre words at the least appropriate moment. Basically, I've just gone completely mad.

I thought about the first two since, even if I was mad, I still had to sort out these problems. If I'd merely fallen out of love with Rob, that would explain entirely why I wasn't overly bothered by his infidelity. But if I'd fallen *in* love with Simon, it was more complicated. Because I could still love Rob and simply not consider myself entitled to feel jealousy when I had been unfaithful myself (since we all know it was only the leggings that prevented me from complete physical betrayal).

I couldn't work it out but I fell asleep from the effort of trying. And don't raise your eyebrows and say none of it matters. It all matters. Rob's pressing me for a decision.

The day after Rob's return was fraught with tension. The girls were running late for school and I was in overdrive trying to forcefeed them breakfast and physically put them into their clothes while all they wanted to do was hug their dad. We'd said that we wouldn't talk about the Wolf Sanctuary until the evening when we'd have more time but that didn't work out quite as planned. Nothing did nowadays.

The girls wanted to know exactly what he'd been doing for the last four days that kept him in the States. He shooed them off his laps affectionately and made calming gestures to them. Claire wouldn't be persuaded. 'I'm not going to school until you tell us everything. Why is it such a big secret?'

Ali caught on. 'Is it a secret to do with us Dad? Is it a holiday?'

Even Jude dropped her cool act and joined in. 'Come on Dad, tell us!'

Phoebe just smiled. She was the first one up and shared a precious five minutes with Rob all to herself before the others emerged.

I shrugged at Rob. It's up to you, I was communicating. I watched him quickly thinking things through. 'OK. If you insist. Right, now there's good news and bad news. Which one do you want first?'

They all screamed at once. 'Good news! Good news!' He held up his hand for quiet.

'Sorry, but I'm going to give you the bad news first.'

303

The girls tutted and groaned. Rob's eyes were twinkling but he assumed a stern expression. 'The bad news is that we are not going to Norfolk for our holidays this year.' There was no reaction apart from a little seed of excitement growing among them as they all wondered if this could possibly be ... no he couldn't mean that. Could he?

'Do you want to hear the good news?' he asked, mercilessly prolonging the tension.

'Yes!' they screamed.

Now I was smiling despite the turmoil going on inside me. Rob took a deep breath. 'The good news is that the reason we are not going to Norfolk is that we are going to ...'

There was utter silence as four shining faces, all holding their breath, stared at Rob, almost fainting with expectancy.

'... Disneyworld!'

The screams that greeted this word scared the dogs, who ran into the study to hide. The girls threw themselves on to Rob and then they threw themselves on to me. Even Phoebe was caught up in it. I had never seen them so happy. All of us for that matter. We were together, a close family laughing together, a dream holiday ahead, difficult times behind us. We were together, intact. That's how it looked and that's how it must stay. Only a monster would do anything that could damage this family portrait. And I was no monster.

Rob held up his hand again. 'There's one more thing and it's not going to be the best of news.' The girls were not overly concerned. Their mum and dad were together and they were going to Disneyworld. Nothing could spoil that. 'You might be wondering how we can afford this,' Rob asked. Blank looks. Of course they

304

weren't wondering, Rob. Kids don't wonder things like that. They are offered a dream come true and they snatch it, no questions asked. They only question the things they haven't got, not the things they have.

'Well, you all know that your brilliantly clever mum here is working on something for the Internet with one of her students. It's the money she's making from this that is allowing us to go to America.'

They politely smiled at me to acknowledge my minor contribution to the occasion. I accepted this accordingly with an inconsequential inclination of my head.

'Is that it? Can we go now?' Ali asked.

Then Jude piped up, 'We want to go to school and tell everyone.'

'I've almost finished,' Rob said. 'Now originally there wasn't going to be any spare money from your mum's job for us all to go away. She'd planned to use it for something else.' He hesitated, struggling for the courage to continue. 'Your mum told me about the surprise you were planning for me.' Thank you Rob. Now they all hate me. They seemed more disappointed with me than angry. That was even worse. 'Don't be cross with her. She had to tell me. Now I didn't know anything about this trip you were planning for me before I went away. And neither did your other mother. So, as we were already in America, she thought it might be a nice early birthday present to send me to the Wolf Sanctuary for a few days.'

Our house became *Gormenghast* once more. Florida was forgotten. Rob had miscalculated badly. He hurried to redeem the situation. They were all developing moist eyes. 'Look we'll discuss this properly tonight. I thought we'd all go out to Pizza Express since I missed the homecoming feast last night.' That's right, Rob, remind them of that too. 'I'm so, so sorry about spoiling your surprise. And your other mother is devastated. She'd never have done this if she'd known about your surprise.' Do I detect a slight accusation there levelled at me?

'I didn't enjoy myself once I knew how disappointed you would be. I really am sorry and want to do anything I can to make it up to you. So we'll use the money you would have spent on me and spend it on us all instead, shall we?'

Phoebe, sweet Phoebe, broke the silence. 'Don't worry, Dad. It's not your fault. We should have told our other mother then this wouldn't have happened.'

Jude softened too. 'And it will be great to go to Florida, won't it?'

'Do they do vegan food on aeroplanes?' Ali asked.

Rob was watching Claire anxiously. 'Is that all right with you, Claire?'

Claire lifted her head slowly to reveal a face streaming with tears. Rob rushed to comfort her but she pushed him off. 'It was *my* idea to get you the tickets for the Wolf Sanctuary. None of the others. Because I knew you'd love it. It was going to be the most special present you'd ever had!'

Rob was getting upset himself. He'd never made his children cry before. 'But Claire, it still *is* the most special present I've ever had. Because of your thought. And all the work you put into planning it. I'll never forget that.'

'It's all *her* fault,' Claire muttered blackly. We all knew who she was referring to. 'If you hadn't gone to America with her, then none of this would have happened.'

Rob didn't know what to do or say to make her feel

306

better. He looked at me helplessly. Thank you. I put my arm around Claire's shoulders, gently making her lean her head against my chest. 'Sweetheart, I know how you must be feeling. But it wasn't Karen's fault.'

Claire pulled away from me roughly. 'Yes it is! If she hadn't come back, everything would be fine now. We'd all be happy, everything would be the same as it always was. Daddy wouldn't have gone to America with her and spoiled my surprise and Mum wouldn't have started wearing make-up and going out to lunch every day and never being here.'

Since nobody spoke, we all clearly heard the time signal beeping from the radio shocking us into the realisation that the girls were going to be late for school. I'd negotiated early returns from their suspensions for Claire and Jude. The headmaster is now my best chum since I removed Phillippa from his office before she caused substantial damage.

Claire was regretting her hasty words and dashed out of the door without saying goodbye to any of us. The others followed having plonked hasty kisses on Rob's and my cheeks. And then we were alone.

Rob sat at the table, buttering a cold piece of toast meticulously, punctiliously. This was his precursor to clearing out cupboards as an antidote to stress. I waited for the question. It came. 'What was she talking about?' he finally asked.

Having started a similar exchange with Karen the previous day, I appreciated the value of skipping all the 'nothings' and 'surelys' and 'oh come on, I'm not stupids'. 'She was talking about me meeting Simon for lunch.'

'Simon?' Rob didn't falter in his buttering rhythm.

'Simon Flynn. The student I'm doing the website project with. I've told you all about him.'

'No you haven't. You've never once mentioned his name.'

I became impatient. 'Don't be ridiculous.' This has become my catchphrase. It's surprisingly versatile and can defend you against an unlimited range of accusations. 'Of course I have. You just never listened.'

Rob looked at me dispassionately. 'I always listened. I know everything about your work. I'm really proud of what you're doing. But you certainly never mentioned a Simon Flynn. And you certainly weren't having lunch with him every day before I went away. Or were you?'

'Don't be ridiculous.' See what I mean?

'Stop saying that.' The problem with a catchphrase is that you have to stop using it once it becomes annoying to the person on the other end. Still, it was effective while it lasted and there are plenty of other people I can use it on.

I had to resort to a more conservative defence – the detailed explanation. 'If you must know, I started meeting up with him this last week because I needed someone to talk to.' I could have just said that Simon and I had to go over our work and Rob would have had to accept it. But I was in the mood for a bit of fact-sharing. Let's put our confessions on the table and see who's really been bad here.

'What do you mean by that?' Rob asked. Here we go again.

'I mean that I was having a terrible time. You were away so I couldn't talk to you. Andrea wasn't talking to me because I said that she was wrong to have an affair with Joe.' Rob raised his knife to interrupt. 'And before you say that I never told you about that, I *did*. I told you I'd seen them in the pub together and you said I was being stupid.'

'I do remember that, now I come to think of it,' Rob conceded.

'Thank you,' I said. 'I'm so glad some of the things I say sink in. What else? Oh yes. I couldn't talk to Phillippa because I felt so bad about hiding Andrea and Joe's affair from her, especially in the light of all that business with Miss Brownlow.'

Rob had by now abandoned the toast, needing all his concentration to keep up with the plot developments. 'What business with Miss Brownlow? I've only been gone eight days. Nothing's happened to any of us or any of our friends for years. Then I'm away for eight days and this part of London has turned into a *Brookside* special.'

'You've never even watched *Brookside*,' I pointed out.

'I don't need to. You only have to see the trailers to work out that all the characters are beset by horrible coincidences and natural and unnatural disasters while indulging in totally unlikely sexual couplings.' He wasn't far off.

'Well anyway, it was awful. I was all by myself and I needed someone outside of all this to talk to. I've been working quite closely with Simon and he's nice enough so I bored him with all my problems.'

'Sounds reasonable enough. So why all the secrecy?'

I was exasperated. 'There was no secrecy. I didn't even know the girls were aware of what I did for lunch. Or that they were bothered. They never said anything. It's all down to this atmosphere of conspiracy that's crept up on us. They must be paranoid about treading on anyone's toes and scared of asking questions. You shouldn't have made them keep the secret of Karen going to the States with you. It really worried them.'

Rob had got up to make more toast. 'That was nothing to do with me. Karen had to tell them because they wanted to know why she couldn't see them that week. And I suspect that Karen didn't tell them it had to be kept a secret. I bet they decided that for themselves. *You* have made them neurotic, not Karen. Every time they mention her name, your face drops and you go all cold on them. So they try not to mention it. You've forced them into this position where they have to watch what they think and say all the time.'

Another failing of mine. Add it to the list if there's any space left. But he was right. I already knew that and had taken the first steps to smoothing out the bumps in our extended family life. The evening before with Karen had turned out to be a limited success. We all sat together, ate together, laughed together. I'd promised the girls it would be like that and it was. I made it better.

Oddly enough, it wasn't that difficult to achieve. There were no embarrassing pauses or awkward glances. I can't for the life of me understand how we could be getting on more smoothly when I now know she had slept with Rob, the one thing I had dreaded since the day she walked back into our lives.

'What's this?' Rob asked, fingering the letter from Betty Speck that I'd stuffed behind the toaster. I didn't feel like going over this but I had no choice.

'It's from my birth mother. Apparently Mum had a letter from her a while back and she decided to pass it on to me when I said I was thinking of making contact.'

Rob looked at me in disbelief. 'But you never said anything. And don't try and convince me that you did and I wasn't listening. I *know* you never said anything

310

about wanting to trace your mother. We've discussed it a million times in the past and you've always insisted that you weren't interested. How could you not tell me something so important?'

'You haven't been very approachable for a while now,' I answered quietly.

We both sat down. This was it. We knew it.

'I know,' Rob said. He surprised me. I'd concluded that he was a man with no self-knowledge, that he stumbled along making mistakes, generally mistakes of omission, unaware of the consequences for other people's lives, which absolved him of a lot of blame but didn't redeem him as a human being.

But he knew. I waited for him to expand on the subject. I'd never bothered waiting for Rob to expand on anything before. He wasn't an expansive man. But this was another Rob.

'It was Karen.' Not the most mind-blowing of observations. But it cost a lot for Rob since he'd resolutely denied that Karen had had any impact on his life since her return. I hoped he would start using longer sentences soon. I was developing a headache and I didn't want to get up and fetch tablets in case it disrupted Rob's momentum.

I couldn't have predicted how strange his confession would sound. It was like listening to the radio, trying to picture the face behind a voice, but never quite succeeding because the image kept changing. I didn't know this man.

'When she came back and I heard her voice . . .' He took a while to compose himself. 'The ten years disappeared. And I know this won't make sense but it didn't have anything to do with how I felt about you. I still loved you the way I always had. But the truth is

'. . . the truth is I never felt the same *profound* love for you that I did for Karen.'

Oh God. I hate this. Don't do this to me. No more of this real love and not-quite-real love. I'll never be able to trust the word again.

'But I held myself together and tried to be objective, to look at it all from the girls' standpoint. They were all that mattered. And you, of course.' You nearly forgot there, Rob. Nearly.

'Then I saw her again. After all this time, she was exactly as I remembered her. Except older and sadder. Not wiser. None of us are wiser, we just get better at looking as if we know what we're doing. So I saw her. And . . .'

He couldn't say it so I said it for him. 'You fell in love with her once more?'

'No, that's just it. You make it sound as if it was new and fresh and different. But it wasn't. It was the same love. It had never gone away, I'd just stuck it in a drawer to keep it free from dust and now I could take it out. It was ten years ago all over again. Except the girls were older, Karen was whole now and . . .'

'I was in the picture.'

Rob took my hand. That hand thing, again. 'I couldn't ignore it but I swear to you that I never intended to act on it. When I said I loved you and would be staying with you, I meant it. I was never going to betray you.'

I removed my hand, but not harshly. 'Then why did you?'

He looked taken aback. 'I know all about it, Rob. I had it out with Karen yesterday.'

Now he was perplexed. 'But how? I don't understand.'

'You don't understand how I could spend the evening with Karen after what she'd told me? Why your belongings weren't flung out in the street on your return? Why I'm sitting here, planning holidays in Disneyworld and listening to you justify an affair with your *wife*?'

'What did she tell you?'

'Not much. I wanted to hear it from you. She just said that it happened. That she wants you back. That you don't want her. That's about it.'

Rob was encouraged by my serene demeanour and became excited, wanting to resolve the whole matter before a more normal hysteria set in.

'No, that's everything! There's no more to it. It happened once. And I knew straight away . . . I knew . . .'

'What?' I prompted, hoping that this wouldn't be something graphic. I'm not that mature.

'I knew that I didn't love her any more.'

I raised my eyebrows. 'And did you tell her this at that precise moment?' I'm joking about it? Scrap possibilities one and two, insanity it is.

Rob looked at me aghast. 'How can you talk so calmly about this? Even make a joke of it? I betrayed you. With Karen. After all the promises I gave you that I felt nothing for her. I lied *and* betrayed!'

His account of the incident was hurting me more than anything I'd envisaged. Televisual images were developing and laying down roots in my imagination where they could do some serious long-term harm. I wanted to get back to my position yesterday when I could cope with it objectively. I tried hard, very hard. 'I knew you were lying. And the betrayal when it happened, wasn't a shock. It was unpleasant and I wish you hadn't done it but I'd always known it would happen.'

That was the truth but it no longer rang true in my heart. My rational analysis was splitting irrevocably from the screaming physical reaction oozing up from within. I breathed deeply and prevented the eruption.

Rob dropped his head into his hands. 'I'm so ashamed. The way it happened, it was ... ridiculous.' Inappropriate use of a good word there, Rob. 'I'd just got off the phone with you and you'd told me about the surprise trip. I felt bad enough but the way you laid into me ...'

'I'm sorry about that.' No I'm not. But it calms me down to say so.

'And when I told Karen, she was inconsolable. She knew they'd all blame her. And she was furious that no one had let her in on the secret in the first place. And we were tired, it had been a long flight with two stopovers. And we'd missed dinner so we just started drinking.'

I held up my hand. 'I can guess the rest, thank you, I don't need details. I don't *want* details.'

'I'm ashamed of myself and I can only hope that you'll forgive me and that Karen won't be harmed by my thoughtlessness. She's not as whole and together as you might think.'

I realise that. One thing bothered me. Well, actually, lots of things bothered me but one thing in particular. 'You looked so cosy when you came off the plane. Then you looked guilty.'

'I know. We'd been talking for hours. Or rather I'd spent hours talking about you, us. Karen was very, very hurt. She thought we'd be getting back together. It took a long time to convince her that it was never going to happen. What we'd done ...' He saw me cringe and squeezed my hand. 'This will be the last time I mention

314

it but it *is* important. It ended it all for us both. She knew straight away. She read it on my face. I'm so sorry, Lorna. I'll spend the rest of our lives making it up to you. But it was the beginning and the end. By the time we got to Gatwick, Karen and I had reached an understanding. We still had the kids to think about. We got there eventually. What you witnessed was the absolute and amicable end of a marriage. And the guilt? Well we had something to feel guilty about.'

'I know. Bloody TV sets for the girls!'

'Oh God, I'd forgotten all about that! I told her you wouldn't like it, but she wouldn't listen.'

'Thank you for at least knowing that I wouldn't approve.'

We spent a minute trying to assimilate all that we'd both said and heard.

Then Rob thought of something. 'The really crazy thing about all this is that it was your phone call that finally made me sort out my confusion. All I could think of was you and the girls planning my trip. The five of you together, I couldn't separate you in my mind. And the pain I was causing to you all. And suddenly it was simple. You were my reality. Karen had just been an unfinished story that had become more of a fantasy the further I got from resolution.

'When she came back here, the fantasy kicked in. I wanted her to step right back where she'd left off, play the story through to the happy finale, tie up the ends.'

'And then what?' I asked.

'Then I'd know. I'd be able to choose.' Rob became thoughtful.

'Between me and her?'

'Between the love I felt for her and the love I felt for you.'

I knew what he was saying. Simon had helped me see this. There were two different kinds of love, the love that is enough and the love that is not enough. He couldn't tell which one he felt for me until he knew for sure which one he felt for Karen.

'And I won?' I stated flatly, without much sense of triumph.

Rob came round to my chair and knelt on the floor holding both of my hands. 'What I felt for her was coloured by the babies. I know that now. She'd given me four children. You can't know how that feels.' I stared at him. He held my hands more tightly. 'I'm sorry, I didn't mean it like that. But I was in love with the whole family, not only with her. She's come to believe through her therapy that she knew this all along and that this realisation contributed to her breakdown.' Poor, poor woman. *Now* I ached for her.

'You see, she'd given me all I'd ever wanted and I loved her for that. But you, Lorna, you. You just gave me yourself. And that's who I fell in love with. The "you" that you brought to us as a family was a gigantic bonus but it was you, first and foremost, that I loved. That I love.'

I believed him with my heart, I could feel that love like a physical force pressing on me. And I believed it rationally. What he said made perfect sense. It was what I'd always longed to hear before. But . . .

'Marry me Lorna. Marry me. I want to marry you and have a child with you.'

Then my mobile phone rang. I had to get up to find it. I saw from the number displayed that it was Simon. Damn. He'd already called twice since seven a.m. 'Hi,' I said.

316

'Can you talk now?' he asked impatiently.

'Not really,' I replied, glancing at Rob who hadn't taken his eyes off me.

'You said you'd call and let me know how things went yesterday. With Rob.'

What do I say to that? 'Oh. Fine.'

'Promise that you'll phone me the second you have a chance.'

'I promise. Bye.' I cut him off without giving him a chance to say goodbye to me. Then I switched the phone off.

'Who was that?' Rob asked curiously.

'Simon,' I answered, feeling odd using the name so casually in our home. After Rob had proposed. Rob has proposed.

He got off his knees and rushed over to put his arms around me. 'I've got a fantastic idea. Let's have a party for my fortieth birthday.' Great. Another surprise blown away. 'But we'll make it a joint birthday and engagement party. What do you think?'

'Oh, Lorna, that's the best news I've heard for ages! Let me put the kettle on!'

'I haven't said yes yet, Mum,' I protested.

'Don't be ridiculous!' I beg your pardon? 'Of course you will. It's what you've always wanted and don't pretend to me it isn't. I know you always said I was a silly old fool for wanting to see my daughter wed, but it was only because I knew that it was what you wanted too. It's broken my heart watching the years go by and you not settled. Good for Robert.'

'Like I said, Mum, I haven't accepted, yet.'

My mum wagged the tea strainer at me, winking cannily. 'I don't blame you at all, my girl. Let him

317

sweat a bit. He's made you wait all this time, now give him a taste of his own medicine. But don't wait too long. His birthday's only ten weeks away, isn't it?' She was checking her calendar as spoke.

Ten weeks. It's as long as ten years to me. I wish I hadn't mentioned the subject to her now. It was only a way of putting off the real reason for my visit.

I knew I had to say it quickly or I'd never get it out. 'Mum, I read the letter.'

She stopped in her tracks, paralysed. She was already making tea, I was already in the kitchen. What could she do?'

'I'll just pop upstairs and turn the heating down a bit.' Nice try.

'Mum, *please* stay where you are. Just listen to what I have to say.'

She began washing clean cups, scrubbing imaginary stains from their interiors. 'I don't need to. I know what you're going to say. You've been in touch and you're going to see her. And you want my blessing. Well, I've already told you it's fine by me. I even gave you the letter to make it easy for you so what more do you want me to say? I hope it all works out just splendidly.'

I went round to the sink and removed her hands from the bowl. This was dangerously intimate for us and she swiftly grabbed a tea towel and started drying the cups. I stood my ground. 'You're wrong,' I said simply.

That got her attention. 'What do you mean by that?' Is it something to do with my diction? Am I not speaking clearly enough? I'm not that cryptic a thinker that my sentences need amplification.

'You're wrong,' I repeated. 'I mean, yes, I did think about getting in touch with ... her, but I'm not going to.'

318

My mum turned to face me. 'But I don't understand. Why not? Why put us both through all this then not want to see her? Is it me? Have I put you off? Are you trying to protect me? Is that it? Or was there something in the letter? I never opened it, you know, not the one addressed to you.'

I poured out the tea since she was too shocked even for that. 'Nothing like that. Really. It was just a short letter and I gave it a lot of thought and decided it wasn't worth opening a lot of old wounds for. I'm happy that I found her, that you helped me find her. That she has a name and address. I like knowing that. But that was all I needed.'

It was after Rob had gone to work that I'd made the decision. I'd sat at the kitchen table for an hour going over the events of the last few months. And every strand always seemed to start with Karen. She walks into our lives to satisfy some maternal urge that she feels entitled to possess and tears us all apart. Because you can't just open doors in other people's existences, wave hello and goodbye and then leave. You leave footprints, whacking great craters in their living rooms.

Look at the legacy that Karen had created. Before she even arrived, her phone call was the unwitting trigger that sparked off Andrea and Joe's affair that led to Dan intensifying *his* affair with Tara Brownlow. That's two marriages and one career going down the tubes. Then when she got here, she really stepped up the pace. One by one, our daughters find their security crumbling underneath them as they watch me fight with Rob, me fight with Karen, Rob go away with Karen, sleep with Karen, come back, shatter their dreams, give them a new one. And would I ever have let things with Simon go so far if it hadn't been for her?

319

No, you don't just enter a life unless you're prepared to accept all the consequences that you can't possibly anticipate. Consequences that I don't wish to wreak on a bunch of blood-related strangers who might be as happy as we all once were. So Betty Speck and my four brothers and sisters (gulp, I have four brothers and sisters, not even half-siblings, the full kind) will have to remain phantoms in an unsubstantiated part of my history.

I told Mum some of that. Not all of it. There wasn't enough tea in the world to get her through the whole saga.

I suddenly remembered that I hadn't switched my mobile back on. As soon as I did, it rang. After I'd spoken to Karen, I apologised to Mum for dashing off.

'Hospital again, love? This is getting to be a bit of a habit,' she said. Even she thought it was funny.

By the time I got there, Karen and Claire were coming out of the cubicle. 'Are you OK, sweetheart?' I asked, rushing to give Claire a hug. She was crying.

'Where were you? They tried to phone you for ages! And Dad wasn't about. In the end, they had to phone her.'

'Her' was Karen, who looked depressed. 'I'm sorry about all this. They really did try to track you down. I was a last resort.'

'They *made* me give them her number,' Claire sobbed. 'I want to go home, Mum.' And with that, she flew into my arms.

'Come on then, my darling,' I soothed. 'You can tell me all about it at home.'

As we walked out, we passed Andrea with a sobbing Isabelle and Phillippa with a miserable Elliott. None of us spoke.

Chapter Twenty

'This is very awkward,' Mr Walters sighed. I sat down in the chair I had come to regard as *my* chair now that these little grillings were getting to be a regular occurrence.

I watched Rob, Andrea, Dan, Phillippa and Joe find seats for themselves, uncomfortable with each other and with the situation. I was quite relaxed. I should be. This is my third time here. I'm an old hand.

It was the first time the six of us had been together since that dinner party. Was that a hundred years ago? It must have been because the picture I have in my mind is of six completely different people. There are Andrea and Dan sitting as far apart from each other as they can on a two-seater sofa. There's Joe looking sullen and Phillippa looking twenty years older. Dan is glancing murderously at Joe who is glancing sadly at Andrea. Rob, on the other hand, has been rejuvenated. He has sat next to me and grabbed my hand firmly. The others look as if they might be sick at this display of affection.

Why am I trying to second-guess what they're all thinking? Apart from Phillippa, they've all made a successful second career out of hiding their thoughts. I look at Andrea and recall all the lies she's told as a matter of course. Of course the worst deceit is that perpetrated against Phillippa. But I'm ashamed to confess that the hurt she made me feel bothers me more.

And do you know the biggest hurt of all? The one I can't shake out of my mind? It's the memory of our lunch in Debenhams all those weeks ago when I first told her that Karen was back. She practically passed out with shock, a reaction I now applaud for the masterclass in Method acting that it represented. She knew all along. Karen had phoned her and told her she was returning. But she couldn't tell me that so she feigned surprise. I believed her. And because of that, I will probably never be able to trust her again. So much loss, I can't stand it.

'Where shall we start?' Mr Walters muttered, looking over the report before him. He hummed and aahed a few times in a very irritating fashion before looking firmly at me and Rob.

'Mr and Mrs Danson,' he boomed making us both jump. 'In this instance, your daughter was apparently acting as mediator.' We both smiled proudly. If your daughter is going to be in a fight, it's always encouraging to be told that she was only trying to break it up.

'On the other hand,' he went on sternly, 'once her mediation failed, she then went on to inflict the most serious injuries on the others, herself and school property.' Our pride was not diminished. If your daughter is going to be in a fight, it's always encouraging to be told that she was a good little scrapper. Still, for the sake of propriety, Rob and I looked ashamed.

The head turned his attention to Andrea and Dan. 'And this is not the first incident we've had with Isabelle . . .'

Andrea jumped in. 'Yes but last time it wasn't her fault, she was led on by Judith Danson!'

322

I say nothing. I am calm, calm, calm. I also consider myself something of an expert in manipulating Mr Walters in the light of recent negotiations. I exchanged a knowing smile with him. He didn't know why he was smiling back at me but he did it anyway. He trusted me. I was the only one in this group of delinquent parents with something approximating a track record of averting potential crises in his office.

He cleared his throat. 'All I am saying is that Isabelle is obviously reacting to some difficulties in her home environment by indulging in anti-social behaviour at school which is, frankly, out of character.'

Dan shifted in his seat irritably. 'What are you trying to say?' he muttered.

'He's saying that it's all your fault,' Andrea intervened. Dan glared at her. He opened his mouth to say something.

Mr Walters quickly turned his chair to face Phillippa and Joe, speaking hastily to cut Dan off before he started. 'And as for young Master Jackson. What can I say? The incident in the sports cupboard was quite unexpected but one which I judged to be largely the fault of Claire Danson who enticed him into misbehaviour.'

Again, Rob and I didn't swerve in our pride. What a well-rounded girl Claire was turning out to be, so accomplished in so many skills that would serve her well in whatever she chose to do with her life – like serving thirty-year sentences in Mexican jails.

Mr Walters was still laying into the hapless Elliott. 'But fighting with girls! Really. That is absolutely unacceptable by anyone's standards and whatever the provocation.' Joe and Phillippa cowered under this attack on their quiet, shy son.

Then the head swung round to face us all. 'Which brings me to the said provocation. I'm having trouble getting to the bottom of all this. But I think you all know what it was about. Would one of you care to enlighten me?'

No we wouldn't. Oh no, no, no Phil, not again. Don't do it.

Phillippa had straightened very slightly but she was still slumped in her chair. 'I think I can clear this up.' The rest of us sat bolt upright, trying to read each other's faces, none of us knowing what everyone else knew. I think this was my cue to bring the meeting to a close, hustling Phil out of the room once more before eruptions ensued. But I couldn't. This had to run its course.

Phillippa thought carefully before she spoke. 'Our children have all grown up together since they were babies.' She gestured to the rest of us. 'We've been friends for all that time.' Bless you for including me in that, Phil.

'But recently, things have happened.' She stopped, trying to settle the quiver in her voice. Then she continued. 'Our marriages have all hit somewhat difficult patches and our friendships have suffered as a consequence. We've tried to protect our children from all that is going on but they are not stupid. They hear raised voices and whispered phone calls. They work it out just as the rest of us work it out eventually.' And her eyes flitted imperceptibly towards Andrea. Imperceptibly, that is, to anyone who wasn't looking for it. We all were.

God. She knows. We all see it immediately. Joe keeps his face down. Dan's expression is unreadable. All the colour has drained from Andrea's face. Rob

324

squeezes my hand reassuringly. And I love him for it. I love him for being here. I love him.

Mr Walters was looking to Phillippa, unsure if she'd finished, as indeed we all were. She had. She had nothing left in her. She was empty.

I had to say something, had to. This was too dreadful to leave hanging over us.

'I think we all accept that our children's behaviour is down to us. We've failed them by letting our own problems drip into their lives. They are still children. They are terrified of change as all children are.' And some grown-ups. 'We should either have kept them fully protected from what was happening or fully involved them. What we've been doing is very wrong and completely irresponsible. But we accept it and we're all going to make things better.'

I looked to the others to agree with me and, reluctantly, they did. Once more I had taken charge of the meeting and once more Mr Walters was painfully grateful. It was I who stood up, encouraging the others to do the same. It was I who said goodbye and shook his hand. Rob stood behind me, acknowledging my leadership in this adventure. The others followed suit robotically. They were still each lost in their own individual nightmares. I could tell they resented me. It must have looked to them as if I'd come through my own particular battle and was flaunting my victory. It was not that clearcut.

I could only avoid Simon for two days. I e-mailed him with all the information he needed on his project, adding brief postscripts begging him to be patient with me. He stopped phoning, but then he knew that he would be seeing me at college soon. I had two days to decide what to tell him. Two days to decide what to tell Rob. Two days to decide what the hell I wanted.

When Rob told me that everything was going to be different, he wasn't kidding. He was a whirling dervish, spinning through the house after me, leaving a trail of kindness, consideration and painstaking attention to my every need. He was driving me crazy. I persuaded him that he didn't need to prove anything to me. OK, what I actually did was scream at him to give me some space but the outcome was the same.

That first night was strained with the girls still confused about the announcements from the morning. Claire's fight turned out to be a godsend. She regaled us with every second of the clash which became more vicious and sustained with every telling. The way she told it, it was miraculous that nobody died.

'But what was it all about?' Ali asked. 'Why won't you tell us?'

'You shouldn't get involved, Ali. It's all horrid. You're better off not knowing.' That was Phoebe's opinion.

Jude was very smug about the whole incident. 'I know all about it. Isabelle told me.'

Ali was incensed. 'You've got to tell me, I'm your twin, twins have to tell each other everything.'

I stepped in. 'That's enough. You may think you know everything but I can promise you that none of us know all the facts. All that you need to know is that Elliott and Isabelle are very unhappy at home at the moment and you should be feeling sorry for them, not fighting with them or talking about them.'

They all looked suitably chastised. But when I left the room, I distinctly heard Jude whisper: 'I'll tell you later. It's juicy!'

We went out for pizza early, mainly to defuse the taut atmosphere in the house. It was an idyllic evening, the restaurant dissipating all the bad feeling with its comforting balm of happy memories and familiarity. I was wrong about clocks never turning back because time reversed for us that night. It didn't matter that we had gone through so much and barely survived. It didn't matter that we must all have changed radically.

Because the important things to us had gone back to how we liked them, loved, needed them. We squabbled over the same pizza toppings, gossiped about the occupants of the other tables, teased Phoebe, shouted at Claire, ignored Ali, tolerated Jude, covered our ears at Rob's jokes. It should have been strange to find ourselves back here as if nothing had happened but it wasn't. It felt right.

And when the girls had gone to bed, Rob and I talked like we used to. About the girls and the things they'd said and done today. About our day. About the horrible scene in the headmaster's office. Rob flicked through the *Radio Times* and pointed out that I was missing *Peak Practice*. I said it didn't matter.

Then he asked me again. 'Marry me?' Again I didn't answer but now my hesitancy was for a different reason. The events of the day had confirmed something for me. I loved our life together. I loved and needed our daughters, that much I'd never doubted, but I'd duped myself into thinking that they didn't love and need me as much. I'd watched Andrea and Phillippa's families crack, the fallout from which no one escaped. I didn't want that for my family. It was so simple I can't believe I ever found the choices complicated.

And that's what I said to Rob. He looked at me thoughtfully. 'You've left out something.'

We both knew what he meant. But I made him say it. 'Do you love me?' he asked bravely.

I know I've said it already. I've been chucking the word around quite liberally since all this began. But that's not what he's asking me. He's asking if I love him enough. He hasn't said as much but I think that's what he wants to know.

'I've always loved you,' I offered.

'That's not what I mean and you know it.'

So I'm right. Here goes then. 'What if I said I didn't?'

He didn't hesitate. 'I'd still love you and I'd wait until you *did* love me. I want to marry you because it's what you've always wanted and because it's what I now want. And we'll have another child because it's what you've always wanted and because it's what I now want. If you need time to forgive me and think things through, I'll understand. But you'll always know that I love you and am waiting here for whenever you're ready to give your answer.'

We'd never talked like this before and I was a bit restrained with him. This was the sort of conversation that I associated with Simon. In fact, Rob was making exactly the same declaration to me that Simon did. A studied statement of feeling and intention, dispassionate and yet utterly passionate.

If I'd written it all down on paper, my choice would be a routine one. Two men, both loving me. Loving me enough. But one is wrapped up in a parcel with four children with equal quantities of love to offer and demand. The other comes with the promise of exclusivity and a quiet bathroom in the morning. One I'd loved for ten years, one I'd known for ten minutes.

But you don't make decisions based on how many

328

ticks and crosses each candidate manages to muster. The final decision, the biggie, comes from a place where the laws of logic don't hold.

And once I accepted that, it was easy. Because all day, all day long, with all the hassles and phone calls and worries and conflicts, there was only one thing nagging at me. Karen.

All I could think of was her appalling manipulation in trying to win Rob back, to destroy my relationship, to disrupt her daughters' stability. All I could see was Karen and Rob together in America. It was a film running on a continuous loop. A burning sensation seared through me, penetrating very nerve, setting me on fire with the most basic, elemental, primeval jealousy.

I didn't feel like this yesterday at the airport, because I hadn't dared to. I hadn't dared hope that I could beat Karen, whose mythological status left her unassailable in Rob's memory. I'd given him up. Pathetic, eh? I hadn't stopped loving him. Not at all. But I'd given up on his love. When I went to the airport, I thought I'd lost. Blocked it out with a superhuman effort. Not let the other feelings through (must be the mystic power of the leggings again).

But I'd been fooled. By Karen. By Simon. By myself. Well, now I was in full possession of all the facts. I loved Rob and he loved me. That's how simple it's always been. And that realisation let in all the agonising pain I'd suppressed yesterday, the torment of jealousy that lit the final flames of resolve in me. Rob was mine and nothing could take him away from me. I was keeping him.

Now all I had to do was tell Simon.

*

We sat in the pub, the same pub where we'd had our first drink. The pub where I'd seen Andrea and Joe together for the first time. Convenience, not nostalgia, took us back there. It was the nearest pub to college.

He was subdued. We both were. We didn't even talk until we had sat down. Simon got me a drink, knowing what to order without asking, knowing what I would want. You can let a man have your body but the final act of intimacy is when you grant him access to your desires from the mundane to the profound. I'd never slept with him but I'd allowed him to know what I felt and wanted on every level. I'd been as unfaithful as Rob.

He knew what I was going to say and had probably planned defence strategies against every argument I might throw at him.

'You're staying with him.' It was a statement rather than a question.

'I'd never said anything about leaving him, if you think about it.'

Simon looked for my hand, but I had both hands firmly in the pocket of my grown-up trousers. 'That's all we talked about if *you* think about it. Not in so many words but it wasn't the words that gave you away. You left him last week. You left him for me as surely as if you'd packed your bags. You had moved into my flat and rearranged the furniture. I saw you do it. You'd given names to our children and planted trees in the garden.'

He was right. Simon was right about everything. Simon was the worst possible person to have as a friend. He would see everything that you wanted to keep hidden, tell when you were lying, even when you were lying to yourself. He'd drag you into the light whenever he saw you when the rest of the time you sat in darkened rooms. I'm not strong enough for him. I'm not sure anyone is.

'Yes I did. And I'm glad I did. I'm glad I had the chance to taste freedom without having to take any risks. I left Rob and gave myself to you as far as I could in my battered state. I tried to release my love from Rob and give that to you as well. But it didn't work. It wasn't real. It wasn't enough. Not for me. If it had been, I wouldn't have gone back.'

'I taught you well, didn't I?' Simon laughed mirthlessly. 'So what's changed?'

'We all have. Well *we* haven't changed but our perspective has. Our reference points have shifted so the picture no longer looks or feels the same.'

'So you think he now loves you enough?' Simon asked.

'He's asked me to marry him. He wants us to have a child together. By your own definition, he loves me enough,' I said gently.

Simon plunged an imaginary dagger into his heart dramatically. 'Hoist by my own petard!'

I didn't laugh. It was too tragic. He'd bought me a pint of cider, knowing that would prolong my time with him. I never leave a drink or a plate of food unfinished. One of my quirks.

I didn't hurry the drink. We wasted another few minutes discussing the project. I would finish it, of course. But we wouldn't be having any further meetings. They'd just been a pretext all along, we both knew that.

Then I stopped talking. I had to let Simon say what he needed to say. This was the last chance he would get.

'What can I say to make you change your mind?'

I smiled sadly. 'There's nothing to say. It was you who helped me make up my mind in the first place. You made me see things clearly.'

'Like I said, I taught you well.' He gazed into his drink. 'I must look pretty silly to you after all my confident pronouncements of how you and I were destined for the big one. How I knew you better than you knew yourself.'

'Simon, you'll never know how close it all came to turning out that way. You weren't silly. You weren't even wrong. There were just variables you couldn't anticipate. Anyway, you got over your twelve-year romance in one day, this little interlude shouldn't cost you more than five seconds.'

'I expect you'll want me to change classes?' he said.

It was the last thing I wanted. 'That might be for the best. What do you think you'll do?'

He didn't hear me. He was lost in thought. I waited for him to share the thought as I knew he would. When it came, it was beautiful in its simplicity and truth.

'I could never win. Contrary to what you believe, I did consider all the variables. It's something I'm good at, it's my job. But it was the weighting, the loading, where I miscalculated.'

'I don't understand.'

'No matter how much you loved me, no matter how much humiliation Rob heaped on you with Karen, no matter what happened, nothing would ever have outweighed your love for your daughters. You were never going to leave them. You never will. If I'd listened to you more carefully, I would have seen that. I could beat Rob. I could never beat those girls.'

But you nearly did. Nearly. You came close but not close enough.

Chapter Twenty-One

'Mum! Claire's used all my shampoo!'

'It wasn't *her* shampoo, Mum, it was everyone's, Karen said so!'

'She gave it to me!'

'Use Ali's, she's got loads!'

'You must be joking, Jude, it stinks!'

'It does *not* stink. Anyway at least it doesn't stink of animal carcasses!'

'Mum, where's my green top?'

'I know why you're wearing that, it's because Steven Billings says you look like Melinda Messenger in it!'

'He did not say that!'

'Mum, have you got vegetarian sausages?'

'Mum this blouse has got a button missing . . .'

I'm in the kitchen surrounded by food. I'm watching the *Home and Away* lunchtime edition on the TV set that I've lugged in from the living room. I can hear them all shouting and I love the noise. I don't need to answer because eventually they'll all come down here and ask me again. By then the requests will have changed. And I will have been spared from futile intervention in a dozen further skirmishes that have fizzled out due to lack of interest.

They'll be down when they realise that *Home and Away* is on. All my fears of losing them to their

333

miniature TV sets proved groundless. While they occasionally used them late at night under the covers, as I used to with the radio, they find them too small to be satisfying. OK and yes, I persuaded Rob to let us have a giant set for downstairs. Good thinking, eh?

Rob is picking up the drink then he has to pick up his mother. Karen is bringing her parents and my mum is coming on the train. There are a million things to think of and I am intoxicated with the joy of being overwhelmed with trivia. I've had a gutful of big and meaningful and significant. Since reverting to trivia, my head had cleared and my Boots bill has halved.

Everything's going according to plan. Well, according to the final plan after the requisite adjustments. While our life is bobbing along its former course, we've had to face some major upheavals around us.

I miss Phillippa dreadfully. I know she was never my closest friend but I'd got used to having her around. She was a reliable link in our chain. I depended on her. And I ended up having enormous respect for the way she handled everything that landed on her. Which is why I was so upset when it ended the way it did.

I was by myself at home the day after the meeting in the headmaster's office. Mr Walters had been so swept away by my magnificent handling of the contretemps that he'd forgotten to impose suspensions as he should have done. I relished the prospect of a normal day. No sweaty phone calls. No lunches. I wasn't even going out so I didn't need to switch the mobile on. That mobile has been the source of a lot of grief.

But you're never safe, I should have learned that by now. This time, trouble came right into my house. The doorbell rang. When I opened the door, Phil walked

334

right in, ignoring the dogs who were slobbering all over her, frantic for affection. They gave up and went looking for crumbs to slurp off the kitchen floor. They are always grateful to have a slatternly mistress.

I followed Phil into the living room where she stood staring at our family photographs on the mantelpiece. It was only when she turned round that I saw the blinding rage on her face. And it was all for me. Maybe I'll switch the mobile back on. Perhaps that nice nurse at the hospital might give me a call. I've still got two other daughters she hasn't met yet.

'How long have you known?' Her voice was hard and ugly.

'What do you mean?' I asked. Now I know why so many people use that question. It's to buy time, that's all. And it works. The downside is that it *really* annoys the person you say it to.

'Don't be so stupid, Lorna!' Wow. This is upping the ante from 'don't be so ridiculous'. Harsh but, in this instance, fair. I sat down, hoping she would do the same. She didn't. So I stood up again.

'I'm sorry, Phil.'

'Thank you. So how long have you known?'

'Not long. A couple of weeks, that's all.' I said it quietly. I thought that might minimise its import. Didn't work.

She exploded silently from the inside out, pain and fury flooding out in tears. 'Why didn't you tell me?' she cried. 'You were supposed to be my friend! Why didn't you tell me?'

I would have gone to her but I knew she didn't want me to try and make her feel better. It would have been an intrusion. Besides, she was beyond reassurance. 'I'm so sorry, Phil. I thought of telling you. But how could I? You would have been crushed.'

Phil stretched her arms out to show me the extent of her ruined life. 'I'm crushed anyway! I was always going to find out. But at least if you'd told me, I'd still have had your friendship!' She was sobbing now, her head shaking from side to side in despair.

I was appalled at the state she was in and the accusations she was firing at me. I knew I'd feel exactly the same if I'd been in her position but it was totally irrational. I couldn't win. If I had told her, I ran the risk of causing all this suffering and possibly destroying her marriage when it might have all fizzled out with her being none the wiser. And she would have hated me, whatever she's saying now, for knowing at all. It would have compounded the humiliation.

But all that's by the by. She knows that I knew and didn't tell her. And it was much much harder for her to take because of who was involved. Like me, she only had two friends (I'm not including Karen here – I wonder if Phil knows the minor but catalytic role that Karen played in this story with her inauspicious phone call). She has two friends, one of whom is having an affair with her husband and the other of whom is colluding in the affair. At least that's how it appears to her.

She's alone. And I know how that feels. I had Simon when I was at my most desperate and isolated. I long for Phillippa to find that sort of comfort, that sort of friend in the near future. Simon. I still think of him warmly. More than warmly.

'Shall I put the kettle on?' I offered feebly with a weak smile.

'Don't bother. I won't be staying.' Her coldness stung me with its finality. 'I just wanted to know if you had any idea of the damage you've caused.'

'Me? That's a bit unfair. Like I said, I'm really sorry about this. I think Andrea has behaved disgustingly and I always told her so.'

'So you won't be having anything to do with her in future, since she's such a disgusting person?' Phillippa sneered.

'It won't be the same again. Not for any of us. Too much has happened.'

'Not to you, it hasn't! You've got it all! You've got Rob back, you've got your family all around you, your lovely house, your future all sweet and rosy.'

I picked up on something she'd mentioned. 'There's nothing wrong with your house, is there?'

She gave me a big, artificial smile. 'Nothing whatso-ever! It's a beautiful house in perfect condition in a sought-after street, as the estate agents say. So they'll have no problem in selling it once they've repossessed it.'

'Oh Phil, I'm so sorry.'

'I wish you'd stop saying that. It doesn't help. Nothing helps.'

'Is there anything I can do?' I asked hopelessly.

'There was only one thing you could do for me and that was to be my friend. You chose not to do that one small thing so there's nothing left.'

'Let me make it up to you in some way, Phil! We've been through so much together, don't just walk away from our friendship because of . . .' I couldn't think of a word that wouldn't upset her so I let the sentence fade. I tried another tack. 'Think about the children. They've been friends all their lives. We can't let our difficulties come between them.'

Phillippa started gathering her coat around her more tightly. 'That won't be a problem. We're moving to Yorkshire.'

337

I gasped. 'You can't do that to the boys just because you want to get away from here. That's selfish! They love it here and the school and their friends.'

'You really are stupid, aren't you?' She meant it this time. 'Do you honestly think I would let the boys suffer because of their father's ... We have to move. We're broke. There's no money. No money for school fees. Not even for a rented flat. We have no choice but to move in with my parents.'

'Oh God, Phil, I'm so ...' I shut up quickly. 'So you and Joe are still together.'

'Only because the boys need him. And because he hasn't got the money to go it alone.' The animosity just kept on coming.

'So I came to say goodbye. And thanks for nothing.' With that she left, crying bitterly, slamming the door behind her.

I couldn't do anything after she went. I was drained. I kept replaying the conversation, searching for clues I might have missed. Did she really come by purely to attack me and then go, leaving me feeling guilty and useless and empty? Surely she would calm down and come back. We'd have a tricky few minutes then we'd make up. Start again. You couldn't just brush off a ten-year friendship like that, could you?

Apparently you can. Because I haven't heard from her since. Her house is on the market and the boys have left Keaton House. I have no way of contacting her in Yorkshire. Her mobile has been cut off and so, effectively, have we.

And that's the only way it could ever end. Maybe one day she'll send me a Christmas card and I'll send her a birthday card and one day she'll be in London, in a few years' time, and we'll have an awkward lunch. It might work out like that. That's all I have to comfort me: not a lot.

Andrea and I are on tentative terms again. Go on, say it. Tell me I'm a snivelling hypocrite after all the things I said about her. Well, it's an agreement based primarily on mutual need. Or that's how we started. Before all this happened, we had our school run schedule worked out to military precision. When Phil left, the schedule fell apart. We had no choice but to meet up and reallocate holes in the kids' timetables. The first time we met was very thorny. We chose a neutral venue and settled on Starbucks.

Once the timetable was sorted out, we were left to fill the time until we finished our drinks. Like me, Andrea never leaves drinks or food. Another thing we have in common. God, here comes that ache of nostalgia again. I need a friend so badly. (I miss Simon.) She looked around at our fellow customers on a Thursday morning, as always predominantly mothers and nannies with hyperactive babies and toddlers. She suddenly grabbed her chest. 'Oh no, I think I'm going to start lactating! It always happens here. They put something in the espresso specifically for the purpose, you know.'

And I laughed. Not much but I laughed. And she smiled, appreciative of my fellowship which she knew wasn't being given easily. We're like new friends, starting afresh. But I'm hopeful we can rebuild something stronger, more honest. We're a long way off at the moment. But at least we're talking.

Not about Joe. That's too raw still. He's gone and Andrea misses him. But at least Dan split up from the ghastly Tara. She got fired too. Or asked to leave, as it's called. Dan wasn't her only conquest. There was a rumour that I heard the girls whispering about concerning Miss Brownlow and a sixth-form boy on a desk in the careers library. Dan must have heard it too because he started spending more time at home.

'Well, that's a good sign,' I said hopefully.

Andrea laughed. But it wasn't her old laugh. It wasn't the old Andrea. 'Not really,' she said. 'We tiptoe around each other, avoiding all the difficult subjects. Which covers just about everything. Anything to do with Isabelle and school reminds me of Tara and everything to do with friends reminds Dan of Joe. Still, we're together. Trying to put things right. We'll be OK.'

I could imagine what they were enduring. Theirs was a marriage that might never be fixed, not without leaving some ugly scars. The rip was too deep for an easy repair. They were going through the motions for Isabelle's sake and maybe they weren't discounting the possibility that they might salvage a future together. Neither of them has got anyone else. That seems to be the basis of other contented marriages, perhaps it'll be enough for them. It might not be what they'd dreamed of when they started out but, on the whole, I think they might just settle for enough.

There was one question I had to ask. 'Was it worth it?' I didn't mean it to sound the way it came out.

Andrea recoiled. 'Worth it? Do you think I weighed up all the possible outcomes and made a rational decision taking all the factors into account?'

I tried to retrace my steps. 'I didn't mean . . .'

She wouldn't let me finish. 'What about you, Lorna? Was it worth it for you?'

I had never discussed Simon with Andrea. I wanted her to understand how much I learned about myself from him, how the almost-affair had helped me to see my relationship with Rob more clearly. How beautiful and loved Simon had made me feel. How it *had* been worth it. And how it had caused me deeper confusion than I'd ever felt before. How I still thought of him when I lowered my guard. Sometimes when I was with Rob. How it hadn't been worth it.

But I didn't say any of those things. 'Let's just say that I was wrong to judge you quite so glibly. I know how you can get . . . sidetracked and distracted. I know how muddled your decisions can get when you're tired and life isn't going the way you always dreamed it would go. I know how you can stop thinking when you have too many things to think about.' I stopped for a moment. I was thinking about me now, not Andrea. 'But when I saw you risking your family . . .'

Andrea's eyes became damp. 'It wasn't worth it. There. I've said it. And do you know what the biggest tragedy is?'

'A cappuccino with skimmed milk and no chocolate on top?' I suggested.

Andrea smiled, the old smile this time. The old Andrea. 'Close. The tragedy is that what I really miss is not my marriage but my friendship. With you and with Phil. In truth my marriage had not been making me happy for a long time. I could live with that. I had Isabelle. I had a good life. I had my friends. But I've lost it all now. Isn't that terrible? A marriage that you don't miss. Is *that* worth it, Lorn?'

It was perhaps the first truth, the first real truth Andrea had ever shared with me. And it signalled the foundation of a new friendship between us. It would take a long time to grow but it would be worth the wait.

*

341

At seven o'clock, the doorbell started ringing. The girls all ran to the door in excitement, announcing the arrivals in high-pitched yelps. The dogs too were being whipped up into a frenzy by all the activity. It's too late to try and calm them down. And I don't want to. It's good to see the children being children, enjoying the thrill of a party, surrounded by all the people who mean something in their life.

It was Karen who arrived first with her parents. 'Granny! Grandad!' the girls shrieked, plastering kisses on the delighted couple's cheeks. 'Hi, Karen,' they added cheerfully. Karen had suggested that they call her by her name. It made life easier for us all and got rid of the hurtful distinction between who was 'mother' and who was the 'other mother'.

It was about a week after her return from the trip to the States with Rob that we settled things. He invited her round to the house one morning when the girls were at school. I'd arranged to be out when she arrived then come in an hour later when he'd had a chance to tell her that he wanted a divorce.

When I got there I could see that she'd been crying but I was no longer irritated or threatened by that. I had no doubts about Rob any more. I sat down at the breakfast bar. Rob got up to make some more coffee.

Karen smiled bravely. 'So congratulations are in order, then?'

'He's told you?'

She nodded, still a little tearful. 'I knew it was coming. I told you in the car coming back from the airport that he didn't want me. So I've been expecting this.'

'It must still be a shock. I hope this isn't going to come between you and the girls. They've come to need you.'

'That's nice of you to say so. It's not true of course. They don't need me. They haven't needed me since the day I left them. They like having me around, especially now we've put all the unpleasantness behind us. But they don't love me and they don't need me.'

I took her hand. I've made this into a little trademark of mine. I mean, I know every variation of holding technique from the erotic to the caring to the conciliatory. And I'm a great believer in utilising all one's experiences, however bizarre, to enhance one's own life skills. I was evidently always destined to be an ace hand-holder.

Karen seemed comforted by it. See, I told you I was good at it.

'They do love you and need you. It's different to what they feel for me. But you will always be the mother who gave birth to them. They may not remember but you will always have that. I'll always envy you those memories.'

She patted my hand and gently removed it. Perhaps I need more practice. 'From what Rob is saying, you could be having your own memories one day.'

I didn't know Rob was going to tell her that and I wished he hadn't.

She sensed my unease. 'It's OK, I asked him outright. I was just concerned about how the girls would react to a new arrival, your own child. I know you'll handle it well. You're a great mother.' A sly smile crept over her face. 'That's why I hate you!'

The tears had stopped and we were both relaxing our facial muscles that we'd had clenched for five minutes in stress. 'So what are you going to do now?' I asked, no longer scared of her answer.

'I've got my contract with the BBC through,' she said.

343

If it wasn't for the fact that I'd won everything she wanted, I would have been jealous. What am I saying? I'm still jealous! I'm writing to the BBC tomorrow.

She went on. 'I'm going to buy somewhere, a small house, but one that's big enough for the girls to come and stay if they want. And I'll be going back to the States every so often. There's a man there . . .'

I knew it! I bet she had a row with him and that's what brought her here in the first place. One day I'll ask her. But not today.

'We'll see what happens,' she said. 'Everything's changing, isn't it? So it might be a good idea of we sort out the names business.'

I didn't see what she was getting at. '"Mum, Mother", that sort of thing,' she explained. 'Anyway, I think it would be best all round if the girls call me Karen. What do you think?'

The girls took to it straight away. It finalised the new structure in their lives that had been built to accommodate Karen; when she arrived at the party, they were as pleased to see her as any favourite relation.

Karen's parents kissed me, without much affection but with good grace. 'Congratulations on the engagement,' they said politely. That must have been hard for them. They were saying goodbye to a lot of dreams with those words. When they followed their daughter into the house that was once her own, they seemed to be a fraction of an inch shorter in stature.

A few other people arrived, doggie people mainly, then my mum arrived, accompanied by Rob's mother. I didn't understand. 'What's happened to Rob?' I asked Mrs Danson. 'I thought he was supposed to be picking you up?'

She shrugged. 'Don't ask me. It's some sort of surprise. He wouldn't tell me. I came on the train with your mother.'

'And a very pleasant journey we had as well, discussing the wedding,' my mum exclaimed, going to join the girls competing with the dogs as to who could eat the most sausages.

I went into the kitchen to finish the desserts. When the doorbell rang the next time, I couldn't go and answer it, I was up to my elbows in whipped cream. I heard someone open the door then it all went quiet. 'Who is it?' I shouted.

'It's Dad, Mum,' yelled Jude. 'Come and see!' I wiped my hands and went to the door.

Rob was standing there with an enormous smile on his face. Standing next to him was a woman I'd never set eyes on before. But it didn't matter that I'd never seen her. I knew that this was my mother.

Chapter Twenty-Two

She's appeared out of nowhere. I mean, she's appeared with Rob and I can see how this has happened, but it's still an apparition. One minute she's a name and a faded piece of notepaper, the next she's a whole person, forcing me to assimilate every part of her, forcing me to see my feelings all the way through.

I looked at her and she looked at me. And then I looked around anxiously for my mum. She was standing in the living room doorway. She knew too. And the expression on her face told me that this was as much a shock for her as it was for me.

'Guess who this is?' Rob announced proudly.

I couldn't move. All I could do was stare at her, drink her in. She was absolutely not the woman that my mother was supposed to be. She was, I don't know, anybody. I might even have passed her on the street every day of my life and never registered her face.

She was thin like me. That was as far as the resemblance went. She was taller than me but looked bigger because she had a huge perm balancing on her head like a busby. Her face was coarse and older than I'd imagined. I shouldn't have been surprised by that. The woman had given birth to five children and had a difficult life, so she said. She was never going to be Jane Asher.

But still. Rob was showing concern now, he was getting embarrassed too. But not as embarrassed as Betty Speck. I had to do something. I went up to ... her, and held out my hand for her to shake. To my horror, she hugged me. But the hug went wrong. Our bodies didn't fit. I went rigid and she pulled me too tightly so we teetered over, almost falling on the floor. That's when she laughed.

It was the sort of laugh that gets you thrown out of cinemas and venues. It was loud, throaty and filthy. It was the sort of laugh that was amusing in a child, sexy in a young siren but anathema in a middle-aged woman. Oh God, what if I develop a laugh like that when I'm that age. I'll shoot myself if that happens.

This wasn't in the articles you read about reunions with birth parents. They talked about the possibility of emotional let-down, of repressed anger spilling over. They said nothing about learning that your genetic blue-print included Albert Steptoe's laugh.

And the only emotion I feel is anger. I'm furious with Rob for doing this to me. I'd told him I wasn't going to contact my mother. Maybe I didn't say 'ever'. Maybe that's where I went wrong. But it's still his fault. And I can hardly throw her out. She may have done that to me but I couldn't do it back. I'm not that bitter. A bit. But not very.

Thank heavens for my wonderful mum. She bustled forward and took us by the arms. 'We can't stand out here. Let's go into the other room and have a good old chat.'

Thank you, Mum, I mouthed to her. Her smile said that she was going to help me get through this.

As we walked, Mum kept the conversation going. 'I'm Rose Fitzwilliam. You wrote to me. I'm Lorna's

347

adoptive mother.' I marvelled at how smoothly she said that. It was the right and proper introduction but I knew how much it cost her. My mum continued, 'Now can I get you a drink?'

Betty looked around to see what everyone else was drinking. 'I'll have a sherry if that's OK,' she asked nervously. She was trying to speak with an affected accent and I was moved by her sad attempt to fit into a world in which she felt out of place. I resolved to make this as easy as I could. For both our sakes.

'So, did Rob come all the way to . . .'

'Braintree, yes! Bless him. He insisted when I said that I couldn't drive. I did say that one of my kids would drive me but he said he'd rather pick me up himself. He wanted to make sure I'd come, I expect.'

Thank you for that, at least, Rob. The brothers and sisters, *my* brothers and sisters, would have been too much. This is hard enough but at least, right now, there's only one of her and loads of us in my family. *My* family.

'He's a nice bloke, your Rob,' Betty continued. 'He told me about you two getting married. Ten years! You took your time, didn't you? Your brothers and sisters were all settled before they were twenty-one. No messing about there. So what took you so long?'

Am I imagining it or did I hear Rob giggle when he heard her ask that? It's not funny yet, Rob. Not yet. Change the subject. 'I'm sorry I didn't get round to writing back, er, Betty. Can I call you Betty?'

She touched me on the arm. Except her anxiety made the touch rough. It was like a slap, a reprimand. 'Course you can love! That's my name!' she said.

I've only known her for five minutes and I'm already a battered child. If she was like this with all her kids, it's amazing they ever made it to adulthood. 'Right. Well, I was going to write but things have been so busy what with the party and all.'

My mum raised her eyebrows at this lie. She knew me well enough to guess that all the food came from M & S. But she kept this to herself. I'm going to be accumulating some serious debts tonight.

Betty nudged me in the ribs, almost pushing me over. 'That's all right love. I'm not a great writer myself. Perhaps you've got that from me.'

Heaven forbid that I've got anything from her.

Once more my mum saved me. 'I hear you've got four children, Betty.' I noticed that Mum didn't say 'other children'. Betty didn't notice. I didn't inherit my powers of observation from her, then. 'Have you got any pictures?' Mum asked.

Betty had her handbag open in a flash and a bundle of photos wrapped in elastic bands came up. The three of us sat down as we were guided through a pictorial history of Betty Speck. Despite my initial reluctance, I found myself fascinated by the pictures. I picked up the names and relationships quickly. 'That's our Adam when he went to school and that's our Rebecca when she joined the Brownies. Dean, now he was always a bit of a terror . . . and that was Sam, she saved up for that bike for a whole year . . .'

With every picture, I tried to imagine me in the background or foreground. Playing on that broken see-saw. Sitting on that aunt's lap or that uncle's shoulders. Eating one of those toffee apples. And Betty changed with each photo. Her face softened, her voice became gentler. This was her world, the one that could have been mine. And I was slowly beginning to realise that it wouldn't have been so bad. Just as I was struggling with this fresh awareness, I noticed that she had stopped turning the photos over. She was looking at one particular dog-eared black-and-white snapshot.

'That's your dad.' She held the picture in front of me. I didn't want to take it from her but she insisted. My dad. He was a young man holding a tiny baby. When you looked at his face, you could see all the lines etched by worries. I looked for me in him. But I wasn't there. Or maybe I just couldn't see it. 'Who's the baby?' I asked curiously.

Betty stroked the photo tenderly. 'That's you, precious, when you were three days old. We knew we couldn't keep you but we still took you home for a day. One of the nurses covered for me with the adoption people.' I remembered Mum mentioning that Betty had a friend at the hospital. Connections were clicking, gaps were closing. 'We shouldn't have. It made it harder to let you go. But we had this photo to remember you by. Just the one. The one your dad took of me and you didn't come out. Still one is better than none.'

Me and my dad. I mean, my father. My dad was someone else. I couldn't take my eyes off the man's face. 'You can keep it, if you like,' Betty said softly. Almost lovingly. Then I looked at her for the first time. The way she deserved to be looked at.

I stopped looking at her through the eyes of a child who had been forced to come to terms with the fact that she was not the centre of somebody's universe. The child who learned that, at the very, very beginning, her own parents didn't love her *enough*. The sulky, judge-mental child who thought that everything was straight-forward, that nothing else mattered as long as you loved someone.

That was the child. And yes I know, part of me (most

of me) even believed that a few months ago. But I see things differently now. I'm different. I'm a mother of four children. I know about love, how complex it is, how *enough* isn't always enough. How it's all messy, how easy it is to make mistakes. And how awful my life would be if I was ever judged for every one of my mistakes the way I was judging my mother.

As she handed me the one, well-fingered reminder of the child that she had loved, still and always loved, I understood her. She was giving me something that she couldn't give me before. And my accepting it would mark an acceptance of her. And it would mean forgiveness. A rebirth.

I looked at the picture again longingly and then at Betty. 'I couldn't take it. It's the only one you've got.'

'Go on. Keep it. I'll tell you what, there are those places you can get copies made without negatives, I've seen the ads. You get yourself a copy made and send the other one back. Or bring it back. Whatever.'

I knew then that there were only two things she wanted from me. She wanted to know she'd done the right thing in giving me up and she wanted to know that I was happy.

It wasn't much to ask. I could give her that. I tucked the photo in my skirt pocket. I patted it firmly so that she would know I had not received it lightly. 'Thank you. I'll get a copy made next week and arrange to bring it over sometime after that if you like?'

Who said that? Was it me? It was as if the photograph of my father and the presence of my mother had unlocked a brave, daring part of me, a part that wasn't scared of consequences, a part that just responded to love instinctively. I liked the feeling it gave me.

Her face brightened. 'That would be nice. Really

nice.' She glanced anxiously at my mum. 'I don't want to tread on your toes, though, Mrs Fitzwilliam. You're her mum, after all. I wouldn't dream—'

My mum interrupted her. 'Nonsense! It'll be nice for Lorna to get to know you and for you to get to know her. She's a very special girl, you see.'

The two of them looked at me with that look that always precedes an analysis of my figure, my hair and my skin. Before they could start on me, the doorbell rang again. I did a quick inventory of the guests and couldn't think who was missing. Andrea and Dan weren't going to be here. I'd invited them informally but Andrea had declined.

Dan was still embarrassed about everyone knowing all the murky details of his and Andrea's affairs. They were keeping a low profile until they felt comfortable in each other's company once more. Then they would venture out. I hoped they would trust us enough to be the first people they came to visit when that time arrived. I hoped that it might happen before our wedding.

I heard Rob answer the door and then call me again. As I approached, I saw his smile again. The last one accompanied a big surprise. How many more surprises could he have up his sleeve? This was supposed to be his party after all.

He'd surpassed himself with this one. 'You're trying to work out how I managed this!' Not really. I was thinking that this was the last person I ever thought I'd see in my house. The last person I ever wanted to see here. Anywhere else but not here. He belonged in my other world, the one without the family calendar.

'Hello, Simon.'

'Hello, Lorna.'

*

I was aware of Rob looking strangely at me. I was not greeting my business partner with the surprised pleasure that he'd anticipated. I pulled myself together abruptly and was about to make normal conversation when I realised that he wasn't alone.

Simon followed the direction of my eyes. She was the most stunning girl I had ever seen. She was nothing like me. She was younger, darker, less shut-in, more open. She was a nice girl, anyone could see that. But I bet I'm the only one that notices the ring on her finger.

Simon took her hand. 'Lorna, this is Cara, Cara, Lorna.' We shook hands. Mine was clammy and shaking, hers was cool and comforting.

Rob was itching to tell me how he'd organised this surprise. 'I found him through the website you're both working on, clever eh?'

'Very,' I managed to say.

Cara leaned forward. 'Could you point me to the bathroom, please?'

I jumped at her closeness to me. Rob took over. 'I'll show you to the one upstairs. Our daughters are queuing for the downstairs one, which means you could be in for a long wait.'

Cara smiled gratefully. 'I'm not very good at waiting,' she said with a strange smile and followed Rob. This left me with Simon in the hall. Neither of us made a move to go into the other room.

'So how have you been?' I asked.

'Fine,' he replied. 'And you?'

'Fine. Until I saw you. What are you doing here?' I hissed.

'You heard Rob. He insisted I come. I couldn't say no.'

'Of course you could have. You could have said that you were busy or ill or anything.'

'Then maybe I wanted to see you.'

'With your new girlfriend?' I asked.

'I remembered that the way you finally resolved your relationship with Rob was to confront all the ghosts and decide which was real.'

'So I'm one of your ghosts and Cara is the real thing?'

'Yes. I'm marrying her, but then you know that. I saw you looking at her ring.' Damn him for noticing too much.

'How long after our last drink did you meet her?'

He answered without thinking. 'Two days.' This took me aback. He noticed that too. 'Yes, a good thirty-six hours longer than it took to get over Sophie. That practically qualifies as a broken heart in my book. Almost a record.'

'But what we had was so flimsy, insubstantial.'

'It was the opposite. It was full to overflowing of substance, potential substance that is. But I consider that real too.'

I'd missed these abstract exchanges. I was talking as fast as I could before Cara came back. I wanted as much as I could get of this man before he went for good. 'So do you love her?'

Simon narrowed his eyes humorously. 'The correct question is: do I love her *enough*. And yes I do. Just enough. No more.'

I don't know why I thought back to the story he'd told me about Sophie but then it hit me in the pit of the stomach. The dash to the loo. 'She's pregnant, isn't she?'

'Yes,' he replied. 'We only found out today but we're both delighted.'

This was so so hard. 'Then I'm pleased for you. I have to be.' I could hear Cara coming downstairs. This might be the last chance I ever had to be alone with him. What should I say? I took a photograph of his face for my memory, making sure that I noted every fleck of his eyes. 'How can you do this?' I asked desperately. Only he would ever understand all the things I was asking with this one final question.

He walked past me to meet his fiancée at the bottom of the stairs. As he passed, his hand brushed mine. As his mouth drew level with my ear, I heard his answer. 'The same way you do it.'

The rest of the party shot by in a blur of activity. I was in and out with the food and drink, making sure I spoke to everyone. I spent some more time with Betty. I would always think of her as Betty just as my girls are happy to think of their birth mother as Karen. It kept the lines clean and definable.

I was so grateful to Rob for bringing her into my life. He was right and I was wrong. It wouldn't be like Karen all over again. I got the impression that Betty's family was tight and strong enough to withstand my big feet trampling huge footprints in their world. Meeting her wasn't as I'd imagined it but it was better. There wasn't going to be any pain in the relationship I forged with her, the love I might find for her, not for any of us. It was time I accepted that pain didn't always follow from love.

All the girls were sick after spiking their Coke with Bacardi so I was up and down the stairs seeing to them. I didn't see Simon and Cara leave. One minute he was there, always in the corner of my eye wherever I was in the house. I kept intending to speak to him but something always prevented me. Usually Rob, now I come to think of it.

Then Simon was gone. He didn't say goodbye. No need really.

Betty got tiddly and emotional when the taxi Rob had arranged arrived to take her back to Essex. I repeated my promise to come and see her, a promise I fully intended to keep. A couple of hours earlier, I hated Rob for imposing this woman on me, for forcing me to confront my past and incorporate it into my future. But now I just loved him. For being right. For not being scared of being wrong. For knowing that some gambles are worth the risk.

I hadn't needed my birth mother. She didn't fill some hole in my life. That was a cliché that insulted my mum and dad. No. Betty Speck gave me something that I didn't need. A gift. And for the first time in my life, I saw myself as someone entitled to that little bit extra. I no longer needed to settle for enough.

The possibility liberated me, thrilled me and scared the hell out of me.

Then it was over. Rob was clearing up a broken glass and saw me flopping over the sink. He came and put his arms around me tenderly. 'Thanks for all you did,' he said. 'It was a wonderful party.'

I put my arms around him. 'But you arranged the surprises for me.'

'Were you pleased? You didn't look pleased.' He looked forlorn.

'I was very pleased. I'm not very good with surprises, that's all. It was lovely of you.'

He stroked my face. 'I like doing things for you. I love you.'

'I love you too.'

We both meant it and this knowledge gave me the strength to get up the stairs. 'See you in bed,' I said wearily.

With each step on the staircase, faces from the evening flashed through my mind. Betty and Simon. Karen and Simon. Rob and Simon. Betty and Mum. Cara and Simon. Rob. Simon. Betty Mum. Simon. Rob. Rob. Rob.

I can't think straight. I'll go over it all tomorrow.

I sat at my dressing table, determined to remove my make-up so that I wouldn't look like a raccoon in the morning. That's when I saw it. Phoebe hadn't left me a note for some time. I assumed she thought I no longer needed guidance. Or maybe she'd grown out of the religious phase. Just when I'd got my mum to find my old school Bible, as well!

I still hadn't found the other quotes and I don't know where I've put them but if this is another one, I'll definitely look it up. I opened the note. Yup. It's another one.

Dear Mum,
John 11:35
Love, Phoebe

The Bible was in my bedside cabinet. I'd put it there in case I needed it. I was letting Phoebe down by not participating in this little correspondence game and intended to deal with this one right now.

It took a while to find my way round the Bible, not having picked one up for twenty-five years. But I got there eventually. I found the book and the chapter and started sliding my finger down the page until it reached the right verse.

Then I sat on the bed and read it over and over again. There were only two words.

They read: 'Jesus wept.'

And finally, I did as well.

Big Girls Don't Cry

Francesca Clementis

Sex, lies and chocolate cake!

Marina has spent most of her adult life going from diet to diet, binge to binge. There isn't a diet she hasn't tried or a type of chocolate she hasn't sampled. But though big girls aren't supposed to cry, in Marina's experience, they don't have much fun either. She's 31, almost fifteen stone and desperate.

Scientist David Sandhurst throws her a lifeline. He's the inventor of a miracle drug – a drug he believes can help people lose weight without dieting or exercise. All he needs to do is prove it...

Enrolled in the year-long test, Marina soon finds herself losing weight and gaining confidence. Soon she's saying goodbye to her hips and hello to her new-improved love-life – and a whole new set of problems! For Marina's about to discover that inside every big woman there's a thin one dying to get out...and eat chocolate!

"Clementis takes humorous chunks out of our skinny-obsessed society"   *Company*

"Incisively funny and terribly sobering... A wickedly funny debut – we can't wait for her next"   *Sunday Post*

"A witty look at our obsession with the battle of the bulge"
Family Circle

The very best of Piatkus fiction is now available in paperback as well as hardcover. Piatkus paperbacks, where *every* book is special.

☐ 0 7499 3143 4	Big Girls Don't Cry	Francesca Clementis	£5.99
☐ 0 7499 3189 2	Bouncing Back	Zoë Barnes	£5.99
☐ 0 7499 3111 6	Hot Property	Zoë Barnes	£5.99
☐ 0 7499 3182 5	Good Husband Material	Trisha Ashley	£5.99
☐ 0 7499 3193 0	Moving On	Emma Lee-Potter	£5.99
☐ 0 7499 3188 4	Mother Love	Martine Oborne	£5.99
☐ 0 7499 3152 3	Pride, Prejudice & Jasmin Field	Melissa Nathan	£5.99

The prices shown above were correct at the time of going to press. However, Piatkus Books reserve the right to show new retail prices on covers which may differ from those previously advertised in the text or elsewhere.

Piatkus Books will be available from your bookshop or newsagent, or can be ordered from the following address:

Piatkus Paperbacks, PO Box 11, Falmouth, TR10 9EN

Alternatively you can fax your order to this address on 01326 374 888 or e-mail us at books@barni.avel.co.uk

Payments can be made as follows: Sterling cheque, Eurocheque, postal order (payable to Piatkus Books) or by credit card, Visa/Mastercard. Do not send cash or currency. UK and B.F.P.O. customers should allow £1.00 postage and packing for the first book, 50p for the second and 30p for each additional book ordered to a maximum of £3.00 (7 books plus).

Overseas customers, including Eire, allow £2.00 for postage and packing for the first book, plus £1.00 for the second and 50p for each subsequent title ordered.

NAME (block letters)_____

ADDRESS _____

_____

I enclose my remittance for £_____

I wish to pay by Visa/Mastercard   Expiry Date _____
